THE
TEMPEST
QUEEN

Tempest Rising Book 5

Elliott VanDruff

Belle Rose Press

Edited: Cayce Berryman at Kingsman Editing Services
Cover Design: Elliott VanDruff
Sword Image: Pixabay: jerycho1960
Rose Image: Pixabay: OpenClipart-Vectors
All Rights Reserved
ISBN-13: 979-8-9869859-7-8

Books by Elliott VanDruff

Tempest Rising Series

Beyond the Shroud

The Last Dusk

A Gilded Cage

Empire of Dust

The Tempest Queen

Tempest Rising Companion Novels

Storm and Sparks

Wind and Wings

Ember and Flames

Steel and Fury

Dedication

To my children, Elena, Charles, and Frederick.

You are the light that illuminates my world.

ELLIOTT VANDRUFF

Map of Lyrica

Chapter 1

I T'S A STRANGE THING that happens to one's mind when the very world is thrust upon their shoulders. I'd been in denial of the role I played in the empire until my wedding day. I didn't want the responsibility.

I wanted away from it all.

Conal once told me that Imor had chosen me to be his champion.

Me.

Of course, that was before Conal turned his back on me. Before he left me to the empire to be their little plaything, putting on shows and selling my talents around the land to those with enough coin in their pocket to pay for it, and enough to get Agramon exactly what he wanted from them. I realized during our campaign that, though Agramon had risen high . . . as high as a sorcerer could go—save becoming emperor—he'd always been met with distrust by those whose support he needed to control an empire.

I should've run sooner. I should never have gone with Agramon across the East. I should've just done it myself and used them as allies for *me*. I could see that *now*. Now that I had a chance to look back on it. There were so many things I wished I'd done differently. Vianne had been right in her message. There was no way I could do it alone.

Though I needed allies, never again would I let myself be the plaything of others. The only person who would be able to wield me, was me. I was nobody's pet.

I began to reconsider my stance on not caring about what happened to the Lyrican Empire. Apparently, I cared a great deal, otherwise I wouldn't be stuffed in a ship's hold for over a month with the royal heir, a shadow, and my best friend as company. I tried not to think about Agramon much. Now with the empire under his control, the possibilities of his actions were endless, and every one of them filled me with dread. I knew him, knew his ambition and ruthlessness, and I was beginning to lose sleep over the idea of him wielding absolute control.

As leery as I might have been of the thought, it seemed the gods had rested the burden of rising against Agramon squarely on my shoulders. After all, I was the one who'd stolen the child emperor from under his nose. He was sure to be quite peeved about that fact. I didn't think I was wrong to figure that my actions had cast a stone into his plans.

There was more I could do too. So much more. I just had to drum up the effort and overcome my fears.

My realization came on that first night, Fin and me huddled around Prince Artian between barrels in the ship's hold, when I first looked closely at my options. Of course, this was after I'd wept in Fin's arms for several hours, unable to believe my eyes that the girl I'd loved most in the world had been at my side the entire time I was in Somme. It was difficult to fathom that type of loyalty when I'd been shunned by those I held dear my entire life.

And Fin?

By all the gods, my friend's metamorphosis into the sorceress she'd become was, quite simply, breathtaking. It took a moment to place where the true shift had been. Though she certainly looked changed, with the smoky blue gem embedded in her brow that matched her eyes and her ash-blonde hair hanging straight and loose over bare shoulders, it was something much deeper. I realized Fin carried herself differently, now so self-assured that I felt as long as we stayed together, we could survive anything. After all, she'd never left my side.

Fin took my hysterics in stride. "You're being silly," she admonished, pulling the small tiara from my hair and handing it to me. I sniffed, wiping my eyes as I took the little crown from her and put it in a bag she'd found. We had no money, and it was sure to be worth something.

"I'm just overwhelmed," I gasped. "I knew Agramon was up to something, but this?" I motioned back to the city lights that blinked through the portholes.

I honestly couldn't believe he'd blown up Del's temple.

I supposed even being in Agramon's favor, like she was, had its own consequences. It hadn't seemed to have been a blessing in the end, and though I'd never trusted Del, I didn't wish her ill. I knew, down to the marrow in my bones, that it had been Agramon who'd blown apart her greatest masterpiece on the day it was unveiled. I didn't regret any choice I'd made since the emperor had been slain, namely because I'd gained my freedom. Now all I had to do was try to keep it.

I looked down, twisting the signet ring on my finger. The rearing bear nearly brought tears to my eyes.

Fin watched my fidgeting. "He's looking for you every-where." Her tone suggested that she was not a fan of Sam.

"I'm sure he is frantic," I acknowledged.

"Will you go back to him?"

I shook my head. "I don't really want to."

"What will you do now?" Fin asked, pulling the blanket up on the sleeping boy between us.

I'd started calling Prince Artian, Omri, a pet name I'd heard his nurse use, which he brightened at hearing. But even with his favored name, Omri didn't say much. He'd watched his father die. He'd fallen asleep crying for his mother.

"I don't know," I admitted. "I'd only ever thought to get away. I figured it never really mattered where I went as long as I could evade those who could follow me."

"Before, you said you would go to Horan," Fin whispered.

"I thought to go there, but more and more I feel as though my place is here, with the humans."

Fin seemed to consider her words carefully. "The fae are powerful, Rowyn. If you ever need to hide or regroup, Horan would be a safe place for you."

I sighed, my heart heavy. "I can't keep running, Fin. I thought that if I could just escape, everything would be all right. But now, now I realize that I can't keep running from destiny. I can't leave the empire to the likes of Agramon."

"But if we can ensure your safety, you will be able to regroup, gather your strength, then strike when the time is right."

My fingers clenched the fabric of my breeches, which Fin had stolen for me so I could discard the wedding dress. I had my sword and the necklace that bore Fin's timepiece, Pedr's queen, and Araceli's key. The holster of knives was strapped to my thigh, beneath a stolen pair of men's clothing that fit well enough that I could be comfortable.

"You could go home, to Morgania. It's always where you wanted to be at Solridge," Fin whispered. "But . . . if you don't want to go to Morgania . . . we could always go on an adventure somewhere . . . together. We could get away from it all, if that is how you truly feel."

"No, you're right," I said. "I should go back to

Morgania. If anything, I could speak freely with Destrian, even if there is a chance he will turn me away."

"He won't turn you away," Fin assured me. "Even at Solridge, when he was fighting his urge to like you, he would never have turned you away."

Silence fell between us for a moment, the only sound being the creaking of the ship and the distant murmurs of the crew above. I let out a shaky breath.

My mind flitted backward to the tower of the citadel. Destrian next to me as the scent of morwood pine perfumed the air, the lights of the city twinkling below us. I'd been so happy then. I would give anything to go back to that moment.

"I should have never doubted him," I whispered. "I made a huge mistake."

I told Fin about Destrian's note before the wedding. He'd tried to get me to leave with him, but I was still clinging to my own dregs of honor. I'd opted to stay and see through marrying Sam before my wedding day was decimated by Agramon's coup. Fin had already told me that he'd blamed the explosions on Lu Shen conspirators. No matter that Agramon and a few other sorcerers had the knowledge and capability to shatter the crystal temple. Nobody thought of that, I supposed. The death of the emperor had completely overwhelmed everyone's faculties, and I needed to focus on the task at hand before I could do anything else.

I had to hide the prince somewhere safe. We would need to do it soon, because being around me was dangerous. I expected the prince to be difficult and spoiled, as he was at the capital, but he was so frightened that he listened to my every word and ate the hardtack Fin snuck us without complaint.

"If he still held fast to you in Somme, then he would want you to go to him now," Fin remarked.

"You don't understand. I did the same thing with Sam that I did to Destrian. The minute we grew close, the moment it got serious, I spurned him." I brushed a tear off my cheek. "Maybe I shouldn't be with anyone. Maybe I'm just irreparably broken."

"You're not broken," she scoffed. "At least, not more than the rest of us. You do have a history of running when things get tough, though. It wasn't just Destrian or Sam— think back to Solridge. That night you caught the arrow when you tried to run away."

"I ran from Espiria too," I whispered. "I ran as soon as I could to get away from the other clansmen."

"I know it's hard, but have you ever considered the fact that Agramon put you on edge for a reason?"

I glanced at her. "What do you mean?"

Fin bit her lip. "He seemed to know this about you. They all do. Master Haris said something on our way to

Horan that I thought about long after. He mentioned that someone like you, being raised in a constant state of fear meant that you were always about to either fight or flee."

I sniffed. "He's not wrong."

Fin patted my knee. "All of your enemies have been fearing the moment you stop to establish yourself. They've put you on edge for a reason. What if you didn't run, Rowyn? What if you put down roots and built a home and fought! You can handle this. You can be the person you—"

"Were meant to be?" I finished with a sob.

Fin reached out and grabbed my hand. "No, the person you want to be."

"I don't deserve you." More tears escaped down my cheeks. "I didn't look for you like I should've," I gasped, rubbing my hand over my eyes. "I was such a terrible friend to you. I don't see how you can forgive me. I could barely see past my own troubles to try to help you with yours."

"I was fine. I was *with* you. You were never alone. I wasn't in danger, at least not in any immediate way." Fin adjusted herself, trying to get comfortable in the dark, cramped space. "After I realized that Agramon couldn't read animals' minds, there wasn't anything to worry about except being seen sending messages to Thorn, but I was so cautious. No one ever saw my face."

"But I didn't know that," I whispered, feeling the guilt crawl over me. "I didn't know you were all right, and I don't think I'll be able to forgive myself. I feel as though I've failed everyone." I sniffed, running my sleeve over my eyes to catch some of the tears. "I gave up on Destrian and he went and did the most wonderful thing. I failed Sam, I ran away, and no matter what you or Echo think, he really didn't deserve that. I never gave the empress the information she needed from Gryse." The tears just rained down harder the more I talked. Luckily the sea was choppy and the men above board were loud in their talking. Omri was still fast asleep. "I just feel as though I've let everyone down," I finished with a wet sniff.

"You saved the prince *for* the empress," Fin hissed. "However she felt about you before, you've more than made up for it now. We can get him to safety. Who better to save the boy than us? Who could possibly stand against us? And Destrian? If you think Destrian has given up on you, think again! Just go see him . . . talk to him. It's not too late!"

"I do want to go home," I said, resting my chin on my knees and studying my feet. "I want to see him."

"Good," Fin said. "*I* would like to be the one who enjoys some luxury for a bit."

I snorted.

"Did you ever think this is how we would end up?" I

whispered, leaning my head against the wall. "Two young sorceresses, stealing away on a boat after kidnapping the young prince?"

Fin chuckled, her blue eyes shadowed in the darkness. "No," she admitted. "But I'm glad we're here now."

HIDING WASN'T EASY on a busy ship that was literally on the hunt for me, but it was one of my more brilliant ideas. Echo kept us informed if anyone decided to venture into the hold, which gave us time to hide. She didn't make herself known often, opting to stay away from Omri so as not to scare him further.

The prince was useful too, his ability to league leap short distances with a companion proving invaluable when they were loading up supplies before setting sail. We had a series of barrels, boxes, and hiding spots mapped out in the hold for when others came down.

We never had to worry about Fin who had opted to transform into a cat aboard the ship. One of many used to keep the rats away. She would wind her way through the stores, stealing supplies before slinking down into the darkness to share with me and the little prince among the barrels.

Admiral Abelard stopped countless times, boarding ships to look for the lost prince and the most powerful sorceress in the realm. Never once did he think to look aboard his own vessel. I'd sat in terror that Agramon would show up and comb through the ship as he'd done to others in the port, but he'd never thought to forage into the admiral's vessel. He was more interested in the ships bound for Morgania.

The navy had given up hope. They came to the conclusion that we'd already reached the western shore, if that was where I was headed, or gone to another land. It was with great relief that the admiral decided to head home, to Iora, to visit his family and regroup.

There was nothing to do in the darkness except entertain the young boy and think.

As I thought, I made plans.

I wasn't running from my calling any longer. Running from who I was meant to be had never worked in the past. I needed to become what they always feared of me.

Chapter 2

THE RHYTHMIC CHIME of bells pulsated through the bowels of the ship, punctuating the cool stillness of the hold. Omri and I sat cross-legged on the floor, our ears catching every faint echo.

From the corner of the dim space, a tortoiseshell cat padded silently across the boards. Before our eyes, the cat began to shimmer and shift, elongating and expanding until the familiar figure of Fin stood in its place. Her blue eyes danced with mischief and her grin was infectious.

"We're at Iora," she announced breathlessly. Her hands settled on Omri's shoulders. "We'll be getting off the ship soon."

I lifted Omri to peer through the porthole as his blue eyes sparkled with curiosity, giving Fin a chance to shrug on her robe. "Ready to see a new world, little prince?"

There wasn't much to see, sadly: a distant pier and gulls swooping over the water. "Will momma be there?"

My heart plummeted. Fin's eyes met mine. I gripped Omri tighter, wishing I could take some of the pain and uncertainty away from him. Wishing that I could make his world safer.

"No," I whispered. "Momma is across the sea."

Omri was still looking out the window when I saw the tear slip down his cheek. I turned him in my arms and held him tight, fighting my own tears at the hopelessness of the situation. I knew it wasn't going to be easy for the child. I knew that as much care as Fin and I took with him, he was still frightened and lonely.

Fin joined us in the hug, her arms wrapping around us as Omri sobbed silently. I began to consider my plan. Was I doing the right thing by bringing him to Iora? Would the empress's friend, Lady Noemi, be the same trustworthy person that the empress had known so many years ago?

All I could do was hope the gods knew what they were doing.

The ship hummed with energy as sailors hurried about, their jubilant voices resonating with the anticipation of being on solid ground again. We listened to them stomp above us, their chatter and laughter filling our ears as noises from shore carried across the water.

We decided to wait until the bustle of sailors died down, replaced by the distant sounds of celebration and laughter from the city. When most of the crew was on land, we saw our chance.

Peering out of the tiny porthole, we studied the harbor. Night blanketed the port in deep shades of blue and purple. Lanterns were hung along the docks, painting the surroundings in a soft glow. Beyond, the houses and stores of the city rose on skinny stilts, connected by wooden bridges and walkways that wound around great trees that towered over the murky water.

Fin pointed to a spot underneath one of the walkways, where the ground seemed to be firmer and which had several trees with low branches that would be easy to climb. "That's our spot."

With my hand firmly gripping Omri's, I nodded. "Ready."

He took a deep breath, his small chest rising and falling with the weight of his power. In an instant, the world blurred around us. The tug at the base of my stomach, the pressure in my ears, almost caused me to let go of Omri's hand, but I clenched it tight. So tight, I worried the little boy's fingers would bruise.

When our surroundings settled again, Omri and I crouched beneath the walkway, listening to the soft lapping of the water. My stomach roiled and revolted as it often did after a league leap. I put my head between my knees, trying to catch my breath.

Omri looked up at me with those piercing blue eyes. "Rowyn? Are you okay?"

Fin, newly transformed and nude, patted my back. "It'll pass."

I nodded weakly, forcing a smile for the young prince's sake. "It always does," I reassured him. I handed our bag to Fin, who pulled out her robe and donned it before rummaging some more and finding the hardtack we'd been using to survive in the hold.

I'd heard Tudor Valdis say that great groves of orange trees were how Iora made their money, along with the brewing of naranj, an orange liqueur that was a favorite to many. We could smell the oranges in the air as we huddled within the shadows of the bridges and trees, listening to the call of insects, croaking of frogs, and splashes of water that wove through the swamp.

"We need to get a message to Lady Noemi," I whispered. I knew fearsome creatures lurked beneath the waters of a swamp and hoped Echo was keeping lookout.

Fin nodded, her silhouette barely discernible in the dying light. "I'll go find her. With hope, she will come to our aid here, at the harbor. It's safer than venturing into the city."

"And if she doesn't come?" The question lingered in the air. What if she gave us away? What if she confided to her husband who seemed to be working under Agramon?

I wasn't entirely sure of Admiral Abelard's alliances. While the ship had been docked in Somme, Fin had left us in the care of Echo and went into the city to get a read on what was happening there. She whispered that the empress escaped to Maryse and was attempting to build a coalition to challenge Agramon. I almost thought to escape with her.

Almost.

But everything in my body told me to stay away from Maryse. There were a lot of sorcerers there with powers I was still ignorant of, and they kept Morganites as pet servants. I wanted to help the empress, but I would absolutely not go anywhere near Maryse and those people.

Ardent was out too. It was too close to Solin, Agramon's holding. I was leery of journeying to Ember Innes, where the empress was from, because I had absolutely no allies there and I was sure no one even knew who I was. Agramon would also think to look for me there, so that would rule it out. Fin mentioned Horan again, but it was too far away, and I needed to hide the prince soon before I was found, which I inevitably would be. Other sorcerers could track power, and eventually I would need to use mine.

The empress had told me of her friend, Lady Noemi, who'd helped with Lady Vianne's escape from the capital. She was Lord Alexander's sister, and a Marendesly too. I'd never even met her, which meant that Agramon wouldn't consider the possibility unless he figured that the empress and I had planned something all along, which was doubtful.

Iora was the best chance I had for keeping the little prince alive and hidden. Just because Admiral Abelard had seemed to ally with Agramon at Somme, surrounded by his army, didn't mean that his allegiance would last. He had far closer ties to Maryse and the Marendesly family than he did to Agramon. Even if the admiral did find out, he would be someone who had materials that kept him safe from mind control, and Omri might actually stand a chance at being safe.

"She will," Fin whispered with reassurance. With a final glance over her shoulder, Fin vanished into the city on the wings of a sparrow.

The soft sounds of Omri's sobs pierced the tranquility. I turned to see his young shoulders trembling, his face buried in his hands.

"Oh, Omri . . ." I whispered, my heart breaking at the sight. Moving closer, I draped my arm around his fragile frame.

"I miss her," he choked out between sobs, his voice full of a pain that no child should ever have to endure. "I want my mama."

I tightened my hold on him, trying to infuse him with every ounce of my strength and comfort. "I know, little one," I murmured. "I know how much you miss her. But you must believe you'll see her again someday."

He raised his tear-streaked face to meet mine. "Promise?"

"It's a hope we hold on to," I replied.

He nodded slowly, taking a shuddering breath as he

tried to hold back further tears.

"Listen to me, Omri," I said softly. "I promise I won't let anything bad happen to you."

"Where are we going, Rowyn?"

"There's a kind lady in this city." I began rocking him gently. "Someone whom I trust. She's strong and brave, and she knows how to keep you safe. I'm going to place you under her care. She'll help us, and together, we'll find a way to reunite you with your mother."

Taking Omri to Lady Noemi might be unexpected, a move that would hopefully leave our pursuers floundering. Agramon's mind would be far from Lady Noemi, yet doubts lingered. Every decision I made wasn't just about my life. It concerned the heir to the throne, a child who had been entrusted to me. What if I was wrong about Iora? What if Agramon decided to search there?

I shook my head, dismissing the negative spiral. Agramon's knowledge of the intricate relationships at the court was not exhaustive, and I had to bank on that. More than anything, I needed to trust in the bond between Lady Noemi and the empress. It was said that the kindness and warmth of Lady Noemi was unparalleled; she would undoubtedly protect Omri with her life. She would understand what was at stake.

DAWN LIGHT THREATENED to reveal our hiding spot under a bridge that led into town. Omri and I had been waiting patiently, brushing off dust that fell between the creaking planks as early-morning risers stepped above us. I constantly found myself reassuring Omri with a gentle squeeze of his hand.

I closed my eyes. Echo was standing on the platform, watching the people as they passed by. A woman carried a basket of fish on her back, her hair tied back with a dirty kerchief as she hollered the day's price. Two little boys ran by, each with a string of dead frogs tied to their belts. Echo moved to the side as a donkey pulling a small two-wheeled cart nearly took up the entire boardwalk. Seeing something drip, Echo glanced over the side of the cart. It was filled with dead snakes. I couldn't contain my disgust and about retched when I felt something drip onto my shoulder.

My eyes flew open and I grabbed Omri, scrambling closer to the anchor post. It was always odd being in Echo's mind. She'd not looked on the snakes with disgust, like I had. She'd merely been curious.

I was about to consider moving to another spot when the familiar rustle of feathers overhead caught my attention. I looked up just in time to see a bird, with a recognizable gleam in its eyes, come to rest next to us.

It was Fin.

She rapidly transformed back into her human form, her

features shifting seamlessly. Brushing herself off, she crouched next to us. Omri held out his blanket for her to drape over her shoulders.

"I've spoken to Lady Noemi," Fin said, her voice hushed. "She has devised a plan. We're going to meet with an elderly woman who lives in the swamp."

"How do we get there?"

Fin pointed toward a distant clearing. "Once I'm positioned there, Omri will need to league leap you to me. From there, we have two more short leaps. After the third, you'll find a boat moored close by. Hide underneath its tarp until someone comes for us."

Omri took a deep breath. "Three leaps . . . I can do it."

With a nod, Fin transformed once more and flitted away.

Taking Omri's hand, I whispered words of encouragement. "Ready?" He squeezed my hand and nodded.

In a blink, the world around us distorted, the feeling of being tugged by an invisible force taking over. Just as suddenly, we were standing beside Fin, the air sharp in my lungs, my head spinning slightly.

Without wasting time, Fin indicated another point a few meters away. Twice more, Omri transported us, each leap pushing him further. By the third, I could feel him trembling with exhaustion, and I wrapped my arms around him protectively.

As Fin had promised, a nondescript boat bobbed nearby, its tarp flapping gently in the breeze. We quickly ducked underneath, concealed by the heavy fabric, and waited, with Fin perched on the edge.

I held Omri tightly, doing my best to keep him steady, my other hand wrapped around the hilt of my sword. The air inside the boat was stuffy, and beads of sweat formed on my forehead. I strained to hear any conversation outside, but the slap of water against the hull and the gentle rocking drowned out any discernible noise.

After what felt like hours, Fin twittered and tweeted above us. I tensed, tightening my grip on the sword as I felt Omri clutch my side.

Without warning, the tarp above us was yanked away, flooding our hiding spot with daylight. My instincts took over. Springing up, I pointed my blade at the intruder, ready to defend Omri and myself at any cost. The bright eyes of a blonde woman met mine. Lady Noemi.

Lowering my weapon slightly, I watched as Lady Noemi's gaze shifted to Omri. Her expression softened immediately. "Oh, little one," she whispered, her voice breaking.

Omri's lower lip trembled. "I'm scared," he mumbled, tears brimming in his eyes.

Lady Noemi gently pulled Omri into a comforting embrace. "I know," she whispered. "I'm so sorry."

I watched the scene, my guard slowly lowering. Lady Noemi was wearing a long, loose tunic and roomy breeches that gathered at her ankle, something I'd not really seen noble women wear before. She appeared to be in the early stages of pregnancy, with her shirt just beginning to swell at her belly.

Omri and I resumed our position under the tarp, with Fin resting on the side of the boat as Lady Noemi untied the vessel and leaped in. Grabbing the oars, Noemi's steady hands began rowing us around a bend and into the swamp that surrounded the stilted city of Iora.

We floated in silence for a while, the splashing of the oars in the water the only sound until Lady Noemi said, "There is no one around. You all can sit up now."

I pulled the tarp back again, and Omri and I each took seats inside the boat to be more comfortable. Fin, now Arden the shadow falcon, perched on my arm as we floated through the dense swampland, ducking around hanging moss and rising mangrove trees.

I took the time to study Noemi and noticed that, though she had not been to court in a long time, she wore a bracelet showing herself as one of the empress's favored. My breathing relaxed for a moment.

"Would you like me to row? I'm sure you must be getting tired," I offered, my eyes on her rounded belly.

"I'll do it—it's better if someone knows what they're

doing." Noemi turned her eyes on me, looking from the black opal gem on my brow, to the gems on the backs of my hands. "So you're the all-powerful sorceress?" She didn't sound condescending, simply matter-of-fact as she took in my threadbare clothes.

I shrugged, moving Arden so that she could grip the side of the boat with her talons. "I wouldn't say I'm all-powerful."

"I was surprised to receive your friend's message." Noemi nodded to Arden. "Surprised, but not disappointed. I was glad Artian got out of the capital safely."

I pulled Omri closer, wrapping him in my arms as he trembled. I assumed he was remembering the explosion and his father's murder. "It was the least I could do," I murmured, thinking back to the last meeting I'd had with the empress, and how disappointed she had been.

"It is good that you brought him here," Lady Noemi went on. "Many people do not consider looking within the swamplands, and I know most at Somme think nothing of The Fens, save Caldeaon. I doubt anyone would search for the young boy here."

"So why do we not go closer to your home?" I asked, my eyebrow raised.

"There are still eyes here, and people whom I trust only to a point, but not with the little emperor's life at stake."

"Who are you taking us to, then?" I asked, looking

around the swamp warily. A large animal with a pebbled snout was gliding through the water, studying us with dragon-like eyes. A prickle of fear crawled down my spine and I gripped my sword. How could I be sure that Omri would be safe?

Lady Noemi nodded toward the trees. "There is an island in the deepest part of this swamp where an old witch lives. It is she who I am going to entrust with the prince's care until we can safely return him home."

"How are you sure you can trust an old witch?" I asked.

A large splash of water to the right drew Noemi's attention. She gripped a dagger that was belted to her side, studying the water a moment before turning back to me. "Because I think she's been expecting this. She's a fortune teller, among other things. You will meet her soon enough and be able to judge her for yourself."

My fingers dug into the rough edge of the boat. "And you trust this woman?"

Lady Noemi resumed rowing, her movements practiced and sure. "I do. There's something about her. I can't explain it, but my intuition has rarely failed me."

We floated in silence for a moment, the swamp's thick foliage slowly giving way to clearer waters shimmering under the sun's muted rays. Arden took off, Fin's falcon form casting a shadow, circling protectively.

It was Noemi who broke the silence, her eyes on Omri

as he peered nervously over the edge of the boat. "How is the empress?"

"I don't know her current condition, but the last time I saw her, she was under immense stress. I hope the Marendeslys are able to protect her."

Noemi seemed to tense at the mention of her family. "Duke Eldred will always do what is best for the Marendesly name," she said, though not as if it was any kind of assurance.

"Do you think the empress and princesses are safe there?" I asked, then chided myself. Omri was sitting nearly on my lap. I shouldn't worry the boy.

Noemi seemed to see this too. She smiled at Omri. "Empress Lesedi and the girls will be well provided for."

Omri attempted to smile back, then went back to studying the passing scenery.

"I just hope I'm making the right choices for him," I whispered.

Lady Noemi placed a reassuring hand on my shoulder. "In times of uncertainty, all we can do is follow our conscience and hope for the best. But remember, we are not alone in this journey. We must try to trust in others so we can all do our part."

With that, she gripped the oars tighter and rowed with more exuberance, taking us deeper into the heart of the swamp.

Chapter 3

THE TREES THICKENED, their twisted gnarls and boughs closing in as we wound our way through the murky water. Somehow Lady Noemi was seeing a path, for as we rounded a bend, she pointed ahead. In the distance we began to make out the silhouette of a crooked house on stilts.

Noemi rowed with determination, her eyes fixed on the structure. I pulled Omri closer. I was about to entrust the very soul of the empire to a witch in the middle of a swamp. I hoped that my gut feeling was correct because it sounded crazy thinking about it.

I noticed a figure standing on the wooden veranda.

"That's Mistress Gladwort," Lady Noemi murmured, guiding the boat toward shore.

A screech from above reassured me that Fin was still watching over us as we bumped into land. I jumped out and helped Noemi pull the boat to shore before reaching out to Omri. He practically jumped into my embrace. I cupped the back of his head with my hand as I stumbled onto drier land, my feet getting sucked into the mud. The unwelcome memory of Ally trapped in the bog so many moons ago rippled in my mind as I pulled my foot out with a squelch and waded inward.

Finally, I was able to set Omri down and breathe. I was a bit out of shape given the year of courtly living followed by a month in the ship's hold. It was embarrassing how easily I'd felt winded.

"The frogs were crooning that I would receive visitors today." Mistress Gladwort cackled, climbing down the ladder with her cane looped over her shoulder. "I told them if they were wrong, I would boil them all in my stew!"

As the stooped woman hobbled toward us, Omri backed into me, trembling slightly. I placed a reassuring hand on his shoulder and tried to get my bearings.

The house seemed sturdy enough. The ladder to the porch would keep away most predators. Around the side of the house was a tidy little garden with chickens and an animal pen. I wondered at the old woman's ability to keep livestock given the animals lurking just at water's edge, but Noemi had called her a witch, so I figured she must know some magic as well, including warding abilities, which Omri would benefit from.

Skulls hung along the top of the porch railing and I shuddered at the different types of animals I could see up there. The old woman must be formidable indeed given the size of some of those monsters.

"Though the frogs tell a whopper of story, they lie too much for my liking," Mistress Gladwort grumbled.

She leaned down and nudged Omri's chest with the bottom of her cane. "Mind you don't listen too closely to anything they tell ya, for more often than not they're taking you for a swim!"

Omri was riveted. Oddly enough, he seemed to be ignoring the pointed ears jutting out from Mistress Gladwort's curly gray hair. Instead, he was intrigued by her blue cat-like eyes.

I was surprised to find a half-breed all the way down in Iora. Usually, the Others could only be found in Horan. Even half-breeds chose to dwell close to Horan's magic. Some had formed circuses and other performance groups to make coin, as those around the empire loved to gawk at them.

Fin appeared next to me, her eyes wide.

Mistress Gladwort raised her brows and seemed to chuff at her nude figure. "You are surprised to see someone like me?"

Fin nodded. "What are you doing here? You're supposed to be behind the border."

"No." Mistress Gladwort straightened, puffing her chest out and gesturing wildly toward the trees with her cane. "*This* is my world. I don't bother the humans, and they don't bother me." The cane landed back on the ground with a squelch as she wiped her nose on her sleeve, fuming at Fin's presumption. "The swamp has everything

I need and I'm too old and too cross to be stuffed into the Canyonlands with the rest of them like a midwinter goose! I'm hurting no one. Very few even know I'm here."

Noemi stepped between them. "She's right. Mistress Gladwort keeps to herself. She's not any trouble, and now she is doing us a favor. We can keep the Others out of this."

Fin looked from Lady Noemi to me.

I grabbed Fin's robe from my bag and flung it at her. It wasn't that I minded Fin's nudity. I really didn't. But I could tell other people minded. Besides, she looked down-right cold. I'd hate for her to catch a chill.

As Fin pulled the thin fabric over her shoulders, she raised a brow at me, as though asking if we were really go-ing to leave the prince there.

I had to admit, even with evidence of the witch's prow-ess for survival, it still felt like the gods were having a giggle at my expense. They wanted me to leave the child emperor in the middle of a highly dangerous swamp with naught but an old half-breed witch and frogs for company?

I chided myself. When I'd asked for Lady Noemi's help, I'd said that I would trust her, and she trusted Mistress Gladwort. Bless the little boy's soul, I did not envy the life the gods had planned for him. I dearly hoped he wouldn't get eaten by a swamp dragon.

Mistress Gladwort leaned down to Omri who still

clutched my leg. I realized it wasn't *so* ridiculous. Omri looked as though he could be her grandson, both with blue eyes and dark-brown skin. Even if someone did spy them together, they likely wouldn't mark the boy as the prince while he was in the witch's company. Why would they? Their features, though uncommon, weren't particularly rare.

Mistress Gladwort's knowledge of magic would help Omri hone his league-leaping abilities. He would learn to survive, to fight. Lady Noemi was near enough that if she ever had to get to him quickly, she was less than a day away. She could also ensure that he had any supplies needed for his studies.

I sighed. I supposed it was pretty perfect, when I actually thought about it.

"Been waiting for you, child," Mistress Gladwort rasped, her voice crackling like dry leaves. "Come on up. We've much to discuss."

Her tone was commanding but not unkind. Omri smiled, a genuine, heartwarming smile, the first since we had left the capital. My heart melted into a puddle at my feet.

"You sure about this, Rowyn?" Fin's question was barely audible as we ascended the rickety ladder toward the porch.

"I have to be," I replied, hoping my conviction sounded

more solid than it felt. "It's the only chance Omri has."

"It'll be this way." Mistress Gladwort gestured for us to follow her into the home. "There's chairs here, for company."

The chairs were arranged around a firepit that had been built into the middle of the hut. Over the fire a large cauldron boiled, the steam filling the house with a tempting, spicy aroma. Shelves and tables lined the outside of the room, cluttered with oddities, herbs, roots, vials, and talismans.

Mistress Gladwort stumped over to her bubbling concoction. She grabbed her wooden spoon and gave it a stir, then brought a ladleful to her wrinkled lips and slurped loudly. She growled something in her throat, then went to a ledge and grabbed a large butcher knife, slamming it down onto something there and tossing what looked to be a couple legs into the cauldron before giving it another stir.

"You can have dinner today," Mistress Gladwort said, her eyes on Omri, "but tomorrow you hunt for it yourself. No room in my home for a boy who doesn't pull his own weight."

Omri looked up at me, his eyes wide and trusting. Was I doing the right thing?

"Do you know who this boy is?" I asked, nodding to Omri.

Mistress Gladwort wrinkled her nose and glared at me.

"Of course. He's going to be my son."

I raised my brows. "Is he now?"

Mistress Gladwort nodded, turning back to her soup. "The seer—not the one who hates you, the other one, Moria—told me that Imor would grant me a son to come ease my suffering in my old age."

"How did she deliver this message?" I asked. I'd never heard of any prophecies from the seer of Horan.

"This was years ago, when I served in her temple. We half-breeds live longer than humans, though not as long as a full fae, who can live a five hundred years apiece."

"You've known we would be coming for that long?" I asked, unable to hide the doubt in my voice.

"I've been waiting my whole life for this one." Mistress Gladwort motioned to Omri with the ladle. "His room is up that ladder."

Omri shot me a questioning look. I nodded. He scrambled to the loft, showing more excitement than I'd seen from him in weeks.

"Rowyn!" Omri cried from above. "There's a bow and arrow here!"

"Aye," Mistress Gladwort said grumpily. "There's a ripe load of chores to do too."

"There's clothes!" Omri continued. "And toys!"

"I have to know," I said, moving closer to the old witch. "Why? Why do this?"

Mistress Gladwort's nose wrinkled as she shuffled about. "I couldn't help myself in the markets, which is why I've been trying to stay away. I'd see something and think, my boy will like that someday, and I'd just buy it. I probably went a bit overboard but Moria was sure he was to be a good boy, and kind to me, so I figured where's the harm?"

"No," I sighed, glancing at Fin and Noemi who were sitting silently next to me. "Why are you so eager to take him in?" I couldn't help the thought that she might have ulterior motives. It seemed almost too good to be true.

Mistress Gladwort added a dash of this and splash of that into whatever she was cooking that smelled spicy and warm and delicious. I'd be happy eating it without knowing what was in it.

"Do you know much? About half-breeds?" Mistress Gladwort asked.

Fin averted her eyes as though she were hiding something. She'd not talked much about her adventure into Horan. I was eager to speak more plainly to her, now that Omri would be out of my care. I had every intention of cornering her later.

I shook my head.

"Half-breed men can produce offspring with the fae or humans, and their offspring can produce offspring, but first-generation half-breed women are barren. We can never have children."

Fin frowned, while Lady Noemi lowered her eyes and rested her hand on her stomach. I wondered how many children she had. I'd thought the empress had mentioned her having at least one already. I would think it a hard life, wanting the one thing you could not have.

"I didn't know that," I said, my voice softening.

Mistress Gladwort shrugged. "There's not much in feeling sorry about it. In my younger days I was a priestess in Moria's temple. They don't let half-breeds do much, but they let us keep the temple. Moria, she'd known I'd always wanted children, but I would never be blessed with my own. I would've loved to raise a little half-breed child, but the fae struggle with child-bearing, and no one is unaccounted for. If a child loses parents, there are always five or six other fae who are clamoring to take them in. There is no way they would let one go to a half-breed. Moria saw my pain and gave me a peek at my future, to cheer me up."

Mistress Gladwort smiled at the distant memory. "She showed me this house, the little boy who would come live with me and give me happy years at the end of my time. That is all I've ever wanted."

"She showed you Omri?" I asked, wishing the boy would come down from his loft.

Mistress Gladwort nodded. "She showed me the boy who would become ruler of a broken empire. I was to keep him safe, she said, or else the fabric of time will be altered."

In the silence after her words, I glanced at Lady Noemi. She was watching me, her eyes bright in the light of the fire. "I will ensure Mistress Gladwort has everything she needs. Winters are mild here, so there is usually plenty of food to be had. As you can see, there are wards to make this spot safe. I think this can work, at least for a time so that the empress can reclaim her rightful spot in court and ensure safekeeping and guardianship of Prince Artian."

I nodded. It was a good offer, but the decision we were about to make had implications, not only for the four of us but for the entire empire.

"I noticed you had a roost of messenger birds," Fin remarked to Noemi who nodded. "I will make myself known to them, so that they will be able to find me in the event of an emergency. Send a message, and I can be here as soon as I can."

"That would be helpful," Noemi murmured. "I'm not at a place right now where I feel I should share this news with Abelard, so in the event that the prince is discovered, there isn't much I can do except try to hide him."

Mistress Gladwort began to dish up bowls of stew. "We'll get along well enough, for a few years at least."

I frowned. "A few years?"

Noemi and Fin also looked puzzled. I'd hoped Empress Lesedi would gain the throne back much faster than that.

Was this a sign of what was to come? The Ylirian War had lasted five years, and we weren't even battling for a throne then.

Mistress Gladwort nodded. "The seer saw it herself."

Her words managed to give me some measure of peace. The gods had made it clear that they wanted to be highly involved in my life, so I needed to learn to listen to the signs.

I accepted the bowl of soup from the woman as Omri clambered back down the ladder in a rush. Mistress Gladwort nodded to a pail by the door where he immediately went and washed his hands.

"Then it is settled," Lady Noemi said, dipping her spoon in her own bowl. "I will check on the prince and deliver anything Mistress Gladwort should require in terms of resources and supplies. I will send word to Fin if anything goes awry, and I will not speak a word of it to anyone, not even the empress or my husband, until we've deemed it safe."

"You have my word too," I said, clasping Lady Noemi's hand. "I will speak of this to no one, save the four of you."

"And mine," Fin added.

Mistress Gladwort looked at each of us in turn. "I will keep the boy safe."

After we ate, we spent the rest of the day preparing for our departure and making sure that Mistress Gladwort and

Omri had everything they needed. When it was time to leave, I hugged Omri tightly, tears in my eyes. The little boy had crept into my heart and leaving him behind was painful.

But it was necessary. He would be easily found if he stuck with me. Wherever I went would be no place for the child.

"I must also be going," Lady Noemi said, her voice heavy. "I have other matters to attend to. But I will return soon to ensure that all is well."

"Next time you come I'll have that nausea tea ready for you, Lady Noemi," Mistress Gladwort said warmly. Those blue catlike eyes blinked. "Master Aydin's ointment will be ready after the next full moon."

"I was hoping you would say that." Lady Noemi smiled as she heaved herself up with a groan. "Take care of the boy." She turned to Fin and me. "And take care of yourselves." She got in her boat and we pushed her away from shore, watching her disappear through the trees.

"I don't want you to go," Omri said, tears glistening in his eyes. His voice wavered, but he held himself together. A brave little warrior.

"You'll be safe here, Omri," I reassured him, kneeling to look into his eyes. "Mistress Gladwort will take good care of you."

"You must become strong and wise," Fin added

tenderly. "We will see you again. We promise."

We each hugged Omri tightly, promising to return, and then it was time to go.

Fin transformed into Arden and took off as I called the wind, feeling its cool caress against my skin as it lifted me into the sky. I'd missed the feeling of the air singing in my ears after being flightless for so long. I took a deep breath and rose higher, relishing the chill.

As we soared northward, leaving Iora behind, I glanced back one last time at the small house nestled in the swamp. I felt a pang of sadness but also a sense of hope.

Chapter 4

W E TORE THROUGH the night, trying to get as much distance between us and Iora as possible. Fin saved energy by coasting on the wind beside me, as she'd done as Arden when I'd flown on the eastern shore. We followed the coastline until a false dawn broke over the sea. When we began to fear discovery, we landed on the banks of the Ballerian near a cave.

"Is it safe?" Fin asked, nodding at the cave's entrance. "Echo, can you check?"

"*Nothing lurks within,*" Echo whispered into the sea breeze. Fin nodded, then collapsed with a sigh onto some rocks and lounged among the beach creatures and plants.

"Well," she sighed, her eyes on me, "I feel good about Omri's place. Fae cannot tell a lie, including half-breeds, so what Mistress Gladwort told us had to be true."

"You have no doubts that we are doing the right thing?" I asked, picking up a stone and tossing it into the water.

"Of course I have doubts." Fin rolled toward me. "But no place is going to be truly, impenetrably safe. Do I think that Omri is the *safest* that we can make him? Yes, I think Iora is about the best we can do, given the time frame and area. Iora was a brilliant idea. I wish I could've taken credit for it, honestly." Fin wiggled her eyebrows.

I chuckled, though the lingering weight in my heart dampened the sound as the sun rose higher. It was a tranquil moment, a brief respite, but my curiosity wouldn't let me rest.

"Fin," I began, my voice hesitant. "You never told me what happened in Horan. You mentioned something about a half-breed named Thorn?"

Fin sat up and brushed a strand of hair from her face. I liked to admire the smoky blue stone embedded above her eyes in the daylight. It looked so lovely with her features.

"He was our guide through Horan. I enjoyed his company, and he was very kind to me." Fin shrugged. "Maybe our friendship will grow if we ever see each other again. I don't know what the gods have planned."

"What about your quest?" I asked, curious how it differed from my own. Fin had surely learned all about my time in the Nightlands from hiding at the capital.

"It wasn't easy." Fin's face darkened. "There was a terrifying encounter with a merman. He tried to force his way with me while we were diving for my gem."

I took a deep, steadying breath. "Where is this creature? Because I'm willing to go to Horan now that I know there is someone I would love to kill."

Fin shook her head with a weak laugh. "He's already dead."

"How?"

"A giant crab snipped him in half a couple of times," Fin said, not meeting my eye.

"That is the single greatest news I've heard in a while." I reached out and squeezed Fin's hand.

"It was gruesome and horrifying, yet it saved my life. But there is something I need to speak with you about concerning the court of the fae." Fin mirrored my movements, sitting up with her arms around her knees as she met my eyes. "King Valon was very helpful to my quest. He housed Master Haris and me when we got to Alden-Ester, he protected us when the merfolk sought retaliation for the deaths of two guides, but he did it all for a price."

I held up my hand. "Two deaths?"

"Oh, yeah, the other merperson tried to drown me when I was returning with my gem, so I killed her."

"As it should be."

Fin tried to hide her smile. She was unsuccessful, possibly because she was naked and not hiding a single thing. "Anyway, in exchange for the King of the Fae's help, I promised that I would give you a message. He wants to meet with you, Rowyn."

I blinked, taken aback. "Me? Why would he want to meet with me?"

Fin fiddled with a shell that had been lying next to her. "I don't think that I can tell you everything—the fae . . . they are different. They would rather speak for themselves than have their words passed through another. I do know he wants you to try to retake the throne of Morgania and claim your birthright. He was adamant that he could help as long as you allow the border to reopen between Horan and Morgania."

My eyes widened. How did Fin know about my family's history? I hadn't known at Solridge. It wasn't until after, in Helena, when Destrian revealed what he'd found.

Fin seemed to notice my unease. "King Valon knew Theramon of Morgania and his family. He says his magic was used to strengthen the shroud when Lyrica crossed the sea, and that's how he gained the knowledge you were there and when you'd left."

I stopped breathing, frozen in the moment. The King of Horan had known my family from a hundred years ago? Had met them? Spoken with them?

"What did the king tell you?" I asked, trying to keep my voice steady. I wanted to know *everything*.

Fin shifted, rubbing her hands along her arms. I tossed her the pack.

"The king didn't share much," Fin admitted, pulling her robe around her. "I just know that he's *very* interested in aiding you in reclaiming your legacy in Morgania, but I can't tell you more than that. He would prefer to 'share his truth.' I've probably told you too much already."

I felt a wave of nausea wash over me. "The fae king wants me to retake the throne?"

"I heard Agramon speak to you, that night when he asked if you would try to claim the Morganite throne." Fin studied me closely. "Is that why you want to go to Morgania now?"

"And take Destrian's inheritance from him?" Tears threatened the corners of my eyes. Was that what she'd thought the entire time we were in the ship's hold? "He doesn't deserve that. He's a good man, and he will probably be a good consul." The tears began to fall anyway. I let them.

It had been a year of veiling my dread and sorrow within the shadows of indifference and submission. I could never show such weakness around the men at the capital who sought to control me. Agramon would've delighted in seeing me break. Sam would've continued selling me lust and control under the guise of passion. Now that I was free and safe, with Fin and Echo, who had only ever loved me, I felt as though I could finally have a good cry.

"I don't want to get in the way of his dreams. But ever since I left home, I've longed to return, and every time I returned, it felt as though I were being pulled away." I sniffed, wiping my cheek with my dirty sleeve.

"But now is your time," Fin urged. "The empire is divided between the empress and Agramon. Are they really going to have the strength to fight each other *and* you if we decide to retake your throne?"

"You say 'we.' I figured you would leave me when we got to Solridge."

"Do you want me to?"

"It's dangerous being around me." I rested my chin on my knees and sighed. "I can't, in good conscience, ask you to stay."

"But what if I want to be with you? What if I want to help? I have nothing waiting for me at Solridge, and there sure as the gods isn't any place I'd want to be on the eastern shore."

"What about Horan?" I asked. "What about Thorn?"

Fin shook her head. "I'm needed here. The change, it's exciting. It feels as though we could remake the world however we want. Can you not see that? There are opportunities everywhere."

"There will be war and bloodshed everywhere." I ached as I thought of all the lives that would be caught in the crossfire of Agramon's quest for domination. I had seen the cold calculation in his eyes, the raw ambition that eclipsed any semblance of mercy.

Stealing Omri, however, had thrown a wrench in his plans. Without Omri legitimizing his control, Agramon's grip on the empire was uncertain, his reign tainted. That didn't mean he would give up, though. On the contrary,

Agramon would stop at nothing to get what he wanted.

Omri's safety was paramount. I couldn't—wouldn't—let Agramon use the boy as a pawn in his deadly game. It's why I had to hide him, why I had to entrust him to the swamp witch, to Noemi. Their homes were off the beaten path, away from prying eyes. I could only hope it would be enough.

"What do you think, Echo?" Fin asked. "Is it worth it to challenge Agramon from Morgania?"

"*Home is where you'll be safest,*" Echo hissed. "*Morgania is where you are meant to be.*"

As much as the thought of Agramon with unrestrained power terrified me, I couldn't allow it to paralyze me. Agramon may have taken the throne, but he hadn't won the war. Not yet. As long as I drew breath, as long as there were those willing to stand against him, there was still hope.

OUR NIGHTS WERE FILLED with the sound of wings and the rush of wind, the moon our constant companion as we flew through the starlit sky. By day, we hid, finding shelter in fruit trees or barn lofts, our bodies weary but our spirits undaunted.

Fin's resourcefulness never ceased to amaze me. She would scrounge up food and supplies, always finding what we needed. I had nicked a satchel from one of our barn hideouts, and it held a coat Fin had stolen from a clothesline.

Echo's whispers guided us to safe havens and hidden places. We avoided towns and cities, knowing that Agramon's eyes would be upon them.

Solridge was given a wide berth. We flew inland, careful not to betray our position. I wanted the empire to search, to wonder, to doubt before I revealed myself. Let them believe I was lost a little longer. Let them underestimate us.

When we reached the outskirts of Ayastaren, a sense of foreboding settled over me. But we had come this far, and we would not turn back. Morgania was just over the border.

We settled into the branches of a tree for the day, our bodies aching, our minds alert. It felt good to use so much magic. It helped me sleep, when I nearly collapsed from exhaustion. I was so tired that I didn't have the energy to worry about what would happen when I finally got to Morgania, or how everything might change.

Chapter 5

I STUDIED THE ROW of tents in the distance. Fin perched beside me on a wide branch, chewing sweet rolls that she'd swiped from the market in Ayastaren when she'd gone sneaking. Now, in the evening hours, we bided our time and waited for the sun to go down, hidden within the boughs of a great oak while watching the marble city in the distance.

Fin seemed distracted, as though there was something on her mind. I looked back to the rows of tents.

"Is that the Lyrican Army?" I asked, glancing at Fin out of the corner of my eye.

Fin's mouth quirked. "The army is still at the capital, moving against the Marendeslys. No one knows what they are planning to do yet."

"The Ayastaren one then?" I prodded.

Fin shook her head. "It's the Baron of Bruin. Him and a large band of mercenaries."

My head snapped back to the camp. "What is Sam doing in Ayastaren?"

"Looking for you," Fin said, validating my initial suspicion.

A flurry of images and memories bombarded me: his

voice, his warmth, his unfailing loyalty to me. And then, the inevitable sting of betrayal. I'd left him a broken man. Was he really so close, searching for me and the prince? "But why Ayastaren?"

Fin sighed. "Duke Roland has provided him men to cut off the border of Morgania with Adair."

"Duke Roland?" My mind wrenched back to a memory in Bruin. I was lying on my stomach, sprawled across Sam's chest.

"What really happened in Ayastaren?" Sam had asked, his eyes on my black locks as they ran through his fingers. "What did Duke Roland do to make you hate him so?"

I should've figured Sam had met the man. Though I knew Sam and Agramon's feelings about the nobles of the Eastern Empire, I had no idea how they felt about the nobles of the West, save Destrian. Neither liked Destrian.

"We had to stop in Ayastaren on the way south to Solridge," I'd said. I told Sam everything, from how the duke treated me in Ayastaren, to the two men who were killed attempting to break into my room, to Destrian's suspicions. I told him how Seith and Elias harassed me at Solridge, and even the time I knocked Elias out and hid him in the privy with Galena.

Sam had fits of laughter about that one. Even now, I could feel the rumble of his chest as he chuckled. I went on, detailing Elias and Seith's fight with me in the marketplace on festival day, ending with Elias's death at the hands of the townsfolk.

Sam was nodding throughout, as though he'd heard most of it already, though he hadn't heard that Teilo and Seith had managed to capture me after I'd returned from the Nightlands. I could feel his body tense beneath me as I told him how Teilo envisioned taking me on as a whore.

"And you were the one who killed him? Not your lord Destrian?" Sam asked, pausing in his petting.

I nodded. "It was one of my finer moments," I admitted, the righteous vindication flooding back to me.

"So strange, now that you are friends with Mellan," Sam muttered, his hand resuming its previous course down my bare back.

"Rowyn, what do you want to do?" Fin asked, pulling me back to the present.

"He knows how I feel about Duke Roland," I said, twisting the signet ring on my finger. "He knows what the duke did to me, and he's allying with Ayastaren anyway."

Sam obviously felt as though I'd betrayed him, but he had to know that Agramon and the empress hadn't given me a choice. Did he honestly think I should've left the young prince to the duke's machinations?

I supposed I was receiving my answer, wasn't I? Sam was camped on the Ayastaren border, staying in the castle of my foe, drinking his wine and recruiting his men.

Agramon had to know about this. Lyrica was closing in once more.

Fin settled back on the branch. She'd always been good at leaving me to my thoughts. The sweet roll finished, she began munching on dried meat. She offered me a piece and I took it, chewing thoughtfully as I watched the fires flicker in the fading light of evening.

"This might be my only chance to talk to him," I said finally. "Once I make myself known, I have a feeling that the time for reasoning will be brief."

Fin sighed. "I will never understand why you hold so much loyalty to a man who wanted to marry you against your will."

"It wasn't against my will," I said with a frown. "I was completely willing."

Fin glared at me, her blue eyes turning icy. "Anyone could see that your heart wasn't in it. You were doing it out of duty to your clansmen, nothing more."

"I know. But I can't stand the thought of him thinking that I planned on leaving. He needs to know the truth. I was ready to be his wife, to fulfill my oath. It was the gods who intervened."

Fin shrugged. "He holds no faith in the gods."

"He didn't . . . probably still doesn't . . . but I want to tell him my side of the story." I sighed heavily. "Who knows what poison Agramon has dripped into his ear?"

"Is there a chance he will convince you to go with him?" Fin continued to study me in the waning light. "There have been whispers in the city. Some are convinced you are married; others insist that since the ceremony wasn't complete, you're free to go your own way. Everyone agrees you're a traitor, though, and that you had some role in the emperor's assassination."

"I can't go with him," I said finally. When we'd hidden in the ship's hold in the port at Somme, I considered meeting Sam and explaining, but something held me back. At first, I'd convinced myself that it was because the prince's safety wasn't assured. Really, it was because I didn't want to chance losing my freedom. "But I still must see him. I have to know what he's doing in Ayastaren."

"*He will not be the man you left*," a voice whispered from my right.

Fin was nodding. "Echo's right. He may do something unexpected. He may be waiting for you to come to him. What if he traps you?"

"I will go tonight. Surprise him while he's asleep. The men at camp don't suspect I'm near, do they?" I asked.

Fin kept her expression cool and blank, blessedly free of judgment. "No, they've been watching the sky and roads closely, but the birds haven't reported that anyone suspects you're near."

I nodded. Perfect.

"Can you find out where his room is? Unless there is someone there to ward, I can sneak in through a window."

"There's something else," Fin said.

I slowed my thoughts and waited.

"Destrian is in Eslin."

"What?" I whispered. "Why?" Eslin was the closest Morganian city to Ayastaren, dug into the cliffs overlooking the Ballerian Sea.

"Probably has something to do with the Butcher of Bruin and Duke of Ayastaren camping out on Morgania's doorstep. Destrian's sister and her husband hold the consulship of Eslin, so he has reason to help protect it. He's been there for over two weeks."

He was so close. "Then after I speak to Sam tonight, we head to Eslin."

Fin brushed the crumbs from her fingers and pulled her robe off. "Very well, I will see what I can find."

I returned my gaze back to the army standing between Destrian and me. "Don't go to Sam as Arden. He will suspect something."

"I won't," Fin agreed.

One moment she was there; the next moment, a little bluebird was perched on the branch. Fin tweeted a brief song, then flapped away.

I sighed, resting my chin on my knees, knowing the wait could be long. "I should've listened to you about him," I told Echo.

"*You needed someone,*" Echo replied, her voice carried stronger by the breeze. "*What's done is done.*"

IT WAS THE MIDDLE of the night when Fin and I flew toward the marble castle, my stomach doing flips the entire way there. I'd been worried about returning to Ayastaren ever since Gillius and I had left two years ago, and my relationship with the duke hadn't improved since.

I was loath to call clouds to disguise my position, knowing that it would likely do the opposite. Instead, I prayed that the late hour would mask my entrance. Fin the bluebird twittered in my ear, directing my attention to one of the towers of the castle. I followed her, landing on the windowsill, my back to the stone.

I was surprised the shutters were open, but it was a warm night. I shut my eyes, using Echo's sight as she slipped through the window. The first place she looked was the bed, but even though it was the middle of the night and the blankets were rumpled, the bed lay empty.

I could feel Echo's confusion as a scraping noise sounded to her left and an arm appeared in her vision, reaching out of the window.

55

My eyes flew open. I screamed as I was grabbed and dragged into the room before being slammed into the wall. My head bounced off the stone with a sickening smack.

Dazed, I scratched at the hand wrapped around my throat, squeezing tightly, hot breath sweeping over my ear. "I knew you would come."

I regained my senses and grabbed one of the knives from my thigh holster.

Sam was expecting it. He took control of my hand and beat it against the wall until I let go of the blade. Sam's foot sent it spinning across the room, then he pinned my hands above my head.

"How did I know that you would be foolish enough to think you could sneak in on me?"

I tried to knee him, but Sam kicked my legs open and moved between them, pressing into me.

"I just wanted to talk," I snarled, furious that he'd gotten the jump on me. "To explain."

"Your actions explained everything," Sam growled, squeezing my hands together so tight that tears swelled at the corners of my eyes from the pain. I was hesitant to use my powers and announce to the army camped below us that I was there, but I also didn't want to be throttled by the man whom I'd almost married either.

"Where is the young prince?" Sam's eyes flicked to the window, as though Prince Artian were hiding out on the ledge.

"He's safe and far away from all of you."

"I'm surprised the empress had faith in you. You don't have a reputation for honoring vows."

I tried to ignore the fear. I recalled Agramon's warnings. Sam was not a man to be trifled with, and I'd managed to earn his ire and anger through the most personal betrayal possible. There was no telling what he would do.

But my mind warred with itself. This was Sam. Sam, who had insisted he loved me. Who hid Nirah for me even though it went against his duty as high commander. Who rescued me from the Ylirian invaders and protected me from the worst of Agramon's schemes.

I tried to wrench my hands free from him, but Sam only tightened his grip, bruising my wrists.

"What are you doing here, Sam?" I gasped.

"Bringing you home."

I strained against him. "I'm not going back."

"You will." His grip was so tight, I worried he would break bones. "You are my wife. Your place is with me."

"You swore to protect me," I hissed. "How is dragging me back to Agramon honoring those vows?"

"You dare to impugn *my* honor?" Sam's nostrils flared. "You've made me out as a fool to the entire empire. Now, what have you done with the prince!"

"I'm not telling anyone where he is," I vowed. "Not

even the empress."

Sam cocked an eyebrow. "You are playing a dangerous game, wife."

My hands clenched in his grip. "Don't call me that."

Sam maneuvered so that both my wrists were held firm in his left hand. "But that is who you are," he said. "To me, at least." Sam's right hand dropped to my leg, and he pulled the straps of the knife holster loose so that it fell to the floor. "You gave me your word. Nothing will change that."

"Everything has changed," I challenged. "You can't see that this was the only way? Agramon was going to control the prince to gain the empire. You and I both know he would kill the boy to get what he wants."

"And who would replace Agramon?" Sam asked, his hand reclaiming mine before he lowered them both to either side of my face, caging me in.

"The empress is a good person. A good ruler. She would be fair, and kind, and generous with everyone in the empire. Agramon would only sow anger and distrust. The empress would create a world where everyone is treated fairly."

Sam frowned. "The empress is hiding away in Maryse. The women at the capital may mourn her absence, but Agramon has Somme in an ironclad hold. If you want protection from him, I am your best option."

I didn't speak for a moment. We just stared at each

other as my mind warred with my heart. It would be easy. Just return with him to Bruin. The Morganites were gone. Agramon had never trusted him. It would make sense for Sam to be relieved of his duty as general.

How long would it take Agramon to force him to relinquish his titles as well? How long would it take for Agramon to call me, once again, to his side to blow the winds in his favor? It could be a coming war. It could be rain. It could be rerouting the weather to punish the enemy. If I went with Sam, I would never be my own person. I would never decide my own fate.

There had to be another way.

Sam's eyes were on my hand. He raised his thumb and stroked my finger, touching the ring he'd given to me for our wedding.

"Sam . . ." I whispered.

Sam's nostrils flared. He leaned closer, his eyes on my lips. I could feel his breath, feather light, as he closed the distance, brushing his lips against mine.

"I can't . . ." I murmured, turning my head away.

Sam nudged my cheek with his, his lips at my ear. "Don't play these games. You made promises to me."

"I know," I whispered, fighting the warmth that always rose at Sam's touch. Despite how we left things. Despite his anger. I couldn't help but miss the way he made me feel. "But Agramon must be challenged."

The tenderness escaped Sam's eyes, replaced by an impenetrable hardness that I'd never seen before. Sam twisted me around, shoving me face-first against the stone and drawing my hands behind my back. "You shouldn't have taken the boy."

"I should've just left him to Agramon's control?" I asked, trying to yank free.

"Since that is what the council decided, then yes," Sam growled into my ear as he reached beside me, pulling a silken cord from the curtains.

"Are you trying to lie to me or yourself?"

"None of that matters, anyway." He wrapped the cord around my wrists and tightened it. "I'm not going to let you drag my name through the mud." Sam had never been so rough with me before.

Suddenly, he stilled.

"Release her," a voice declared.

His grip on my hands disappeared and I spun.

Fin was behind Sam, one of my knives in her hand and held to his throat.

I drew my sword and, nodding to Fin, backed away.

Sam looked over his shoulder, his eyes widening at Fin's nude form. He raised a brow. "General Ivar's daughter, I presume?"

Fin held the knife aloft, her hand steady. A year as an animal had made her body a muscled work of art. If I looked as she did without clothes, I probably wouldn't have minded prancing around naked either.

Sam was less distracted than I expected him to be. His eyes flew back to me when I took another step toward the window. Fin and Echo were right. Coming to Sam had been a mistake. I should have traveled around Ayastaren to reach Morgania and not alerted Sam to my whereabouts. Now he knew exactly where I was. He would also come to the correct conclusion about where I was headed.

"I'd heard you found your friend," Sam growled.

"I didn't come here to fight," I said. "I came to explain. I didn't plan for what happened. I didn't walk down the aisle that day intending to betray you."

"Then why did you?"

"You can't tell me that you believe Agramon's lie that Lu Shen attacked!" I was starting to shout, but I didn't care anymore. Sam used to listen to me. He used to hold me with gentle care, as though I were the most breakable thing on earth. He used to give a damn about right and wrong. At least, I'd thought he had.

"It doesn't matter what I believe. Agramon has control of Somme!"

My throat stopped working. "You're working with Agramon? You chose his side?"

"You didn't leave me a choice."

"How could you?" Anger flared in me. "You know how

I feel about that man. You know what he is. How could you take his side in this? How can you take Duke Roland's side?" Tears began to drip down my cheeks.

"I am a man of the empire," Sam said. "I have to do what is best for the people."

"You *hate* him."

"I don't hate him. I just have never trusted him."

"Yet you trust him now?" I asked, throwing a hand out while keeping my sword pointed at him. Sam was not someone to let my guard down around. He became head of the army through skill and merit alone. He had never been one of the soft nobles from the capital.

"It's because of the empress," Fin said, her eyes never straying from Sam's back, poised to attack.

"Why wouldn't you even give her a chance?" I asked.

"The army is firmly against her," Sam said. "As well as the common people of the empire. The only allies she has now are the Marendeslys, and even their loyalty is weak. Duke Eldred just wants the throne for himself."

"So, you become Agramon's lapdog, is that it? You come here, allied with Agramon and the duke of Ayastaren, the two men I hate most in all the world? After all this, you dare to demand that I come back to you? After what you've just done?"

Sam's jaw clenched. "I need you to return with me."

"You think he'll give me to you?" I laughed. "You know

he wanted to keep me for himself. Right before I accepted your proposal, he was talking about marrying me. Why do you think he would just give me back to you?"

Sam straightened. "Because he needs me."

"But why do you need him?"

Sam didn't say anything. Fin's eyes flicked to me.

"Right," I said with a mirthless laugh. "Because you thought the only way I would return to you was by force, and you needed him on your side."

"Am I wrong?" Sam asked, his hand sweeping out. "Look where we are. It can't be a coincidence that we show up on the border to Morgania after combing the entire *fucking world* for you, and suddenly you're here," Sam yelled, stepping into my sword point. "You may think nothing of your vows, but they mean *everything* to me!"

I took a step back, still not willing to hurt him. "I came to speak to you, Sam. I didn't desert you." I tried to keep my voice calm. "But when the emperor was killed, it became about more than just us."

"You've stashed the prince," Sam said, his voice dropping. "You've escaped from Agramon. So why are you going to *him*?"

It was a plea. Sam's hand opened, reaching toward me. I took the signet ring off my finger and placed it on the table next to the window, Sam's eyes following my every move.

"You knew," I whispered. "When we got married, you knew I was still in love with him."

"Rowyn." Sam's voice dripped with warning.

I stepped onto the window ledge and leaped off, letting the wind take me higher. Within moments, Arden flapped beside me.

I looked down and saw Sam with the knife that Fin had dropped.

He drew his hand back.

He wouldn't.

If I'd thought there was truly danger, I would've called a mass of clouds. In my subconscious, I must have been testing him. I wanted to see how far he would go. How much he really loved me, despite what he claimed.

Sam threw. The wind I called to deflect it came too late, and the knife lodged in my shoulder, sending me careening through the air.

I used my magic to catch myself just in time. A powerful blast sent me flying into the clouds and miles away within moments. I managed two more strong gusts before the throbbing in my shoulder began to distract me. I looked down and noticed blood soaking my tunic. My head began to swim. Feathers flashed before my eyes, and Arden flapped behind me. She screeched a warning and I looked down. The ground was fast approaching, a rugged, rocky coast.

64

I barely had time to cushion my landing, and I might've hit it too hard, for the next thing I knew was darkness.

Chapter 6

I am in a storm that I cannot find my way out of.

I cannot fly . . .

I cannot fight . . .

I can only endure it.

Chapter 7

WHEN I CAME TO, I was blinded by a bright light. I tried to lift my arm, to cover my eyes, but it was stone beside me. The best I could do was lift a single finger. I moaned, pain fogging my brain. Pain in my side. Pain in my leg. Pain damn near everywhere.

Something brushed against my forehead and a shadow fell over me. I cracked my eyes open a little.

"You're awake," someone whispered, their hands gentle. I couldn't remember the last time someone touched me in such a way. Gentle . . . soothing. "How are you feeling?"

"Like I'm dying," I croaked.

The voice chuckled. An arm snaked behind my shoulders and lifted me. A rim pressed to my lips. I took a drink and was thankful it was just water. I took another drink, and another, finding myself parched the moment I gave it a thought.

I lay back down and met the eyes of my visitor. I lifted two fingers and brushed them against a balled-up fist.

Destrian looked down and took my hand in his. "I'm glad you're awake."

Tears welled at the corners of my eyes, threatening to

spill. "You found me."

"I will always find you," Destrian murmured, ducking close to my ear. "You might never be rid of me now."

"How?"

"Fin tracked down a group of my soldiers and brought them down to the beach to help. You were being guarded by a particularly vicious pack of wolves." Destrian placed the cup of water on a table beside the bed. He turned back to me and leaned forward.

"Fin is amazing," I sighed.

"You're not wrong there." Destrian chuckled. "She has half my men pining after her now. Several spent an entire barrel's worth of ale to produce the worst poetry I've ever heard. Luc had it worse though."

I attempted a smile; it came off more like a grimace. "Luc's here?"

Destrian nodded. "I guess he recognized Fin as some falcon who traveled with you at the capital. He got quite a shock when a naked woman suddenly appeared."

"Tell me about it," I mumbled. "I hadn't realized Arden was Fin, either, until I was running." I tried to sit up a bit more, but the shock of pain from my shoulder laid me straight back down with a cry of pain.

Destrian rose with a frown. "Gillius is here. I know you're angry with him, so I didn't let him near you while you were asleep." He met my eyes, his fingers gentle on mine. "But you might consider . . ."

"Why is Gillius here?" I gasped, trying to catch my breath. I didn't need to sit up, anyway. It would probably just hurt worse. "How bad is it?"

"My sister's healer said you would live. Gillius wants to help in case the fighting begins. He might get drained quickly, and soon." Destrian's voice dropped. "Fin said you went to see the baron?"

In my half-delirious state, it was difficult to read his emotions.

I nodded, feeling like such a fool. Why had I been so insistent on throwing myself into danger?

"I'll fucking kill him for this," Destrian muttered. Now there was no mistaking his barely restrained rage.

"He was angry." A tear slid down my cheek when I remembered the look on his face. How much I'd hurt him.

"We won't let him near you again," Destrian assured me, leaning onto his knees. "It's been weeks of watching and searching the borders for any sign of you. Morgania is ready to protect her own."

The tears were coming faster now. I hated how I let myself become as close to Sam as I did. Even if I ran, Sam would attack Morgania in the hopes of ferreting me out of the shadows. Destrian didn't deserve this. Now everyone would be after him.

"I'm so sorry." I mourned every choice I made since

leaving Morgania's shores. "I know I've ruined every-thing."

Destrian looked stricken as he ran his fingers along my arm. "You've ruined nothing. You've fought valiantly for us all. It's time to give us a chance to return the favor. Tell us how we can help. What do you *want*, Rowyn?"

"I don't want to be afraid of them anymore." I sniffed.

Destrian brushed a tear from my cheek. "Come home, and you won't be."

I cried harder. Everything just came flooding out and I couldn't make it stop. "Sam thinks we are married."

"The entire empire knows the ceremony was never fin-ished. As far as anyone else is concerned, you are still free to do as you please," Destrian assured me, his fingertips lightly brushing the back of my hand, the touch disappear-ing as it grazed over the gem.

"But he's on Agramon's side now." I still couldn't be-lieve that Sam was allied with Duke Agramon. After their bickering on the journey through the empire, I figured there was no chance that the two would unite. I was a fool for not considering that Sam's entire force would be against the empress *and* me. Sam would follow duty over all else, always. He'd shown me as much during our time together in Bruin.

"It's what you believe that matters. Do you feel you are married?" Destrian asked, hesitant.

"We are not married," I said finally. "But I feel as though I've gone back on my word."

"Did you know that Agramon was going to incite a coup on your wedding day?"

I shook my head. "I had no idea."

"Then there is nothing that was your fault, and you didn't go back on your word. You fulfilled a duty by hiding the prince. It was the baron who betrayed you."

I sighed. "It's hard to see it that way."

"He vowed to protect you. He vowed to keep you safe, and look what he did." Destrian motioned to my shoulder. "If I ever get the opportunity, I want you to know that ending the Baron of Bruin is first on my very long list of things to accomplish. Him and Duke Agramon. Fuck the lot of them for what they did to you."

"I survived," I said weakly. My feelings were so . . . complicated. It was hard to decipher how I felt.

Destrian's hand tightened around mine, his anger palpable. "That doesn't excuse what they did. Echo showed me enough to prove that neither your baron, nor the duke are innocent."

I met his eye. I couldn't leave it unsaid. "It was hard being alone," I murmured. "I was just . . . left to them." I fought the tears. Tears from the pain. Tears from the agony I'd gone through while trapped under Agramon's control. Tears from having no one to go to except Sam, who pulled me out of my misery for a regrettable price.

The muscle in his jaw clenched. "Well, I hope that you will someday find it in your heart to forgive me," he murmured.

I tried to lean closer, looking up. I still couldn't believe that we were so close after having been so far before. "That's not what I mean. It is you who must forgive me."

Destrian cupped my cheek. "I don't forgive you, because you did nothing wrong. The only reason that I stayed away was because Arda the seer had told me to do whatever you said. So, I did that. I wrote down everything that you told me you wanted for Morgania in the Nightlands and then when you ordered me to stay, I did. I just worked on your list, counting down the days until I could see you again, wishing that fate would have been kinder to the both of us."

I stared into his eyes, searching for any trace of blame or anger, but there was none. Only the warmth I'd come to crave in the Nightlands. The softest of smiles that he always seemed to reserve just for me. The lingering touch of his fingers.

He leaned down and kissed my temple, whispering, "Rest now, my love. I'll be here when you wake."

I allowed myself to drift into a peaceful sleep, knowing that when I woke, I would not be alone. I had found my way home.

THE SCENT OF THE SEA and clean linens permeated the room, while outside the window, the sunlight tried its best to filter through the clouds that blanketed the sky above. I wondered how long it had been that way. I could feel my magic seeping from every pore, rising with the fog that curled lazily over the sea that beat against the cliffs the castle of Eslin was built into.

My shoulder throbbed with an insistent rhythm, a gnawing reminder of the wound inflicted by Sam. I was not on the brink of death, but I was weakened, confined to a sickbed in a quiet tower. The door creaked open, casting a sliver of light across the floor. It was Master Gillius, his face tight with worry. He glanced in my direction, then to Destrian who'd been dozing in his chair at my side.

Seeing me awake, Destrian nodded at Gillius. "She can decide for herself now."

I was struck by how different Destrian was from Sam and Agramon. They wouldn't have hesitated. If getting me well furthered their own ends, they would've held the door for Gillius and let him have at it, no matter how I might've felt about it. My throat began to close as I got weepy all over again from how much I'd missed Destrian.

Gillius took a step forward, his gem glowing a bright

green. "Rowyn, I . . ." His voice broke, laden with remorse. "I know you may never forgive me, and for that, I'm sorry."

I looked at him, my expression cold, my eyes filled with hardened steel. "You did what you thought was best," I said, my words void of any emotion. "For the empire. For the commoners . . . like yourself."

A heavy silence lingered, the air thick with tension. Gillius deflated slightly under my cold demeanor. Yet, I knew Destrian was right. I needed to be well, and fast. I needed to be ready for when Sam inevitably crossed the border to crush Morgania under his blade.

"Why are you here, in Morgania?" I asked.

Gillius looked down, his shoulders tense. "All of the students went to the quinquennial. Many have not returned to the academy yet, as war seems to be looming on the horizon. I fear what's to come."

"So you're here to spy on us for Agramon?" I asked, anger flaring in my chest. I was ready to face down anyone who threatened my home, even someone who once posed as my mentor.

"No, Rowyn, I swear it. I will not spy for Agramon. I cannot help what the Council of Five asked me to do before, but now I'm just looking for somewhere to be safe," he pleaded, his eyes wide and earnest.

I shifted, my grip on Destrian's hand tightening as

though he were about to be torn away from me. "Why do you think Morgania would be safe?"

His expression softened, and he looked at me with a kind of longing. "Because I thought you would be here."

My heart ached for a moment, but I shoved the feeling away. "Why should I protect you?"

"It's not just me," he said, his voice catching.

"What do you mean?" But before he could answer, Destrian intervened.

"Rowyn, we can discuss the rest when you're healed." His voice was firm but gentle.

He was right. I needed to be strong again, and Gillius could help me. I nodded slowly. "All right, heal me. But Gillius, know this: my trust in you is shattered. You'll have to earn it back, if that's even possible."

Gillius's eyes filled, but he nodded. "I understand, Rowyn. I'll do whatever I can to make things right."

"Go ahead." The sooner I was better, the sooner we could move forward. The sooner we could rein in the chaos.

Nodding, he pressed his palm to my shoulder as his gem glowed green. The room fell silent as the warmth spread, easing the pain and knitting together the raw edges of my wound.

Once finished, Gillius took a step back. He looked as though he wanted to say something more, but instead, he gave a curt nod and left, the door closing softly behind him.

Destrian stood. "You already look much better," he said, rubbing the back of his neck. I could tell he was nervous. I suddenly felt self-conscious. "I'm glad you let Master Gillius heal you . . ." He trailed off as though there was more he wished to say.

I ran my hand over the coverlet, afraid to meet his eye and see all the emotions bubbling forth that he was holding back while I was injured. "It was the smart thing to do anyway," I mumbled. "No matter the other feelings I might have had about it."

He smiled. "We're in this together, Rowyn. Always."

I took his hand. "Thank you." No words could express the depth of my gratitude. "I'm so sorry."

Destrian's brow furrowed. "For what?"

"For Sam . . ." I choked and wiped my cheek again. "I'm sorry that I let it go as far as it did with the Baron of Bruin. I'm sorry about what happened to your father. I'm sorry I didn't have faith in you. I betrayed your love for me so many times, and I know I don't deserve you." I looked down. "I never have."

"No," Destrian said, sitting on the edge of the bed and nearly crushing my fingers in his grip. "You have nothing to be sorry for." He twisted me to face him, his hand on my cheek, tilting my face to his.

"The thing with Sam . . ."

"Don't," Destrian said. "You are here now, and I want to look to the future, not the past."

"I didn't encourage him in the beginning," I said with a gasp. "I wish now that I had never taken that step."

"No, Rowyn, listen." Both hands held either side of my face. He refused to let me look away. "Every step you took brought you here, into *my* arms . . . home to me. There is nothing else that matters."

A wrenching sob broke through me. I shuddered as he wrapped his arms around me and crushed me into him. I wished I could stop the tears. Since when had I become some weeping woman who cried at the drop of a hat?

"I never wanted any of this," I choked out. "All I wanted was peace. For us, for Morgania, for everyone."

Destrian was being so kind. I hadn't done a thing to deserve his kindness. Not ever.

"Promise me something." Destrian's voice barely broke a whisper.

"Anything," I replied without hesitation.

"Promise me that no matter what happens, we'll face it together. Promise me that you'll never leave again."

My hand tightened around his. "I promise. I will never leave you again. Not in this life or the next. We will face everything together, as we were meant to."

Looking into his eyes for the first time in a long time, I

felt hope. Hope that love and courage could conquer even the darkest of foes.

Chapter 8

I AWOKE TO the sound of insistent knocking on my door. My eyelids fluttered open, and I stretched out my arm and its sore muscles.

The door opened, followed by murmuring, before a woman's voice said, "It's *my* house, brother," and footsteps approached the bed.

A lady with auburn hair pinned up in a plait strode into the room, bearing a tray with a steaming mug and rolls. Her vibrant smile lit up the room, and her dark eyes sparkled with curiosity and warmth. Fin followed, licking her fingers coated in frosting.

"I was just trying to bring you some breakfast," the woman said, shooting Destrian an admonishing look. She carefully set the breakfast tray on my lap.

"Rowyn, this is Onora Everett, lady of Eslin," Fin said, motioning to Destrian's sister when Destrian himself just stood there and glared. Onora bustled cheerfully about, tidying the room.

"You look much better today." Fin sat next to me on the bed and readjusted the dressing gown that Onora had seemingly given her to borrow. It was a pretty shade of green that made Fin look lovely, but it didn't look to fit her quite right.

"I've heard so much about you," Onora chattered, her voice filled with genuine interest. "We're happy you finally made it safely back to Morgania."

"Thank you, Lady Onora." Her warmth immediately made me feel at ease.

Onora glanced at Destrian out of the corner of her eye. He was clearly unused to someone else taking charge in his presence. "Destrian, relax! I'm just being hospitable. You've been hovering over Rowyn for days. It won't hurt to let someone else pamper her for a change."

Destrian blushed slightly, a sheepish smile on his face. "I know. I know. But it was such a bad injury, and she's already been through so much."

"I can see that," Onora said, her voice softening as she looked at me. "But she's here now, and she's safe. We'll take good care of her."

I smiled, touched by her kindness.

She gently nudged her brother. "Go, get some rest. You need it."

Destrian hesitated, glancing at me as if asking for permission. I gave him a reassuring smile and a nod. With a reluctant sigh, he left the room as Fin eyed another roll.

"I'm grateful that you let Gillius heal you," Onora said, lifting the cup of lady's tea for me. "It just made sense to have you at your best."

"I can be stubborn sometimes, but it would've been far too foolish to send Gillius away," I replied with a sigh as I sank back onto the pillows.

"Stubbornness seems to be a trait among sorcerers." Onora chuckled, handing me the cup.

Fin picked up a roll from the tray and offered it to me before plucking another one for herself.

Onora's eyes moved from Fin to me, and she sat on the edge of the bed. "Speaking of Gillius and Master Haris, they've decided to stay here in Eslin."

I took a bite of the roll, interested. "Really? How come?"

Onora exchanged a glance with Fin who leaned against the footpost. "Gillius feels that it might be best if he stays away from Helena, and particularly from you."

I scrunched my nose. "He's not wrong. I would be more comfortable with a bit of distance, especially right now. I've no wish to be around anyone who reminds me of Agramon, even inadvertently." I hoped Destrian's sister didn't think my words cruel or mean.

Onora's eyes met mine, soft and understanding. "You don't have to worry, Rowyn. You're among friends here, and sometimes that means knowing when to keep our distance."

"But it's not just Gillius," Fin interjected, pausing to take a bite of her roll. "Lady Vianne and Lord Alexander are in Helena as well. Anger is high against mind readers after Agramon's coup."

"That's troubling," I muttered, finishing my tea. "I guess we'll have to navigate through some uneasy waters."

"Well," Onora said, taking my empty cup and refilling it. "Kendrew has already found a place for Gillius to set up a hospital. He said that we can send anyone wishing to learn the healing arts to him and he can train them. It's quite exciting! Eslin could become the hub for healing care in Morgania." She paused, her eyes gleaming with a far-off look. "You know, it feels as though we actually have the power to change the world in this moment."

"I am glad that he is finding a new place for himself in the world," I offered.

Onora rested her hand on her stomach. "It will certainly be nice having him here, especially since I'm expecting our second."

My eyes widened. "Congratulations!"

Fin echoed my sentiments.

Onora waved her hand in thanks before leaning toward me. "Now, down to the question on everyone's mind. Are you going to do it?"

I blinked in confusion. "Do what? What are you talking about?"

Onora searched my gaze with a mixture of hope and determination. "Are you going to take the throne?"

I was at a loss for what to say, my mind racing to catch up. How many people knew of my legacy? My throat felt dry, and I struggled to find the right words. The room was still, the silence thick with tension. Finally, I looked up, meeting Onora's earnest eyes, and whispered, "I don't know."

It was the truth. I didn't know if I could do it—if I should do it. But as I looked at Onora and Fin, I realized that this was a question I needed to face. The path before me was uncertain, and the choices I made would shape, not only my destiny but the destinies of those around me.

Onora's smile softened, and she took my hand, giving it a reassuring squeeze. "You, Fin, the empress—there's something remarkable happening here. It's rare to have so many powerful women in the same cycle. Perhaps it's time for us to be given a chance to remake the world."

I smiled faintly, but still, the fear and uncertainty lingered. "But what about Destrian? I could never take his birthright from him."

Onora's face went from bright and encouraging to shocked and confused. "Don't you know?" she asked, her eyes wide. "What do you think he's been doing the entire time you were away?"

I felt the color drain from my face. "What do you mean? What has he been doing?"

Onora's mouth opened, but no sound came out. It was

as if she'd said too much, and now she wasn't quite sure how to proceed. I watched her carefully, my heart pounding as I waited for her to explain.

Her eyes darted to Fin, then back to me, and she looked truly remorseful. She reached forward and took my hand again, her touch gentle and warm.

"Rowyn," she said softly, "Destrian loves you. I've never seen my brother like this before. He's ready to support you, and he's completely bent over backward remaking Morgania into what you wanted, just so that you would have a home to come back to and a place where you could thrive."

"But why didn't he tell me? Why didn't anyone tell me?"

Onora squeezed my hand. "I don't know, but he believes that you can do this, and he's willing to give up everything to see you succeed." She stood, her expression still warm but her posture hinting at her need to attend to other matters. "Think about it. That's all we ask." With a graceful nod, she swept through the door, leaving Fin and me to ponder her words.

Fin took Onora's vacated spot, leaning back against the footboard with her legs stretched out beside mine. "I like her."

I raised an eyebrow. "It's because you want me to take the throne, too, isn't it? Since you're an emissary of King Valon now and that is what he wishes."

Fin combed her fingers through the tangles in her hair. "No, I'm much more selfish than that. I want you to take over Morgania so that I can have a home where no one can own me."

I looked at her, really looked, and saw the longing in her eyes. This wasn't just about me. It wasn't just about a throne or power or responsibility. It was about hope, safety, freedom, and a chance to reshape our world after we opened our eyes to the mistakes of those before us. It was about everyone's future with the possibilities of a new world.

FIN SLEPT IN the room with me for the better part of the day. When I awoke later, she helped me bathe and put on a dress that was borrowed from Onora. Just as we finished, a soft knock was heard at the door.

"I'll see you at dinner," Fin said with a wink, before disappearing.

"How do you feel?" Destrian murmured, stepping in. His gem gave off a soft red glow, and the fire grew brighter, sending waves of heat over me.

"Much better. You were right. I needed Gillius to heal

me."

Destrian nodded. We stood there, oddly awkward, while I shifted my feet. "Can we please sit?" I asked finally, motioning away from the bed and toward the two chairs that faced the fireplace.

"Of course," Destrian said, cutting across the floor and pouring two cups of water before bringing them to the table between the chairs.

"Your sister seems lovely," I began, taking a seat in one of the chairs. "But what did she mean when she said you'd made changes to Morgania?"

Destrian slumped down into the other chair as though he carried a world of weariness upon his shoulders. "I've been enacting what we discussed in the Nightlands."

"Why?"

Destrian's face grew serious. He paused, as though gathering his thoughts. "I remember what you said, when you were wounded by the arrow. When you tried to flee Solridge. You said you wanted to go home. That always stuck with me. In what you thought might be your final moments, that was what you wanted most in the world. So I tried to give you that." His voice trembled slightly. "I knew that's what you really wanted. That's what Fin wants. That's what Vianne wants. That's what the Morganites have wanted all along."

"That's what Agramon wanted." I exhaled sharply,

shaking my head. Were people really that simple? "I still think Vianne is just trying to help the empress." I thought back to Empress Lesedi's anger at my failure in Gryse and her resistance in helping me with Agramon.

"Vianne said that when Agramon made his move, there would need to be a haven for resistors, and Morgania was the perfect spot to hold important people of the empire who had no wish to bow to Duke Agramon's command. Considering how perilous it would be for them to head to Maryse, being so close to Somme and Bruin, it made sense. There would need to be a place in the West for those allied to the empress."

The ever-present feeling of uncertainty crawled through my bones. Destrian seemed to trust Vianne, but I didn't. She had enchanted me to forget Gillius's betrayal. I still wanted to know why that was, and I supposed I would have the opportunity to find out.

Then again, I was pretty sure it was she who sent Obi to give me the Girdle of Ephema, which had saved me from Agramon's mind reading. How much more danger-ous would my time on the eastern shore have been if Agramon had been allowed to go through my mind, mak-ing me do whatever he pleased? What shell of a person would I have become?

Who was left to trust? Who could I count on? I'd thought I could trust the empress, but she turned around and threw me to the wolves the minute I'd blundered, not going to Gryse to see what Agramon had intended with Count Balthazo's mercenary fleet. I'd not gone, still recovering from the trauma of being kidnapped, and the empress had deemed that enough reason to cast me aside, except when she needed me again, of course. I'd fulfilled my duty to her. I'd hidden the young prince in the swamps of Iora, right under the nose of Admiral Abelard Valdis. I'd done my part, sending the empress information of my travels with Agramon, working with Countess Mahira to end the war with Lu Shen and then hiding the prince in the safest place I could think of.

What had the empress repaid my loyalty with? The same as everyone else. She had decried my friendship the minute she was angry. I'd received a few coins to help Luc escape and she sent a letter to Destrian, warning him of the Count of Gryse trying to make a claim to his seat in Helena. That was it.

I clenched my fists. I could never trust someone completely. I would never make that mistake again.

"I'm not entirely inclined to ally with the empress yet. She essentially turned her back on me."

Destrian looked taken aback. "But you hid the prince."

"Yeah, because I knew Agramon would kill him. Just because I didn't want the prince to die doesn't mean I'm entirely on the empress's side."

"But I don't think Lady Vianne is working for the empress. Lady Vianne was always going to bet on you. The best hope for survival was to break away from the empire, to make a safe haven, and Morgania was the natural choice."

"Why Morgania?" I asked, genuinely curious how Vianne had sought my rise more so than I did.

"They nearly beat back Lyrica during the invasion. The only reason Lyrica succeeded at all was because they assassinated the sorcerers loyal to the Morganite kingdom. Nobody is going to break away from the East because anyone who controls the Eastern Empire will hold the land together through force and a history of control, but the West? We are a sea away. Though there are loyalists in Adair and The Fens, Morgania has always had a rocky relationship with the crown, especially since the drought. We have a lost princess who is home now. It makes sense that we become our own once more."

I studied Destrian as the information poured from him. I would've thought that the idea of breaking away from the empire would give him cause for alarm, but no. He was . . . excited.

"So, Vianne wants Morgania as a place for others to hide?" I tried to mask the disbelief from my voice.

Destrian nodded. "Vianne and I worked on this together. Other sorcerers will want to come too. Those who don't wish to become too involved in the infighting will flee. There are many who are afraid of Agramon, who would escape if they knew where. We could be that haven, Rowyn. You were meant to be queen."

"So what now? What do you think I should do?"

Destrian took my hand. "Now? I'm prepared to do whatever you want. If you want to run, I can go with you. If you want to stay and fight, I am prepared to fight."

"As a consul?" I met his eyes. "Onora said that every-one is waiting for me to take the throne back, but what of your future?"

Destrian chuckled darkly. "Agramon will not let me have Morgania if he remains in power. What do you want to do? Just tell me what your next greatest wish is, so I can fulfill that one too." He waggled his eyebrows.

I snorted. He'd released the men of Morgania from conscription, a practice I'd grown up hating, especially af-ter Luc was ripped from my life so quickly. I'd always dreamed of those men coming home, and Destrian was not wrong when he said he'd made my dream a reality.

His profile was illuminated by the soft glow highlighting the stern lines on his face. He had not flinched once, and there was something that unsettled me about his unwaver-ing support.

"Destrian," I began, my voice just above a whisper. His eyes met mine. "Why are you doing this? Helping me to take the throne, I mean. This would effectively end your reign as consul. It doesn't make sense."

There was a long pause as he considered my question.

"I believe in you, Rowyn." He shrugged as though his words meant so little. Not knowing that they meant the absolute world to me. "And I believe in what you can do for Morgania. This isn't about power or position for me. It's about doing what's best for everyone."

I held his gaze. "And what will you do, if not consul-ship?"

His answer was immediate. "The empire is being torn apart from the inside. Morgania doesn't need a consul loyal to Lyrica. We need a queen who is loyal to her people." Destrian leaned forward and took my hand into his warm one. "I want to be by your side. I want to be your right hand, supporting you in your reign. I want to be part of this journey, Rowyn, in whatever capacity you'll have me."

"What of your dreams?" I asked, still in disbelief that he would willingly give up everything and hand it to me—and more. "What of everything you've worked for?"

Destrian's fingers caressed mine. "I am my father's son. It was one of the more admirable traits he passed down to me. We only love once, but we love big. It will only *ever* be you." He cupped my cheek. My blood quickened at the heat of his fingers. "Rowyn, I look into your eyes, and you conquer me. I will lose none of that if I help you."

"What are you saying? We would marry? You would be king?"

Destrian pulled away. My flesh mourned the loss of his. "Actually, despite what my wishes might be, I would advise against it. You being unclaimed, and as powerful as you are, it would make much more sense if you left yourself open for an alliance. Lu Shen, Ember Innes, Shea Innes, and Yliria are all strategic possibilities in the trials to come, that is, if we can find anyone to legitimize your claim."

I furrowed my brows. That wasn't what I expected him to say. Nor wanted.

"I don't want to do this without you."

Destrian smiled. "I'm not planning on going any-where."

Destrian, out of all my would-be lovers, was the only one who actually listened to me and didn't try to force me to conform to his ideals. Unlike Sam, Agramon, and even Luc, he heard my wishes and acted on them, not for his gain, but for my happiness.

A lump formed in my throat, and I swallowed hard, un-able to find the words to express my gratitude, my aston-ishment, my respect for this man who had gone to such lengths for me.

"We can think on it later," I conceded, a sense of ur-gency creeping into my voice. My gaze was drawn to the window. The world outside was filled with both possibilities and threats. "Did you say there would be fighting soon?" I asked, a chill running down my spine.

Destrian's face was grave as he nodded. "The baron has been calling back a few of the forces along the border, and we believe he plans to mount an attack soon, especially now that he knows where you are."

A fire ignited within me at his words. "Well," I said, determination settling in, "let's slow them down, shall we?" My feet carried me to the window, and I peered out at the sky, closing my eyes to envision where Ayastaren lay to the south of us.

The plan formed in my mind with startling clarity, a straightforward feat considering the short distance. It was within my reach, an act of power that I could unleash.

Destrian stepped beside me. "What are you doing?"

A smile tugged at my lips. "Ayastaren wanted rain, right? Well, I'm going to give it to them." My hands rose to the sky. Feeling the energy rise within me, I sent a boiling mass of clouds south on a strong wind, feeding an enormous amount of power into it. More than I normally would to create a storm that would be a true monster.

I could almost hear the howling winds and feel the torrents of rain that would descend upon Sam and his forces. If he thought he could bully me with his little army of mercenaries, then he didn't know me at all. He would soon contend with a sodden army, flooded terrain, and an impassable river.

I sent the wind south, the power coursing through me as I waited, tracking the clouds until they were right where I wanted them. And then, I unleashed everything I had at Duke Roland and the Baron of Bruin.

It was a declaration of defiance, a reminder of my strength. I would not be bullied—I would not be cowed. I would stand my ground and let them feel the full force of my wrath.

As the storm raged, I relished the satisfaction. They wanted a fight? They would get one.

And this time on my terms.

I looked at Destrian. "So how do I accept this dream offering of yours? Do I make a formal request?"

Destrian's eyebrows perked up. "Oh, my Queen, I thought you'd never ask."

Chapter 9

THE TOWER OF ESLIN was actually many towers built into the cliffs that bordered the chilly northern Ballerian Sea. It had been built by my Morganian ancestors. While Helena's architecture featured heavy columns and simple windows, Eslin was built later, and the winding columns and windows were smaller, with delicate carvings throughout.

Over the great hall, a balcony overlooked the cliffs below and sea beyond where I could get fresh air under the watch of guards. Spiraling around the columns and balustrade were carvings of thorny vines. Looking closer, I realized they were Morganian rose blossoms. Even in the hands of Lyricans, the homes of my ancestors still bore the symbols of the past.

"Rowyn!" Luc shouted, running up and gripping me in a big hug. I turned and laughed, returning his hug with a tight squeeze, thankful that my shoulder was fully healed.

"Do you recognize these?" Luc asked. His finger brushed the rose blossoms on my neck. "We've been worried sick about you. I'm glad to see you up and feeling better."

I'd always thought Luc and I were meant to be. I'd been

raised to believe that we were destined for each other. But now, I wanted something different for my life. Destrian was my future. Destrian was who I wanted to spend my days with. The one who constantly dwelled within my thoughts, haunting me the farther I traveled from his embrace.

"Destrian suggested Master Gillius heal me," I explained.

"You love him, don't you," Luc whispered, watching me closely.

I nodded and looked back out to sea. "It feels strange. We were promised to each other for so long, did you never stop to consider if you really did care for me the way the others wanted?"

Luc gripped the delicate balustrade in his big hands. "I've always cared for you."

"No, you didn't care in the East," I said, pushing back the sadness.

Luc frowned and looked down at his hands. "I know I fucked up. I know I'm shit at showing it. But I have always cared for you. When I was in the pits, I thought of you often." He watched the sea lapping easily below us on the rocks and cliffs at the base of the towers. "I would think back to our childhood—you, me, and Ferris—and all the adventures we went on. Even then, I wished to return to those moments."

He turned to me. "But that was then. As I think on them now, I know we can never go back to that life, even if we wish to. When the realization hit that I might never return home again, I gave you up and pushed you from my thoughts and entertained myself with the present. With the next bloody battle, the next woman who offered me comfort at night. I never dreamed I would see you again. If I knew then what I know now, I wonder if I would have let myself turn into the man I was."

"It doesn't matter anyway." I wiped a tear from the corner of my eye. "The truth is that none of that matters anymore. It's only a matter of time before Samael and Agramon come for me."

"I know," Luc murmured. He took my hand in his. "Thank you for what you did. Your sacrifice to save us."

"That's what you do for the people you love," I said, looking somberly up at Luc. He had not sacrificed himself for me. Quite the opposite, in fact. "I am taking the throne."

Luc stopped breathing for a moment.

"Please don't tell anyone." I glanced over my shoulder at the guards. "We need to get to Helena before it's announced, but as my oldest friend, I thought you should know."

"I know you're still angry with me," Luc said gruffly. "We may not be fated to each other for the rest of our days, but we are fated to be together now. The empire is crumbling around us, and the rise of the Morganites is at hand. You will determine whether or not the Morganites come into their own again. So, my place is here with you, now, to do what I can to help you succeed. Imor has called me to it."

I turned back to the sea, its waves ever constant, a reminder that even in times of tumult, some things remained the same. I took a deep breath, filling my lungs with the salty air, as if I could draw strength from the very earth that had birthed my ancestors. With Luc by my side and the promise of battles to come, I faced the setting sun.

WE GATHERED IN the courtyard of Eslin, preparing to depart for Helena. Men were busy saddling horses and checking equipment. Among them were the Morganites, marked with imorets, and a few Lyrican soldiers readying themselves next to them.

As we made the final preparations, I noticed Onora standing near the edge of the gathering. I approached her, extending my hand in gratitude.

"It was wonderful meeting you. I cannot thank you enough for the risk you took in keeping me sheltered and helping me heal."

She took my hand, her grip firm and reassuring. "You're like family now, Rowyn. I'd do it again in a heartbeat. Just take care of my brother," she added, a playful glint in her eye.

I smiled back. "I'll do my best."

Destrian approached leading horses. "Are you ready?"

"As ready as I'll ever be."

"I've already sent word to prepare Helena for the return of her princess," he told me as he lifted me into a saddle, his hands warm and steady.

"Did you just know I would say yes to taking the throne?"

He paused and met my eyes. His lips curved into a slight smile. "Not exactly," he admitted. "I had multiple plans ready, depending on your decision."

I shook my head, taken aback by his preparation. "And what if I had said no?"

"Then another series of orders would've taken this one's place," he said before mounting. "I believe in being prepared."

He turned back to the others to issue more directions. There was an elegance to his command, a smooth confidence that put everyone at ease.

For the first time, I allowed myself to consider that maybe, just maybe, I was ready to rule. And with Destrian by my side, I knew I had the support I needed to face whatever was to come.

Destrian leaned toward me as we waited for the gate to rise. "Things will move fast when we get to Helena, and I was worried about Bruin's army, but now it looks like we won't have to worry about them for a while."

"How are things looking in Ayastaren?" I asked. As soon as I'd woken up in the morning, I located the storm that was still raging in Ayastaren and added as much power as I dared before getting ready to leave.

"They are miserable," Destrian said with a grin. "Cold, wet, and miserable. That was an excellent idea on your part."

As we rode out, the host of men falling in line behind us, I couldn't help but feel a surge of energy and anticipation.

We began our journey through the a city perched on the edge of cliffs, with the Ballerian Sea stretching out below. Its cobblestone streets were narrow and winding, flanked by stone buildings that clung to the cliffsides. The morning sun cast a golden glow on the sea, and the air was filled with the cries of seagulls and the salty tang of the ocean.

As we moved through the city, I marveled at the bustling markets where merchants hawked fresh fish and salted meats. The sounds of hammers rang out from the blacksmith shops, and children darted between the legs of horses, their laughter mingling with the rhythmic *clip-clop* of hooves.

But beneath the lively façade, I noticed the furrowed brows of citizens and the weary looks of soldiers patrolling the city walls. Eslin, like the rest of the land, was on edge, caught in the grip of uncertainty. And change was coming.

Past the city gates, the land opened up to hilly farmlands and forests. Green fields rolled into the distance, dotted with houses and windmills. It was a peaceful contrast to the anticipation that thrummed within our ranks.

"What of allies in Morgania?" I asked, now feeling doubtful. "What of the consuls of Rudin and Eslin? I can't imagine they would be so quick to give up their titles just because I want to pursue the crown."

Destrian nodded. "If Emperor Arthello were still alive, it would've been much more difficult, but as it is, the chaos gives us more opportunity to solidify our position while the nobles of the East fight among themselves. Onora's husband, Kendrew, has been pissed at the empire for years, so he was easy to persuade to our cause, considering the unrest at the capital right now. It shouldn't be too difficult to negotiate."

I nodded. "What of Rudin?"

Destrian glanced at me. "We'll be our own kingdom, which means we have all sorts of higher noble titles we can hand out to people whom we wish to ally with. Maybe we can let him be a viscount? He would like that. Honestly, he would follow my decisions no matter what. It's the people we need to focus on. We must win their trust."

Chapter 10

THE NIGHT WAS COOL as we made camp on the road to Helena, the stars shining brightly above us. The soldiers had gathered around the fires, their faces illuminated by the dancing flames.

A rustle in the trees caught our attention, and we looked up to see Arden gliding down from the sky. She landed gracefully on a nearby branch, her eyes gleaming. With a shimmering transformation, the falcon's form melted away, and Fin stood before us, unashamed.

The soldiers' eyes followed her as though in a trance. Luc was the first to snap out of it, quickly removing his cloak and draping it over her shoulders.

"Thank you," Fin said to him, her smile genuine.

"Arden was you the entire time?" Luc asked.

Fin nodded, her eyes twinkling with mischief. "Yes."

Luc's face turned a brilliant shade of red, and he began to stammer. "Then you've seen me . . . you've seen me naked?"

Fin shrugged, her smile widening. "And now you've seen me naked. You have nothing to be ashamed of. Most of the time I *barely* looked."

Luc's sputtering grew louder as Fin walked away, still

wearing his cloak, to get some food. He stormed after her, his words a jumbled mess of indignation and embarrassment. Destrian and I burst into laughter.

After our giddiness died down, Destrian led me to the tent that Fin and I would share.

"We should work on our plans," he said, serious once more. "Every detail must be accounted for, and I don't like speaking too much in front of the men until we reach Helena."

I nodded, my mind shifting to the task at hand.

The interior of the tent was spacious, with a hole at the top to let out the smoke from the central fire. The light cast a gentle glow on the maps and parchments spread out on a makeshift table.

"How will we unify everyone?" I asked, settling down on a cushion to pick at a plate of food that a soldier had brought while Destrian pulled out a journal and quill. His mind was clearly deep in the details of our strategy. "There will surely be those who have no wish to go against the empire."

"Possibly, but you weren't wrong at Solridge when you argued that the unrest in Morgania was due to overreach. In the end, it's not just been the Morganite clans frustrated." Destrian looked up from his journal, his eyes thoughtful. "And I've brought the Morganites into the fold. They're fractured, but the leaders are willing to support you. They see the opportunity for a new future."

I frowned, dubious about his claims. "Just like that?"

He smiled with a touch of pride. "I've been working with them for some time. Trust takes time to build, but it's there. I created my council in Helena with the intention that you will choose some people you might be interested in utilizing. People you could trust. Your cousin Ferris is now the captain of the guard."

My eyes widened. I didn't speak for a moment. "Ferris is the head of your guard?" I asked, unsure if I heard correctly. What had happened in Morgania while I'd been overseas? "I can't believe that Morganites are any part of the guard!"

Destrian nodded. "Morganites and women. The pay is good enough that we've had a few female recruits already. But, now that we have all those conscripted men back, I say we do exactly as Duke Agramon feared and use them as an army. Keep in mind, my father was a hoarder of money; we are plenty able to fund what you desire."

I nodded, my eyes on the fire. Watching it with Destrian in the room was the most comforting feeling in the world.

"I want to spend it on people," I said, resting my head on my hand. "Let's pay the soldiers well. Morgania has the best-fed people in the entire empire, even with most of our crops going overseas. We would be a formidable force, but I want people to be paid well."

Destrian grinned and nodded. "Urdua is also in Helena. She's currently a judge, but the council duties will shift once you become queen, and we will need to elect masters to each position."

"All right, let's start there. If I'm to take the throne, what kind of people will I need to surround myself with?"

Destrian's grin turned almost predatory. "I will be your greatest help, of course, as a seneschal," he said. "But beyond that, we will need . . ." He flipped through the pages in his journal until he found the right one. I studied the cover, thinking I should probably steal it from him so I could get insight on what the gods he'd been up to.

"Let's start with the main ones. We need a Master of War. Especially now that the Baron of Bruin is pounding on our doors with Ayastaren. Your rain won't hold them off for long. Most of the conscripted men who have returned are willing to join the army," Destrian went on, "but we need a commander. Someone capable and loyal."

I sighed. The commander of forces would be the hardest one to assign. "Did you have anyone in mind?"

Destrian shrugged. "Lord Alexander is in Helena. He'd do tolerably well in the role, if we needed him."

I looked down at the map of Morgania. "No. We need to have someone who knows the land. What about Ferris?"

Destrian grimaced. "I don't want to move him. He's done really well with the guard, and I worry that if I bring in someone new so quickly, it will all turn to shit."

"Luc would actually be a good general," I said, my eyes back on the fire. "Even Sam said so."

Destrian raised his brows. "He has already proven to be a traitor to you."

I bit my lip. "He wants to protect Espiria. If we make all of Morgania safe for Morganites, he will want to protect that too."

"It is your call, but I don't like it. Are you sure you can trust him?"

I frowned. How did he even know about Luc betraying me?

"Echo showed me what happened with Ena and Agramon," Destrian said, slipping a finger in his journal as he closed it.

I wished Echo wouldn't do that. Destrian probably wondered why I had chosen Luc over Ena. I honestly didn't even know the answer to that.

"I know, but Luc would be really good at it. He was ready to take over from Father at home, and he's an excellent strategist. That's how he did so well in the fighting pits, and Sam remarked that he had some really good ideas."

Destrian sighed. "In the end it's your choice, but I want Lady Vianne to look into his mind to see if Agramon's planted anything that could cause a problem later."

I sighed. "Fine, but I would like to appoint Luc as

Master of War for now. The others will look up to him. They know him already as Mordog."

"We will need a Master of Law. Especially if you want to reform the Lyrican laws still in place. New judges will be appointed by that person. New laws suggested. I know you want changes for the Morganites, so we could ask for suggestions from Kaelan or the others."

I shook my head. "Didn't you say you appointed Urdua as a judge? She should do it. We need reforms for Morganites and women. Urdua satisfies both."

Destrian's eyebrows peaked. "She's definitely someone who commands respect." He opened his journal once more and began to write. "She's unhappy with her scribe though. She can't read or write, and the boy I assigned to the task has been taxing her nerves."

I shrugged. "Get her a new one then. Either way, I want her as Master of Law. The clan she brought to Espiria was large, so if we want to keep them happy, giving Urdua more power to make changes is the way to do it."

Destrian nodded. "It will be done."

I almost laughed, my eyes on him. "It's as easy as all that, is it?"

Destrian's lip quirked. "Do you doubt my ability to help you?"

I shook my head. "No, I just thought you would argue more. Everything with Agramon and Sam always ended in an argument where I was wrong and they were right, and I needed to stop being so pigheaded."

"I am glad I am not them," Destrian said. "I need to know who you trust. We will find spots for everyone you want close to you, and I will try to fill in the gaps from there. Now, ideally we would have a spymaster, but those are the most difficult to come by. It requires a very specific set of skills."

"Vianne?" She'd spent more time in Morgania than I'd initially thought.

Destrian shook his head. "She's too conspicuous. Those on the eastern shore know her face from her time at court. League leapers are ideal, but Lord Obi isn't in his right mind, and Elgar the Swift already works for Agramon."

"Fin," I breathed, my eyes widening. "Fin would be perfect."

"She can understand what is said as an animal?"

"That's what she was doing in the East the entire time I was there. She sat right under Agramon's nose, and he was none the wiser. Never once was she caught."

"How did he not sense her?"

"I don't know. He has never spoken about reading an animal's mind."

"I wonder if she would do it." Destrian looked thoughtful. "It's the riskiest job on the council. Elgar the Swift has the scars to prove it."

"I only need to ask." I fiddled with a loose thread on my skirt. "She already knows the risk."

"I thought it too optimistic to think we could have a spymaster so early in your reign, but you do make some very good points." Destrian dipped his quill in the ink before scribbling some more in the journal.

"We need banners," I offered, my mind racing. "Symbols that people can rally behind. We need to show them a united front."

"Yes, symbols are powerful," Destrian agreed, jotting down more notes. "We need to choose wisely. Your reign must be a new beginning, not just a continuation of the past."

I studied him. Everything my parents, my clan, had dreamed of was beginning to come true. But at what cost? "You will lose everything if we fail to break away," I whispered, meeting his gaze. "We all will."

Destrian placed his hand on mine. "You are my everything."

My heart began to quicken. "And you are mine," I whispered back. I wanted him to kiss me. I wanted to feel the heat of him.

Destrian squeezed my hand and then let go, a determined glint in his eye. "Then let's make sure we don't fail. Let's build something that will last."

I nodded. No matter what Destrian told me, I wasn't convinced that I hadn't wounded him in some way when it came to Sam. "Yes. Let's do that."

"I love you," Destrian murmured with a smile.

"I love you too." I placed as much feeling as I could into the words. I just had to show him that I meant what I said.

I was done running.

Chapter 11

THE SPELL'S SOFT GLOW danced across the fabric of the tent, painting it a mystical shade of red as Destrian placed the protective barrier around us. Fin and I watched from the pads we'd fashioned on the ground.

"He's good at that," Fin whispered, her eyes wide as she watched the ward take shape, leaving no holes.

I nodded, my thoughts still tangled with the emotions from earlier. "It saved me the night we'd stopped in Ayastaren on the way to Solridge."

Once the ward was complete, Destrian's shadow retreated, leaving Fin and me alone in the cozy space. Quiet, save for the murmurs around camp that swam in from beyond the canvas.

Fin eyed me. "I'm sorry about the baron. I didn't think he would throw."

"I didn't either," I sighed.

"I know you still had feelings for him, even if they weren't as strong as they are with Destrian," Fin whispered.

"I thought there was a chance I could be happy," I confessed. "It wasn't terrible when we were in Bruin. I'd actually enjoyed myself most of the time."

Fin rolled her eyes. "Oh, I know."

I took a deep, calming breath. "I didn't know you were Arden. You didn't have to stay and watch."

Fin pursed her lips. "But Echo did."

"By all the gods, Echo! What's wrong with you?" I hissed into the darkness. Fin snorted. "You're so damn nosy sometimes."

"*I wanted someone to share my pain*," Echo whispered back.

Fin broke out into fits of laughter, and the murmured voices from the tent next to us stopped.

I threw a pillow at her. My life was a mess, and I wished every intimate moment I'd ever shared with somebody wasn't so much on display. That's the way it was with magic, I guessed. It always wanted to be out in the open. Agramon had hinted at seeing glimpses into my love life with Sam, and of course Echo had apparently stuck around for every detail. There wasn't much for her to do, though, considering Agramon and Luc had been away at Gryse, so there was no one to follow, nor information to seek.

"Wait a moment. Echo, did you know Arden was Fin?" I asked.

"*I knew Arden was different. I didn't know how.*"

"Why didn't you tell me?"

"*She was guarding you. I assumed she had reasons not to reveal herself.*"

"I'm just surrounded by liars," I huffed.

"Hey, that's not fair," Fin said. "You were spying for the empress."

"And you're spying for the fae king."

"And you ask Echo to spy for you," Fin reminded me.

I suddenly remembered my earlier conversation with Destrian. "Yes, about that. Would you be able to see what Agramon is doing overseas in Somme?"

"Who's to say I haven't been all along," Fin replied. "There's a flock of pigeons that keeps me updated."

"What's he doing?"

"Trying to keep his hold on Somme. He seems to be working closely with the Sons of Sol and Chassandre the seer, so if I were you, I wouldn't be trying to get back to the capital anytime soon. He blames you for the emperor's death. He's made up some story about how you allied with Lu Shen."

I rolled onto my back. "I just love how, in just two full moons, Agramon and Sam, who were supposed to take care of me and keep me safe, have become the two greatest enemies I have on this earth."

Fin sighed. "I know. Men are baffling."

I turned back toward her. "Destrian says that we would need a Master of Spies, someone to take messages and gain intel from our enemies. Naturally, I thought of you, but you might have other ideas about what you want to do with your life. It's dangerous work, after all."

"I'd half a thought to travel," Fin said, a smile tugging at the corners of her lips, "but I could certainly travel with a purpose and learn what I can."

"Even if you don't help me," I clarified, "you will always have a home in Morgania. I can't make promises for when Agramon discovers my sedition and razes this place to the ground, but as long as I am living, and in control, then I would be honored if you made your home here. You can have rooms at the castle, or in the city—wherever you want. I'll have Destrian arrange a tour for you; he said that the majority of rooms are empty or storage anyway. You would receive a salary as well. Just for sticking around and helping out, if you wish. I was already going to pay you for your help in getting the prince and me back from the eastern shore."

"We're friends, Rowyn. I will not take payment for that."

"I insist," I said, brooking no argument. "You've had nothing to yourself for the past year. You need clothes, Fin. Clothes, good food, comfort. I can't imagine what it must've been like for you as Arden. I wish I'd spoiled you more!"

Fin laughed. "I would be honored to accept a position at court. I like the idea of my best friend being a queen. I feel as though my life is going to be bigger than what I'd ever dreamed."

"Anyone would be lucky to have you, Fin. I've always said this. But I'm not going to lie—we need you here. Just think about it," I said, feeling as though Fin and I were on better ground than we'd ever been.

"Absolutely I will do it."

That was a little unexpected. "How can you agree so quickly? Did Destrian say something?"

Fin shook her head. "I was born for this. Claw, the goblin who taught me how to transform, told me that there was another of my line who was spymaster for one of the emperors."

"What of your bargain with King Valon? Will it interfere?"

Fin shook her head again. "Just meet with him, and I will have fulfilled my end of his deal."

"Well . . . thank you for accepting. I don't want to drag you down or anything, being involved in a rebellion—"

"Will you stop already?" Fin murmured. "This isn't bringing me down. This is raising me up."

"It's still a gamble though," I reminded her.

"Yes, a gamble that I get to choose to make."

"Have I told you I love you yet?" I asked.

Fin shook her head.

"Well, I love you, Fin . . ." I paused. "Wait, what do you go by?"

Fin looked down. "When I was in Horan, they called me Fin Of-Cheapside. Before that, I had my mother's surname."

"What do you want to be called?" I asked.

Fin shrugged. "Well, since I'm going to be the spymaster and all . . . what about Fin of Morgania?"

I grinned. "Are you not worried you might hate it? You haven't even been there yet."

Fin wrinkled her nose. "I won't hate it. I'm absolutely planning on turning Morgania into something I love. There is power in change. I want my voice at the table."

"I love you, Fin of Morgania."

"So," Fin began, her eyes filled with curiosity and concern. "You're going to take the throne. You're really doing it."

I sighed. "It seems the gods have been pretty firm about what they expect me to do."

"It's exciting, too, isn't it? I mean, I know it was kind of thrust upon you, and you haven't been interested in leading, but now you have the opportunity to build Morgania into what you want it to be."

"Yes," I said slowly, "but that's exactly what scares me. Having one person in control of an entire country. Just look at the emperor. A single death to upend a kingdom . . . it's not a very secure way to build a land. I don't want to be in a position where I, or whoever sits on the throne after me, can do whatever they want based on a whim."

Fin's brow furrowed, and she sat up, leaning on one elbow to face me more fully. "You won't be like that, Rowyn. You'll be just. You'll rule with compassion and integrity."

"But what about after me?" I asked, my voice trembling with doubt. "How can I ensure that what follows will be for the good of the people?"

Her expression changed, becoming more serious. "What about Destrian? Will you two get married? That would make him king. At least then you would have a partner."

I shook my head, remembering the conversation I'd had with him. "He advised against it. He said that I might need to make an alliance with another empire. Marriage might be necessary for that."

Fin's eyes widened slightly, but she nodded in understanding. "That makes sense. It's wise to keep all options open."

I couldn't help myself. "What about Luc? What's going on between you two?"

"What do you mean?"

"I can't tell whether he is in love with you, furious with you, or both."

Fin's voice softened. "Did you know that Luc would sit

outside your bedroom at night with a chair to the door, just to ensure that Agramon didn't bother you? There were many nights that I sat on his shoulder, and it felt like the two of us were guarding you."

Silence settled between us once more, but it was Fin who broke it again. "You know, King Valon will want to see you, especially now that you are actively taking charge of Morgania as queen."

I sighed, feeling the weight of the responsibilities ahead. "I won't be able to leave Morgania very soon. There's too much to do."

"I'll send him a message," Fin offered, her tone firm. "I'll tell him that you're taking the throne. He'll want to know, so he can help you."

"Why would he want to help me?" I asked.

Fin thought for a moment, her eyes distant, as though searching for the right words. Finally, she looked back at me with a steady gaze.

"Because he wants to open the borders between Morgania and Horan," she said carefully. "So the fae can begin to pass through once more."

I was surprised by the news, my mind racing with the implications. "We were allied in the past, and though there were issues that came with cohabiting with the fae, Morgania was a stronger place for it," I thought aloud.

Fin nodded, her expression grave. "The fae are getting

crowded in Horan. The king believes that by working together, Morgania and Horan can both benefit. He might be able to help in the trials to come, especially if Agramon decides to make things hard for you."

I felt a chill at the mention of Agramon's name and remembered his threats. "Agramon told me he wouldn't let Morgania break away if he was put in power. He will eventually come for me, won't he?"

Fin's eyes darkened with concern, but she didn't shy away from the truth. "Yes, he probably will. But with allies like the King of the Fae, you won't have to face him alone."

"You're right," I said. "We'll need all the help we can get. Does he really just want to renegotiate the border?"

Fin sighed. "No, but it's best if I let him tell you himself. I know it seems like I'm being secretive, but he'll be so much happier if I just let him say it."

I let out a gust of frustration.

"I know, Rowyn, I know. There's so much going on, and it's all so overwhelming. But let's take things one step at a time."

We lay in the dark, the tent filled with the soft sounds of our breathing. I stared at the stars through the opening above us. It seemed only yesterday I was still in Somme, standing as still as possible while my wretched handmaid Gree tied me into an extravagant showpiece. Agramon would be sitting outside of my door, waiting to parade me around the entire court to display how powerful he was.

Sam was always at my heels, trying to guard me against Agramon but being woefully ill-equipped to do so. Gods, they'd all just left me to that man. He'd murdered Ena. He'd entrapped Luc, entrapped me, and then murdered the emperor. Now, he was in charge of the entire empire.

I would not let that stand.

When I'd considered running, I thought I'd be alone. What else was there to think? Destrian hadn't tried to reach me at all, a fact that Agramon had informed me with glee. Fin had disappeared, and the masters at Solridge hadn't said a word. The very clan that raised me had turned their backs. First my uncle, then Conal, Luc's father, had thrown me to the empire like I was worthless trash. There was no one who reached out and offered me escape. Now, all of a sudden, I was surrounded by allies.

Gillius was a surprise. I was sure that he'd be the first to offer help to Duke Agramon. After all, it was Gillius who Duke Agramon used to gain information about me from Solridge. It was Gillius who sent the portrait. It was Gillius who spent Agramon's coins on me and bought my trust.

But Gillius had come to heal me. When the choice mattered, he'd chosen *my* side. He and Vianne.

I still couldn't gather my feelings about Lady Vianne. She'd taken my memories. She'd kept me trapped within the empire. Had she done it because Gillius told her to?

Then again, Vianne was also the one who ensured I receive the Girdle of Ephema. She went to Morgania to help Destrian build a regime. Vianne also hated Agramon more than I did. There was a reason for her loyalty, and I knew it better than anyone. By the gods, was this really how it was going to be?

I glanced over at Fin's sleeping form. All this time she'd been by my side.

Even Destrian, who'd stayed a world away, had shown his loyalty countless times. I'd thought he'd moved on with his life. I'd assumed that after the rumors of Sam and I had reached his ears that he would've found solace in someone else's arms and tried to forget about me.

How wrong could I've been about him? Destrian had busied himself with getting a throne ready for me.

Even my clan had redeemed themselves. When we were planning together, Destrian had told me how Ferris had captured Conal, and Urdua had sentenced him to prison for killing Destrian's father, the Consul of Helena. I couldn't believe they'd even spoken with Destrian. Now, the clans were rallying to Morgania's cause.

Our cause.

When I asked if we would be married, I hadn't realized I'd been waiting for the admission of Destrian's true desire. It would've made sense for him to want to be king, and I was prepared for it. I would've probably taken it too.

But Destrian hadn't sought to benefit himself. How did he go from saying everything wrong to saying everything right? I'd fallen completely in love. Destrian was my everything, and I hoped to all the gods who could hear my pleas that we got more time. I couldn't lose him again. My heart wouldn't be able to take it.

Now that I knew what it felt like to be surrounded by love, I refused to be alone anymore.

Chapter 12

I AWOKE TO AN unusual emptiness in the tent. Rubbing my eyes and sitting up, I realized Fin was already gone. The warmth of her presence was missing, replaced by the distant sounds of the camp coming to life.

Rising and dressing in the utilitarian garb suitable for a day of travel—breeches and a tunic—I quickly ran my fingers through my black hair and braided it, hoping it looked somewhat presentable. Thoughts of yesterday's discussions swirled in my mind—the plans, the hopes, the uncertain future of Morgania.

But I was already beginning to doubt myself. It was maddening to have so much thrust upon you, and though I had many resources to help me shoulder the burden of prophecy and change of fortune, I was ill-equipped with others.

I hated being around people. I hated being the center of attention. Though I played the part as best as I could for Agramon, I was still woefully inadequate, despite the amount of teaching and training that had gone into me learning how to survive at court. I'd barely managed it, if I was honest with myself.

I might have good ideas. I might have a strong belief in

justice, but I was not really someone to inspire people in a speech to change long-held ideas and prejudices and put aside their fear for something greater.

That was Destrian.

Even Fin was probably better at that than I was.

What made me so special that my opinion counted so much more than everyone else's? There was still so much for me to learn, and I already felt behind.

I let out a sigh of frustration as I belted Iranoct to my waist. It seemed stupid to continue the same illogical process that had put the empire in this entire mess. They put all their faith and the integrity of the empire on one voice. One person could cause everything to crumble. It didn't seem like the empire was that sturdy to begin with.

No, if I was to take over Morgania, there had to be safeguards. What if Sam and Ayastaren attacked? What if something happened? I was absolutely target number one.

Sometimes I wondered what they were thinking. Everyone loved Destrian, but me? Most people didn't really like me. I was used to it now, but it was difficult for me to believe that thought would just magically change the moment they called me, "Your Highness."

There had to be another way. We couldn't just keep propping up the same failed system and creating unrest for the people. I realized, after hearing Destrian describe what he did for the council, that what we really needed were more voices. We needed people who everyone could believe in.

Stepping out of the tent, the morning sun greeted me with a kiss of warmth. Soldiers were moving about, breaking down tents and stomping out fires, the laughter of camaraderie brightening the day.

I found Destrian immediately, as if my body was always aware of his presence. He looked like he'd just finished sparring with some of the guards. His shirt was off, like the rest of them, and his chest was dark from days spent in the sun.

My eyes were instantly drawn to his arm, where the marking of a dragon seemed to come to life on his bicep. Its wings were outstretched across the muscle, and its tail wound around his forearm. My heart galloped in my chest. He didn't have that marking in the Nightlands. I was sure of it. He must've gotten it while I'd been in Somme. Just seeing it made me . . . look at him differently. With his red beard growing out, he was beginning to look more like a Morganite than a Lyrican.

I'd always thought him handsome, even when I didn't like him. Now? He was becoming impossible to resist.

I approached. Destrian nodded the guardsmen off, though one or two tossed him a teasing comment, which he ignored. He grabbed a shirt that had been tossed on the grass and mopped the sweat off his brow.

I couldn't resist reaching out, my fingers brushing the marking.

"Careful, Rowyn," Destrian teased, flexing his arm slightly, his eyes twinkling. "It might bite."

I was unable to suppress my smirk. "I heard the songs, but the way I remember it, I was actually the one who succeeded in killing the dragon."

Destrian laughed. "Oh, come on, you wouldn't begrudge me this one glory. Do you like it?"

I bit my lip. "It's not fair." I met his eye. "You're the one who took romance off the table. Now you just dangle it in front of me?"

Destrian stilled, his eyes drinking me in. "I said we shouldn't." His voice lowered. "I never said that I wouldn't." Destrian's nostrils flared. Heat burned in his gaze.

I glanced to the side, starkly aware that we had an audience and fervently wishing we didn't. Destrian rested his hand on my cheek, running a finger along my jaw as he watched my lips, licking his own.

"Consul!" someone shouted behind us.

Destrian gritted his teeth. "What?" he snapped as he turned to see what was needed.

It was as if the gods themselves were playing a cruel game with us.

I tried to calm my heart as I made my way to the large

fire where Fin and Luc were enjoying breakfast, though I supposed *enjoying* was a bit of a stretch. Fin was staring at the flames, deep in thought, while Luc was staring at Fin. She *did* look resplendent in that dressing gown that Onora let her have. I'd carried it in my pack so she'd have it when she wanted it.

I grabbed a bowl of soldier's breakfast mush and settled next to Fin. Destrian, now with a shirt on, accepted his meal and sank down next to me, absorbed in a list in his journal. We both tried to ignore the charged atmosphere from earlier.

Luc's gaze shifted to me. "Did you know that the bird was her the whole time?" he asked, pointing at Fin with his spoon.

"No," I replied, still a bit distracted with Destrian so close to me, practically leaning against my legs, his head nearly in my lap. By the gods, I'd missed him at the capital. It had become far too easy to touch him in the Nightlands, and now? My entire body seemed to be drawn to his warmth.

"Will you get over it already?" Fin snapped. "Why are you so against me seeing anything that you did at the capital?"

Luc gritted his teeth. "Because you were spying on me."

"No," Fin replied, sweeping her hair off her shoulder. Luc's eyes followed the movement. "I was spying on

Rowyn. I wasn't there for you at all."

"You saw me at my weakest. You don't get to decide whether that matters or not." Luc's face twisted into a grimace. "Besides, I miss the bird," he lamented, glancing at Fin with a touch of melancholy. "You never minded riding on my shoulder when you were a falcon. Why are you acting so cold now?"

Fin shrugged nonchalantly. "I only rode on *your* shoulder because the view was better."

I snorted into my bowl, unable to contain my amusement, while Destrian seemed to determinedly ignore the whole exchange, absorbed in his endless lists.

Luc's face turned a shade grumpier. "That's not an answer."

Fin smirked and rose from her seat, her dressing gown flowing behind her. "I'm going to freshen up before I change form," she announced, leaving us in her wake.

As her footsteps receded, I turned to Luc. "Why are you so upset?"

"Because, she won't tell me what she saw!"

"Are you embarrassed?"

Luc's eyes darkened, and he looked away, clearly struggling with the question. "Yes," he finally admitted. "But it's more than that. I'm worried about what she might think of me. The capital was a difficult time, and knowing that she was there, watching without my knowledge . . . it's unsettling."

I placed a hand on his arm. "Luc, Fin is not one to judge."

His eyes filled with uncertainty. "I would talk to her, you know, as the bird. I had no one to talk to, except you and Agramon, and neither of you liked me at the time. By the gods, I didn't even like myself. But Arden liked me. I talked to her all the time . . . told her my thoughts and how much I hated my life.

"But now, every time I try to bring it up, Fin brushes it off with a joke or a sarcastic comment. It's like she doesn't even want to be friends, and it's upsetting. Next to you, Fin knows me best, and she barely even looks at me."

Luc buried his face in his hands.

"Just give her time," I offered. "I don't know what's going through her head, but I know it had to have been difficult for her at the capital too."

"We need to move soon," Destrian said, his eyes on my hand still resting on Luc's arm. A muscle tensed in his jaw. "Fin will be ready, but the rest of us must pack up. Helena awaits."

While the guardsmen packed up camp, Fin rode on my shoulder as Arden. She'd told me that she preferred to travel as a bird because she liked being able to see the long distance and know what to expect. I had to admit, it was damned useful.

I grabbed her robe and stored it in the pack on my horse. Arden had just flown off when Destrian appeared behind me, his hands on my hips.

"You're still trying to lift me in the saddle?" I asked, unable to keep the smile off my face.

"Always," Destrian murmured into my ear with a smile. It was a simple act, one he'd performed countless times, but now it carried an awareness I couldn't ignore as he lifted me onto the horse, his fingers lingering along my thigh.

With Luc at the head and Arden circling above, we kept our distance from the others, and as our horses fell into step, Destrian's voice was a comforting murmur at my side.

"We need Marc. I would offer him a title and some lands."

"He isn't a friend to me," I said. "Why should I give him such honors?"

"Because Marc is the only tracker in the realm," Destrian said, his brows raised. "If you think that he can't re-trace your steps and find the child emperor, you'd be mistaken. He's also a man who knows the West better than anyone. He is friendly with the families of Adair and The Fens. He travels often, and interacts with the other nobles. He's experienced and he's resourceful. What more do we need?"

"I suppose," I grumbled. I hadn't thought of that.

Destrian, it seemed, had thought of everything.

"But he's also stubborn and . . ." I paused, trying to find the right word, ". . . prickly."

Destrian let out a small laugh. "Prickly, yes. But wouldn't that serve him not to be easily swayed or bullied?"

"Would he even agree?"

"I think he would, if the offer were sweet enough. The second son of a consul to be granted lands and a title? He would get to travel the West and visit his friends. What would he possibly say no to? His life would be infinitely better than what his current prospects are, in charge of the guard of Korballis. That would be a huge waste of talent."

"He's not fond of me, to say the least."

"He may not like you, but he respects you. And that is far more valuable. I'd trust him with my life, and he's fair at strategy too. While my father kept me from visiting with other nobles, Marc was meeting everyone. His family would likely be in line to overtake Duke Roland Lyon as the western overseer if something were to ever happen to that family. He knows the relationships and things that you only know when actually meeting with people."

I bit my lip. "What are you saying? Obviously you've given this some thought. What role would you have mapped out for him if I did comply with your wishes?"

"He should be given a duchy. We could build him someplace out west, near the border to Korballis."

"Or he could break Korballis off and take part of Morgania with it. Name himself a king."

Destrian shook his head. "Marc wouldn't be a good king and he knows it, but he's the best choice for ambassador. Can you imagine if your voice across the Western Empire is Marc Trinidan of Korballis? I know you didn't like him, but you are very much in the minority there."

"He hated me." I couldn't be more sure of that.

"You made him uncomfortable. He didn't act the same around you as he did around the rest of us. And just think, most of the time, he would be far away from you. Who better to send to the other nobles than a tracker? If there were some mystery to be solved, or whisper of information, he would be able to find the story out for you. He loves traveling, and the other nobles and he are all friends. In their circles, Marc vouching for you would not be taken lightly. You want him, even if you don't realize it yet."

"You're right." Even though I said the words, I wasn't happy about it. "When the empire came in before, they made sure to assassinate all our sorcerers, and even then we weren't easily defeated. Any sorcerers we bring onto our side could tip the scale."

Destrian was nodding. "The mark of a good leader is not how good they are at governing themselves. It is that they surround themselves with the best of their jobs. The emperor was mistaken in who he chose for his council because he surrounded himself with sycophants clinging to his every word. You should have those on your council who do not like you. Who will disagree with you and make you uncomfortable."

I thought back to Sam, how he refused to speak sense to the emperor. The emperor never changed his mind about the war because of Sam's advice and council—he changed his mind because Countess Mahira interfered. As much as I hated to admit it, Destrian was right. Again. And yet he still wanted *me* to be queen?

I rode in silence, processing his words. It was a gamble, no doubt, but perhaps a necessary one. I finally turned to Destrian, giving him a small nod. "All right, we'll do it."

Destrian smiled. "It's a good decision, Rowyn."

The landscape rolled by in a tapestry of greens and browns. Mountains loomed in the distance, stark and beautiful, beckoning me home.

"We will need Pedr." I stared ahead. If he got Marc, then I wanted Pedr, if he cared to come.

I could practically feel Destrian tense. "You always had a partiality to him."

I rolled my eyes. "Pedr could give us loads of ideas and options when it comes to Agramon's response, and he can work with Urdua on the reforms we want to make into laws. I'd bet he would have plenty of ideas on that count. That is, if he's interested in coming."

Destrian's teeth clenched. He'd always been jealous of Pedr, despite it being for no good reason. "A Master of Ink wouldn't be a bad idea. They are in charge of keeping historical records and drafting treaties. He could actually be useful."

"I *still* don't understand why you didn't like him," I said with a frown. "He likes men."

"No," Destrian corrected. "He's attracted to *both* men and women. I actually used to like Pedr before you showed up. Then I thought he had romanced you away from me, and I hated him with a burning passion." Destrian was staring ahead, an absent look on his face. I unfolded my arms and leaned forward.

"But," he continued, turning to look at me as he returned from wherever it was he'd gone, "he was top of the class in both history and governance, and he has read way too much information that is good for a man. If I was putting together a council to create my own country, I *would* want Pedr Tore on my side."

"I didn't realize he was top of the class," I said, wrinkling my nose.

"Oh yes," Destrian said with a nod. "Your closest friends at Solridge were all at the top of the class. Fin was loads better than the rest of us at mathematics, and Pedr was the golden pupil for Lord Obi and Lord Alexander. Not to mention Araceli, who so exceeded Lady Vianne's expectations in deportment that she simply ignored her."

"And there I was, dragging them all down," I said with a grin.

Destrian snorted. "Right, the most powerful sorcerer of the generation was that group's weak point."

I rolled my eyes.

"Seriously," Destrian said, leaning into Valor's saddle. "From the very beginning, I hated how intimidating you were."

"I was the intimidating one?" I laughed. "You had all the eligible ladies at Solridge swooning after you."

The tips of Destrian's ears turned pink.

"What were you and Ingrid doing here in Morgania while I was away?" I asked, half teasing, half curious. I wasn't sure I wanted him to answer the question, to be honest.

"Nothing happened." Destrian's nostrils flared. "But it could've."

I nodded. I'd known that Ingrid would probably try to make herself available to Destrian. I guessed I wouldn't have blamed him if he'd taken her up on her offer. It wasn't like I had room to talk. Still, it made me feel better that he didn't. That probably made me a hypocrite, but I didn't have room in me to care. It still made me happy.

"Do you think they will come?" I asked.

Destrian shrugged. "All we can do is extend our hand."

He scanned the road that wound up a steep hill before us.

Suddenly, a screech tore through the air. It was Arden. My heart lurched, and Destrian's head snapped up. The guards stopped in their tracks, their faces alert and tense.

Fin transformed, her body contorting and reshaping, her wings folding back into her shoulder blades. When she returned to her human form, she strode over to us.

Destrian and I both dismounted.

"We've got a big problem," she shouted, her voice taut, her eyes wide with fear. "There's a group of mercenaries closing in on the road up ahead."

My blood ran cold. I looked at Destrian, who was frowning as though he couldn't believe it.

"The baron is there," Fin continued, her gaze fixed on me.

"How did he get ahead of us so fast?" I asked, my voice shaking with dread.

Fin shot me a steady look. "I think I saw Elgar the Swift with him."

Chapter 13

E LGAR THE SWIFT meant that Sam could get any-
where he wanted within a moment. At the capital, the powers of the sorcerers seemed to be on
my side since I was Agramon's ward. Now they would be
against me. What other sorcerers would Agramon throw
our way, and how could I prepare for it?

Destrian looked over his shoulder. "Eslin is too far to
be any help."

I nodded. "Can we avoid them?" I asked Fin as Luc
strode up behind me.

She shook her head. "They've already spotted us. The
baron recognized me. They tried to shoot me down with a
crossbow."

I turned to Luc. "Now's your chance to prove your
worth."

Luc's eyes narrowed, and he straightened his back.
"What do you need?"

Fin used a stick and the dusty road to show us where
the mercenaries were and where she thought Sam was
planning to attack. When we heard the number of men
they had, all the guardsmen groaned audibly.

"That's five to one," one guard murmured to another.

I raised a brow. They might've been scared by numbers, but I sure as the gods wasn't. "How many sorcerers are in their party?" I asked sharply.

Fin shrugged. "Only one I saw was Elgar."

"And we have three," I said, meeting the eyes of the guard who had complained. "We have three of the most powerful sorcerers of our generation. We'll be fine."

Destrian raised a finger. "Actually, I would prefer if we just stuck with two. You really shouldn't fight."

I took a breath, trying to control my temper, aware of the guardsmen around us, their faces grim but ready.

"Absolutely not. Do we remember the Nightlands differently? I can hold my own."

Destrian began to shake his head, but one of the Morganite guardsmen piped up. "I fought beside her at the Battle of Espiria, and she's right. She is very good in a fight." He pointed at me. "It is known."

"See?" I said, my hand on my hip, gripping Iranoct's hilt. "'It is known.'"

"Fine," Destrian conceded. His voice dropped lower as he leaned toward me. "I still don't like it. The queen should be protected."

"And yet the king is always supposed to ride in front," I hissed back, then glanced at Luc. "Let me lead, and Destrian can protect our back." I glanced at Destrian. "I would bet you could make some pointed shots from that vantage point. It's better if I'm ahead of our men since my aim is worse than yours. Once I use lightning, it goes everywhere."

"Luc, you place the guardsmen wherever you want with that plan in mind," I went on. "I'll take out as many as I can with a first strike. Ayastaren has seen me battle with my full powers, but none of these men have, so Sam is in for a surprise. Fin, keep watch above and make sure nothing goes awry. Help when you can."

The nods were firm.

I touched Destrian's arm. "You can make a ward over me, can't you?"

Destrian nodded.

"Then shield me, and we can win this."

"What if he takes you?" Destrian asked, reaching out to cup my cheek. Just then, I understood his worry.

"We'll get through this."

My eyes shifted to Fin, her body trembling as she prepared to transform. I nodded at her. With a cry that resonated in the very core of my being, she transformed into Arden and rose above us, her keen eyes watching for the enemy.

I turned to Luc, his body poised and ready. He signaled the guardsmen, who moved into position to flank the road, their faces grim, their swords gleaming in the fading light.

The dust on the horizon heralded the approach of

Sam's men.

Sam had manipulated me—had played on my fears and desires, twisting them to his advantage. He had tried to kill me. He showed me that he was exactly the man Agramon and everyone else had warned me about.

He was dangerous.

I forced the guilt back—silenced the voice that whispered of what might have been. I was done with being used.

I called the wind and felt it wrap around me, lifting me above the others. I was a tempest of noise and fury as I flew over the landscape, the thunder of hooves echoing over the hills around us. The gems in my hands and in my head pulsed with warmth. Above, clouds gathered, dark and ominous. A warning for all below.

Studying the terrain, I decided to blanket the northern section of the road and hills it had been dug into with the wettest fog I could manage. It would help to confuse Sam's men and spook their horses as they battled a slick road and poor eyesight.

The waiting was the worst part. I studied the edges of the cloud as the sound of hoofbeats and neighing drew nearer. The Morganian guardsmen were approaching from behind me, led by Luc. Destrian looked up as Fin swooped past, her call shrill.

I flew lower.

Suddenly, the mercenaries broke through the cloud. Sam was in front. His eyes widened when he looked up and saw me.

Time seemed to slow. I landed hard, feeling the ground give as I dropped to a knee and looked up through the swirl of fog. My arms outstretched, the veins of color on my gems glowed, snaking the green, orange, and blue over my hands. My braid whipped in the wind, pulling strands out of the plait.

I straightened.

Sam reined in his horse and shouted to his men, but the mercenaries ignored him, their eyes on me, their minds fixed on their mission. They veered toward me, exactly where I'd wanted them to go.

A crossbow bolt burst into flames when it hit Destrian's ward and the red wall flickered. The magical shield continued to sizzle as the mercenaries peppered me with arrows.

I raised my hands and lightning leaped from my palms. A sizzling path of destruction struck the mercenaries. Their bodies convulsed on the ground until the shock rendered them lifeless.

My breath came in ragged gasps, my body alive with power. The road was littered with bodies, and rain began to fall in thick sheets.

I was just getting started.

I sent another bolt, catching the mercenaries who'd

been riding behind the first line. It exploded as it hit one of them, sending those riding beside him into the mud to be trampled by horses.

Luc's men began to overtake me, riding past so fast that it nearly knocked me off my feet. Iranoct's steel sang as it left its scabbard. Gritting my teeth, I squared my shoulders and gripped my sword tighter. I refused to be the scared girl Sam remembered. The cascading rain made the ground slick beneath my boots. But I would not falter.

They did not get to have me.

I braced myself for the clash of steel that was seconds away. Ahead, the thunderous charge of cavalry shook the ground, their horses kicking up sprays of mud, a storm of man and beast. Sam's eyes were alight with the thrill of the fight. He spurred his horse and barreled toward me.

I clashed with a horse, slicing through its leg as it passed. A mercenary on foot swung at me. I deflected his blow with a loud ring of steel against steel. He was large, his blows heavy, but I moved with the rhythm of the storm, dodging his strikes and countering with a swift slice that dropped him to the wet earth.

Behind me, a blast of fire sizzled through the air, a searing heat that scorched my back. I turned, my sword a deadly arc that cut through a man, and I felt his body give beneath my blade.

My thoughts were a jumble. I was spinning around,

trying to see through the rain as others battled on horse and foot beside me. A mounted Morganite was struggling with one of Sam's men. I ran forward and hacked at the mercenary with Iranoct, feeling the blood spray across me as I hit an artery. Sam's man fell. The Morganite fell, too, a dagger in his throat.

I saw Elgar in a flash of movement. I stepped toward him, my sword raised, my eyes fixed on his face, my heart pounding with anticipation, but he was gone before I could swing.

I heard something behind me and then a scream as Destrian's ward flared. I turned and found Elgar the Swift on his knees, holding his hand as it blistered before our eyes. I stepped forward, but then he was gone, in the blink of an eye.

My breath came fast, my body aching with exertion, my mind whirling with the chaos of battle. And then I saw him.

Sam.

Unhorsed, fighting with his sword.

My heart lurched. It was both exhilarating and terrifying.

The sizzling flash of magic filled the air, and a man fell beside me. I caught a glimpse of Destrian, his face set in concentration. His magic surged and crackled with power. Fierce pride welled within me. In the Nightlands I'd always been able to rely on Destrian to watch my back. Always.

I was fighting toward Sam when Luc appeared beside me, his movements swift and sure as his blade cut through the enemies.

A man careened into him, a knife in his throat. Fin stepped back, her body smeared with mud and blood, her eyes wild and fierce. She pulled another dagger from a belt that seemed to have been taken from a fallen soldier and gripped the blade, ready for another kill.

I turned back to Sam, my heart pounding as he glared at me, his sword raised. A ball of fire hurtled toward him. It seemed destined to engulf him. But as it neared, a ward revealed itself, shimmering and pulsing, deflecting the fire with an almost contemptuous ease.

My eyes flicked to the gems on his sword, noticing for the first time that they were all different colors. Shit. I knew one gem protected him from mind readers, a shield against intrusion and manipulation. But the rest, the myriad of colors and facets—they must be his armor.

I sent a bolt of lightning toward a group of mercenaries, leaving them convulsing on the ground. Smoke mixed with the scent of charred flesh.

Sam's eyes followed my attack. "You betray my love for this?"

Another fireball blasted toward Sam, whose ward came flashing to life once more. I ducked as it was deflected toward me. The heat seared my skin. My voice was laced with frustration and sorrow. "Betray *you*? You're the one who turned against everything we believed in."

"But we could have been together!" he shouted, his voice cracking. "You were my *life*."

Sam moved in, his blade overpowering mine. We'd fought before, at Somme, when he was working with me on my fighting techniques. Then we'd mostly focused on hand-to-hand combat since I was underdeveloped in that area, so I hadn't really seen him use a sword much. His strength was a force that I struggled to match. I felt the pressure, the power, the determination in every move he made, every strike he landed. I fought with everything I had, but he was relentless and unyielding.

With a final, mighty swing, he beat me back so far that I lost my footing and fell. The ground met me with a jarring thud, and I looked up, dazed, only to see Sam's face twisted with anger and something else—something that looked almost like desperation.

I heard shouts behind me, and as I sat up, I saw Sam's gaze lift, his eyes widening as he took in the chaos around us. Several Morganian guardsmen were beginning to circle him.

Suddenly, Elgar the Swift appeared at his side, his uninjured hand reaching out to grab Sam's. In an instant, they disappeared into the ether, leaving me standing in the midst of battle, struggling to draw breath and calm my racing heart.

Luc stood beside me and held out a hand. As I righted myself, I found Destrian storming toward me. He reached me in a few strides and tore me away from Luc, sweeping me up into his arms and burying his face in my hair. I clung to him, closing my eyes for a moment as I breathed him in, relishing his scent. I'd been more afraid than I realized.

"I understand, now, what the soldier said about you being good in a fight." Destrian had never seen me use lightning in a fight before.

I tried to smile. "You shouldn't doubt me anymore." The words were meant as a jest but carried a weight of truth.

He tightened his hold, as though fearful that Elgar the Swift might return and wrench me from his arms. In truth, it was what I worried about too. "Wanting you safe doesn't mean that I doubt you, Rowyn."

"Thanks for saving my ass," Luc muttered. I looked around Destrian to see Fin nearby.

She shrugged, her eyes narrowing as she surveyed the damage. "It was nothing."

I caught the way Luc's eyes lingered on her.

Destrian released me. "The baron must've snuck those men over the border before Rowyn sent the rain. He used the fact that they were planted to try to head us off. Let's hope there are no other forces like that within Morgania."

Luc nodded, his expression grim, and Fin put her arm over my shoulders and squeezed. "You were brilliant out there," she said with admiration.

I wrapped my arm around her waist and returned the hug. "The only reason we were able to mount a proper attack in the first place was because of you."

Fin grinned at Destrian. "We made a pretty good team today, didn't we?"

Destrian's ears turned pink.

I couldn't help but smile.

Chapter 14

THE SMELL OF BURNING reached us long before Fin landed to break the news. Sam's mercenaries had turned the nearest village into a graveyard. Bodies were laid out for the scavengers, burnt remains of all shapes and sizes scattered over the blackened land. Animals, men, women, children. None had been spared. Homes were reduced to skeletal frames, still smoking in the fading light.

Sam's message was unmistakable. He was punishing me by preying on the weak. He was driving the knife where it would hurt the most. I was a fool for allowing the Butcher of Bruin to know my weaknesses better than anyone. He'd heard me speak of Ayastaren. He'd known my anger surrounding the enslaved Morganites in Maryse and the men who'd been conscripted to his cause. By the gods, he'd seen me steal away Nirah *and* Prince Artian to ensure their safety.

Looking at the remains of what was once a thriving farm hamlet, I could see his message was clear. The children he'd laid out specially for me.

To frighten me.

To bait me.

To make me second-guess myself.

To make me second-guess Destrian.

It was working. A sob caught in my throat. I stumbled forward, my legs weak and my heart heavy. This was not war; this was butchery.

Destrian stood silently beside me. His head bowed. His hands clenched. He'd seen Sam's work before. He'd told me stories of the mindless slaughter he'd witnessed in Yliria. Destrian's greatest wish had been to end the wars, the senseless bloodshed. Now, I saw exactly what he'd meant.

I tried to keep myself together as my body trembled uncontrollably.

Now . . . because of me . . . this.

Clouds gathered above, mirroring my fury and grief.

I took a deep breath.

Then another.

Sam, Agramon, Duke Roland Lyon.

They were *all* the same.

A peal of thunder sounded from above.

"Rowyn, it's not your fault," a voice murmured behind me.

I jumped and frantically wiped my cheeks with shaking fingers.

Fin stepped forward.

I pointed to the body of a small child lying on the

ground. "Tell them that."

I walked away. The world had turned back to the dark and cruel place that I'd always known it to be. The world that I was most frightened of. It was Ayastaren all over again, with the duke using the woman's family as bait for my torment. It was Ena, whom Agramon used to keep me in line and constantly afraid. It was the entire reason I'd told Destrian to stay away.

I didn't want those I loved to get hurt. I didn't want the blood of innocents on my hands. But no matter what I did, the innocents were always used against me. They were the ones who paid for my choices.

When I came to the edge of the forest, I collapsed onto the earth. The air was growing cooler the farther north we got, and Morgania was getting ready for autumn. Wind carrying a hint of chill snuck through the rustling leaves to further deaden me.

I had fought, and I had lost. The battle was over, but the war was far from won. How could I live when all around me was death?

How could I love when all I felt was hate?

How could I hope when all I knew was despair?

Tears streamed down my face.

Then Echo's voice reached me. *"He is not the man you wanted him to be."*

"I didn't know him at all," I gasped. "The Sam I knew

would've never done this."

"*He is not the man he wanted to be either*," Echo replied.

"I see now why you were so concerned about him." My throat felt raw.

"*Everyone must choose their own path.*"

I took a deep breath of the cool, crisp air tainted with smoke and ash. And then I heard a noise behind me, a soft rustle. I turned and saw Destrian leaning against a tree, his hand on Phyranox. He stepped forward, his movements deliberate and gentle until he stood before me, holding out his hand.

He pulled me up and brushed his thumb across my cheek to wipe dirt away. He cradled my head, his fingers threading through my hair.

"I know what you're feeling," he murmured. "But we can protect the others if we get to Helena and mount a defense."

I nodded, knowing exactly who to take my anger out on. I tried to step around him, but Destrian held my arms fast and pulled me to him, wrapping his arms around me.

"I hate it too," he whispered. "Hopefully we can end it soon."

"But at what cost?"

Destrian tipped my head up and wiped my cheeks. "It's worth it, if it means that hope and freedom do not die."

I sighed and buried my face into his chest, breathing

deep. I never wanted him to let me go.

THE DAYS FOLLOWING the grim discovery at the village blended into one another as we continued our journey north to Helena. The somber mood began to lift as we reached the outskirts of the city where people ran to greet us with smiles on their faces and hope in their hearts.

A young girl, with imorets tattooed around her eyes, waved flowers at me as she called, "Welcome home, Princess Rowyn!"

Destrian looked a bit sheepish at her words. "The bards have been singing your story ever since I sent word to Bernard to enact our plan."

I glanced around as the people pushed forward, calling me "The Morganite Queen" and "Rowyn of the North." I should've felt joy, but the bitter fangs of fear had sunk into my throat, stealing my breath.

I immediately grew envious of Fin, who soared above us as Arden. She didn't have to be a spectacle if she'd no wish to be. I took a deep breath, feeling a chill creep up my spine, knowing there was something wrong with me. Morganians welcoming me home with open arms should've made me feel on top of the world. It was my parents' greatest dream. It was the end my clan had worked toward for a century. So, why didn't I feel better?

The crowd. The shouting. The many faces staring back. It brought me straight back to Somme. My heart began to race. Nervous energy, swift and unwanted, rippled through my muscles. I couldn't help searching through the crowd, more focused on potential enemies than the faces of the Morganians who were celebrating my return. A dream I'd paid dearly for and now couldn't seem to enjoy.

Were the Sons of Sol in Helena? They seemed to constantly be lurking over my shoulder in the East, and it was too much to hope that the West would be any different.

I took a steadying breath, but worry continued to poison my mind. Was Elgar the Swift in the city? Was Sam watching from the shadows? Could Agramon simply be biding his time, waiting to reveal that he'd outwitted me? It would be like him to stall until I got to Helena, to only show his hand when he knew it would wound deepest.

I closed my eyes, trying to fight back the tears as my hands began to shake. I knew the people were trying to be kind. I knew that I should be thankful for the crowd's support, but I was fraying at the seams. It was Bruin all over again. I was constantly looking over my shoulders, knowing there was someone who wished me ill getting ready to stab me in the back.

I hated to admit it, but at least with Agramon, I'd felt reasonably safe from everyone but him.

At least . . . most of the time.

A noise turned my head, and I found Destrian's dark eyes taking in my trembling fingers and quivering lip. Red light domed around us, and I emitted a gasp of relief, my eyes tearing up when I wished they wouldn't. I really needed to stop blubbering.

I wiped my cheek and attempted a smile. "Thank you."

Destrian pointed out the temple of Imor, his voice filled with pride. "I had it rebuilt while you were in Somme."

I admired the smooth marble columns, climbing with jasmine and moonflowers. A couple was entering, the man bearing imorets and markings along his neck. The woman was Lyrican.

What Destrian had managed to accomplish while I'd been gone was beyond anything I could have imagined. How could I ever hope to deserve him? He had believed in me, supported me, and loved me through it all, and I was overwhelmed with gratitude.

Destrian drew Phyranox and stood in the stirrups, raising his sword. The people cheered and screamed, shouts of "Dragon" echoing off the walls.

I laughed, immediately distracted from my anxious thoughts. Clearly the people of Helena *adored* Destrian. He grinned and waved, calling the names of those he knew, seemingly unburdened by the weight of countless gazes. I'd never seen the crowd behave that way for the emperor, nor Agramon, nor me. These people clearly felt like they knew him.

Destrian met my eyes and smiled, nodding in my direction, encouraging me to engage. I took a deep breath, plastered the most winning grin I could muster on my face, and raised my hand to match his. The ward flickered away a few seconds before Arden swooped down to land on my shoulder. I had to admit, it felt better having Fin watch my back.

"Shows of strength are good for morale," I remembered Agramon telling me. As much as I hated my time with him, I'd bled for the knowledge, so I would be a fool not to use everything I learned to give me the edge in the battles to come.

I called on my power. A calming sprinkle of rain began to fall, each drop catching the light and emitting rainbows throughout the entire city. The effect was enchanting. Cheers and laughter filled the air, and this time, the joy was contagious.

As we approached the castle of Helena, trumpets heralded our arrival. A flag was being hoisted, bearing the old Morganite sigil, black with a silver crescent moon and three stars.

I glanced at him, and the hint of a grin played at the

corner of his mouth. In that moment, I'd never seen some-one so handsome in all my life. How the sun shined brightly on his hair, his dark eyes warm and inviting. Everything about him was beckoning me. The minute I got him alone I wanted to kiss him until I forgot my past.

"Do you ever stop to think that you're almost too good at this?" I shouted at him. "Aren't you essentially working your way out of a seat?"

Destrian shrugged. "It's more fun to run a kingdom."

I shook my head. "I still think it's a bad idea to have a kingdom rely on having a single person breathing," I murmured, my words only for him.

His face changed instantly, the playfulness replaced by sudden anger. "You need to stop talking about your death, Rowyn."

"Not talking about it doesn't change the risk," I shot back.

He leaned toward me, his voice low and intense. "Just enjoy the moment. The people are celebrating their queen coming home."

Fin disappeared when we reached the citadel steps. Dismounting, I looked up to see faces watching from the windows, and most of the castle staff was waiting outside, their eyes wide with wonder. Among them, I spotted Sir Bernard. He was clapping along with the rest of them, a twinkle in his eyes.

I felt a lump in my throat when I met his gaze.

I couldn't help myself. I gave him a hug.

"We're glad to see ya to rights, yer Majesty," Sir Bernard rumbled as he returned my hug with a fierce one of his own. "We missed ya here in the West."

"I'm glad to be back," I said, breaking away and turning back to Destrian who was beaming beside me.

We entered the castle, and though I'd seen it before, it felt as though being inside with completely different emotions was enough for me to look at the place with new eyes.

"Take Princess Rowyn's things to the lady's room," Destrian ordered one of the servants. The maid had imorets around her eyes and was young, maybe twelve.

"I didn't realize the citadel was in the business of hiring Morganite servants," I said, watching the girl leave, followed by the young hostler who had brought in my bag.

"About that . . ." Destrian winced. "When I heard about Ena, I went to see her family."

I frowned. "What?"

Destrian refused to meet my eyes.

I looked back after the girl. "That wasn't . . ."

"It is," Destrian said, taking a deep breath. "Ena's sister, Rosie."

Tears sprang to my eyes. "Why? Why bring them here? You're putting them in danger!" I started to panic. "The entire empire is about to come after me in Helena, and you brought them here? Right into the thick of it!"

"When I went to see them, to break the news about Ena, they were not in a good way. Her father had lost a large number of pigs to a shadow panther that had been stalking their grounds. They were out of money and her father was desperate. I brought the whole family here."

I raised my brows. "They *all* work here?"

Destrian nodded. "The older ones do anyway. Her father helps watch the pigs that we use here at the citadel. Rosie and May are maids, little Flynn is a scullery, and her twin, Peri, is a stableboy. They also have a good-sized apartment here, that way they can stay together."

My anger washed out of me like a wave. I hadn't even known all the names of Ena's siblings, yet Destrian could call them by name—and personally made sure that they were taken care of, exactly as I would've wanted to do myself. Ena was trying to help with her wages earned with me. With four or five of them earning wages now, the family would surely be fine. That is, if Lyrica didn't turn Helena into rubble first.

"You trusted me to handle things here," Destrian whispered, his fingers rising to my cheek. "I did not take that trust lightly."

I smiled through the threat of more cursed tears. "I should know better than to doubt you now, surely."

"Just tell me what you dream," Destrian murmured, his

thumb brushing my lips. "Surely there must be something I can grant or solve for my queen."

"That's the thing." I tried to keep my fingers off of him, uneasy with eyes around us. It was incredibly difficult when all I wanted to do was throw my arms around his neck and kiss him until I couldn't breathe. "I don't really have one. Nothing in my life has turned out how I thought it would."

"May I offer you a new one?"

I tilted my head, curiosity piqued. "A new dream?"

"A new life," Destrian replied, taking my hand.

Chapter 15

ESTRIAN LED ME down the halls and stopped at a set of large wooden doors at the end of the corridor. One was ornately carved with ivy leaves and roses.

"This was my mother's room," Destrian said, pushing open the door. "In the days of old, it was the queen's chambers."

Flames flickered to life in the fireplace and I was able to see the room more clearly. It was a large bedchamber, with ornate carvings similar to those in the hall. A massive four-poster bed draped in white linen sheets sat at one end, while a fireplace warmed the other. Before the hearth sat a sofa and several simple chairs, flanked by small end tables, with one bearing a decanter of wine and four goblets. The scent of vinegar and lemons hinted at its recent cleaning.

I raised my brows and walked around the same chamber that Queen Helen had dwelled in when Morgania was first built. "Why would you bring me here?"

"Because it is yours." Destrian walked to the window overlooking the city, his eyes on the lights below. "No other person has more right to this room than you do. No matter what happens, this is your home."

I ran my hand over a large wooden vanity next to the bed and chanced a glance at myself in the mirror. I looked quite the sight. My hair was mussed in its braid, and I had dark circles under my eyes from sleeping in fits.

"I didn't want to decorate for you," Destrian went on, looking around the chamber. Though it had been cleaned, there was nothing on the walls, and the bed linens were practical more than anything, though they were soft as silk. A door to the side led to a grand bathing chamber equipped with a pump and large mirror. "I know Onora and Ilisa have always enjoyed that part, so I figured you would too."

Agramon hadn't let me choose even the smallest of furnishings or clothes in my wardrobe. Every part of me had been meticulously crafted to his taste. But Destrian was giving me a completely blank sheet of parchment. I wondered if he understood the gravity of what he was offering.

I walked around one of the sofas, running my hand along the back. I'd never been one to shop before. I didn't know what I was doing. Everything I'd had growing up was either caught, made, or stolen. Markets had been new to me, and the only time I'd ever really "shopped" for myself was when Gillius took me to get clothes for Solridge.

Destrian walked me to the set of glass doors at the end of the room. He opened them with a flourish, and my breath caught in my throat as I stepped out onto the balcony.

A rush of cool night air swept over me, carrying with it the sweet scent of northern flowers. My eyes widened in surprise and delight at the sight before me.

It was a garden, right there on the balcony. Roses climbed the balustrade, their blooms a deep red. Several small morwood pine trees stood as sentinels in pots toward the edge, their sweet scent perfuming the night. Little plants were scattered all over the balcony, arranged with a graceful elegance that was both wild and cultivated. It reminded me of the forest. It reminded me of home, in Espiria.

"I didn't want to decorate the room," Destrian said again, coming to stand beside me. "But I couldn't just leave it with nothing, so I hired an artisan from the city to decorate your balcony."

I was silent for a moment, taking in the beautiful scenery. I would never be able to deserve this man. The thought of Sam was an unwelcome torment poisoning my mind. He was still out there. He was still coming for me. He was still a danger to us both.

But now? In this moment, I wanted to enjoy the beautiful gift of time I'd been given. It wasn't so long ago that I despaired of ever seeing Destrian again. "Thank you, this . . . it's more than I could've dreamed of."

"I wanted you to have a place of your own, somewhere

you could make your own mark," he murmured. "And yet, I wanted it to feel like home too."

"You've done a very good job," I complimented.

He chuckled. "It was Simon, the artisan, who did the work. I merely told him what you might like. I even mentioned that watering the plants wouldn't be a problem."

Destrian took my hand, squeezing it gently. "I wanted it fitting for a queen."

As the sun began to dip below the horizon, casting a golden glow over the flowers, I felt a profound sense of contentment and peace. In this moment, everything was perfect. I truly felt as though I were home.

We stepped back into the room, the heady scent of the garden still lingering. Destrian shut the door and was about to speak, then seemed to catch himself.

"Is this too much? Because there's more."

I clenched my fingers, my hands cold and clammy. "How could there possibly be more?"

Destrian chuckled and went over to a wardrobe. He opened the door, blocking my view for a moment, before turning, holding a silken cushion. Sitting atop it was a black crown. Sideways crescents, made of silver, lined the base, mirroring the blessing that had been tattooed onto my chest. Connecting them were filigree spires, and atop each of the five spires was embedded a black opal.

I clutched my chest, unable to catch my breath. Queen

Helen's crown had been destroyed. "Did you . . . did you make this?"

"Yes." Destrian's voice was tinged with pride. With his fire magic, he was an excellent forger and blacksmith. His talents were evident in the delicate workmanship of the spires, the way the metal was shaped with precision and artistry.

But what truly captured my attention were the opals. They seemed to glow, my magic reaching out to them. I stared in wonder at Destrian, the words tumbling from my lips. "I thought it was horrible luck from the gods if you took more than your allotted gem."

"That's true for the pilgrim, or the person who's gaining their gem on the quest," Destrian explained, his eyes locked on mine. "The mentors can take gems if they manage it."

"You could've sold them," I breathed, still in awe of the crown and the man who had crafted it. "You could've made mountains of gold."

"Or," Destrian said, "I could've made a crown for my queen." He held it out to me, the silver and opals glinting in the candlelight.

I stared at the piece, at Destrian's outstretched hand as he offered me the chance to remake the world. The crown was a promise of what could be, of what was meant to be. It was what the gods had demanded of me, if only I could stomach the courage to take it.

The weight of the crown, the beauty of the room, the love in Destrian's eyes—all of it overwhelmed me, and tears began to slip down my cheeks. Destrian's expression turned to one of concern as he gently set the crown aside and reached out to me. "What's wrong?"

"I just . . . I don't feel like I will ever deserve you," I said once again, feeling more at a loss to match his gestures. "Because of all that I've done."

He shook his head and gently lifted a strand of hair from my face, tucking it behind my ear. "You deserve everything, Rowyn."

I was unable to resist. I gripped his arms, lifted myself up, and kissed him. Destrian pulled me close as he returned the kiss with an intensity that matched my own. Our lips tumbled as we reacquainted ourselves with each other. It had been so long ago, and our time had been short. It had been but a few weeks of truly loving him before being snatched away by fate. But now, I had him back. I had my life back.

Time seemed to slip away as I lost myself in his arms. His tongue played with mine, the heat of him, the intoxicating smell drawing me closer. I leaned against the massive bedpost as Destrian's lips trailed down my neck, his hands pulling at my waist, drawing me into him.

Our passion was shattered by the sound of the door

creaking open. We scrambled away from each other, breathless and disoriented, to find an older woman with silver-red hair standing in the doorway, her eyes wide.

"I—oh! I'm so sorry!" she stammered, her cheeks turning a bright shade of red. "I didn't mean to interrupt. I just—"

"Aunt Maureen," Destrian said quickly, his voice still husky from our embrace. He was trying to compose himself, but I could see the flush in his cheeks and desire in his eyes. "I'd like you to meet Rowyn. Rowyn, this is my aunt Maureen."

She was a graceful woman with silver hair and piercing blue eyes who greeted me with a warm smile. I couldn't help but be slightly intimidated by her. According to Destrian, she had raised him as a mother would.

"Princess Rowyn, it's a pleasure to finally meet you," Lady Maureen said. Her voice carried a hint of elegance and sophistication, just like her appearance.

I curtsied and hoped to mask my lingering embarrassment. It was unnerving having others call me princess. "I've heard so much about you."

Lady Maureen's eyes sparkled with amusement. "Likewise, my dear."

Destrian cleared his throat, his eyes shifting between us. "Aunt Maureen has taken over management of the citadel to help me," he explained, carefully steering the conversation away from our earlier indiscretion.

"That's wonderful," I replied, genuinely grateful for her support. I sensed that Destrian was leaning heavily on those closest to him.

Lady Maureen's eyes softened, her demeanor shifting from amusement to genuine concern. "And as for you, my dear, I noticed your bags were quite meager. We're going to plan a market trip to pick out fabrics and choose your room furnishings as well as a wardrobe. We must have you properly outfitted."

"Thank you," I whispered, touched by her thoughtfulness.

She then turned her attention to Destrian, her voice taking on a more serious tone. "They are waiting for you in the morning room. Consul Kendrew has sent word that Ayastaren still may mount an attack any day."

Destrian's jaw tightened and he glanced at the door.

Lady Maureen turned back to me. "I'm putting your friend, Fin, in a room close by. I feel as though both you young ladies need some proper care and comfort."

"She'll need to go shopping with us," I told Destrian. "She has nothing as well."

Destrian nodded. Lady Maureen's face broke into a pleased smile, her eyes twinkling with approval. "I suspected you'd feel that way, dear. Consider it arranged."

I felt a flutter of relief, grateful that Fin would be looked after. But as I turned my attention back to Destrian, I sensed a weariness in his eyes.

"Who is waiting?"

Destrian shook his head with a sigh. "All the others have been clamoring to see you. We must get started with our work right away."

He turned to Lady Maureen. "Send someone up to help Rowyn dress and freshen up."

Lady Maureen nodded. "Of course, Destrian."

He leaned to me, giving me a chaste kiss on the cheek, his touch lingering just a moment longer than necessary. I felt a rush of warmth.

"I'll escort you to see the others soon," he promised in a low voice.

He followed his aunt out the door, but turned at the last moment, shooting me a look of pure, unbridled lust. My heart skipped a beat. The thrill of anticipation penetrated my thoughts. I wished he would stay and throw me back on the bed and reacquaint himself with the rest of me.

Then again, a bath didn't sound too bad either.

Chapter 16

I STARED AT MYSELF in the mirror, mulling over who waited down the hall. I hadn't seen Lord Alexander or Lady Vianne since I'd left for the Last Dusk. It felt like a lifetime ago, and in many ways, it was. Now I knew what Vianne had done to both help and hinder me. She'd stopped me from running away. She'd taken my memories and wariness that I'd been right to feel toward the empires. She'd helped keep me chained.

Still, I'd be remiss in not acknowledging that she'd ensured that I received the Girdle of Ephema. She'd protected me when it counted. I never wanted to imagine what life would've been like with Agramon if I'd never had it. How low he would've brought me.

I wanted them to be impressed with me. How could I make them see that I knew what I was doing? Even though my education in courtly intrigue hadn't been as long as the others, I'd been tutored by Agramon the Divine himself. My lessons had been etched in the blood that we spilled across the empire, in both Agramon's and my folly.

Vianne would know this. It seemed as though she'd always seen the potential in me. Now, I had to embrace that role. I needed to start presenting myself as a queen, not a lost girl fumbling for her place in the world. I had to know exactly who I was.

My thoughts were interrupted as the door swung open and in came Daisy, the maid who'd served me before when I'd visited Helena. Her face was flushed with excitement as she greeted me.

"Lady Maureen has sent me in to help you get ready to meet in the council rooms. Lord Destrian has called a meeting before dinner."

Daisy then unveiled the dresses she'd brought from Onora's closet. I recognized the one on the bottom.

"The black one," I said without hesitation. The memory of wearing that dress, the emotions and revelations it was tied to, all came flooding back. It was the perfect choice for the occasion. The silver stars had looked brilliant that night Destrian and I'd returned to Helena, bathed in the success of our quest. We'd been given one night of pleasure before fate swept me in its unending current and pulled me to another world.

But I'd found my way back.

Daisy helped me bathe, then step into the dress. The last time I'd worn it, I'd been half-starved from my quest to the Nightlands, and the gown had been obviously too loose on my figure. Thanks to the eastern shore's hospitality, I now had curves the silk could hug.

Daisy had left most of my hair down, and even brushed

on some subtle paint that I quite liked, before she left.

Rising, I belted Iranoct around my waist. I always pre-ferred to wear my sword, even though I missed the thigh holster that Sam had given me, and the daggers from Agramon and Luc. Sam had pulled them off me in Ayasta-ren, and I felt their absence.

Then again, Lady Maureen had mentioned we would go shopping. I resolved to buy another set.

A knock at the door pulled me from my reverie. Open-ing it, I found Destrian standing there, looking as hand-some as ever. His eyes widened slightly as they took me in, and I saw a spark of appreciation flash in his gaze.

"You look beautiful," he said, his voice low and filled with warmth.

I felt a flush creep into my cheeks. "Thank you," I mur-mured, my heart pounding.

Then, someone squeezed in beside him.

"Mellan?!" I practically shrieked, incredulous that the only good Lyon I'd ever met was there. "Why did you leave the capital?"

Mellan sighed. "The Butcher was coming after me, picking my brain to try to figure out if you'd told me any-thing about your plans. Destrian had already told me that I was welcome to make a home in Morgania if I had a mind to leave Somme, and it was as good an offer as I was going to get given the circumstances. It's not like I can go home to Ayastaren. My father and Agramon have always worked closely together."

"What about the work you were doing?" I asked, glancing at Destrian and wondering how much he knew about Mellan's illegal ring of slave rescuers.

"Destrian actually invited me to continue my work here," Mellan said, clapping Destrian on the shoulder. "He asked that I work to free other Morganites who were taken in the consulships and noble houses. Since I'm already familiar with the network, I will be the point man here in Morgania, and we can give people the option of returning home or making one here."

"And the skin-traders?" I tried to keep the anger from creeping into my voice. Melbo still left a sour taste on my tongue.

"We are dealing with them," Destrian said, glancing at me. "Ferris is having them hunted down and brought to justice."

I nodded. "What are you doing with them?"

"Hanging them."

I didn't have much to say to that, except good job.

"So, you are staying here?" I asked Mellan, though I glanced at Destrian.

He nudged Mellan, who was busy glaring at him, clearly missing the nonverbal signals being thrown his way. After another not-so-subtle nudge, realization dawned on

Mellan's face. He stepped forward and bent the knee.

"I am here to serve you, my Queen," Mellan declared with firm resolve.

I glanced at Destrian again, my eyebrows raised. "What should I do?"

"Pull out Iranoct and bless him," Destrian instructed.

Doing as I was told, I unsheathed Iranoct and gently tapped Mellan on each shoulder. "I accept your vow?" I glanced at Destrian again, still not sure. I wasn't quite sure how anything worked, if I was being honest with myself.

Destrian clapped his hand down on Mellan's shoulder when he tried to rise, pushing him back down. "Say it again, only this time with more authority."

I took a deep breath, glad that I was practicing without others watching. I slowly lowered Iranoct onto Mellan's shoulders and said, with all the solemnity I could muster, "I accept your vow to serve as guardian to the kingdom of Helena, Sir Mellan Lyon."

Destrian nodded approvingly. "I thought Mellan could act as captain of your queen's guard."

My eyes lit up at the suggestion. "Really?"

Destrian smirked. "Mellan asked for a job with the least amount of responsibility and work."

Confused, I faced Mellan. "Why would the position of captain of the queen's guard have the least amount of responsibility?"

Mellan looked at me as if the answer was obvious. "You're the most powerful sorcerer in the land, and you know weaponry as well as any knight. Realistically, I'll barely have to do anything."

I rolled my eyes, both amused and exasperated. "Fine, captain of the queen's guard it is, but don't think that gets you out of training sessions."

"I just wanted that lovely apartment Everett was offering me, a manservant to follow me around and clean, and a weighty allowance for the bribing of freedom smugglers."

I raised my brows. "You will no longer be the poor lost son beholden to your father's purse?"

Mellan shook his head with a smile. "Nope! And he's promised to help me get Aureliana out of Ayastaren if an opportunity presents itself. I can't believe my luck. I think I'm the happiest man in the empire."

"Morgania will no longer be part of the empire," Destrian reminded him.

"Whatever gets my family wiped from the face of this earth. You've already killed two of us. I'd be a fool not to ally with you. We've always had the same aims, you and I."

I smiled. "I can honestly tell you that I'm glad you're here, Lyon."

Destrian offered his arm, and I took it, allowing him to escort me down the corridor. As he opened the door, a wave of anxiety washed over me at what I had to face. I knew I had to be strong, but I couldn't shake the feeling of vulnerability that gnawed at me.

I took a deep breath, then entered the chamber. Everyone along the table stood.

Lady Vianne's purple gem was glowing as her dark eyes measured me. She hadn't changed much in the year that I was gone. She was still the most stunning woman I'd ever seen next to Empress Lesedi. It was Lord Alexander, her husband, who held a weariness I hadn't remembered in Solridge.

Suddenly, a broad chest was in my face and I was being lifted in a bruising hug. I laughed, recognizing Ferris's dark hair, and clapped him on the back.

"Let her down please," Destrian growled.

Ferris looked annoyed but set me down all the same. "She's *my* family." He looked back down at me. "I'm glad you made it back, and you brought all our brothers with you."

"It wasn't just me," I said, looking over to Destrian.

He was already turned to Luc and Fin who'd joined us also.

"Was it bad?" Ferris asked, his voice dropped low. He had to have heard the stories. I wondered how much of it he believed to be true.

I shrugged, thankful that Destrian was keeping the

others away and giving me this moment. "I certainly learned a great deal. Some lessons, of course, were harder than others."

Ferris's lips drooped. He seemed to be searching for scars, but of course, there were none he could actually see. That was Agramon's way. That was the capital's way.

"The daughter of Imor has returned," a husky female voice said from behind Ferris. Urdua stepped forward, gently pinching both my cheeks in an old Morganite blessing that mothers would use on young children. I beamed, throwing my arms around her. I remembered who Destrian said had helped him while I was away, and Urdua's assistance had been nothing short of a surprise.

"We are glad that you are back," she whispered in my ear. She glanced pointedly at Destrian and raised her brows at me. "Some of us have been working very hard for someone's approval."

A nervous giggle shot out of me and I clapped my hand over my mouth.

Ferris squeezed my arm before taking a seat next to an older, scary-looking Morganite man covered in tattoos. A couple of Lyricans followed, a Solston and an old sage wearing spectacles, their eyes filled with wisdom and curiosity. Sir Bernard shot me a wink as he took his chair.

Destrian led me to the head of the table and we all settled, Destrian taking a place at the side, leaving me to look down the entire length of the council alone. The end of the table was far too big for one person, and I couldn't help but wish that Destrian or Fin were beside me, filling the empty space.

An expectant silence fell over the room. All eyes were on me, waiting, watching, and I suddenly realized that I had no idea what to say. I felt a rising panic, my mind going blank as the weight of their expectations bore down on me.

Destrian straightened in his chair. He cleared his throat to address the room. "We are gathered here to discuss the preparations for Morgania as it will soon be under the rule of Rowyn the Morganite. She will take her rightful place as the leader of our kingdom."

Destrian met each council member's gaze before he spoke again. "Before we proceed, I believe it is necessary for everyone to make their loyalties clear. All who wish to remain at this table must bend the knee to Rowyn, last heir of the Morgans. You must give an oath to uphold her as the sovereign of the Kingdom of Morgania."

The first to stand was Luc. He walked purposely to my side. I glanced at Destrian again and he held his hand to mine, helping me to rise and then nodding toward Iranoct.

Right. The sword. I glanced at Destrian out of the corner of my eye. The sword that Destrian had given me, I was using to bless the council that Destrian had made for me, in the city and land that was his gift. Who was this person? He didn't even feel like the same boy I'd gone with into the Nightlands. Before, he seemed so unsure. Now, he acted as though he knew exactly what he was doing.

One by one, they came forward and bent their knees, and one by one I blessed them for their oath. Destrian always followed to speak of their duties to the kingdom. I was just glad when I could sit once more. Then again, I had to sit, alone, at the head of the table, staring at everyone before me as they watched me expectantly.

Lady Vianne was the first to break the silence. She looked at me with a strange mixture of empathy and resolve. "Rowyn," she began, her voice gentle yet firm. "How are you? Truly?"

I met her eyes. "I suppose I'm still trying to figure that out."

Vianne frowned before looking away. "I can understand why you might feel that way, especially after everything that's happened."

My mind flashed back to Solridge, to the moment when my memories were stolen, and unresolved anger flared within me. "Why would you want to help me now, Vianne? You were the one who took my memories at Solridge, putting me further into Agramon's grasp. Why should I trust you?"

The room went still, the silence punctuated by the sharp intake of breaths. Vianne's face paled slightly. I gathered she was seldom surprised by someone's words. "I did what I did because you needed to stay to get your gem. The prophecy would not have been fulfilled if you hadn't."

Her words were measured, her voice calm, but I noticed the flicker of uncertainty in her eyes. "At points in our lives," she continued, "there are times when we have to work through someone else's wishes." As she spoke, her gaze shifted pointedly to Fin, who looked back at her with a blank expression.

I felt a surge of indignation on Fin's behalf. "I know Fin is acting on another's wishes, but at least she was honest about it. You manipulated me, played with my mind."

Vianne's face tightened, but she didn't look away. "I am here to help you, Rowyn. You know that I will not ally with Agramon. You can accept my oath or turn me away. The choice is yours."

Her words hung in the air, a challenge and an offer all at once. I looked around the room, at the faces of those who had gathered, each one a part of this complex web of alliances and betrayals.

Finally, my mind cleared with a decision. "I'll accept your help, but I'll be watching you. I won't be manipulated again."

Vianne nodded. "I wouldn't expect less."

Destrian cleared his throat, anxious to get the meeting back on track. "Sir Bernard, what's the update?"

Sir Bernard nodded. "I've sent the appropriate letters to the consuls of Eslin and Rudin, giving them the titles Duke of Eslin and Count of Rudin. They have been ordered to call their arms and make them ready for war to the south. I think with people traveling here in the next few weeks, we should probably try to have the coronation by the end of the month."

Destrian was nodding. "In the meantime, we are attempting to shore up alliances. We've already sent word to Marc Trinidan of Korballis and Pedr Tore of Livian inviting them to join the council. In addition, we will need to seek out foreign allies and continue developing Morgania's military and defense."

Ferris jumped in. "Our weakest point is the coast, especially DarkPort and Eslin, because we have no navy. It would be easy for Agramon to take both cities with a relatively small force, given that we have no real way to retaliate."

"You do not necessarily need a navy to take out a fleet," Lord Alexander said, leaning back in his chair, his eyes on the others at the table. I wondered how much convincing Vianne had to do to get Lord Alexander to join her in Morgania. He didn't seem happy to be there.

Lady Vianne raised a finger and commanded the attention of the room. "I'm not sure which way Admiral Abelard is leaning, but we should send word to the empress that we'd like to ally."

I raised a brow. "Since you were such close friends with the empress, could you . . . ?"

Lord Alexander shook his head. "I'll go. They are my family. I don't want Vianne putting herself in danger so close to Agramon."

"But Alexander," Vianne started, only to be silenced by a reassuring touch from her husband.

"I insist," he said firmly.

"As an adviser, I wonder it wise that you give up everything for a rash feeling of love," someone said.

My gaze zeroed in on the Solston who was angrily trying to meet the others' eyes, but none bothered. "Really? The Everett title? Your lands? Your right to rule? All for a girl you fancy? The consulship of Helena was given to you by Sol, and you just decide to give it away?"

I felt silly for not noticing his saltiness before, but holy men did not bend the knee. The imorati had stayed seated also.

Destrian's eyes hardened. "You make it sound as though I've done all this on a whim, Solston Ignace. Unlike you, I've considered the ramifications of what it means now that Agramon is in power. You assume that his rise would mean life as usual for Morgania, and that perception will not do you justice. My job has always been to protect the people here, and that's exactly what I'm doing."

Solston Ignace's brow wrinkled. "How? How is breaking away from the empire protecting your people? It disrupts trade. We will have to renegotiate borders, not to mention the army is sure to descend on us soon. The Butcher is already at our doorstep. The rest will soon follow."

"Because I know how Agramon works. The minute he chose Rowyn as his ward, the entirety of Morgania was in danger. Ayastaren's attack on Espiria was just the beginning. How long until he brought Morgania to its knees in order to keep her in line? How long until the people of the land were used in one of his punishments?

"You ask why I gave up my title as if I only did it for love. I did it because it was the best chance we had to keep the people safe. I won't let Morganians become puppets for Agramon to use to dispense punishment to Rowyn every time she steps a toe out of line, and he would. He did it with Ena. He was prepared to do it with me.

"We've all heard the stories of what happens to cities and villages that get in the way of a powerful noble with a grudge. Rowyn is the strongest sorcerer in the empire, and there are powerful people who will want to stay out of Agramon's reach. Some will have nowhere else to go. I do not feel it will be hard to find allies."

The man's nose wrinkled in disgust, but he looked away, chastened by Destrian's words.

Destrian made it sound so easy. "People distrust me though," I said. "There is a whole sect of people who want me dead." My mind went back to the Sons of Sol and their attacks on my tour across the empire. "It's not as easy as what you're making it out to be. I have more enemies than allies."

Destrian shook his head. "*That* was the people of the Eastern Empire. Here in the West, you're celebrated."

I snorted. "I doubt that. Ayastaren still has a target on my back."

"Ayastaren has tried to hit that target multiple times and failed. The other nobles have taken notice. You had to have realized that the Lyons are far from loved and re-spected. They've ruled through fear, and you are not afraid of them."

I looked over at the council members, then the faces sitting in front of me.

"What news is there of the empress? Is there the possi-bility of an alliance?"

I was looking at Lady Vianne, but it was the Solston who answered.

"She barely has any allies in the East except with the Marendeslys. The other nobles who matter have all sided with Agramon."

My eyes sharpened on him. "Maryse hasn't. Ardent hasn't. They will never side with him." I looked at

Destrian. Really it was him I wanted to convince. "I've declared my throne. As my first act of foreign diplomacy, I will be moving to declare myself an ally of the empress. We need to work together on this. Ferris is right, we could use a navy, and Admiral Abelard's wife is from Maryse. It could be that he sides with them."

"The more foreign allies you have, the more legitimate a foe you will be," Lady Vianne added. "And I'm sure the empress would recognize your claim to the throne."

"Does she have a choice?" I asked, my voice hard. I glanced at the bracelet on Vianne's arm, wondering again if the empress was using it to communicate with her kindred women of the realm, or perhaps it really was just a token of affection and nothing more. I wondered if I would ever know. "There is a far better chance of foreign countries legitimizing my throne than hers. She will know this."

"I don't understand why no one has mentioned Horan," Fin cut in.

Destrian looked almost angry.

"I've been to the land of the fae, and they would be a formidable ally, enough to turn the tide of war," she said.

Kaelan, the scary Imorati, shook his head. "The fae don't offer to fight in wars, Fin."

"But we will still hear what he has to say," I offered, shooting Fin a smile. After all, I was pretty sure she already sent a summons to the fae king.

We continued the discussions well past dinnertime until we decided to reconvene the next day. As the council members began to file out, talking among themselves or examining the parchments and plans laid out before them, I took a moment to look around the table. I'd seen and heard council meetings in the capital, and the table at Morgania was a world of difference to what I'd witnessed in Somme. Already it felt as though we'd won the war. I smiled inwardly, feeling as though Morgania might actually be able to weather whatever storms lay ahead.

Chapter 17

IN THE RESTLESS THROES of sleep, my consciousness flickered and shifted, settling somewhere unfamiliar yet deeply intimate. I was looking out of my own window but not through my eyes. The city of Helena sprawled below, illuminated by the moonlight, its architecture a testament to the long history of the city.

I—Echo, rather—felt an odd sensation, a presence that wasn't there before. Turning around, I found a spectral figure. Her visage was as familiar as any painting or tapestry that hung in the halls of this very castle. Queen Helen.

"Sister," she spoke, her voice echoing like the softest chime of a bell, a haunting melody of loss. "You have protected her well."

Echo looked down upon my sleeping form sprawled out on the bed. "I did the best I could," Echo replied. And she had. Echo had been a guardian, a confidant. A family once lost, but now unforgotten.

"Can you bear it?" Queen Helen whispered. "Being around me?"

Echo paused. Nirah, she had been called in another life. Sister to Morius the Black, the man who had been in love with the queen who haunted the castle of Helena. A myriad of complex emotions, centuries old but fresh as any wound, swelled within her. "Being with Rowyn has helped me forgive you. Time heals, but love heals better."

"How much longer will you stay?" Queen Helen asked. "Does the northern darkness not call to you as the castle calls to me?"

"It does," Echo agreed. "But I don't want to go back. I will stay until she has no more need of me."

"She is stronger than when you left," Helen remarked, her ghostly hand reaching out to brush the coverlet.

"She has experienced enough to make her cautious and wise," Echo agreed.

Queen Helen nodded, but before either could speak again, the world around us began to dissolve. The dream, the connection, was fading.

My eyes blinked open, the first rays of dawn spilling through the windows. Helena greeted me with its waking life, the sounds of a city coming alive with the morning sun. But even as I rose to meet the day, the memory of the dream, the conversation between Echo and Queen Helen, clung to me like the remnants of morning mist.

DAISY BUSTLED AROUND my room, her face alight with

excitement as she presented three more of Onora's dresses for me to choose from.

"I think the light-purple one will do," I said, smiling at Daisy's enthusiasm.

Her eyes sparkled with delight. "Oh, it's a lovely choice, Your Majesty! And I'll be accompanying you and the other ladies to the marketplace today. It's going to be quite the adventure!"

My cheeks flushed at her calling me majesty. I supposed it was something I would have to get used to if I continued on this chosen path.

Later that morning, we made our way through the bustling marketplace, Fin strolling around in her dressing gown, casually looking over various items, while Lady Maureen walked gracefully between us. We stopped at a stall filled with beautiful dresses, and I found myself admiring one of the gowns.

"I'd like one of these," I said, touching the soft fabric. "Perhaps in several colors?"

Lady Maureen leaned close, her voice gentle and kind. "Rowyn, all of the tailors of Helena will want to get their clothes on you. It's kinder to share the outfitting of your wardrobe with all of them, not just one stall."

That made an enormous amount of sense. I nodded in agreement, while wondering if I was supposed to know that. Agramon always just had one tailor in the city that he called to outfit him.

Beside me, Fin was engaged in conversation with one of the seamstresses, explaining her unique problem of needing to get a gown off quickly so she could transform. The lady was nodding, pointing to various parts of Fin's body and taking meticulous measurements, intent on creating gowns that would suit Fin's particular needs. Apparently, she sold highly decorated dressing gowns to the few brothels in Helena. Fin's garment needed similar accommodations, though for different reasons.

I found a vendor who sold leather harnesses and I explained my wish for a knife belt on my thigh. The Morganite said he could make something for me and agreed to have the bill be sent to the castle where Lady Maureen would take care of it.

As we left, Lady Maureen guided my attention to a building in the distance. "See there, Rowyn? That's the new sage school that's being converted. Quite the project, isn't it?"

I studied the structure. "It's incredible," I murmured. Still I was learning of more things Destrian had done.

"He's a fine young man, born to lead and rule. It would be a shame, wouldn't it, if such a dedicated soul were pushed to the sidelines, given that he's so good at what he does?"

I considered her meaning. She wasn't telling me

anything I didn't already know. But her words resonated, affirming something I'd been feeling but hadn't quite articulated.

I wanted Destrian at my side, not walking behind me.

We continued making our way through the market, our day proceeding delightfully when Mellan came riding toward us, his frown evident from four stalls away. I could tell he was cross, but I wasn't quite sure why until he reached us.

"Rowyn, why did you leave without me?" he demanded, his voice filled with frustration.

I blinked in surprise. "I didn't know you were supposed to come with us."

Mellan's face grew even more disgruntled. "I am the captain of the queen's guard. It's my duty to go with you."

I felt a pang of guilt at having overlooked this detail but decided to make the best of it. "Well, you're here now. Let's continue."

And continue we did, purchasing from as many stalls as we could. All bills were sent to the castle, and Lady Maureen was keeping track of our purchases with a practiced eye. We bought paint for our faces, gowns of varying fabric and occasion, fancy hairbrushes and hair decorations, cloaks and shawls, breeches and tunics, boots and socks. We even found curtains for our rooms and bed coverings.

We savored the joy of choosing and buying. I felt invigorated, connected to the people and the life of the city. I felt like a new person in a new world. I felt alive and, truly, I felt happy to be.

By the time we finished, Fin and I were starving. Lady Maureen, ever the gracious host, took us to her favorite bun shop in the market. The old widower who sold rolls there had a twinkle in his eye when he handed Lady Maureen her purchases, and I couldn't resist teasing her about it.

Fin and I rode back to the palace, the sounds of the market still faintly echoing in our ears. Mellan trailed behind us, his ear on our conversation and his eyes on the surrounding crowd.

"How's your room?" I asked Fin, knowing she was in one that I'd used in Helena before. "Are you settling in well?"

"Oh, it's lovely! I'm excited to make it my own."

Mellan chimed in from behind us, his words tinged with feigned indignation. "I should get an allowance to outfit my room too!"

Fin shrugged. "Talk to Destrian about it, Captain."

Mellan huffed in mock exasperation. "Destrian Everett is as stingy as his father."

"No, he's not," I shot back. "He's spared no expense."

"Maybe for you he has lavished riches," Mellan

retorted, "but not for everyone else."

Fin flipped her hair over her shoulder. "Well, I've already negotiated a rather nice salary from him, and permission to take messages myself to Horan or the gatekeeper if need be."

I shook my head, admiration mingling with amusement. "You never cease to amaze me."

Mellan huffed to himself, but I knew he wasn't truly mad. He was definitely treated far better in Morgania than he'd been in Somme. He certainly wasn't drinking as much.

Returning to the palace, Fin and I were met by Sir Bernard, his weathered face breaking into a smile at our approach.

"Your Majesty," Old Bernard greeted, inclining his head. "His lordship wishes to meet with you both."

We followed him through the familiar corridors, Mellan hanging back. I assumed the room Sir Bernard was leading us to was Destrian's, but as he opened it, I realized it was a morning room.

Destrian sat at a desk, a mug of tea beside him as he pored over maps and charts, while Lady Vianne, Lord Alexander, and Luc debated the importance of Admiral Abelard's allegiance.

"The support of a navy is crucial," Luc was saying as he pointed out DarkPort and Eslin. "We simply cannot leave the coast so unguarded."

"The empress and the Marendeslys must understand the importance of their role without being privy to our entire strategy," Destrian replied before he turned to Fin and me. "How did shopping go?"

"We had a good time." I smiled, somewhat guiltily. I was having loads of fun while Destrian was at the castle working.

"I'm glad Lady Maureen accompanied us," I added, settling into the chair beside Vianne while Fin sat on the couch and lifted her feet onto the cushions. Luc watched her for a moment before meeting my eye with a wishful gaze.

I swallowed. He was on his own with Fin.

A servant girl arrived carrying a tray laden with lady's tea and biscuits. I smiled in thanks as she poured the tea, the aromatic blend of herbs filling the room.

"Indeed," Lord Alexander chimed in. "It is Admiral Abelard who we must ensure is loyal to our cause. His control over the northern sea could tip the balance in our favor."

Lady Vianne's eyes flicked to mine. "We must be cautious with the Marendeslys. I would urge you to ally with the empress directly, not with them."

Lord Alexander didn't say anything, but I noticed him shaking his head a bit, a subtle sign of his disagreement.

As the servant handed me my cup of tea, I caught a

flicker of something in Vianne's eyes. It was a look I hadn't seen before, a sudden sharpness that was both alarming and confusing. Before I could even raise the cup to my lips, her hand shot out and slapped it out of my grasp.

It shattered on the floor, tea splattering everywhere, and I stared at her in shock.

"Lady Vianne!" My heart pounded. "What on earth—"

But her eyes were still fixed on the servant girl, who was now pale and trembling, backing toward the door.

"Do not leave," Lady Vianne commanded, her voice cold and imperious. The girl's eyes glazed over in a dull purple light.

Lady Vianne's eyes were cold as she studied the trembling girl. "You slipped poison into the queen's tea, didn't you?" she accused, her voice sharp and cutting.

The servant girl's face crumpled, and she immediately started crying, her sobs racking her slight frame. "He didn't say it was poison!" she wailed. "I swear, I didn't know what I was doing!"

Lady Vianne shook her head, her expression one of deep disappointment and anger. "Ignorance is no excuse," she said, her voice steady but filled with disdain. "You have betrayed this household and your queen."

Luc was at the door, calling Mellan who hurried in and grabbed the girl roughly. Her cries echoed as he and Luc dragged her away. I could see the fear in her eyes, and though I was angry at her betrayal, I also felt a pang of sympathy for her.

"I will go through the entire household staff myself," Lady Vianne offered. "I will make sure that no one is hiding a false allegiance. We will root out the traitors and deal with them accordingly."

I was pretty sure it was Agramon, and I had a feeling Vianne suspected the same thing.

Destrian's face was dark and clouded, his eyes on the door. "I'll send Aunt Maureen to assist you. She knows the staff."

Lord Alexander stood with Vianne. As they prepared to leave, Vianne gave Alexander a soft kiss on the cheek. It was a simple, gentle gesture.

My heart warmed. I had never seen them exhibit much affection at Solridge, nothing that hinted at the grand love story that the empress had implied. But there, in that small, private moment, I saw a glimpse of something deeper.

As Vianne and Alexander left, Destrian steepled his fingers and sighed, his eyes on Fin and me. "Why didn't you tell me about the King of Horan?"

I blinked. "For some reason it slipped my mind, but Fin just mentioned that he wanted the borders open. I didn't think it was *that* big of a deal."

I heard Fin shift behind me. I glanced at her over my shoulder as Destrian glared at her. "No, it's not just about the borders. I was hoping we could avoid working with the Others. They're powerful, yes, but they can also be incredibly tricky. Unpredictable. We should try to avoid them if we can."

"I disagree," Fin said with a sigh. Her bare leg peeked out from her robe, and I felt a twinge of jealousy. Fin had grown stunning in her transformation. Her skin was golden from her time in the sun. Her hair was always loose and flowing over her shoulders as if she were sitting for a painting. "The fae are much more advanced than us in many ways. We could learn a lot from them. It was the fae who taught me how to transform."

I glanced at Destrian, wondering if he'd marked how different she seemed now. Luc had surely noticed, though he hadn't ever known the girl before. But Destrian wasn't looking at Fin. He was studying me, a wrinkle of worry on his brow.

"King Valon is the same king who allied with Theramon the Conquered while he lived. They made a blood pact." Destrian and his fingers through his hair. "I think Valon's going to want something more than what you're imagining. Something we might not be prepared to give."

"We'll approach this with caution, then," I offered. "We'll learn what we can and make no promises until we understand the full scope of what's being asked."

Destrian tapped his finger on his desk nervously. "Promise me you'll be careful, Rowyn. The fae's favors are never as simple as they seem."

I crossed my arms. "I trust Fin's judgment on this, Destrian. She's been to the land of the fae. She knows them better than we do."

Destrian's eyes narrowed at Fin. "I see I'm going to be overruled on this one, but the decision to open the border to the fae will be an unpopular one, just to warn you."

Fin's expression was insistent. "The king is urging me to set up a meeting."

"Then bring him to Helena," Destrian snapped. "Rowyn must remain here, especially since she will be newly crowned. It wouldn't do for the people to watch her leave, especially with Lyrica lurking beyond our borders. The King of the Fae will have to come to her, just like everyone else."

Fin shook her head, her lips set in a thin line. "He honors the border."

"Bullshit," Destrian retorted, leaning back in his chair. "I'm positive the king would be able to leave Horan if he needed to."

Fin's face remained impassive, her silence speaking louder than words. I looked between them, realizing that Destrian was right.

"Mellan is unhappy with his salary," I said, trying to

lighten the mood. I didn't like the two people I loved most in the world angry with each other. I understood Destrian's worry, I really did, but I also understood Fin's unwillingness to go against her promise to the fae king.

Destrian's went back to the documents before him. "He should've had Fin negotiate it for him then." He glared at my friend. "But I'll be furious if you do."

"Was it really that bad?" I chuckled, looking between the two of them.

"Fin is a lady who knows her worth." Destrian made a face, a mixture of admiration and exasperation in his voice.

Fin simply smiled, her expression radiating smug satisfaction.

"Lady Vianne looked through Luc's mind," Destrian said suddenly. "She found several triggers."

Fin sat up. "What's a trigger?"

"It's when Agramon plants a set of actions or orders in someone's mind that goes off when something specific happens." I turned back to Destrian. "I'm guessing the trigger against me was still there."

Destrian nodded. "Luc would still hurt you if you did something to harm Agramon, but Lady Vianne can unravel it."

I let out a breath of relief. "That's wonderful news."

"Lord Alexander is working on locating a ship to take him across the Ballerian Sea to meet with the empress and the Marendeslys, so I'm having Luc work with Sir Bernard and Ferris to build up the army," Destrian went on.

I leaned back in my chair, a new thought dawning on me. "I can send a signal to the empress through a storm," I said, looking between Destrian and Fin. "But I'll have to hold off on reinforcing the rain at the border."

Fin shrugged, her eyes straying to the window.

"Have you been watching the border?" I asked, curiosity getting the better of me.

Fin shot me a look that was slightly reproachful. "You made me spymaster, remember?"

Destrian tried to hide a smile.

"They're pretty bogged down," Fin went on, her voice more serious. "The baron is trying to figure out how to move his forces. Duke Roland is getting annoyed with Sam's mercenaries being there."

"That's good news," I said, allowing myself a small smile. "I'll use my magic to send a message to the empress. Hopefully, when she sees the storm, she will know that an alliance is coming."

Destrian nodded, distracted as he shuffled through the things littering his desk. I rose and stood behind him, my hands resting on his shoulders, scanning the papers and letters. Destrian took too much on himself. I resolved to find ways to lessen his load.

"What now?" I asked. "All the letters have been

dispatched, so what comes next?"

Destrian took one of my hands in his, his fingers gently stroking my skin. "There's still a lot to do. I'm requesting everyone to make it to Helena by the end of the month to see you crowned."

I felt a flutter of excitement mixed with nervousness at the thought of the upcoming ceremony. My life was about to change in ways I could hardly imagine. It almost didn't feel real.

"I did have a dress commissioned for you," Destrian added, looking up at me. "If that's all right?"

I smiled, touched by his thoughtfulness. "Of course, that's fine. Thank you, Destrian." Neither Agramon nor Sam would've ever asked.

Fin rose from her chair and stretched her arms. "I'll leave you two," she said, winking at me. "I have some unpacking to do."

I watched her leave, realizing that I needed to do the same. But as I looked around the morning room, which had now become Destrian's office, I noticed a desk at the other end.

"Whose is that?" I asked, pointing to it.

Destrian followed my gaze. "It was my father's," he said quietly. "But now, like everything else of mine, it's yours if you want it."

I moved around Destrian, sitting on his lap and

wrapping my arms around his shoulders. He seemed tense, his mind clearly occupied with weighty matters, and not seemingly interested in me ripping his clothes off, which I'd been craving to do. I kept wishing he'd walk me to my rooms or find some time for us to be alone, but after dinner, he stayed up late into the night, planning and meeting with others. By the end of the day, I imagined he was so exhausted that he must just collapse into bed.

"I would love to take the desk," I said softly. Then, I ruffled my fingers through his vibrant red hair, admiring the way it felt. "You seem stressed."

He let out a small laugh, though it didn't reach his eyes. "Treason will do that to a person," he admitted.

My heart ached at the worry in his eyes. I drew him closer, wanting to offer comfort. "Are you sure we're doing the right thing?" I asked, searching his face for reassurance.

"It's impossible to tell," he said, his voice honest and raw. "The seers have said that the outcome will probably work in our favor."

"But?" I prompted, sensing there was more on his mind.

"I'm worried about the fae king and what he could want," Destrian admitted. His brow furrowed. "Vianne has warned me to be wary of the fae, and I think Fin is clearly keeping something from us."

"I know," I said. I understood his concerns, but I trusted my friend. "She's keeping it from us because the fae king will want to reveal his agreement himself. That's their way."

Destrian sighed, his body still rigid.

"I think you need to find a way to unwind," I suggested, a smile tugging at the corner of my mouth as I twirled a lock of his hair around my finger. I would dearly love to take his mind off his duties for a while. Perhaps here on the desk even, since he was looking so delicious in his green, brocade coat, with all manner of blades strapped to his waist. Something about the number of weapons he now carried sent my mind reeling into the most indecent thoughts. I wanted to ease the coat off his shoulders and slide my hands up the planes of his stomach, rediscovering everything I thought had been lost.

He kissed me, soft and gentle, filled with tenderness and affection. Not the hungry, all-consuming desire that I wanted from him.

"I will always love you, Rowyn," he whispered. "But I want you to succeed more than anything."

"What if I want to be with you?" I moaned. "You're one of the more powerful sorcerers in the West. Why couldn't *we* make an alliance?"

"Because you already have my power at your disposal." He tilted his head up to meet my eyes, his fingers running lightly down my back, far too chaste for my taste. His hands should be climbing up my skirt. "Others may need more incentive to back your side—other than being madly in love with you."

I understood his reasoning, but my heart ached with longing. "Maybe we can't be married," I said, nipping at his lip, "but I want us to be together."

He tightened his grip, finally pulling me closer, catching my lips in his. "I have no plans to leave your side," he murmured, breaking away far too soon, "but I don't want to step on anyone's toes or get in the way of an alliance."

"It's not worth it if I have to keep my distance from you." My voice broke. "In the capital, I would've given anything just to have another day with you. I don't want to keep our distance when it's not assured that Sam and Agramon won't be able to get to me."

His jaw tensed as the flames on the hearth licked the air wildly. "Rowyn, don't think like that."

I shifted, my skirt hiking up as I straddled him. "If this is all we have, I want to enjoy it."

Our lips met again, this time with the passion and urgency that I'd been craving. Our world narrowed to just the two of us, without politics or duty or the evils of the world that seemed to follow us.

I drank Destrian in, biting his lip as my fingers twisted in his hair. His hands went firmly to my waist. I ground into him, wanting desperately to be closer. Wanting to feel all of him. To take everything he would give me and more until he was mine and mine alone.

"Gods," he groaned, pulling my gown off one shoulder and freeing a breast from my corset. His teeth nipped at me, sending shocks of lightning to my core. I sucked in a breath, his roaming hands growing more urgent as clothes began to shift. Just as we were teetering on the edge of crossing the line, Destrian broke away.

"I've got to go," he panted, his voice thick with regret.

"No," I pleaded, my lips breathless on his. "Stay with me."

He pulled my sleeve back up, his eyes filled with a longing that mirrored my own. "I wish to the gods I could stay, Rowyn. But I'm already late. I have to meet with Sage Rasmus."

I tried to calm my racing heart and quench my lust. "I guess I should send the empress her message."

He nodded, his eyes still locked on mine. He leaned in to give me one more searing kiss, lingering as if he couldn't bear to pull away.

"I love you," he said with conviction.

He lifted me as he rose from the chair, then set my feet gently on the ground. After resting a final, lingering touch on my cheek, he left the room, leaving me feeling both fulfilled and empty at the same time.

With the shadows deepening outside the windows, I returned to my room and set to work organizing the new clothes and various items delivered from the marketplace. I'd cracked the balcony doors to let in the garden's irresistible perfume, and the fire crackling in the fireplace made the room seem cozy and peaceful. I breathed deep, the smell of the fresh mountain air making me feel as though I were finally home, and I realized how quickly I'd grown to love the place.

I hung the dresses, each one more beautiful and intricate than the last. I smiled and admired my new knife set and thigh holster, recalling Destrian's huffy reaction when I'd told him of my wish for the blades. He'd insisted that he could make weapons for me, but I gently reminded him of the importance of supporting the artisans of the city. He didn't need to beggar the blacksmiths of the city.

It was hard though . . . being alone was not kind to my thoughts. Without distractions, the weight of the crown loomed large in my mind. It seemed foolish, this collective faith that everyone seemed to be placing in me. I was one person, a single soul tasked with leading a kingdom, making decisions that would impact lives and shape the future of Morgania.

I pondered the gods, how even they shared the weight of ruling, each one responsible for a different aspect of existence.

Why, then, should I be expected to carry this burden alone?

Chapter 18

U NCLE BAYLIN SHOWED up in Helena with a contingent of people from Caymir's Rook the next afternoon. Tall, broad-shouldered, and exuding authority, his arrival drew the attention of many in the hall when he was announced. Yet his face was creased with irritation, his mouth set in a tight line.

He began making his way to where I was standing. My stomach tightened when I noticed Pria limping behind him. Neither Uncle Baylin nor his daughter were ones to mince words, and their irritation was palpable even from across the room.

I excused myself from my conversation with Lady Vianne and went to meet them, wondering what he could possibly want. He had never sought my presence before. Quite the opposite, actually. So why would he come to Helena now?

"Rowyn," Baylin said, his voice deep and resonant. But there was no warmth in his greeting.

"Uncle," I replied, trying to keep my tone light. "Welcome to Helena." I had no cause to make a scene . . . yet.

His eyes narrowed slightly, and he looked me up and down as though assessing me. "I wish to speak with you."

His tone grated my nerves. He was treating me as though I were still a child, not the ruler of this land.

Urdua stepped up to one side of me, while Mellan flanked the other. Baylin shot his wife a look of absolute loathing. Perhaps he felt unsure of his position since Urdua had given both men and women the right to divorce in her update to the council on my first day in Helena. It seemed a more self-serving change then I'd initially realized.

Destrian was away with Luc overseeing the arms training, so I followed Sir Bernard to the council room, leading Mellan, Baylin, Pria, and Urdua.

Though I wished Destrian was with me, it was both unfair and foolish to rely on him for everything. My family, I could handle myself. As we sat, I could feel the weight of my uncle's gaze on me, and I met it squarely, daring him to ask something of me.

"What is it you wish to discuss?"

His eyes flickered, and for a moment, I saw a hint of uncertainty. But it was gone as quickly as it had come, replaced by a determination that was all too familiar.

Urdua's lips had flattened to a thin line. She seemed . . . exasperated.

"My role," he said, leaning forward. "How I can help. How I can be of service to Morgania."

A laugh escaped me, tumbling out of my lips and shocking everyone in the room. He couldn't be serious.

"I suppose I don't understand what you mean," I explained when he was clearly affronted. He rolled his shoulders back and eyed the others in the room.

I wondered what he would've said if they hadn't been there. In Espiria, he would go out of his way to say the most terrible things to me. I'd always wondered if he'd wanted me to lose control that day. In my darkest thoughts, I considered him capable of using me to kill his own brother. Baylin had always been jealous of Father. When I was younger, I'd overheard other women gossiping that Baylin had been the initial one to pursue Hania, my mother.

I wondered if he understood that he should fear me. He had manipulated me at home, then sold me away to the empire we'd been raised to hate. Now, he had the audacity to try to come make peace? As though none of his previous betrayals mattered. As though he didn't owe me so much more.

I'd survived in the Nightlands, battling the beasts of darkness. I'd survived in Somme, escaping the monsters roaming in the daylight. Yet there I sat, with three gems, a throne, and a crown, and the love of a man who was bending over backward to give me the world.

Nothing my uncle could say or do would ever faze me again. If he irked me enough, I could just send him to the dungeons to keep company with Conal, the other traitor.

I set my mouth in a grim line. "Espiria must be manned and available, so whether you like it or not, you will remain there or in Caymir's Rook. After all, that is where you were elected to be."

"I am the chief of the Espirians," Baylin said, straightening. "Whether you like it or not, I am an important figure among our people."

"No, *I* am their chief," I scoffed. "I am Espiria's chief, I am Rudin's chief, I am chief to *all* who dwell within Morgania. Your betrayal was never taken lightly, and you should count your blessings I don't have you down in the cells with Conal."

"I did what I did for the clan," Baylin snapped. "If you weren't so selfish, you would've seen that it was the only way."

I slammed my hand onto the table and felt Mellan shift behind me. Sir Bernard leaned forward, as though to cut in, but I shook my head sharply. I didn't need his help.

"It was *not* the only way. You allied with Lyrica against your own clansmen, and now you must pay the price. You *will* keep Espiria manned with a small host of men. You *will* protect whoever decides to dwell there as refuge, and you *will* keep your distance from me. Supplies will be sent regularly so that you can live your dream of never raiding again, but *this* is as far as you go in the story of how Morgania came to be in her own once more. Your role in how

I rebuild Morgania is over."

I rose and gestured toward the door. "Ignore my order at your own peril, Uncle. Conal is lonely."

My uncle stood, Sir Bernard at his side. "I will wait for you in the hall," he told Pria, resentment clear in his every movement. But I was unapologetic. The presumption that he was somehow necessary to me was laughable. Sir Bernard led Baylin out of the chamber and shut the door behind them.

Urdua had also risen with Baylin, but now she held her hands out. "Rowyn, Pria had written to me before they left, wanting to see you about an idea she had that I thought was very good. I assured her that you would hear her out."

I took a measured breath. Of course she would want something from me too. Of course, when I needed help the most, my entire family up and abandoned me, but now that I could help them, I was in their company once more.

Pria assessed me shrewdly. She leaned on her cane, the walk through the castle probably wearying her.

"I learned," she began, her voice trembling, "that Urdua has made allowable under law for women to divorce their husbands."

I nodded. It was a groundbreaking change, one that had already seen many women come forward seeking to have their relationships dissolved. I looked at Pria, waiting for her to continue, but she hesitated, her eyes flicking to

Urdua.

Urdua nodded gently. "Go on, Pria."

Pria squared her shoulders just as her father had. "For women looking to divorce, they might not have another home to go to. I had an idea that I thought you would like, though I'm not sure you'll like it at all if it comes from me."

Irritation seared through me at her hesitation. "Just go on already, Pria," I said more sharply than I intended. We'd been close growing up, but time seemed to ravage the open wounds of our relationship. First, it was Luc. Then it was my mother. Then it was the lack of control over my magic.

Pria and I would never be close again. I didn't want to be. Yet, I would be a fool not to mark her words. If I wanted to make improvements, I would need to listen to others.

Pria's eyes narrowed but she pressed on. "Some women's families won't take them back in, and the only other place to go are brothels, since most landlords in the city refuse to rent to women. It would be helpful to have safehouses for them. For the women and the children."

My frown deepened. What she said rang true.

"Those were unintended consequences of the law," Urdua explained. "And now there are women who would seek divorce if there was a place for them to go."

Sitting back down, I dipped my quill into an inkpot and began to write out a list. "We can ask the advice of ladies

Vianne and Maureen," I said as they returned to their seats across from me. "We can start one here in Helena—try to find what works and what doesn't before we expand to DarkPort, Eslin, and Rudin."

I looked over at Pria. "Would you like to head up the safehouse?" Although we'd disagreed over the years, she was well-versed on managing a large home, having learned it from my mother.

Pria glanced at Urdua with a guarded expression. "I didn't think there would be room for me," she said, her voice edged with a hint of snark, "since you sent Father away."

My eyes narrowed at her tone. "This isn't about you. It's about what's best for the people of Morgania."

Pria's hand clenched her cane. I forced myself to calm down. I knew Pria was hurting, but getting things right was too important to let personal feelings get in the way.

"I can't think of a better use for your talents than having you help women be more independent," I added softly.

There was silence, and then Pria nodded, her face pale but determined. Urdua smiled warmly.

"Funds must be appropriated for use in the venture, and they will be overseen by the sage. Report your work to Urdua so that she can then bring updates to the council."

I set the quill down and handed Urdua the parchment. "Though we've had issues in the past, Pria, I always want to hear good ideas that may make things better for our people."

Pria's face tightened, and she stood, grabbing her cane. I watched her limp out of the room, noting that her step had worsened since she'd left Espiria. My heart ached for a moment, but I pushed the feeling aside.

"Wait outside, Pria, and I'll be there shortly," Urdua said. Then she turned to me. "Haplin wasn't good to her, Rowyn. The tribe of Espirians is breaking with my absence and Baylin being shut out of ruling Morgania."

"Ferris is well respected, and so am I, but Baylin is seen as a failed man, and Haplin has been at his side since I've been gone. I don't really see it functioning as a clan the same way anymore."

"Why is that?" I asked, stepping around the table and pouring myself a glass of wine that Mellan stared longingly at. Too bad, he was on the job.

Urdua shrugged, her eyes troubled. "They don't see a need to, because they look to you for leadership."

"Woe to all, then." Bitterness tainted my words as I took a sip.

But Urdua frowned, shaking her head. "There are more trials to come, surely, that will test this kingdom. Do not allow self-doubt to be one of them."

Her words stayed with me long after she left. I glanced over my shoulder at Mellan.

"I keep wanting you to be Destrian," I admitted, feeling a pang of loneliness.

Mellan glared at me, then went to stand in the corner and pout.

IN MY DREAMS that night, Echo drifted through the halls of the castle, unseen, and arrived in a dimly lit chamber where a large map of Morgania was laid out on a heavy wooden table. Dark figures hunched above it, the low hum of voices, mixed with the crackling of the fire, made it hard to discern what was being said, but Echo, ever the spy, snuck closer.

Destrian stood at the head of the table, his fingers gently tracing paths on the map as if he could foresee the steps of a future battle. Worry clouded his eyes every time his fingers brushed over Ayastaren. Lord Alexander was sitting beside him, his chin resting on his hand as he studied the young men in front of him. Luc and Ferris sat next to each other, both sporting new markings on their bulging forearms that denoted their new ranks.

Ferris was talking, his black hair pulled back into a knot common to the Morganite clansmen. "I've got my own patrols monitoring the areas, and our spies have reported that

Rowyn's storms completely ruined all the Butcher's supplies and Duke Roland is having a damned of a time just managing his own city. I doubt he's interested in losing even more men on a foolish attack on Eslin."

"Now, I've managed to patrol most of the border, but Morgania is big, and it's stretched my forces too thin already. We're barely watching the western edge near Horan."

"That's unacceptable." Destrian scowled. "The fae are up to something, and I want to make sure we aren't caught unawares."

Luc and Ferris shot each other a glance. "We Morganites have no qualms with the Others."

"You Morganites weren't used as trophies to their bloodthirsty brethren," Lord Alexander grunted. "Lyricans are wary of them, and rightly so. We know precious little about their magic."

Luc snorted. "Well, if we don't ally with the fae, what do you suggest? Would you rather us rely on your royal family to support us?"

Lord Alexander took a moment to weigh his words. "The Marendeslys have lost a lot of favor, especially with the late Emperor having none of our family on his council. Duke Eldred let the throne fall to Agramon, and he's going to want to get it back by any means necessary. Sadly, the family has lost support over the years, and the other nobles are either flocking to Agramon's side, or waiting to see who's standing when the dust settles."

"According to Fin," Destrian said slowly, "Agramon is mostly occupied with solidifying his grip on Somme. He probably won't launch an attack soon, but we shouldn't rule anything out."

"That sounds less than promising," Ferris grunted. "The Morganites won't support shirking the favor of the fae to get the support of some fallen royal family from Lyrica. What if we negotiate with Duke Agramon? He'd have to rein in the Butcher of Bruin, wouldn't he? Could be a simpler solution than going to war. Doesn't he like Rowyn?"

Lord Alexander shook his head, his weary eyes flickering with warning. "The Duke of Solin is not the type to let useful assets slip through his fingers. Rowyn would be far more valuable to him tethered than untethered."

"We also shouldn't assume the Butcher of Bruin is following the duke's orders," Luc added. "They never got along during Rowyn's tour of Lyrica. The Butcher will attack based on his own agenda, not the duke's."

Ferris's blue eyes darkened as he let out a gust of frustration, his casual demeanor shifting abruptly. "Well, it's a damn pity Rowyn wasn't more selective with who she bedded," he snapped, the words escaping like a shard of glass.

Luc took a deep breath, studying his hands as he

clenched and unclenched his fists. "Rowyn was lonely," he finally said. "It's not right to judge her."

Ferris scoffed, rising and flinging his hand out. "Lonely? She had you. She had Fin!"

"She didn't know Fin was there. Ena, her closest friend, was killed by Agramon. And me? I promise you, I wasn't any help to her. You have no idea what it's like under him." Luc shook his head, a muscle in his jaw flexing. "He had me far too angry to be much use to anyone. Rowyn didn't have a choice in most of it. The worst men at the capital saw her power and tried to take advantage of it. That's what Somme is. And the few times Rowyn tried to fight back, Agramon tortured her . . . carved into her. As a lesson for her to follow orders and not make a fuss. I saw it with my own eyes," he added, looking at Destrian, his voice tinged with a mix of rage and guilt. "He made me wait outside . . . knowing he was hurting her . . . and I was unable to lift a finger about it. I could only stand there like a fucking fool."

Destrian's reaction was immediate. He pushed himself up, his whole frame trembling as the fire in the fireplace roared higher, light streaming to all four corners of the room. I'd wondered if Echo had shown him that particular memory. I found myself glad that she had not. Some things I preferred to keep hidden in the shadows.

"She told me he'd drugged her once . . . tried to put her

in the arms of Count Balthazo of Gryse," Luc went on. His gaze was sharp on Destrian, as though trying to make him understand.

"Fuck him," Destrian breathed, running his hand over his face. His breath was coming sharp and fast. The torches on the wall burst into flames. Destrian strode to the windows and began slamming them open.

"Do you want to know who saved her from that particular incident?" Luc called to him.

"Mellan?" Destrian snapped, his gem emitting a bright red glow.

"The Butcher," Luc finished.

"I know I failed her," Destrian yelled. "Every person in this room has failed her. You were the one who told Agramon about her." He pointed at Luc. "You were the one who kept her leashed." Destrian shifted his finger to Lord Alexander. "And her own family sold her." He finished with Ferris, who had the decency to look away. "We've all failed her in the past, but it ends today. We do not negotiate," Destrian snarled with finality. "The Butcher himself said he would never let Rowyn go. If we want to protect the kingdom, we need to find other ways to stave off a war or prepare for battle."

A sudden shriek echoed off the stone walls. Arden was perched on the windowsill. In the blink of an eye, she transformed, revealing a nude Fin.

Most quickly averted their gazes—everyone except Ferris, whose eyes were locked onto her with a heated stare. Luc rose and smacked him, harder than necessary. Ferris reluctantly turned, his cheeks aflame.

Luc pulled off his tunic. "Here," he said, offering it to Fin. She accepted the garment with a smile of thanks. Luc stood in front of her, his arms crossed, scowling at the others while she slipped the garment on.

"My lords," she said stepping from behind Luc. "I was hoping to catch you together."

"What is it?" Lord Alexander asked, leaning forward.

But Fin wasn't listening. Her head was tipped to the side. A little mouse appeared on the windowsill. She offered it her arm and it scampered up the sleeve of the tunic to sit at Fin's ear. She stilled, her mouth tightening into a thin line.

"Who mentioned negotiating an alliance with Agramon?" she asked the room. Destrian looked down angrily. Luc said nothing.

It was Ferris who gave himself away. "I was just proposing that we look at all of our options."

Fin raised a brow, her eyes flashing dangerously. "Are you suggesting we put ourselves under his thumb? Would *you* like to be Agramon's new little Morganite pet?" Her voice dripped with disdain as she sidled up to Ferris. Her eyes flicked briefly to Luc. "You could volunteer to replace the ones he's lost. We can include that in your little . . . negotiation."

Ferris grimaced. "It was just an idea."

Fin straightened, her fists clenched. "Yes, it was just an idea to negotiate peace with the Lyricans by selling Rowyn to Agramon in the first place. If you are really suggesting we take that path again, then perhaps it should be your precious neck on the bargaining table."

Ferris's face reddened, looking properly chagrined.

"Furthermore, you will lose any help from me if you all go behind Rowyn's back to speak with the baron or Agramon. I will leave, and I can't promise I won't take Rowyn with me if she has a mind to go. I won't keep something like that from her."

"I'm with Fin," Luc said, his eyes on Ferris. "I will stand down too. It's not worth it."

"There will be no negotiating with Agramon or the baron, not now, not ever," Destrian cut in. "We'll defeat the Baron of Bruin's forces and show Agramon that Morgania bows to no one."

"It was just a suggestion," Ferris muttered, rubbing his face with his hands.

Fin looked around the room, her eyes resting momentarily on each man before speaking. "Now, what I came to discuss was our defenses. What about the castle? Have the wards been examined? How do we know Elgar the Swift can't leap into the room as we speak?"

"Destrian and I looked into the castle wards and reset them," Lord Alexander said. "There are remnants of fae spells from long ago, though I'm not certain how to manage them."

Fin's eyes glinted with a new kind of interest. "Well, we can ask the king when he arrives for negotiations."

Everyone froze, eyes widening in unison. "The fae king is coming here?" Destrian broke the silence.

Fin nodded confidently. "Yes, I've sent him a letter. He's very interested in speaking to Rowyn."

Lord Alexander immediately began shaking his head. "Inviting the fae into our affairs is a mistake. We have to remember that they operate on a completely different set of morals. They can't be trusted in the way that men can be."

"We need help," Fin insisted. "We need something that gives us an edge, something more powerful than what the capital has. The fae are the answer."

"I still don't think-"

"Rowyn requested it herself," Fin interrupted. "And as we've all sworn fealty to her, I suggest we accept her judgement. Still, that's not the main reason why I've come. I think I've worked out a way to improve messaging across Morgania and with each other." Fin's gaze settled on Ferris. "I propose working with the guards to train a network of messenger birds and animals. They could help us send information quickly throughout the kingdom."

Ferris perked up immediately, a grin spreading across his face. "I'd be more than willing to help with that."

Beside him, Luc's expression tightened ever so slightly. "The army could use the same structure to smooth communication between units."

Fin barely acknowledged him, focusing instead on the two most authoritative figures in the room. "Destrian, Lord Alexander, what I envision is a well-coordinated network where each key person selects a familiar—a creature that can report to me or designated others. I can find willing animals, and individuals can choose from there."

Lord Alexander adjusted his posture slightly, his eyes narrowing. "Is this a reliable method? When I spoke with Master Haris, he mentioned that animal cognition is far simpler compared to humans."

Fin nodded. "That's true, but while I was at the capital, I started experimenting. Feeding small threads of my magic into the same animals repeatedly made them more intelligent, more capable of nuanced communication. I believe I can train them. Slyfoot here is a perfect example." She plucked the mouse from her shoulder and set it on the table where it promptly ran to the dish of fruit and began gorging itself.

Fin rolled her eyes at the mouse, then continued. "The

massacre in the village at the hands of the Butcher of Bruin might have been avoided or at least mitigated if we had such a system in place."

Lord Alexander exchanged a glance with Destrian. "Agramon has Elgar, we have Fin. Honestly, I'm starting to like our odds more and more. Animal informants might be far more helpful and reliable than human ones."

Fin looked pleased with herself. The others pushed in their chairs as the late hour made itself known in the yawn Lord Alexander tried to suppress.

Luc came up behind Fin, taking hold of her arm and leaning in as though to whisper something to her, but before he could, Fin wrenched herself from his grasp.

"Don't!" Fin snapped, her eyes wide, her breath coming in gasps. "Don't grab me like that!"

Everyone froze, their eyes on her. Fin took in their questioning gazes, but instead of explaining, she shrunk back into the form of Arden, the tunic falling to the floor, and disappeared out the window.

Luc looked stunned. "I don't understand. I wasn't trying . . . I didn't grab her hard or anything."

Destrian shrugged, he and Ferris appearing just as perplexed.

It was Lord Alexander who spoke. "She couldn't see you." He ran fingers through his blonde hair. "If women . . . or anybody really . . . have encountered a certain form of . . . violence, they can have aversion to touch. Especially if it's sudden and they can't see you. It takes them back to the moment. Vianne is the same way."

Realization dawned on the others. Luc's shoulders slumped. "She was an animal at the capital. I thought no one knew she was human."

"I didn't say it happened at the capital."

"Not at Solridge, surely?" Destrian asked.

Lord Alexander shook his head. "It came up in Master Haris's debrief of her quest to Horan."

"The fae?" Destrian choked. "The fae that she's been insisting we bring to Morgania?"

"To be clear," Lord Alexander said, opening the door for the others. "You speak as though it doesn't happen here, too. If Vianne were here, she would tell you that this is the world she is trying to unmake with Morgania."

"What happened?" Ferris asked as he and Luc walked to the door.

Lord Alexander scowled as he followed them out. "That's none of your business. Just act accordingly."

Destrian remained, appearing pensive. He glanced at the mouse, still munching on a plum in the dish of fruit and tentatively reached out, allowing the mouse to sniff his finger. When it went right back to eating, Destrian gently stroked down its back. I felt as though I could read the thoughts on his face as clear as if he'd voiced them: Will all these preparations, these innovations, truly be enough?

Chapter 19

THE GREAT HALL of Helena was a buzzing hive of activity in anticipation of my first grand dinner. Nightly festivities had been the thing in Somme, but when I mentioned it to Destrian, he shook his head. "You would hate that, and I am not in the business of making you do things you hate. We can have dinner wherever you want."

We still ended up just eating in the great hall with the rest of the castle, since that was how I ate growing up, but this event was supposed to be my official unveiling as future queen. Destrian had opened the invitation to all the important men and women of Morgania, sparing no expense for my first grand entrance as a royal.

"Quite the sight, isn't it?" Fin asked, rotating slowly underneath evergreen boughs hung through the rafters of the starry ceiling. Her dress was the color of the sea, not quite blue, not quite green, the nearly sheer gauze pale as seafoam. Her hair was curled, hanging loosely over her shoulders.

"It's beautiful," I whispered, almost to myself.

Living ferns and vases of roses decorated the tables. Everywhere I looked, greenery and blooms filled the room, twining around pillars and draped over balconies. Banners of the Morganite flag, black silk with a silver crescent and three silver stars, hung proudly from the walls. The scent of pine and roses mixed with the savory aroma of roasting meats and baking bread from the kitchens.

Simon, the artist behind the vision, was directing the placement of a massive centerpiece at the head of the banquet table. His dark skin suggested ancestors hailing from Ember Innes. The man was a lover of the earth, with a mischievous smile that seemed permanently etched on his face. His spectacles caught the light as he turned and noticed us.

"Your Majesty!" he exclaimed, hurrying over. "I hope you like what you see." He bowed with a flourish.

"It's stunning. I've not seen its equal in Somme." It was true too. Miyu didn't use many plants to decorate the halls of the capital. The drought had made them far too expensive.

Simon chuckled, brushing a stray petal from his tunic. "When you use live plants, nature's spirit lends herself to the design, Your Majesty."

"You were the one who set up Rowyn's balcony?" Fin asked, coming to join us.

Simon beamed as he nodded. "His lordship was very clear about wanting it to be a refuge. So that's what I envisioned, a little mountain oasis."

"I appreciate your use of morwood pine," I said. "It has always reminded me of home."

"And the smell!" Simon laid his hand on his chest. "I can't seem to get enough of the smell of these trees."

"Does that mean you'll stay?" I asked, glancing at Fin. Lately, all I could think about was how to horde my friends in Morgania. The urge to ensure everyone's safety needled at me daily.

"Not likely," Simon admitted. "I'm a man of the wind. I go where it blows me."

"What about you?" I asked Fin, who was dipping to smell a bouquet of flowers.

She looked up in surprise. "I think anyone would count themselves lucky to call Morgania home."

"So . . . you like it here?" I asked when Simon bowed and hurried away to finish preparations. Fin seemed happy, but I still found myself unable to judge her true emotions. She kept so much in. I wanted her to love it. I relished seeing her every day, and she was good at what she did. She was brilliant actually.

Fin snorted. "Like it? Rowyn, Morgania is the most enchanting place I've ever been. I *adore* it. It's close to Horan too." She raised her brows pointedly as she took my arm, and I remembered her mentioning that she was looking forward to seeing Thorn Beyond-the-Border again. She hadn't yet found time for a visit, but she was hoping soon.

Poor Luc . . . it seemed her affections were firmly fixed elsewhere.

"Come, we must get you ready," she murmured, guiding me toward the stairs. I allowed her to lead me away but cast one last glance at the beautiful hall. As Fin chatted excitedly about the evening's events, I let myself get wrapped up in the flutter of excitement.

The passing days had left me with hardly a moment to breathe. Destrian wanted me involved in every aspect of our fledgling kingdom's planning and growth. From council meetings and strategizing about Morgania to dinners with important community members, every waking moment seemed to be filled with responsibilities. One day, we were slogging through mud to watch the new army recruits go through their training regimen, the next we were scouring the library, searching for evidence of old treaties and possible allies we could bring back to our side.

I'd purchased a journal for myself from the market and copied Destrian's endless lists, transferring them to my own pages so I could at least give the appearance of having my thoughts as well planned as he. I now saw the importance of writing down my tasks, because there was absolutely no way I would be able to remember them all if I continued relying on memory alone.

I should've been happy things were going so well, but it was hard to be when Destrian hadn't found any time for us to be *alone*. Apparently, ravaging me senseless was not a high priority on his list of to-do tasks, but our days were so filled that at night I was exhausted anyway. Even Echo let me sleep. If we *did* get a few precious minutes and found ourselves in each other's arms, Destrian insisted on *waiting*.

"I want to take my time, and enjoy it," he'd murmur, his teeth on my throat, teasing me. But he never went further, and it was both exhilarating and maddening at once.

I felt as though I needed to live for the moment, considering the threats that still loomed on the horizon. Lady Vianne found out that, not Agramon, but Elgar the Swift had purchased the loyalty of three servants within the castle and the orders were to try to kill me. Mellan quickly dispatched them, but Lady Maureen was shaken and worried more would find their way inside.

It was also imperative that we got a handle on our situation with Lyrica. Lord Alexander was scheduled to leave for the East before the coronation, acting as our emissary. Both Marc Trinidan and Pedr Tore had sent word that they were on their way to Helena, though Pedr would likely take longer. We already knew the Duke of Ayastaren was against us, but he'd been hesitant to send *another* army of men over the border. It was no wonder, considering the last time he'd done it, he'd lost the army and a son. Still, the peace was temporary, and Destrian was right in urging us to take advantage of the brief pause and move quickly.

Hopefully, formally announcing my intentions to the world with the formal dinner would bolster others to my cause. Despite what I'd said to Destrian, I was glad that Marc was coming. We needed more sorcerers.

Fin guided me to my chambers, her steps light. Once inside, she plucked a peach from the fruit bowl and tossed herself onto my new bed covering—an embroidered weave of blue and purple threads that shimmered under the sunlight streaming through the windows. Taking a bite of her peach, she looked around, studying my new furnishings. Gossamer curtains hung from the windows, the same sheer ones that I'd admired from Ardent, fluttering softly in the breeze. A chair covered in vibrant green silk, another in blue, echoed the precise vein of color running through the stones on my hands. The couch was made with animal leather.

Daisy waited beside a bath of scented water. I'd agreed to have her as my official lady's maid, since I found her to be cheerful and kind. Fin, meanwhile, had hired Rosie, Ena's sister, a choice that sent a twinge of fear through me, but ultimately, it was Rosie's decision, not mine.

Fin took another bite of her peach, licking the juice that had begun to drip down her arm. "Does being here feel like it did in Espiria? Is everyone still afraid of you?"

I shook my head as I stepped into the bath. "In Espiria, I was uncertain of my power. I was afraid of what I could do, of what I might become. But here, I know the extent of my abilities and my control is as good as I can make it. I feel better than I ever did in Espiria."

Even though Agramon and Sam still cast their shadows over me, their tactics and capacities were not entirely unknown. And knowing your enemy is half the battle, they say.

Fin nodded solemnly as Daisy helped me bathe. When I finished, she helped me slip into a black silk dress and cape lined with silver embroidery that draped around my shoulders. Slipping into the dress felt like sinking into a dream; the fabric soft as butter against my skin.

Fin's gaze met mine once again as I took a final turn before the mirror. "Destrian is going to go mad with you in the room."

"Am I doing all right so far?"

"You're doing fine," she answered, but her eyes were unreadable. "But you don't seem to be enjoying it much."

I paused, contemplating her words. "It's not that I don't enjoy it. I'm just . . . worried. If you were in my shoes, would you do things differently?"

Fin shrugged. "Doesn't matter. You're the one destined to be queen. Everyone down there is waiting for you, not me." She rose and extended her hand toward me.

"You and I both know that there are several men down there pining for you." I studied her for a moment. "I worry that Morgania won't hold you."

Fin's eyebrows pulled together beneath her smoky blue gem. "Why would you say that?"

"It feels as though it might be too small a stage for someone like you," I explained, struggling to articulate my worry.

Fin moved toward the door. "I have no intention of going anywhere, Rowyn. This is where I want to be, for now."

"Did you meet your father when we were in Maryse?"

Fin shook her head. "No, I never had the chance." The corners of Fin's mouth twitched into a smirk. "But I would love to see his face now. His little bastard turned spymaster for a kingdom."

Her smirk grew wider, now fully reaching her eyes. "I'd pay good money to see the look on the faces of everyone who ever underestimated me."

"Especially now that you can afford it," I added as she swept open the door.

Mellan, in an official uniform, black with a silver crescent embroidered on his tunic, leaned against the wall, picking his nails with a dagger. His brown curls were longer and he hadn't shaved for over a week. He looked up and slid his dagger in its sheath when he saw Fin watching him.

His eyes danced between the two of us. "Have they left the two most eligible ladies of the kingdom to be escorted by a rogue?" He bit his lip. "My job keeps getting better and better."

"Destrian isn't escorting me?" I tried to hide my disappointment. Mellan was a perfectly acceptable escort. He'd done it many times in Somme, and I'd had fun. Still, Destrian made the night out to be a major thing. It rankled that it wasn't enough for him to come take my arm himself. I hadn't even thought to ask him about it. I'd just assumed. Just like I assumed he would still want to be with me after I accepted his seat for myself. Was he protecting his heart? Was he worried to begin something new just to bring about more disappointment?

Bother holding out for an ally. I would marry him tomorrow.

I let out a sigh of relief when Destrian turned the corner and strode down the hall. He looked me up and down, his eyes darkening. "We'll meet you two there."

Mellan and Fin stared after him as he grabbed my arm and guided me back into my room. I frowned, wondering if there was something wrong. Had Elgar the Swift managed to sneak someone into the banquet? Had Sam attacked?

Destrian slammed the door, then promptly spun me into it, his mouth hot and heavy on mine. "Fuck if I'm going to be able to keep my hands off you," Destrian murmured when he broke away, his fingers threading through my hair.

I peered up at him through my lashes, heat rising to my cheeks. "So . . . I look all right?"

Destrian's nostrils flared. He gripped my hair tight in his hands, leaning his forehead against mine. "You look as though you stepped out of my dreams." His mouth crooked. "Apologies in advance if I act untoward." His fingers were already climbing my thigh, wrapping it around his waist.

I leaned up to his ear. "You're the one who says we should keep our distance."

"Ever the fool am I," Destrian breathed, his lips capturing mine. I moaned, wrapping my arms around his neck, wishing his fingers would go higher. His hips ground into me. Tingles ricocheted over my skin.

Forget the party. Forget the dinner. I just wanted to drag Destrian to my room and get lost in his fire.

"We really shouldn't be late, though," Destrian murmured gruffly, pulling back and lowering my leg.

"I'm sure no one will miss us," I whispered, trying to lure him back.

Destrian shook his head with a laugh and opened the door. His hand on my lower back, he leaned in and whispered, "They await your grand entrance, my love."

It wasn't easy to stem the tide of lust. I wondered if Destrian knew what he was doing to me. Did he realize how much I craved him?

"So what is it tonight?" I asked, letting him guide me down the hall. "Do we divide and conquer?"

Destrian pulled me closer. "Tonight, I will stay by your side. I don't trust the Lyricans not to sneak in and snatch you from the crowd."

I couldn't help but feel relieved. It was much easier meeting new people with Destrian at my side. He knew them, after all, and spoke so easily that I learned far more about them with him around than if I were just awkwardly on my own. I never knew what to say.

When we got to the entrance of the hall, Destrian broke away to speak to the herald. I shifted from one foot to the other, trying to calm my racing heart. It wasn't like being in Somme with Agramon. Those people didn't want that much from me. In Helena, everyone was either looking at me with hope or hoping I'd fail.

I set my teeth when Destrian returned to me with a smile. "Are you ready?"

I nodded and let out a slow breath.

The doors opened.

The crowd within craned their heads, trying to glimpse the new entrants. Destrian strode forward first, announced as lord of Helena. Then, it was my turn.

I found Fin in the crowd. She was smiling at me from next to Lady Maureen. I smiled back and strode forward, stopping just within the doorway to hear my name called.

"The lord of Helena is proud to present Princess Rowyn, heir to the Morganite throne."

Destrian bowed as he offered my hand, which I took, squeezing my fingers in thanks. The entire mass followed his movements.

Chills danced up my spine as I surveyed the room. My breath caught in my throat. My family's dream of an independent Morgania was finally being realized.

Everyone rose and the hall filled with noise. Talking. Laughter. The clinking of cutlery and glass. It was a whirlwind of faces and emotions as Destrian led me around the room and helped introduce me to others. Most were gracious and offered a kind word or blessing to my reign.

As the hall began to fill, the party grew more raucous, a buzz of excitement that thrummed in time with the music.

Urdua approached me while Destrian stood nearby, whispering to Mellan under his breath as they eyed the guests. "Magnificent, isn't it?" she breathed, coming to stand by my side.

"It truly is," I agreed, smiling at her. "And you, Master of Law, how are you finding your new role?"

She chuckled. "Difficult at times, but Anya, Sir Bernard's granddaughter, has been helping me."

"Destrian made a wise choice in you."

Her cheeks flushed, but she waved it off. "I'm doing

what I can."

Lady Maureen joined us and we began discussing the necessary reforms to the list of punishments for crimes. My suggestion to include language that would apply the new laws not only to Lyricans and Morganites but also to the fae seemed to be well-received. It was a preventive measure, just in case the King of the Fae managed to convince me to open the border between our worlds.

Lady Vianne approached soon after. Lady Maureen and Urdua turned abruptly and walked away while continuing their conversation.

I shot Lady Vianne a questioning look. "Did you just use your powers to send them away?"

She shrugged, unremorseful. "You looked like you could use a minute to yourself."

I glanced around, marking Destrian nearby, but out of earshot. Taking a deep breath, I asked the question that had been gnawing at me since I'd gotten my gem. "Why did you really erase my memory at Solridge? Everything I know of you suggests you wouldn't perform such a thing if it went against your conscience."

Lady Vianne's expression turned somber, almost wistful. "I knew what you would be to Agramon, Rowyn. If you'd run then, you would have lost the potential allies you'd made in Solridge. Agramon would have found you, no matter where you went, and you would've gone friendless and without any means of escape. The only reason I got away from him was because I had friends, people who loved me, to help me."

"I know Empress Lesedi aided you," I said. "She made much of your friendship in Somme. She really admires you."

Lady Vianne nodded, smoothing the purple and gold fabric that was wrapped around her body in the style she preferred. "And I admire her. It takes a lot of courage to do what she does every day. But Alexander was also crucial to my flight." She glanced at Destrian, who was still engrossed in conversation.

Wait a minute . . .

"You wanted me to stay for Destrian?" I asked, dumbfounded.

"I knew he loved you, and Destrian is powerful in his own right. A powerful ally, a powerful love. Sometimes those two things align. The strongest magic happens when it does."

"It was all to play matchmaker?" I hissed, trying to calm my shaking hands.

"Do you question the veracity of his love?" Vianne asked pointedly. "Or is it, I wonder, whether or not you question your own feelings. I promise that I made no attempt at swaying your heart. All thoughts you've had of Destrian have been your own."

"Still," I grumbled, shaking my head. "You could've just tried to convince me to stay."

Vianne's gaze swept the grand room. "I know you're waiting for me to say I'm sorry for what I did," she said softly. "But I can't be sorry when this is the result."

Just as Lady Vianne was about to continue, I felt someone step beside me.

"May I?" Destrian asked, extending his hand toward me.

I glared at Vianne who was beaming at me, then took Destrian's hand and allowed him to lead me away.

"Are you all right, my love?"

"I'm fine," I said, taking a deep breath. I couldn't let Vianne rile me. As much as I despised her methods, it wasn't like she was being dishonest now. She had everything to lose, and we both knew it. That was simply how she was, and I either accepted that or banished her. I bet she would get along in the court of the fae quite well.

No, I couldn't banish her. She'd been far too useful already, rooting out spies and assisting Urdua when needed. Lord Alexander was also more helpful than I'd initially predicted, and if I banished Vianne than he would surely go to.

It was a silly thought anyway.

Destrian's lips brushed my ear as he whispered, "Now that the work is over, we can finally enjoy ourselves."

Mellan fell into step beside us as we approached the small gathering of our friends. Luc and Ferris were joking with Pria and Fin. I'd wondered at Pria staying at the castle. We'd given each other space, and she was given a room near Fin's in the guest quarters. It turned out that Fin, though not forgiving of Pria's treatment toward me, did manage to always be kind to her. Ferris and Luc being there also helped.

We joined the circle, the conversation shifting to the messenger animals.

"Inkwing and I are beginning to understand one another," Ferris was saying, his arm on the wall as he leaned over Fin.

She grinned. "Ravens are incredibly smart, so he will learn fast." Fin ducked out from under Ferris's arm and grabbed a goblet of wine from the table. "How's the wolf?" she asked, turning to Luc who was openly glaring at Ferris, clutching the sword at his side.

Luc's eyes softened as they met Fin's. "It's taken time for him to adjust. He misses his pack."

Fin reached out and patted Luc's arm. "He was cast out, so he will still have feelings about that. He never desired to be a lone wolf."

Luc nodded, but his attention was on her hand, still resting on his sleeve.

"So you grew up with Rowyn?" Mellan asked Pria who

leaned on her cane beside Ferris.

She nodded warily, glancing at me.

"I want to hear every embarrassing story you have of that girl," Mellan demanded with a smirk. Apparently he'd completely forgotten his duties to guard me and was now openly drinking. "Tell me all the worst parts. The more details the better."

"Don't," I snapped with a glare as Destrian shifted to hear better. "I mean it, Pria."

She snorted into her wine, but Mellan bowed to Pria. "I can ply you for information on the dance floor, if such a lovely lady would deign to accept the hand of a lowly soldier."

Her smile faltered. "I can't dance," she said, lifting the cane.

"Nonsense!" Mellan announced. He scooped Pria up by the waist. "Rowyn and I used to dance like this all the time in Somme."

Pria let out a delighted squeal as Mellan spun her into the crowd of dancing couples. Her feet dangled behind her, her black curls tumbling over her shoulders.

"You should join us," Luc was saying to Fin as she swayed in time to the music. "There are other girls who train with the soldiers."

Fin looked annoyed. "Other girls? Let me know when you're ready to handle a woman."

I think I was the only one who saw the smirk as she turned to Ferris who had held out his hand in front of her. "Would you care to dance?"

"I would be delighted," Fin said with a genuine smile, taking Ferris's hand. I caught Fin glancing over her shoulder at Luc. There was a question in her gaze, almost as if she was daring him to come forward, but Luc only watched them, looking defeated.

He turned to me, his eyes desperate. "Rowyn, you have to help me out here. I just can't seem to win with that woman."

I shrugged, offering a half-smile. "I wish I could help, Luc, but Fin is . . . complicated."

Destrian shook his head. "Complicated? She clearly wanted to dance, and Ferris simply had the courage to ask her first."

Luc straightened. "I'm not exactly lacking in courage," he retorted.

Destrian looked him over. "You're used to women falling at your feet. You have no idea how to actually woo one who challenges you."

"Well *that* is simply the pot calling the kettle black," I muttered, craning to try to see Fin and Ferris dancing. They were both so handsome. They would actually make a pretty good couple.

Destrian turned to me, his lips pursed. "Are you

insinuating that I've done nothing to woo you?"

I belatedly realized my mistake. "Absolutely not," I assured him. "Luc, you need to take a leaf from Destrian's tree of knowledge. He's very good at the woo part. Too good, in fact." I squeezed Destrian's hand and he relaxed slightly.

Destrian turned back to Luc. "Anyway, maybe it's time you learn how to chase instead of being chased."

Luc glanced over the crowd, probably seeing far more than I could since he was a head and a half taller than I was. He seemed to calculate his chances, his eyes narrowing. Then, as if making up his mind, he stalked forward to the edge of the dance floor, lingering like a wolf on the edge of a clearing, ready to pounce the moment Fin and Ferris glided within his reach.

Destrian turned to me. "Would *you* care to dance, my love?"

"Of course," I murmured, wrapping my arm around his. I'd gotten marginally better at dancing since being at the capital. Only marginally because I tried to get out of dancing at parties unless it was the crazed ridiculous fancies Mellan and I found ourselves in from time to time, much to Agramon's displeasure.

"Are you pleased with how tonight turned out?" Destrian asked, his eyes searching mine as we turned and swayed in time to the music. This time, I relaxed in his arms, letting myself just enjoy the moment.

I recalled what it felt like when I'd returned from the Nightlands. How everyone stared. How I couldn't seem to find any confidence or enjoyment in being a spectacle. But now I felt like I belonged. I was surrounded by those who wanted me to succeed, and it made a world of difference.

"It feels like a dream," I whispered, "a dream I haven't woken up from yet."

His arms tightened around me. "I feel blessed to finally enjoy dancing with you without someone on the sidelines, waiting to rip you away from me."

My heart fluttered, but another, more primal desire clawed its way up from the depths of my stomach.

"You should come to my room tonight," I whispered, half emboldened by the wine, half desperate for something more between us.

Destrian smirked. "Whatever will we do, so late at night?"

"I figured you had some ideas," I said, trying to be flirty but worried that my desperation for his touch was evident in the heat of my cheeks.

Destrian's lips grazed my ear. "We shouldn't leave together. I will meet you there in a few minutes." Warmth spread through me like wildfire, my skin tingling, every nerve alive and alert.

"No," I pouted. "You leave first. If you stay, you're

bound to let something distract you."

"You think I would let anyone tear me away from this?" Destrian asked, his fingers walking down my back before he jerked me closer.

I gasped just as a trumpet sounded at the door, startling the entire hall. The music faltered, conversations halted, and all eyes turned to the door.

Destrian's grip tightened reflexively around me as the room froze. Fin stepped forward, flanking my other side.

"My lords and ladies," the herald shouted. "May I present, King Valon Of-the-Castle, High Lord of Horan and the court of the Fae."

Chapter 20

THE ARRIVAL OF King Valon was a spectacle that none in Helena's court would forget. In stepped a Woltari, his silver-white hair hanging in braids between massive ram's horns that grew from the top of his brow. A gilded vest was buttoned across his waist, while his shoulders were cloaked in a coat made of peacock feathers. His golden eyes surveyed the room, leading a line of fae, some with wings, others with hulking arms and large heads, and some whose height reached only to our knees.

"Princess Rowyn Of-the-Shroud," he said as the crowd parted before him. He stopped in front of me, his hand at his chest, and bowed. "I have long awaited this meeting." He looked up, his golden eyes flicking to where Destrian's hand was clasped in my own.

I sucked in a breath and let go.

"Why is he here?" someone whispered behind me.

A chill crawled down my spine as the silence in the hall seemed to grow stifling.

Right. People were waiting for *me* to do something. I inclined my head, attempting to collect my thoughts. "Your Majesty, welcome to the Court of Helena. We are honored by your presence."

"I come in good faith, bearing the wealth of Horan." King Valon straightened and waved. Two of the larger, hulkier fae stepped forward heaving a massive trunk between them. "We wish to bring tidings and welcome to our sister kingdom."

The trunk landed on the floor with a heavy clunk before the fae with tusks grabbed the lock and ripped it straight off the lid with a splintering crack. He looked at the piece of twisted metal in his hand for a moment, as though his own strength surprised him. The other fae grunted and smacked his partner upside the head before dragging his comrade back to the line.

King Valon sighed, watching the two fae retreat out of the corner of his eye before kicking the chest open.

Unsurprisingly, it was filled with treasure. Ridiculously excessive, though pleasing nonetheless. Gold coins spilled over the edge, a glittering stream dotted with various gems that bounced onto the marble floor. Many looked similar to Fin's jewel. She peered over and gasped, her eyes shooting back up to the king who regarded her beside me with interest.

Why was the king seeking to butter my friend up? Of course, he would know that a sorcerer could wield greater magic if they had jewelry containing stones that matched their gem of power. Agramon had a staff containing one such jewel. Was the king simply performing a kindness? Or was there something more to his schemes?

For half a moment, I was ashamed to say that I doubted Fin.

While everyone else admired the hoard of coins, I found myself studying the king. He didn't seem that old. In human ages, he would've appeared to be in his mid-thirties. Near Sam's age. Yet he was several centuries my senior.

I didn't like the way King Valon kept glancing at Destrian, though; it was the same look I'd seen in Sam's eyes, and it set my nerves on edge.

"If I may," I said, "allow me to introduce Lord Destrian of Helena."

King Valon's mouth quirked into a half smile. "I've heard stories of the Dragon of Helena. Tell me, Your Majesty, will he keep his title once a crown is set upon your head?"

Destrian bristled beside me as a murmur rippled through the hall.

Stepping forward, I offered King Valon my arm. "You have traveled far, Your Majesty, and clearly it seems we have much to discuss. Might we continue your greeting in private?"

King Valon's brows shot up, his nostrils flaring as he gently took my fingers in his and rested my arm on his own. I sucked in a breath, realizing his muscles were like stone, and met the fae king's eyes as he grinned wickedly.

"I would be delighted as long as my voice can accompany us." King Valon nodded at Fin.

"Of course." Fin grabbed a goblet of wine from a server and held it up, showcasing she was ready.

"Prepare the formal receiving room," Destrian ordered, sending servants scurrying about the hall. Lady Maureen slipped out the door ahead of us, her steps quickening as soon as she entered the corridor.

King Valon watched me curiously as I stalled, smoothing my skirt and nodding to others. He was handsome, of course. Most high fae were beautiful in some way. I wondered at Fin not mentioning how handsome he was, though. Quite breath-taking really. His amber eyes were striking, given the paleness of his skin. A white sheaf of hair hung down his back, with braids woven down the front and hanging over his shoulders. I could feel the formidable muscles under his coat, and it occurred to me that Thorn Beyond-the-Border might not be the only fae to catch Fin's eye in Horan.

Finally, we began to move, me smiling and trying to look comfortable as the entire host of Helena watched me leave with the King of the Fae on my arm.

"Do not forget the rules," King Valon reminded his party as he passed. Many grumbled audibly. He shot them a stern glare. "They will be good," he assured, patting my arm with his massive hand.

"Do they always follow your orders?" I asked.

"Naturally," the king replied. "They cannot disobey orders if they are dead."

My eyes widened. What were we getting ourselves into? I looked over my shoulder, glad that Fin was still behind me . . . drinking heavily. She must be nervous. I tried to calm my breathing as we walked through the palace halls. Mellan was nowhere to be seen. Destrian was going to be furious when he tracked him down.

I tried to rally my thoughts. Though I'd intended to end the evening quite differently, I supposed it was important to find out what the King of the Fae wanted. It was also important that I help Fin fulfill her end of the deal she'd made with the king in exchange for his assistance on her quest. She'd already helped me in so many ways. It was the least I could do to pay her back.

Destrian led us into a room that I'd never seen before. I supposed it was nice, something Destrian's family would trot important guests into to show that they were powerful. I took a seat on the silk couch and immediately wished that someone would sit beside me so I wouldn't have to be alone.

Flames erupted in the fireplace as Destrian loomed behind me, probably glaring at the fae king over my shoulder. Fin took a seat near the wall, her eyes also glued to the king.

"Rowyn Of-the-Shroud," King Valon began, sweeping his coat beneath him with a flourish before sitting in the chair across from me. "I would bridge an alliance between our lands. We fae and Morganites have always been brothers and sisters under Imor's gaze."

I glanced at Fin before nodding. "I welcome the benefactor of my greatest friend. We were allied in the past, so it only makes sense for us to ally again, now that Morgania seeks to become sovereign once more."

King Valon bowed his head in response. "And we, fae, are ready to share the burdens of a shared world." I tried not to frown. It sounded like he used a lot of words to say absolutely nothing.

"Lyrica will come soon for me." Even though I figured what his answer would be, I still needed to say it. "We need an army. Any help you can offer our fledgling military would be welcome."

"War with formal armies and battles is not the fae way." King Valon leaned back in his chair, seemingly completely at ease, his hands folded in his lap.

"Are you not king?" I asked, curious. "You cannot command them?"

King Valon raised his brows. "The magic in our kind makes it so that we lead lives far longer than your own mortal ones. I knew your great-grandfather—and his father before him. I remember well the paths and roads over your land. But we tend to guard our lives as the precious things they are. I am sorry, but as king, I do not have the authority to command another fae to give up their life for mortals. The title, king, is one that you all have pinned upon me. To my people, I'm merely the shepherd and final judge."

"If you cannot aid us with war, why come to speak of an alliance at all?" Destrian growled.

King Valon's golden eyes turned molten. "We fae have grown restless behind our borders. Too much time has passed where nothing has changed, and life has become boring. There are far too many of us living too close. Imor willed that if we congregate too closely together, our births drop considerably. There is infighting, rebellion. We wish to travel once more, to mingle beyond our borders. One thing fae miss most is the excitement the short lives of mortals bring. Many are eager to rejoin the world."

"You're offering something else, aren't you," I said.

King Valon's mouth crooked. "Though we cannot aid you as cannon fodder, we are well-versed in magic, and we've heard that since Morgania's demise, you've lost your sorcerers. What I propose is this: you open your borders to the fae of Horan, and any of us who crosses must owe you a favor. The people's abilities are versatile and could help you in any number of ways. I feel you will find our favors far more useful than dead bodies. We have many who can travel quickly, brew potions, cast protections . . ."

Destrian leaned forward. "We will want assurances that any who cross aren't doing so to hunt."

King Valon shrugged. "There are those who are pining for their trophies. I will leave my ambassador here with you. He worked in Morgania during the time of kings and has already asked for his old position back."

"So free rein for a fae who gifts us a favor," I said, folding my hands over my knees. "What is it you request of us in return? How do we seal this alliance?" My posture stiffened. "How are we to know you'll not turn around and offer the Duke of Ayastaren or Agramon the Divine the same thing, offering a back way into Morgania?"

"There is only one way to seal this alliance," King Valon said, his eyes narrowed. He looked from Destrian to me. "I require a bride."

I took a calming breath and smiled. "Well, you are free to choose someone within our borders, as long as she is willing."

"If only it were that easy. You see, I require a royal bride." King Valon looked to the fire, studying the flames as they licked the air. "Theramon's oldest was a daughter, lovely as a rose. That first night I saw her, watched her dance in the moonlight on the Winter Solstice, it was her spirit that called to me." He turned back to me and smiled.

I admired how perfectly shaped his lips were, then immediately chastised myself. Destrian's lips were perfect too. Did King Valon affect all women this way? Did he have a potion or something to make himself more seductive? I wouldn't doubt it. It was hard not to . . . gawk. "Princess Gwyneph would've done well in Horan. She was playful. My court was ready to love her, as I did."

The king paused. I wondered if he was waiting for a question or just got caught up in a memory. After a moment, he continued, his eyes seeing me once more. "We were to be wed the next year, after proper ceremonies and treaties and all the other details required for a royal wedding were ironed out."

"You did not marry," I said, my voice barely above a whisper. "Fin said you had no wife."

Fin nodded. King Valon's eyes met mine, a flicker of something unreadable in their depths. "A lot of life can happen in a year," he said softly.

His eyes raised. "But the blood pact must be fulfilled, Rowyn Of-the-Shroud. I have waited a long time for my bride."

"Don't listen to him, Rowyn," Destrian snapped from behind me.

Despite the sadness I might've felt at his story, anger rose, strong and sudden. "Are you saying I was sold to you? A century ago?"

King Valon tented his fingers in front of him. "You're coming onto a throne. One would expect you to be available for an allied match. That is one of the burdens that comes with a throne."

"We will require more than a few favors if you wish to entice Her Majesty into forming a marriage alliance," Destrian said stiffly.

"Oh?" King Valon remarked. "We have fae who can sing wood back into its former tree, who can will the seas to toss ships over. The future queen knows how powerful we can be. All the Morganites do."

I gritted my teeth. King Valon was right. If we received a favor from every fae wishing to settle in Morgania, it could turn the tide of the upcoming war. What if we didn't even need to fight it? We *needed* that kind of magic.

But marriage? I'd just escaped a marriage that I'd felt necessary. I wasn't ready to commit again. Not yet, anyway. Even with Destrian thinking that an alliance may be the only way to legitimize my throne, the only person I could bring myself to face marriage with was Destrian, and even then I might not have the courage to do it.

"Would the pact still bind me if I hadn't sought the throne?"

"It was made between the Morganite royals," King Valon replied. "Claiming yourself heir is the condition for its fulfillment."

"Is it not too late to walk it back?" Destrian asked, somewhat desperately.

I betrayed myself and glanced up. The look I gave Destrian was shattered, heartbroken. The idea of relinquishing the throne to escape a fate I had no hand in choosing? My entire world felt as if it were crumbling around me.

"The moment you stepped forward to claim your birthright, the gods themselves decreed your fate. You cannot ignore it."

Fin, who had been silent until now, burst out angrily, "So that's why you were so focused on me encouraging Rowyn to claim her seat. This was your game all along!"

"And what if I decline this deal?" I cut in, dread curling its fingers around my heart.

"Then everything will go wrong for you, Your Majesty. It will be as if the entire world were launching an attack. Sickness will ravage the land. War will be lost. Death would come swift."

"He does not get to decide for you, my love!" Destrian snarled.

King Valon's eyes shifted from me back to Destrian, and for the first time, his impeccable composure seemed to crack. His golden eyes flickered, disappointment clouding his features. It was as if he'd tasted something bitter, something unpalatable.

And it wasn't hard to guess why. King Valon was

starting to understand that fate had ensured I would never love him, for my heart was already in the hands of another, and perhaps for a being as old as he, that was a disappointment more poignant than any other.

"I see now, how the gods continue to make a fool of me." He sighed. "You're thinking that you hold the love of a good man. It will spoil you for me, I think, as I am not good. I am fae, and 'good' is not our way."

King Valon tilted his head. "I have no wish to compete with love magic. Since you are insistent, our way allows for another choice, even in the direst circumstances. You must honor the blood pact and marry me, or you must promise me your daughter in your stead."

He smiled at Destrian. "I've waited a hundred years already. What's twenty more?"

"How dare you," Destrian said, starting forward.

"I'm just giving you options." King Valon shrugged. "But this is not about the alliance to open the border—this promise was made centuries ago by your grandsires. I'm sorry it falls to your shoulders, but that is the way of magic. It likes to play. Either you or your daughter must join me on my throne." He rose, straightening his feathered coat and folding his hands in front of him.

"I have no children," I said, following him up. This was what I'd always hated about being a woman in the empire. Was I going to do what I always feared? "How can I make a promise on a child whom I don't even know will come to be?"

"You forget your tales," King Valon said. "We have our seer, Moria the Maiden. She has said that your firstborn will a daughter. That is all the assurance I need to trust the blood pact will be fulfilled."

A parchment appeared in the king's hands, and he offered it to me. I unrolled it and glanced over the treaty before handing it to Destrian.

"You know," King Valon began, lowering his voice. "Had you come to us sooner, you would've already been safe on your throne." He glanced at Fin. "Your friend said that you always talked about running to us, and I always wondered why you didn't seek our help. I suppose now I know why."

"You could've helped me control my magic?" I asked.

The king nodded. "We are very familiar with sorcery, though our magic works a bit differently."

I glanced at Destrian, the treaty clenched in his fist. But King Valon was focused on me, waiting.

"Do you agree, Princess Rowyn Of-the-Shroud, for the wheel of fate is turning, and the choices we make today will echo through the ages."

I held out my hand to his raised one. "I feel as though I do not have a choice," I admitted as he kissed my fingers.

King Valon glanced up. "If you want to live the rest of

your life in relative peace, then you don't."

Shit. No matter what I did, no matter what choice I made, I knew fate would always ensure that I would regret the decision. There was nothing to do but go with my gut.

"The daughter then," I said, refusing to look at Destrian.

Chapter 21

MARC TRINIDAN ARRIVED two days later. Our meeting was in the morning room. The smell of parchment and burning wood drifted in the morning breeze while I shuffled through a pile of letters sitting behind the old oak desk.

"Lord Marc," I began, looking up from my papers when he walked in. "Thank you for coming on such short notice."

I glanced at Destrian beside him, then looked away, waving them into the seats in front of me. He was still extremely upset about the visit from the fae king.

That was an understatement.

He was furious I made a deal with Valon promising my daughter to him when she came of age. I didn't really see that I had any choice, considering marrying the King of the Fae would definitely remove me from Destrian's arms once and for all.

I wouldn't leave him again.

I couldn't.

Though I didn't like promising my daughter, I figured if she was raised to know her future, that would be infinitely better than having it thrust upon her suddenly like what was being done to me. Furthermore, King Valon had made clear that whoever married him would need to join him on his throne. I didn't miss his little word play. I wouldn't leave Morgania. I couldn't. There was still far too much to do.

Destrian didn't speak to me at all after our meeting with the king. We returned to the great hall only to find pandemonium. Everyone was drunk and frolicking and having a grand time with the fae visitors who were drinking in the debauchery like creatures parched. By the time King Valon rounded up his entourage and swept them away, the hall was in absolute tatters. Greenery and roses were strewn over the floors and onto tables, next to couples who'd completely lost all sense of decency and were romping in full view of everyone. It was disgusting.

Having to see it wasn't even the worst part about it.

No, the worst part was that everyone *else* was getting their fill of love and touch and fun. Meanwhile I had to sit there and watch Destrian spark at the fingertips while he snarled at everyone around us to get it together and begin cleaning up.

The fae king had effectively ruined any chance I had of getting close to Destrian that night.

And the night after that.

And the night after that.

Stupid fae. He just had to come in and ruin everything.

It took an entire day and a half to bring the hall back to sorts, a day and a half that Destrian avoided me. If we did happen to run into each other, the torches or candles nearby would burst into angry flames.

I hoped he would forgive me.

But King Valon was right. The gods didn't really leave me a choice.

I knew that Destrian was worried about the daughter, but fate was forcing me to be pragmatic. Tales told of people being forced to give up their child to the fae, and most ended happily enough. The problem that King Valon and I understood, and that apparently Destrian did not, was that it was unwise to try to work against fate.

Disastrous even.

Clearly a Morganite princess was fated to marry the fae king. There was a hundred-year-old blood pact that the king handed over in pristine condition, so clearly the gods had made up their minds about the whole marriage business. Who was I to question it?

I'd already learned the hard way not to try to work against fate. It didn't bring anything good.

It brought Agramon.

It brought Sam.

It brought the loss of Ena.

It brought the wasted years spent in the East.

I'd been forced, in a moment, to take a good hard look

at my choices in life. The times I'd followed fate's guidance, things turned out well. Wonderful even.

I'd been fated to go to the Nightlands with Destrian and I came back in love. I'd been fated for three stones and now had more power than I could've dreamed of. I'd been fated to love Destrian and now Morgania was unified under one cause.

But I was not fated to be with the King of the Fae.

And if I was not, then that meant that my daughter was.

I had to begin trusting my gut. The king was right. The Morganites needed the help of Horan if we were to break away and stay protected from Agramon and Lyrica.

I glanced up and watched Marc, another person whose help I apparently needed, take the opposite seat with an easy grace. Marc seemed to be studying me, his brow slightly furrowed. I wondered if I looked much changed since he last saw me. He looked the same. Same wavy, chestnut hair and green eyes. His coat was richly embroidered with golden branches, a nod to the tree of Korballis on the Trinidan's sigil.

"When Destrian sends a letter asking me to travel to Helena, I presume it's important."

Heat rose to my cheeks as I tried to smile. "Indeed, it is. We have a proposition for you."

Marc raised an eyebrow.

"As you've probably heard, I'm claiming my crown.

We're breaking away from Lyrica."

Marc pursed his lips. "Everyone's heard the great sorceress committed treason and dragged a perfectly respectable family down with her." He seemed to be glaring at Destrian out of the corner of his eye.

Destrian didn't seem to notice. He was too busy staring at me.

I took a deep, calming breath, and went on. "We need an ambassador to the West, to Adair and The Fens. Someone who is familiar . . . friendly even . . . with the families who rule there."

"I suppose I fit that description," he admitted with a hint of wariness.

"Yes, you do. And, more importantly, you are respected among them," Destrian added.

Marc shook his head, staring at his boots. "I knew you would drag me into this."

He clearly wasn't speaking to me.

Destrian didn't respond for a moment. Finally, he shrugged. "We aren't offering you scraps, Marc. This isn't a friend's favor. It's an opportunity that we are presenting to you first."

Marc was silent for a while, looking thoughtful. Then, he asked, "So you just want me to what? Travel and talk?"

"Isn't that what you do best?" Destrian asked, his hand out. "You told me yourself that you weren't looking forward to the duties your father had mapped out for you. You said that all you wanted was to stay in a new hall every night and soak in all the world has to offer. You said those words to me. Do you remember?"

Marc let out a slow breath. He nodded.

Destrian glanced at me, as though asking permission to go on. Touched, I offered a timid smile. Even angry, he still thought to take my feelings into account.

"That's all we're asking you to do. We're working to draft possible treaties now. In time, we ask that you take those, and the discussion topics, to the families of the South. Get them to come to the table. Convince them to sign. Just because we're breaking away from Lyrica doesn't mean we want to give up on trade. Only this time, the terms will be more in our favor."

Marc shifted. It was impossible for me to tell whether he was pleased or angry. "And what do I get out of this?"

"In addition to serving your people," Destrian replied, "you will be granted a title: lord ambassador. And, when the time is right, you'll have the promise of land within Morgania. A duchy."

Marc's expression turned contemplative. "And how do you intend to get messages safely to Morgania?"

The door opened and Fin strode in. Marc glanced at her, then looked again as she took a seat on a couch and smiled at him. "How are you?" She sounded relatively pleasant.

"Well," Marc replied, his tone guarded as he took in, what I assumed, the confidence Fin exuded—the Fin she'd become now that she was given freedom to be herself. He, like everyone, apparently, liked what he saw.

"Fin is our spymaster and also in charge of messages," I said, motioning to her. "She will ensure you are able to communicate with us."

Marc raised his brows as he glanced at Fin. His mouth quirked. "I want Ayastaren."

My eyes widened. He couldn't be serious.

"I'm risking my family's censure, my reputation, and even my life." Marc folded his hands over his knee. "I believe the reward should commensurate with the risk."

Hmph. Since when did people think I had the power to hand over a duchy that I didn't currently control, nor did it ever exist within the kingdom of Morgania? I hadn't considered the possibility of gaining Ayastaren in the war to come, but Marc apparently had.

He continued, and this time I caught his ambition. "You will need to address Ayastaren soon. With the upset at the capital, there is opportunity there. If you ever acquire the city, I want that duchy."

Destrian was nodding to me. I met Marc's gaze. "Very well, we can promise you Ayastaren as long as it falls under Morganian control. You will not make your own kingdom,

Lord Marc."

Marc shrugged. "I've never had a wish to be king. Being wealthy without looming responsibility is more my league. Des is the one who enjoys work."

"What would stop you from just selling us out to Agramon?" I had my own reservations to address.

"That would require me to put my trust in a mind reader." Marc crossed his arms. "Many have made that mistake, including our late emperor. I will not be one of them. We would like to see the empress win this war, but even so, I'm not the oldest. My brother, Ajax, will inherit Korballis. I would like some land of my own, a title to pass down to my children. Morgania isn't so far from Korballis that I couldn't visit, and it would make sense for us to ally with you if you are also building an alliance with Horan. We would like to be included in the safeguards if the Others are going to be allowed past the borders again."

"Your father is extremely unhappy about the border being open to the fae," I said, watching him closely.

"I know there are bad fae, but King Valon has kept them behind the border. I don't see why the king would go back on his word."

"What do you say then?" Destrian asked. "Do you accept?"

"Very well." Marc nodded. "We have a deal."

After hammering out a few more details, like how long

Marc would be staying—he promised to witness the coronation—and which rooms he could choose from at the castle, Marc left through the door, and Fin through the window, her robe fluttering to the ground in a cloud of silk.

"I still don't think we need Marc," I complained, frustration threading my voice. "I believe it's more important to ally with empires rather than consulships. The West . . . it's just a patchwork of territories. Have we even reached out to Yliria yet?"

"No, we need him," Destrian said gruffly. "I need him. Nobody knows which way the empire will go. With the coming war, Lyrica could lose all of the West, and it might revert to separate kingdoms again. The empire's hold on those lands is tenuous at best."

He paused to let his words sink in, and I felt a knot of anxiety in my stomach. "It's best to make *allies* with our neighbors rather than enemies. You know that. If Pedr were here, he would tell you the same thing."

As much as I wanted to disagree, I knew he was right.

"What's next?" I asked, hoping the change of subject would keep Destrian talking to me again. It felt like we were almost back to normal. I wanted to move forward, to focus on the next challenge.

Destrian consulted his journal, flipping through the pages filled with neat, precise handwriting. He met my eyes. "We should probably go over the terms of the fae treaty."

I glared at him. So much for moving forward.

"I know you do not agree with what I did, but I stand by it," I murmured, reaching out to take his hand. "I don't even regret it. I know that's horrible of me, and I've honestly been waiting for that feeling for the past several days, but it hasn't come. I can only assume it's because I made the right choice."

Destrian's lips thinned. "I hope you can appreciate how hard it is to see it from your perspective."

I rose, walking to the window. "You're the one who is putting me on the throne. I'd hope that you would trust my judgment on the more serious matters. I'd hope that you had more faith."

"I have faith in you." Destrian snapped his journal shut, setting it on his desk. "You know I have faith in you. But let's not dance around the real issue here." He ran his fingers through his auburn hair glowing bright in the late-morning sun. "Is it our daughter that he's talking about?"

"You know I don't have an answer for you," I replied. "I am not with child now, if that's what you're wondering."

Destrian frowned. "I wasn't wondering that." He rose and joined me at the window. "In the end I know it's your decision. It's just . . . it's not how I would've preferred it to be." He cupped my cheek in his hand. I looked up, admiring the warmth of his eyes. The red bristles of his beard framing his perfect mouth. "But you can't think I don't have faith in you. Quite the opposite. Running a kingdom suits you."

I chuckled mirthlessly. Yes, I learned how to rule. At the cost of my freedom and innocence, I learned how to take on the world. "I can't take all the credit. I've learned from many."

"Oh? And who might these teachers be?"

"Agramon, Sam, my father," I admitted. Now that I thought about it, their influence on my life was great, and perhaps they were why I could feel some semblance of confidence in myself now. I learned what worked, and what didn't. I learned where I wanted to draw the line, and what I would give up if I crossed it.

"Agramon," Destrian echoed, an edge to his voice. "That's a surprising choice."

"I'm not saying I admire him," I clarified, "but he taught me a lot about how to work with people." I looked down, unable to believe what I was about to say. "In many ways he was misunderstood. He was fighting for a world that suited him, the same as us. But his tyranny, his disregard for the people . . . I don't want to be that kind of ruler."

"And the Butcher?" Destrian prompted.

"Sam had a knack for winning people over. He knew

how to unite people—he inspired loyalty by working alongside his soldiers. Much like Father." I smiled as I looked out over the city. "When I was growing up, Father would walk me through the tunnels, meeting each family, talking about what they needed and how they were doing. He loved his people. He would have given anything for them. He taught me sacrifice and duty."

Destrian stayed silent for a moment, his gaze fixed on the horizon. "And you're the best of them all."

Chapter 22

THE DAY BEFORE my coronation, all I could think about was my past. I walked through the now-familiar halls of Helena, running my hands along the wall as I considered everything that my parents had ever hoped for me. In the end, I'd shattered them all. I would be crowned Queen of Morgania on the morrow.

The rise of the Morganites was at hand.

I saw Luc and fell in step beside him as he strode down the hall. "Have you seen your father lately?"

Conal, the imorati who had foreseen me on the throne, had killed Destrian's father, Consul Colman, and was currently imprisoned in the dungeons beneath our feet. I'd tried not to think of him, but it was impossible on the very day he'd kept insisting was always on the horizon. Of course, all of that was *before* he'd taken Baylin's side and handed me over to the Lyricans.

Luc looked a little surprised but nodded. "I visit him every other day. I even dine with him, if you can call it that."

"Has he . . . asked about me?"

Luc's mouth quirked, his hazel eyes meeting mine. "He has, actually. Several times."

All of a sudden, the air felt too heavy. "Let him know I'll visit soon."

I went to return to the morning room, but a sense of urgency stopped me. Why wait? Some conversations shouldn't be postponed.

"Mellan," I called behind me, catching his eye. He was usually at my side during the day, with another guard from the castle on watch outside my door at night. Though he seemed to enjoy being in Helena, he still seemed . . . brooding.

"Your Majesty?"

"Will you please take me to the dungeons?"

Mellan's eyes widened, but he nodded. "Very well." He offered his arm and I took it, smiling mischievously at him. He missed it, his mind elsewhere.

"Is something wrong?" I asked as we descended the winding steps to the lower levels of the castle.

"What do you mean?" His gray eyes scanned the staircase.

"I mean, you're not acting like the Mellan I know," I replied, suddenly unsure of myself. I shouldn't be saying anything. It wasn't like I was unhappy with his job or anything. He just didn't seem . . . entirely well. At the very least, he wasn't the same man I knew in Somme.

Mellan shook his head. "I just keep thinking about Aureliana." His shoulders slumped. "At the capital, it was easy to get lost in the gilded lives of the nobles and make a show of forgetting about us." A mirthless chuckle tumbled from his lips. "Most of the time I would collapse into a dreamless sleep, while my life passed by in a haze.

"Here, I can't escape her. She's too close, and with the turmoil in the West, for the first time I'm being forced to reckon with my situation. I've never had to face it like this before."

I frowned, my heart breaking for my friend. What is there to do when your father forces your love to marry him? Where did you go from there? "I'm sorry," I murmured. "It's got to be hard for you."

"It's not good, it's not bad, and it's certainly not your fault," Mellan murmured, his other hand squeezing mine. "I would've had to face it eventually."

I wished I knew better how to help my friend. What Marc Trinidan had asked for was niggling at the back of my mind. He'd wanted Ayastaren, and we'd said we would give it to him if it fell under Morgania's control. What did that mean for Mellan Lyon, the duke's son? It was one thing to take the duchy away from his father, but a completely other thing to take it away from Mellan.

Ugh, Marc Trinidan. I hoped Destrian was right about him.

After what felt like an eternity, we reached the doors of the dungeon. The guard looked up, surprised to see me, but he quickly hid his emotion.

"Your Majesty," he greeted, shoving the iron key into the lock.

The guard opened the door to Conal's cell, and I stepped inside, feeling a mix of dread and curiosity. Who I saw was not the Conal I remembered from my childhood, the strong and charismatic friend of my late father. Instead, I was greeted by the image of a broken old man. His spine was curved, and his skin had turned sallow and wrinkled from the lightless cell. For a fleeting second, I wondered if my father would have looked like this had he lived to old age. But I quickly pushed that thought away.

"How are you treated here?" I asked, my eyes falling on a simple but surprisingly well-made bed in the corner. The cover looked familiar, and it took me a moment to recognize the blanket that had graced his bed in Espiria. Luc's mother, who'd died in the plague, made it.

Conal looked up from a simple, wooden chair, his stare vacant. "Well enough, I suppose. Especially considering everyone is waiting for me to die."

"Luc is happy to see you," I offered, taking the seat across from him. A plate of food sat half-eaten on the table. A crust of bread. A hunk of cheese.

"He is not happy to see what I've been reduced to, though," Conal growled. "You know, that's the funny thing about life." His gaze shifted away from me to some invisible point on the wall. "In our youth, we spend so much time waiting and pining to live, to grow older, to achieve. But when old age comes, it's nothing but a wait to die. Living to old age means that others only remember the deeds they disagreed with, no matter how well intentioned. Perhaps you will live long enough for the same to happen to you."

I frowned. I wasn't there to listen to some old man's platitudes about how he dignified selling away the daughter of his best friend and clan to his most hated enemies. "Are you not sorry at all?"

Conal's eyes snapped back to mine. "Ah, yes. Sorry about you going to Lyrica instead of standing with the Espirians," he grumbled. "Quite the betrayal, that."

"Betrayal?" I echoed, the word sticking in my throat. "The only reason I ended up in Lyrica in the first place was because your son, Luc, betrayed me to them. Has he mentioned that little detail to you? He betrayed me. He revealed my existence, and whetted their appetites. You and Uncle fed me to them."

A flicker of something—surprise, maybe guilt—crossed Conal's face. "No, he hasn't," he admitted softly, looking down at his hands.

"Your dreams told you I should go to Horan," I continued, pressing the point. "And you know what? Those dreams were probably right. If I'd gone to Horan, maybe things would have been different. But we'll never know, will we? We both made choices, Conal, choices that led us to where we are now, talking about betrayal and waiting—for life, for death, for something to change."

"Dreams?" Conal asked, his mouth twitching. I couldn't tell whether it was from nerves or age. "That is how the gods like to torture you in the end. They give you time enough to consider what could have been." He licked his lips. "In your father's and my youth, our dreams felt so real, we could almost taste them. We'd had it all planned out. We would unite the tribes. We would rise as one."

I tilted my head. "So you never had faith in me?"

"Faith?" Conal hissed. "It was never meant to *be* you. It was meant to be him."

I closed my eyes, shaking my head. Conal was such a fool. Even now. Even faced with the consequences of his choices, he still couldn't see where he'd gone wrong.

"Take care, Conal," I said, nodding to him as I stood.

"Luc said you're to be crowned tomorrow." Conal watched me walk to the door.

"I am."

"Wear it well," Conal grunted. "Imor will see to it that you wear it well."

I nodded, then left the old man. He might dwell on what might've been, but that didn't mean I had to.

I climbed the stairs toward my chamber, my thoughts

still with Conal. When I entered, leaving Mellan outside, I found Daisy rummaging through my wardrobe with the sort of intense focus only she could muster for clothing.

"What are you doing?"

Her head popped up, and she beamed at me. "Ah, Your Majesty, Lord Destrian sent your coronation gown up for me to look after. Would you like to see it?"

My interest piqued, I nodded. "Yes, pull it out."

With a flourish that would've made any stage performer proud, Daisy pulled a gown from behind her. As the fabric unfurled, my breath caught.

It was black, as dark as the night sky, cut in the Morganite style—high-necked, long-sleeved, and reaching all the way to the floor. The wool was soft as silk. Intricate designs had been stitched along the front and the bottom hems. Bright multicolored threads formed an almost electric pattern that appeared to be lightning bolts.

My fingers trembled as I reached to touch it. The threads matched the colors of my opals exactly, the reds, blues, and greens in perfect harmony.

"Lord Destrian had it commissioned a while ago," Daisy said, breaking the silence.

A while ago? My brow furrowed at that.

After Daisy readied me for bed, I stood on the balcony, admiring the pine trees and roses, sipping a cup of tea and contemplating the garment that hung near the door.

"Echo," I said, raising my voice slightly. "Can you find Destrian for me, please." I was tired of waiting. If we wanted to be together, if we were meant to be together, then why weren't we?

As Echo flitted away, my thoughts wandered to the fleeting moments we spent in the Nightlands. It felt like a dream, bright but brief. We'd made promises, lying under a blanket of stars with nothing to hold on to but each other.

I wanted to go back to that moment. To those feelings.

"Destrian is in his room," Echo whispered suddenly.

I turned, shutting the glass doors carefully behind me, before making the short walk to Destrian's chamber. It was a walk I'd made countless times in my mind but never in reality.

For a moment, I hesitated, my knuckles hovering just above the wood. Then, I knocked.

My breath caught as I waited, and I wrapped my dressing gown tighter around myself as a cool breeze wafted through the corridor, sending a nearby torch sputtering.

Destrian opened the door, a wooden pick dangling from his lips. The moment he saw it was me, his eyes brightened and he smiled—a genuine, heartwarming smile. He stepped back into the room, pulling the pick from his mouth and tossing it onto a shelf.

"Are you ready for tomorrow?" he asked, stepping

aside so I could view the organized chaos within. A tall bookshelf lined one wall, crammed with scrolls, books, and other trinkets. A stack of books also claimed residence on the bedside table, each appearing well-read and often referenced.

"As ready as can be expected," I replied, my eyes traveling to the weapons. Unlike the books, these were organized with meticulous attention to detail. Swords, daggers, and axes hung neatly on one wall. "Lady Maureen has drilled me in how to walk and accept the crown, so hopefully I won't make an ass out of myself."

Destrian grinned, looking particularly handsome this evening, a detail my mind lingered on. I couldn't help but admire the definition in his arms. And the beard he'd kept since our time in the Nightlands gave him a mature, worldly look that I found irresistible. I wanted to run my fingers through it as the heat of his mouth . . .

"The dress you chose is perfect," I said, finally breaking the silence. "I can't thank you enough for it."

Destrian's gaze softened. "I can't wait to see you in it," he said, his voice husky and low.

"Are you sure about not getting married?" I asked suddenly. I couldn't help but wonder if that's why he kept his distance. "To keep me open for a political alliance?"

He nodded, his gaze never leaving mine. "We'd be fools not to leave that option open. It's better for Morgania, if not for us."

Feeling a burst of courage, I leaned into him, my arms wrapping around his neck, and sank into his heat. "But I love you. There's no future I can envision, not one shred of happiness I can imagine, unless it's a future with you."

Destrian made as if to close the distance between us before hesitating. He hesitated, and it felt like my heart was being ripped from my chest. "Why do you hold back?" I murmured, my voice nearly breaking.

Destrian leaned his forehead against mine, our gems brushing together. "Every time we got close before . . . it wasn't long after that you'd tried to leave." His fingers threaded through my hair, gripping it tight. His burning eyes met mine. "You will ruin me if you leave again."

I captured his face in my hands, running my fingers through his beard like I'd dreamed about doing. "I'm not leaving again," I whispered. "I promise, nothing will keep me from your side."

Something shifted within Destrian's eyes, his smoldering gaze morphing into a raging fire. His fingers in my hair tightened and his lips crashed into mine, urgent and needy and everything I'd been craving for weeks. His tongue toyed with me, drawing me in until all I wanted to do was get lost in his fire. Teeth nipped at my lip, shooting sparks of warm feeling through the length of my body that pooled into my core.

Pulling away just enough to speak, Destrian murmured, "Do you have any idea how impossible it's been to stay away from you?"

Suddenly, his hands were untying the dressing gown and pushing it off my shoulders to pool in a silken heap on the floor.

"Then why have you?" I gasped.

His hands went to my waist, pulling me closer, dragging the fabric of my chemise up.

"Now, Your Majesty," he murmured. "I told you that I've been waiting so that I can take my time." He pulled the thin fabric over my shoulders, but it caught on my arm and ripped down a seam. Destrian growled, finally releasing me from its hold so he could get to the skin underneath.

I tugged his tunic over his head and wrapped my arms around his neck as he lifted me, wrapping my legs around his waist as he carried me to the bed, giving me the opportunity to get lost in his scent and heat and everything that I'd missed since I'd last been close to him. I ran my tongue along his neck, biting and nipping and drinking him in as he growled beneath me.

He lowered me to the bed, far too gently for my taste, and much too slow. I immediately went for the laces on his breeches, hungry for more, starving in fact, but his hands captured mine, yanking them above my head.

"Oh no, my Queen," Destrian scolded. "I've been waiting far too long for this." He transferred his hold on my wrists to one hand, leaving his other free to skim down my arm. "Me first."

The heat in his eyes was scorching as he finally released me to scan my body, laid bare before him. I wondered how different I looked. In the Nightlands I'd felt self-conscious, far too thin and worn to feel pretty. Now I had shape to my curves. Curves that Destrian was drinking in as he ran his palms from the sides of my thighs to my waist. He threw my legs open, his arms propping up my knees, the dragon tattoo on his bicep flexing and rippling with the movement, doing terrible things to my restraint.

Destrian's fingers toyed with me, nimble and quick. A whimper of want escaped my lips as warmth flooded my body and I arched toward him. Destrian cursed as he kissed a path along my inner thigh, his breath hot on my skin, as he worked his way around to devouring every bit of my flesh.

Losing myself in his fire had always felt like coming home.

And I came again.

And again.

And again.

Chapter 23

THE SWELL OF WARM SKIN on my cheek woke me. I remembered, as I came to my senses, the ills of speaking as my dream self. Of putting voice and words to my innermost thoughts. That day in the carriage when I'd said Destrian's name while Sam held me burned in my mind. Still, as I squinted into the light, dread filled my stomach at the thought of being back in the capital with Sam and Agramon. Tears began to fill the corners of my eyes as the arm holding me tightened. Then the smell hit me, and I remembered I was home.

My eyes adjusted to the light. A smattering of red chest hair tickled my cheek. I looked up, taking in Destrian's other arm curled behind his head, his eyes closed as he slept. I gently rested my head back down and closed my eyes, sinking into him, breathing in his smell. It felt just like the Nightlands. I felt safe despite everything else. My heart calmed as though it had been racing for a damn year.

The night before had been ... incredible. Destrian made damned sure I knew how much he'd been craving me. A delicious ache threaded through my muscles as I sank into the feeling of contented weariness. But I knew I couldn't lie there forever, as much as I might wish to.

"I have to go," I whispered as he shifted, shading his eyes from the harsh morning sun streaming in through his windows. Lifting my chemise from a chair, I noticed that the ripped seam had been sewn shut. I frowned. "Did someone come in?" I asked, holding out the evidence.

Destrian shook his head. "I didn't want the others to whisper about you—about us."

A smile broke out on my face. "You sewed this?"

Destrian tried to contain his grin but was unsuccessful. "I listened to you more than was probably good for me. It must come from being . . . in love."

My smile softened, and I crawled over him, straddling his hips and kissing him gently.

Destrian broke away all too soon. "Are you ready for today?" He stroked my cheek with his thumb, studying my features as though hunting for worry or fear.

Of course.

It was coronation day.

"Are *you* ready?" I whispered, threading my fingers through his red chest hair. I liked it. Probably a little too much if I was being honest with myself. I just wanted to bury my face in it and rub it around. "Now that you've given me my dress *and* crown?"

Destrian grinned as he propped himself up. "I can't wait to see you in them. I will be able to die a happy man."

My breath caught in my throat. I clambered off him.

"Don't ever say that."

He shrugged, watching me pull the chemise on. "It's true, though. You'll be the most beautiful queen this kingdom has ever seen."

I felt heat climb up my neck. "You're distracting me from what's important."

He pulled the covers off and sat at the edge of the bed, scouring the room for his own clothes. My breath caught as I noticed his arms and back, threaded with muscle, in the daylight. His bare body was . . . doing things to me. Things that would be welcome if I had a day free of responsibilities. As it stood . . .

"And what is that?"

"That we're putting an awful lot of faith in one person," I said, gesturing to myself. "In me."

He found his breeches and began pulling them on. "Rowyn, if there's anyone I would place my faith in, it's you."

I sighed, slipping my arms into the dressing gown that was now wrinkled from a night spent in a pile on the floor. "That's not what I meant. I have plenty of faith in myself now. It's the structure that worries me. One person should not have so much power. One person shouldn't be the key to holding the entire land together."

Destrian frowned. "I thought what you wanted was the kingdom of Morgania," he said, grabbing a fresh tunic and pulling it over his head.

"It is," I said, tightening the sash of my robe, unsure of what I was trying to say. "I just want the changes we're putting in place to last past me."

"Now it is you who needs to stop," Destrian snapped. "Stop talking like you're about to die."

I shook my head and sighed. "You don't understand what I'm trying to say," I whispered. "I have to go." I had a coronation to prepare for, after all.

I hurried from his room, darting back into my own before Daisy arrived to get me ready for the ceremony. For a moment, I leaned against the closed door, my heart pounding. The day had finally arrived, and everything was about to change.

I stood in front of the mirror, examining my reflection. Daisy had done wonders with my hair, plaiting it low in preparation for the crown that would rest on my head by end of day. My hands moved hesitantly over the stiff gown, tracing the designs stitched in the bright colors of my opals. I looked like a queen—felt like one too—but there was still a tight coil of nervous energy in my stomach.

Destrian had always gotten it right about me—always understood who I was and who I could be. I just hoped he wouldn't be too angry about what I was about to do.

It didn't matter how good I was at being queen, if nothing remained after I was gone. But I had realized a way to ensure our legacy, and I was going to take it. They would either celebrate my choice or eventually forgive me for it . . . I hoped.

I walked to the door and swung it open. Mellan stood guard outside, wearing his usual uniform. I was surprised to find Sir Bernard next to him.

"I'm ready," I announced, trying to keep the nervousness from my voice.

Sir Bernard hurriedly wiped away moisture from his cheeks.

My brows raised. "Are those tears?"

"It's just me emotions gettin' the best o' me is all." Sir Bernard's burly frame trembled ever so slightly. "To think, meetin' a princess by the side o' the road. Then to bow down to her as queen."

The dam nearly broke for me right then. I strode forward and wrapped my arms around the old soldier. "I've been grateful for your friendship through it all," I said softly.

"And I've been honored to serve you, Your Majesty," Bernard blubbered. I broke away as he wiped his sopping eyes with a kerchief. Mellan patted him on the back.

As they followed me through the hall, whispered conversations fell silent. My heels clicked on the stone floor. People had begun to line the corridor as I moved toward the great hall. Some carried roses and waved them to me.

I smiled, accepting one, then another, and another, until my arms were filled with blooms.

When we reached the bottom story of the castle, Ferris's guardsmen lined my path, holding back the pressing crowd who craned for a better look. When they realized they couldn't get the roses to me, they threw them onto my path, the fragrant petals curtaining the corridor.

I took a deep breath.

I held my head high.

I hated every minute of their eyes upon me, but the gods insisted I do this part alone.

Trumpets sounded my entrance and a deafening cheer greeted me. My attention was immediately caught by several pairs of horns, jutting above the crowd. Near the throne was King Valon. He stood with his attendants, some with iridescent wings folded behind them. They watched the crowd of humans with muted expressions. Some of their eyes sparkled when they saw me. They turned to each other, whispering behind their hands.

I wondered if they, too, had known my ancestors. Did they recognize them in my features? Could my father, mother, and grandmother see me from their places among the stars? Was I doing them proud?

Waiting behind the dais was Destrian. By the gods, I wanted to melt into a puddle at his feet, he looked so gorgeous. I didn't care if I was the one who defeated the dragon, I found the dragon pattern on his doublet, the same one that adorned his arm, so fitting. Not to mention how easy he looked in the midst of being gawked at. I remembered before, how insufferable I'd found him when I'd first gotten to Helena. I thought him a spoiled heir. His dark eyes were warm as they met mine, and everything else faded into insignificance for that moment.

Right below the dais stood Fin and Lady Vianne. It was evident that the separation of Vianne from her husband was painful. Fin's information from the East made it seem like Agramon was busy and distracted, but we could never know for sure. Even so, Lord Alexander had left the day before, bound for diplomatic talks and an audience with the empress in Maryse.

Solston Ignace and Imorati Kaelan waited for me at the very top of the dais. It was odd, seeing a Solston and Imorati standing together. The first wore the ceremonial colors of Sol, white and gold. Ignace was older, and not a huge fan of me, but he trusted Destrian. Everybody did.

The new Imorati, Kaelan, was fearsome-looking but hid a tender heart. His robes were black and silver, the colors of Imor nestled in the night sky.

I liked the two together and enjoyed their back and forth when they bantered with each other in the council rooms. It was hard to decide whether they hated or loved each other. Probably a bit of both. Others in the crowd had dressed to mirror the colors, but there were no Sons of Sol. No shouts of derision or hisses that I was evil and must be taught to bend to their world.

My eyes caught on what sat between the holy men. The crown on its little silk pillow. The opals seemed to call me forward, beckoning me with their power.

So perfect for me.

So perfect for this moment.

The icy chill came suddenly. A pang of a memory. Another walk down another aisle toward another destiny, one with Sam.

I took a long, slow breath, stepping carefully up the steps, trying to hide my trembling fingers in the skirt of my dress. That was the only bad thing about Morganite dresses, they were too stiff to hide anything.

When I reached the top, I faced the holy men standing together and raised my head high.

Solston Ignace stepped forward. Clearing his throat, he gestured wrinkled hands toward the crowd.

"People of Morgania, we gather here under the eye of Sol to witness the rise of a new era, the coronation of Queen Rowyn the Morganite. Sol, the eternal light that watches over us, we beseech you: shine your brightest rays onto our queen. May her reign be luminous, her judgments enlightened, and her path unclouded. Grant her the wisdom to guide us through the darkness and into a future where your light touches even the most shadowed corners of our land."

He paused, then stepped back, making room for Imorati Kaelan.

"Queen Rowyn, as the night sky embraces the stars, so shall you embrace your people. As Imorati, I call upon the darkness to bless your reign. May you find wisdom in the stillness of the night and strength under the people raised to the stars. I ask the night to be your ally, and may you find meaning and truth that dwell in darkness."

Both men stepped to the crown. I kneeled, bowing as they lifted it together, then shuffled toward me. I heard Solston Ignace counting his steps under his breath as they got closer. Closing my eyes, I felt the weight of the crown come to rest on my head.

Everything the gods had insisted I become was nigh.

I was taking my rightful place on the throne of my ancestors, and I was damned determined to leave behind a legacy of justice. And I was going to ensure it was a legacy, not another short dream that the Lyrican Empire seemed to enjoy crushing.

"By the gods, who've deemed us their voices for Morgania, and demanded sovereignty, long live the queen," Solston Ignace intoned, his voice reverberating throughout the hall.

"By the people, whose voices have risen from the mist,

crying out for liberation, long live the queen," declared Imorati Kaelan.

"Long live the queen," the crowd chanted.

I opened my eyes. Destrian was smiling at me from behind the holy men. For a moment, I felt invincible.

"Long live the queen" echoed over the rafters.

I stood and faced the room, my eyes meeting a sea of bowed heads.

"Long live the queen!" The air trembled with the unified cry that erupted from everyone gathered.

I brushed away several tears that had slipped down my cheeks. Overwhelmed, I glanced down at the foot of the stairs and found Fin's glowing smile. I held out my hand, stretching my fingers toward her.

"Long live the queen!"

Fin's brows furrowed, then rose. She beamed as she ascended the steps, then came to stand beside me, her fingers curling around mine.

"Long live the queen!"

I looked over my shoulder at Destrian. He'd stepped behind me, flanking one side, while Mellan flanked the other. He shot me an encouraging smile when he noticed my eyes were on him. I held out my hand, wordlessly asking for his support.

"Long live the queen!"

He came to stand on my other side. I squeezed

Destrian's hand on my right and Fin's hand on my left as I faced the sea of people and held my head high.

"Long live the queen!"

The chanting gradually lessened, until all of a sudden, I could hear a pin drop in the grand hall of the citadel, despite that it was filled to bursting with every manner of person to be found in the kingdom of Morgania.

Holding the hands of the two people I loved most in the world, I took a deep breath and began to speak.

"The notion of home was ingrained in me at a young age." My voice carried clear in the silence. "It's a place we fight for—that we protect at all costs, a sanctuary that offers comfort and love. Morgania is such a home—a home to all who stand here, a home to those who have left us and to those who have yet to join us. As your queen, it is my foremost duty to protect our home."

I paused, locking eyes with as many as I could.

"But I believe that the strength of a home—of a kingdom—relies on the harmony of its voices and the strength of the throne. This has been demonstrated amply by the crumbling Lyrican Empire."

I could feel the crowd's rapt attention, their energy feeding into my words.

"We've lived for too long with the idea that one voice, one crown, should hold dominion over all. The gods themselves—Sol, Ada, and Imor—rule as a trinity. As such, I refuse to rule alone," I continued. "My first decree as your queen is to ensure that our home, Morgania, hears the voices of all its people." I squeezed Destrian's hand. "Today, I wish to crown Destrian of Morgania to serve as the voice of the Lyricans among us." Fin started beside me as I continued. "And I wish to crown Fin of Morgania, who may serve as the voice of the animals and fae who share our world. I would offer for them to join me upon the throne, and to rule by three, as one."

There was a stunned silence, a collective holding of breath.

"Rowyn, what are you doing?" Destrian hissed into my ear.

I met his eyes, then turned and met Fin's. "Well? Do you accept?"

Fin regarded me, her brows high, clearly in shock. She turned and looked out to the crowd. Her hand shook in mine. King Valon was glaring between the three of us, the fae behind him whispering and watching the scene with pure delight at the turn of events. I shuddered to think what the coronation party afterward might look like if the fae chose to stay.

"Rowyn, you can't think we want this, to take it from you . . ." Destrian continued to murmur.

Fin snorted softly. "Speak for yourself," she told Destrian before turning to the crowd. "I accept the honor of serving as queen to the kingdom of Morgania. Together, we can begin an era of peace and bounty within our shared world."

The crowd erupted into cheers. The wave of sound filled the hall.

"You're not taking anything from me," I insisted. "This is what's best for the people . . . for *all* the beings of Morgania. We need this."

Destrian looked dumbfounded. I'd expected him to feel honored, or even be expecting the move, at least for him. I knew Fin was going to be a surprise to everyone, but I preferred the idea of ruling with three and needing a majority instead of one person overruling another.

Three was best. I was sure of it.

I nudged Destrian with my elbow and nodded to the crowd.

Destrian faced the people. Guardsmen who had lined the path to the dais were raising their fists, saluting him and shouting, "Dragon!" The people who screamed the loudest were from the castle and city of Helena. They'd watched Destrian grow up. He was the future they'd been looking forward to for years. I'd wondered how the denizens who'd supported the Everett line felt about my taking of the throne. Destrian always acted like they'd get over it in time, since he was the one giving it up, but I wasn't prone to Destrian's constant optimism.

It was the only way to unite everyone.

"I accept," Destrian finally said, but it was far too quiet, and the crowd grew unruly in their screamed demands.

"I accept!" Destrian shouted, raising his hands as though in surrender. "As everyone knows, Morgania has always been my home. The only one I've known." He looked to me and raised our hands. "Together, we can move forward from the mistakes of the past and begin a new dawn!"

My mouth was starting to hurt from smiling. I squeezed Fin's hand, a bit overzealously I might add, and held it up on the other side as the noise in the hall reached a deafening volume, reverberating off the stone walls.

We were now strong. I felt a joy so profound, it nearly broke me. I was home, and for the first time in my life, home was a kingdom, a family, and a future, all rolled into one.

Chapter 24

GUARDS SURROUNDED US and we practically ran from the hall to get away from the crush of the crowd, mindless with excitement. Luc appeared at Fin's side and helped Mellan hurry us through the corridors toward the easier-to-guard family wing.

After the door to my room closed behind us, Destrian's eyes fixed on me. "Why?"

Fin crossed her arms. They were probably wondering why I hadn't told them of my plans. The truth was, I didn't want to chance someone talking me out of it.

"If something happens to me," I began, choosing my words carefully, "I want to make sure Morgania continues to flourish. The old way, with a single monarch wielding all power, is outdated. It's vulnerable."

"And you think a triarchy is the solution?" A hint of skepticism crept into Destrian's voice.

"Yes," I replied firmly. "Three thrones, three voices for Morgania. We can divide responsibilities a bit, but mostly, each voice our own conscience at the table when it comes to any major decisions or things we might disagree with. Furthermore, we could each name our own heir. We can decree that it doesn't have to be a blood descendent either . . . we can decide based on who is the best fit for our role."

Destrian sighed, shaking his head, but I continued regardless. "It's about balance, Destrian. It's about making sure our kingdom is resilient, adaptive, and most of all, fair."

Fin cleared her throat. "I'm not sure I can adequately represent the voices of the fae. I'm not one of them."

"Then why have I heard King Valon refer to you as his voice here in Morgania?" I replied. "Besides, it doesn't change our plans very much. You would still oversee the Others coming into Morgania and monitor any favors owed or offered."

Destrian stared at me for a moment longer before his expression softened. "This changes *some* things, though. You realize that, right?"

Before I could answer, Fin chimed in. "It's a lot to take in, but Rowyn's right. We're stronger together, and this . . . this could really work."

Destrian reached out and cupped my cheek in his hand. "You are too wondrous to be believed sometimes . . . do you know that? Even for me, someone who pretends to know you well, you keep finding ways to surprise me."

Heat suddenly flared between us.

Fin's eyes were flicking between Destrian and I. "Wait, so are you two going to get married?"

I shook my head, taking his hand in mine. "No. But think about it. If we ever need a marriage alliance, now we have three options. For now, I don't care if we're married. I just want to live happily, surrounded by the people I love, building a home strong enough to protect them."

Before I could say another word, Fin swept me into a tight embrace. I hugged her back, unable to restrain the emotion flooding through me. And then Destrian's arms were around both of us, his head resting atop ours.

"You should have a room closer to us," I whispered into Fin's hair. I was already planning in my mind how we'd rearrange things.

Destrian pulled back. "Which room would you like? Mine or my father's old room? It's next to Rowyn's."

Fin smiled slyly. "I want the room with the balcony next to my greatest friend."

He chuckled, letting out a sigh as if he expected no less. "Of course you do."

"The council is asking to meet with you all," a voice said at the door. Luc had come in, his eyes on Fin. "And the party is starting to get out of hand."

Fin broke away, her face flushed with the excitement of the day, and took a moment to admire the general. Luc had taken care in his dress for my coronation day. Most of his hair was slicked back into a knot, and I'd noticed he'd oiled his beard as well. His leather breastplate was stamped with images of crescents and stars, and he wore his falconer's arm and shoulder guards.

Fin glanced back at Destrian and me. "I'm going to go think for a bit before we hash all this out."

"You're queen now, you can do what you want," I said as Destrian draped his arm over my shoulder and drew me to his side.

Luc was nodding. "I understand if you need time to—"

"Would you like to go for a ride?" Fin asked him suddenly.

Luc froze. "I am at your disposal . . . I mean . . . I would be honored," he stammered before quickly adding, "Your Majesty."

"What about the party?" Destrian asked.

"Captain Ferris can deal with that mess, can't he?" Fin said, shooting a smile to Luc whose face blazed scarlet. "I'll meet you in the stables." She morphed into Arden, her dress falling in a puddle of silk before she hopped to the window and flew off with a screech.

I raised my brows at Luc, who was still blushing as he scooped the dress off the floor and mumbled a hurried goodbye.

Apparently, Destrian was waiting for us to be alone again, because his arms suddenly enveloped me, his lips hot on mine. "You wondrous little thing," he murmured as his mouth moved over my cheek and down my neck. His hands went to the lacings at the back of my dress. The very intricate lacings.

I got lost in the moment, meeting his lips with mine while unbuttoning his embroidered coat and pushing it off him. His tunic came next.

I could tell Destrian was getting frustrated when he started yanking on the ribbons. "By all the gods," he cursed. "I can't bring myself to rip this dress."

I responded by exploring his chest with my tongue. Destrian groaned, lifting me against the wall and trying to gather the skirt in his hands, but the fabric was too stiff.

My hands went to the ties on his breeches.

His fingers went back to the laces on the gown. After a moment, he cursed again.

I couldn't help myself. I laughed.

Destrian shot me a pained look before striding to the door and flinging it open. "Get Daisy in here!" he barked to whomever was outside. Probably Mellan. "We'll meet with them tomorrow," Destrian added as he slammed the door again, then came toward me. "Turn around," he murmured, his hand on my waist as his soft lips kissing my throat, sending tingles over my skin. He lifted my crown and set it gently on the table before returning to kiss my neck and pull pins from my hair.

"What's got you in such a mood, Your Majesty?" I

whispered, gasping when his teeth nipped at the curve of my throat.

His arm tightened around my chest as he pressed my waist into his, showing me how excited he was. "Say it again."

I reached up, wrapping my fingers in his hair while I twisted, wanting to taste him again. "King Destrian Everett, the Dragon of Morgania."

"Fu—"

"You called for me?" Daisy asked as she entered. Destrian and I sprang apart.

"Get her out of that thing," Destrian ordered, his eyes scorching as he settled shaking hands on his hips. I loved seeing him with his shirt off. The dragon tattooed on his arm, the smattering of red hair across his chest, I was ready to melt right then and there.

Daisy dipped her head. "Yes, my lord . . . er . . . I mean, Your Majesty."

Destrian waved his hand. "It's fine, just get the dress off."

I leaned against the wall as Daisy unraveled the laces. My poor maid kept glancing at Destrian who was watching her with growing impatience as she painstakingly unwove the back of my dress. I didn't miss the flames in the fireplace crackling with heat the longer she took.

Finally, I was able to step out from under the gown so

she could take it to be cleaned, as fast as her little feet could carry her. The girl wasn't even completely out the door before Destrian grabbed me by the arms, crushing his lips to mine. He didn't feel the same about my chemise as my gown. He tore it off me in a flicker of thread and flames. I giggled as he lifted me effortlessly and tossed me into bed, before prowling toward me.

Squealing, I tried to scramble away, but he was quick to capture me, trapping me beneath his fire. I soaked it up, like the greedy wanton woman I'd turned out to be.

IF AGRAMON HAD been in Morgania, he'd probably figure the reason I appointed Destrian and Fin as co-rulers was to have them sit beside me at the head of the council table. He wouldn't be wrong.

I leaned back in my chair, trying to stifle a yawn. Destrian had kept me up all night, and I couldn't help but think that during my year-long absence in Somme, he must've kept a list in that little notebook of his of all the things he'd wanted to do to me. Last night, it felt like he was on a mission to tick off every single one. I found myself smiling at the thought, my body still tingling with the memories.

But, the entire council was staring at me expectantly as I sipped my lady's tea.

"In my view, each of us is equal in power," I began. "There's no need for a main one among us. With three, if one goes rogue, the other two can outvote them."

Sir Bernard raised a finger. "Will we have three thrones?"

Destrian nodded. "And three crowns. Thanks to King Valon's gift, I have the jewels we need for Queen Fin's. Mine might take more time."

I tried to suppress my excitement. We'd talked about it the night before, wrapped in each other's arms, too excited for sleep and making plans in the light of Imor.

Fin leaned forward. "King Valon will be staying another day to review entry protocols before he takes the information to the gatekeepers. There are long lines of fae clamoring to cross over."

"Good gods," Solston Ignace muttered. "Are they going to inundate us?"

Imorati Kaelan narrowed his eyes at the Solston before bowing his head toward Fin. "How are you planning to keep track of favors, Your Majesty?"

"And how will you keep track of the fae if they get out of hand," Marc Trinidan added, his steely gaze on me. I wondered if Destrian had told Marc his own misgivings. Had he told him of the deal I'd made?

Fin held her head high, looking down at Marc. "Unless they have a unique gift we can use, the standard favor will be a year or more of service to the crown, and that can look like anything. Cooks, workmen, guards . . . you name it. Once our Master of Ink is in place, we will devise a way to keep meticulous records."

I couldn't wait until Pedr arrived.

"We've already talked with Her Majesty about the possibility of fae being added to the guards," Luc added, with Ferris nodding beside him. Luc had been a complete mess when he'd disappeared with Fin the day before. Now, he leaned back in his chair, a smug look of satisfaction on his face. I glanced over at my friend. Fin was pointedly looking at anyone but the general of our forces.

Lady Vianne had her eyes on all three of us from her seat beside Urdua. She took in Destrian's barely restrained yawn and hid a chuckle behind her hand.

"What of the news from Korballis?"

Marc tapped his fingers on the table, aware that everyone's gaze was now leveled at him. "I have spoken to my father. Korballis is willing to support the Marendeslys maintaining the throne of Lyrica."

"You mean, the empress?" I asked with a glance at Vianne. She shrugged. I wasn't sure if that meant that Marc and his father really didn't care, or if Vianne didn't care about their opinions.

"For whomever they put on the throne," Marc said. "We're one of the furthest consulships from the capital. It's not our battle."

Destrian leaned onto his arms. "What about military aid against the Butcher?"

Marc ran his tongue over his teeth. "We would prefer to stay out of it. With the fae about to come over, you can't ask us to spare any men."

Luc frowned, pointing to the map stretched out on the table between us. "Well, we still need some way to secure the borders along the south, namely Ayastaren." The border between Morgania and Adair looked uncomfortably exposed, even in ink on parchment.

A knock interrupted our discussion. Mellan, who now served, not just me but all three of us monarchs, moved to the door. Guards stood there, their faces grim.

The sound of glass shattering cut through the council chamber. Lady Vianne had risen, her face devoid of color. She stared at the open door where the head guard was whispering to Mellan. He turned and found Vianne, his eyes saddened.

"I'm sorry," was all he said.

Those seated around the table rose as Vianne straightened and walked slowly from the room, her back ramrod straight. The guards parted at the door, giving her room to pass.

"What is it?" Destrian asked.

Mellan faced the room. "A large number of bodies washed up in DarkPort with pieces of a wreckage. Lord Alexander was among them."

Chapter 25

A HUSHED SILENCE fell over the room. Destrian looked as though he'd been struck, his eyes searching for something beyond the walls, beyond the immediate reality that had just shattered. The air thinned, as if a shadow had been cast on all our futures.

Though I'd spent time with Lord Alexander, I would never claim to know him well. Destrian had traveled with him to Yliria. He and Lord Alexander were what Master Gillius and I had been.

And Lady Vianne.

Without thinking, I rose and hurried after her. Lord Alexander was who Lady Vianne had escaped Agramon to be with. Alexander had helped rescue her from darkness, and now he was gone. Snatched away by the powers of the world that hungered for violence.

My breath came in quick bursts as I nearly ran down the hall. It was what I feared for Destrian.

Lady Vianne's room was in the guest wing. She was just at the door, fiddling with her key, when I came upon her. She looked up, her cheeks stained with tears, her gem dull. Footsteps behind me announced Mellan, but I held up my hand.

"Wait outside please," I said.

Mellan shook his head. "At the very least I need to check the room."

Vianne and I stood within, waiting silently as Mellan looked in the corners and behind doors. When he stepped outside and shut the door, Vianne collapsed onto a chair by the window.

"I'm sorry," I said, going to a pitcher of water and pouring her a glass. I placed it in front of her before taking a seat at her side. "I know what he meant to you."

Lady Vianne shook her head, choosing instead to look out of the window as the tears fell. She sniffed and wiped her cheeks. "I knew Agramon would get Alexander in the end, but I had hoped . . ." Her voice trailed off.

"It could've been Baron Samael," I whispered.

Lady Vianne turned her steely gaze onto me. "No," she said harshly. "It would only be *him*."

I gritted my teeth. "You fear him so, yet you sent me to him."

Lady Vianne let out a sharp, barking laugh. "I knew *you* would survive him. You would never break for a man like that. That's both the best and worst thing about the two of us. We will always survive, to carry the guilt as everyone we love succumbs."

My heart froze in my chest. She wasn't wrong. I'd

known, in the end, that Agramon wouldn't ever really hurt me physically. Not in any permanent way. It was always the others. It would be Destrian, or Fin, or Ferris, or anyone who dared to be close to me. I clenched my fists, feeling a sick swell of fear. I couldn't let Agramon get his hands on them.

"I understand that you probably want time to be alone," I told Vianne. "Please know that we meant what we said. Morgania is your home if you choose to stay. We will protect you as best we can. Let me know if there is anything you need. I will speak to Lady Maureen about beginning funeral preparations."

Lady Vianne just nodded, her eyes going back to the window. I stepped out of the room and shut the door behind me, leaning against it with a sigh.

"How is she?" Mellan asked.

"Not well. Where is King Valon?"

"I don't know, but we can find out," Mellan said, falling into step beside me as I headed back to the council room. "How do you think Agramon knew where to strike? More spies?"

I shook my head. "There was a sorcerer who I met in Solin. Solston Navar . . . have you heard of him?"

Mellan shook his head.

"His magic is used to see great distances. I know Agramon used him to watch me on my journey to the

Nightlands. I'm betting he's at the capital now, as we speak, watching us and letting Agramon know our every move."

"So what's your plan?" Mellan asked.

"Lord Alexander had said there were old fae wards on the palace. I want to know if King Valon can help reset them."

"Destrian is sure that you're putting too much trust in them," Mellan remarked, his eyes darting around the halls. His hand gripped the sword at his side tightly. Though there were three monarchs in Morgania now, only I had a regular guard.

I sighed. At least it was Mellan. "What do you think?"

Mellan snorted. "Don't ask me about politics, I don't really know." He sobered quickly. "Just be careful."

We turned the corner and came upon Destrian who'd seemed to be looking for us.

"What happened with the council?" I asked.

"We'll meet later," Destrian murmured. "I still can't believe he's gone. And because of water, of all things."

I took a deep breath. "About that, we need to meet with King Valon immediately. We should reset all of the wards on Helena."

Mellan stepped back, apparently avoiding any lines of fire.

Destrian's nostrils flared. "He will want something for

it."

"Of course he will. So let's go find out what that is."

"He's in the formal meeting room," Destrian replied, turning to lead the way. "Fin went to meet with him."

I quickened my pace, Mellan keeping in stride. We reached the large doors of the meeting chamber, and Destrian pushed them open. Inside, King Valon and Fin were seated across from each other, Fin on the couch and King Valon in the chair beside the fire, his hands steepled in front of him.

The king rose as we entered, taller than any man I'd ever seen, his silver-white hair cascading in braids between the massive ram's horns. Someone had woven flowers through the horns, which only served to make him look more . . . interesting.

"Your Majesties," he greeted. Despite the formal address, his gaze lingered just a moment longer on Destrian, as though weighing all he saw. Perhaps he was just put off by the scowl on Destrian's face.

Fin was frowning, confused and worried at our sudden appearance.

"We are pleased that you came to witness the coronation, King Valon," I said, stepping farther into the room. I'd never seen someone so exotically handsome before. Good gods, was I going to faint? Did he weave some type of spell that drew me to him?

I gritted my teeth. If there was, I would resist. I nearly reached for Destrian's hand, then reconsidered, gripping my skirts instead. It was not Destrian and me. It was Destrian, Fin, and I who made the decisions of Morgania. We needed to maintain a distinction between our three separate selves.

"How are your companions enjoying the city?" I asked, settling onto the couch beside Fin. Destrian stood behind us, his arms crossed. Mellan chose to wait outside. It made sense. After all, what help would he be with a fae king when the three people he was protecting were the most powerful sorcerers in the kingdom?

"We are finding Helena to be far different from what we remembered," King Valon said, his eyes moving between the three of us.

"But we are stronger for it," I maintained, folding my hands over my lap as I straightened.

King Valon let out a slow breath, a bemused smile on his face. The flare of attraction grew stronger and I tensed. The King's smile widened.

I tilted my head up. "Before you begin discussion of entry protocols for migrating fae, there is a favor that we would like to request that may or may not change your negotiations."

Fin's brows rose, then she slowly sat back on the couch, waiting for me to continue. King Valon smiled in a very creepy and predatory way that shattered whatever enchantment he might've had.

"A favor, you say?"

I took a steadying breath and went on. "Your Majesty, we seek your assistance in resetting the fae wards around the palace."

King Valon's brows rose. "You are fearful, now that one of your own has perished?"

I looked to Fin. "Did you know who Solston Navar was?"

Fin's expression morphed from puzzlement, to realization, and finally to anger. "That's how he knew." Fin and Lady Vianne had gone over the palace with a fine-toothed comb, with the aid of Lady Maureen, weeding out any and all liabilities or possible spies in the servants. Lord Alexander's departure had remained hidden from everyone except a select few on the council, and he'd gone in disguise.

I nodded. "Would the fae wards be able to hide Helena from magical sight?"

"They would," King Valon said, tapping his fingers on the arm of his chair. "The wards on the palace protect you from scrying, league-leaping, bad intentions, and also provide luck. You will probably stop having plumbing problems, for example."

"Gods," Destrian said from behind me. I glanced up. He shrugged. "That's just really useful."

"I will happily reset the wards," King Valon said, his eyes dancing with mirth. "In exchange for a favor of my own." The request had clearly opened a door for him, an opportunity he was keen to exploit.

I could sense Destrian's unease behind me, even with the promise of a future free of castle maintenance. "We come to you prepared to negotiate." The kingdom's safety was paramount. Destrian, Fin, and everyone who sheltered in the safety of Morgania would always be my first priority.

King Valon inclined his head. "I confess, I was so moved by the words at your . . . the coronation. Declaring that every voice would be heard in Morgania. You even named Fin as the voice of the fae. However, Queen Fin is no longer beholden to any of my wishes, as her favor has since been fulfilled."

King Valon smiled at Fin who didn't return it. Instead, she shifted uneasily beside me.

The king went on. "Therefore, in exchange for resparking the wards around Helena, I require that a seat on your council must be held by a fae of my choosing. Furthermore, any new laws or issues regarding fae in Morgania be seen by this individual. They will need rooms here at the palace and be provided for as members of your court."

"We should all have a say in the appointment to the council," Destrian said from behind Fin and me.

King Valon looked over our shoulders at him. "Do you

know of any fae who you would prefer for this role?"

Destrian shook his head, his reluctance apparent. "No, I do not."

I met Fin's eye. "What do you think?"

Fin offered a single shrug of her shoulder, her fingers absent-mindedly stroking her lips as she studied the fae king. "It seems rather fair in my mind. If they are to be here, they should have a true voice. It would also be helpful to have someone around to help monitor entries and track them."

I looked up at Destrian. He was biting his lip.

It was the first decision we were making where the three of us were not in agreement. But it would not be the last.

"It is agreed then," I said, my eyes going back to King Valon.

King Valon nodded. "We have a pact then. I will let Yew know of his new position when I return to my rooms."

"And the wards?" Fin asked, her brow raised.

King Valon smiled. "They are already in place."

My face fell. "What?"

King Valon leaned back, perfectly at ease. "I took advantage of last night's celebration to respark them with the members of my party. It is best to do it when there is high excitement and energy in the air. It helps feed and carry the magic."

"Trickster!" Destrian snapped from behind me. "Yet you forced us into a deal anyway?"

King Valon straightened, looking remarkably intimidating despite the fact that I could feel the heat from Destrian's magic behind me.

"Her Majesty said it herself; it is only fair for my people to claim a seat at your table," King Valon snarled.

"But why did you go to the trouble?" Fin frowned. "Knowing you could've used it for a favor?"

King Valon's fists clenched, his amber eyes glinting. "I am promised a bride, and this time, I will risk nothing."

Chapter 26

THE TEMPLE OF SOL stood radiant in the bright, late summer sun. Stained panels of glass, richly colored in golds, crimsons, and blues, depicted Sol's struggle against darkness. At the altar lay Lord Alexander, covered in a ceremonial shroud of white and gold. Behind him, on a raised dais, stood Solston Ignace, watching the people file in for the ceremony.

Though Lady Vianne was grieving, she remained composed. Her head high, cheeks dry, she stared at the altar, flanked by Lady Maureen on one side and Urdua on the other. The former held Lady Vianne's hand in support; the latter held her great sword with both hands, her eyes darting around the room as though Agramon were waiting in a corner to jump in and snatch Vianne.

Mellan, beside me, was standing much the same way. On my other side was Destrian, then Fin. Behind us stood the rest of the council and court, including Yew, the new fae councilman King Valon had left in our care. Another Woltari, his tall stature and grand horns made sure that nobody standing behind him could see a thing.

"Welcome to you all, standing in the light of Sol, here to honor Lord Alexander, a son of the noble Marendesly line," Solston Ignace began. "A man who dedicated his life to teaching the youth of Lyrica, and who showed great bravery and courage in rebuilding the kingdom of Morgania." Solston Ignace went on, extolling Lord Alexander's virtues to the somber audience.

Lady Vianne didn't really seem to be listening, her eyes downcast, her breathing even.

Marc Trinidan stepped up to the dais to speak about Lord Alexander as a teacher and friend. Destrian spoke of Lord Alexander as a mentor.

"Above all, he was a man who wished for peace between us. A wish that I share," Destrian finished before bowing to Lady Vianne. She momentarily roused herself from her stupor and nodded in acknowledgment.

With the words and blessings over, one by one, attendees approached the altar where Lord Alexander's body lay. Each laid a stone, branch, or flower. Lady Vianne did her best to acknowledge the gestures of sympathy, but by the end, she was utterly worn down.

Finally, Luc, Ferris, and a few other guardsmen stepped forward and lifted the wooden bier, carefully bearing Lord Alexander's body from the altar.

I, along with the rest of the assembly, watched in silence as the procession made its way out of the temple. Lady Vianne followed her husband's body, her arms now threaded through both Lady Maureen's and Urdua's, with Imorati

Kaelan walking as guard behind them.

The rest of us gathered back at the palace, in the great hall draped with black banners. I spoke with my cousin, Pria, for a bit, happy to hear that they'd secured a women's home.

"There is also equipment for a brewery," Pria was saying. She looked better than I'd ever remembered her looking in Espiria. There was color in her cheeks, and she'd begun wearing her black hair in intricate braids. I wondered if the change was due to her now lack of husband, or if it was because she'd already found another. "So once we can get that up and running, the women will have a trade as well, which might eventually earn us enough money to run the home."

I shot Pria my first genuine smile in years. "I'm pleased that you are happy and that it is going so well."

Pria mirrored my grin, her mood lighter, seemingly without the lingering weight of the past.

I spotted Fin standing with the new fae councilman, Yew, beside the refreshment table. She'd said she met him briefly in Horan when she'd gone to get her gem but hadn't known him well. I excused myself to Pria and joined them.

"Good afternoon, Yew Of-the-Castle," I said in greeting, just as Fin had taught me.

Yew and King Valon, though both bearing the horns and tails known for their kind, were quite different from each other in the best way. While King Valon was all seriousness and melancholy, Yew was prone to good-natured, sly humor and wit. Already I liked him.

"Your Majesty, I hope the day has found you well, despite the grim proceedings of the morning," Yew replied, bowing to me while raising his glass of wine. The fae drank our wine by the barrelful. It seemed they were accustomed to much stronger drink. It was good that only Yew remained of their party, or we'd get drunk out of Helena.

"How do you find your rooms here at the castle?" I asked.

Yew let out a long breath. "I find them to be blissful, if I'm allowed to be perfectly candid. The palace of Alden-Ester is quite crowded, and all of us share space frequently. The solitude is a new and welcome change."

"I am glad that you are enjoying yourself so far," I replied. "When those in the procession return, I would like to introduce you to Urdua, our Minister of Law. You will need to work closely with her to enact any new fae laws that you're concerned about."

Yew bowed his head. "I am at Their Majesties' disposal."

Conversation was interrupted by the sharp twittering of a bird that had found its way into the hall. Small and frantic, the little creature flew in a circle above our heads, trilling a warning, before darting out of an open window.

Fin gripped my arm. "Something's wrong."

Mellan was at my side in a moment, one hand on my arm, his sword in the other. Destrian joined us, his own sword unsheathed as we faced the door.

Imorati Kaelan burst through, carrying an unconscious Vianne in his blessing-marked arms.

Destrian stepped forward. "The formal meeting room is close. Let's go there."

"What happened?" Fin asked as we all hurried after Destrian.

"Her bracelet," Kaelan gasped, trying to catch his breath. "It blazed scarlet, as though on fire, and then she screamed before I caught her."

I looked down. The bracelet now appeared unmarked. I looked closer. The same bracelet that Empress Lesedi used to give to her closest friends and confidants at the capital. The bracelet that marked a woman as loyal.

"Get smelling salts," Fin told a servant we passed. The girl nodded and ran off as we filed into the meeting room where the candles blazed before calming into a flickering glow.

The serving girl stepped in soon after, a vial in her hand. Fin gave her a smile as thanks and waved the open vial in front of Vianne's nose. It wrinkled, and she coughed, then sneezed, before trying to sit up.

"Here," Kaelan said, propping her up with his arm.

When Lady Vianne's eyes focused on me, she leaned forward, bruising my arm in her grip. "Empress Lesedi, she's dead."

I froze, the world lost to me as I attempted to understand her words. Empress Lesedi gone? It couldn't be. She was safe in Maryse, with the Marendeslys.

My heart stuttered. Omri. The little prince, hidden in the wilderness of the swamp. I'd promised him he would see his mother again someday.

"How do you know this?" My hands began to shake.

Lady Vianne's fingers went to her wrist. "The bracelets were how she communicated with us. You need to use your blood to send messages. The last one she sent was just a loud, brief, dying cry. She's gone, Rowyn. I can't feel her connection at all anymore."

"Is that Ember Innes magic?" I asked, nodding to the stones woven through the fine metal strands. I remembered the rumors from the capital. Some had accused Empress Lesedi of witchcraft. I wondered why I had never earned a bracelet myself. After all, it was me who she entrusted the prince's care to. It probably had everything to do with Agramon.

Lady Vianne nodded.

I straightened. "Call the council together."

Destrian nodded, then left. After accompanying Imorati Kaelan to Lady Vianne's rooms and ensuring that she was safe in bed with the Imorati standing guard at her door, I hurried to the council room where people were just beginning to process the news.

"That's just like Agramon to go after the women," Fin snarled upon my entrance.

Marc and Destrian exchanged a loaded glance across the table.

"It might not have been Agramon," Marc said carefully.

Destrian nodded in agreement as I took my seat between him and Fin. I was glad the others had also returned from the funeral. Urdua and Maureen had gone to see to Vianne. It was just as well. My only thought was a roar for vengeance and blood.

"Duke Eldred of Marendesly has ambitions of his own. He'd want the throne and wouldn't appreciate the competition," Marc finished.

My heart began to race. "You're saying he could have killed Lesedi to clear his path to the throne?" To believe such treachery was unconscionable. Yet, I hated how little I'd be surprised if Marc was right. But if there was no Empress Lesedi, then I wasn't really interested in having anything more to do with Lyrica.

Destrian placed his hand on mine. "It's a possibility we can't ignore."

"What about the princesses?" I asked.

"The last report I received had the princesses in Ardent,

with Count Ariz and Countess Mahira," Fin said.

I let out a relieved breath. Of course, Empress Lesedi would've seen to their safety. She would've never trusted the Marendeslys with her children, which was why she sent Artian with me in the first place. Countess Mahira was her cousin and would honor blood.

"There is no reason to kill them. They are not a threat and can be used for marriage pacts later," Marc explained.

"For who?" I asked, raising a brow. "Duke Agramon or Duke Eldred?"

Marc met my gaze. "Either."

I had to stop myself from throwing a dagger at him. Of course, Empress Lesedi had been dangerous because she was full of ambition and ideas. Her daughters, malleable and powerless young girls, could be used as pawns in their games. I pulled my hand from Destrian, hating them all in that moment.

Whether it was Agramon's ruthless ambition or Duke Eldred's sadism, Lesedi's life had been lost. And each life lost brought us one step closer to a reality I didn't want to face.

I closed my eyes for a moment to collect myself. "I want to stand down from supporting the Marendesly claim to the Lyrican throne," I announced. "Let Agramon and El-dred rip each other apart."

Destrian tensed. "I do not feel we should act rashly.

The Marendesly claimants have a large number of sorcerers at their disposal, as well as a navy presence. We cannot so foolishly give up on a potential ally."

"And if he had her killed?" I snapped.

Destrian refused to look at me.

"I agree with His Majesty," Fin announced to the room. "We should not give up a potential chance at strength so quickly."

I stopped myself from snarling at both of them. It wouldn't do, not with most of the council staring at us, waiting for my grand experiment to fail. I took one slow breath, then two. Swallowing, I said, "Very well, we will maintain that we are open to an alliance with the Marendeslys, however, I do not wish to chance another death by sending one of our own. They have better means to travel to us for an audience, if they wish to make a deal."

"I can agree to that," Fin said softly.

Destrian nodded. "Me too."

I glared around the room, daring someone to argue. It was Luc who finally broke the heavy silence. "What should we do now?"

"We need to consider the implications of the empress's death on our strategies." Destrian scanned the room. "Our defenses should also be reevaluated."

"There is no one scrying through the fae ward," Yew offered.

Destrian turned to glare at him. Yew grinned back, his face innocent. "I helped respark it myself, so I can tell when the Solston of the East makes an attempt. He's now rendered quite blind." Yew winked at me. I supposed I was but one of a few who were in on his little joke. The Solston he spoke of, Solston Navar, was already quite blind to begin with, and could only see through magical sight.

"Yet Agramon's power grows by the day," I countered. My steady voice masked the turmoil within. I was afraid. Oh, how I was afraid. But never for myself. "We can't afford to be caught off guard. I won't allow Morgania to fall prey to the whims of Lyrica's out-of-control nobility."

My voice grew louder when I saw Luc nudge Ferris with a smirk. The look he shot him was one I knew well. The fevered excitement before battle. Even Marc was nodding as I went on. "Duke Agramon, Baron Samael, Duke Eldred, let them kill each other over scraps of a crumbling empire. We need to know the moment one has decided to strike us, and we must be prepared to crush them. We must show the world that Morgania will no longer yield to the whims of men a sea away."

I noticed a bird perched on the windowsill. It chirped hesitantly before hopping forward and fluttering to Fin's shoulder. She leaned down and listened, the entire council watching her.

She ran her finger over the feathers on the bird's head

before it flapped up, rising above our heads, and darting out of the window.

"The Baron of Bruin has set sail with the navy of Gryse," Fin declared. She looked at Destrian. "They are bound for Eslin."

"Then we will meet them," I declared. "For there is no better way to honor the dead than to avenge them." Empress Lesedi, Lord Alexander, Ena. I would get vengeance for all of them.

Destrian slammed his fist on the table. "Agreed."

"Agreed," echoed Fin, taking my hand in hers.

Luc and Ferris began thumping the table with their fists, their voices rising in a Morganite war chant. We were going to war.

Chapter 27

WHEN WE ARRIVED in Eslin, I couldn't help but admire the banners that flew over us. A favor from a fae who wanted nothing more than passage into Morgania. The outline of the flag was black, and within were three partitions. One purple, stitched with black roses and a silver star, another blue, with a black dragon and a golden star, and another with a green background and a bronze falcon. The fae woman responsible had set up shop in Helena and was bringing in excellent business, especially with the new influx of nobles eager to part with their coin.

Glancing back, I saw a blend of determination and apprehension lining the troops' faces. Fin was riding on Luc's shoulder as Arden, her sharp eyes scanning the landscape ahead. Luc's wolf, Graywind, was trotting beside his horse, his nose perked up, sniffing the air around us.

We finally reached Eslin's gates, and as we entered, we were greeted by Consul Kendrew. Destrian didn't waste any time.

"Consul Kendrew, you're now Duke Kendrew. I'm going to add the northern coast to your duties. If you want a ceremony, we can arrange it, but we're short on time."

Kendrew's eyes flickered to me, a momentary assessment or perhaps a weighing of this sudden proclamation. Then his gaze shifted as Fin rode up to join us, her hair flying freely in the wind.

"It's an honor that all three of you came to our aid," he finally said.

I met his eyes squarely. "It shouldn't be a surprise. Morgania will protect its dream, and we expect all who follow to do the same."

Duke Kendrew nodded. "Very well then."

He bowed, the weight of the moment not lost on him. "Welcome to Eslin, Your Majesties."

As if on cue, the entire court of Eslin bent the knee. I noticed Onora and little Galvin among them, the boy's face showing a mixture of awe and apprehension. Onora's belly had gotten bigger during our absence. I hoped she was well. The stress of a siege on her city couldn't be helping her pregnancy.

As soon as the formalities were over, we made our way to Eslin's council chambers. Maps were laid out on a large table, and Duke Kendrew took the lead, motioning to the ships who were crossing the Ballerian to the West.

"It's lucky you all came when you did. The fleet will be here soon, and I have a feeling that Ayastaren will attack with them."

Fin nodded as she picked up a colored stone and set it

near one of the ships. "Sam is on the largest vessel, and I've seen Elgar the Swift too. The ships have been outfitted with some type of weaponry that I've not seen before."

Kendrew nodded, his finger tracing the southern regions on the map. "Ayastaren has been busy pillaging our southern borders, but the recent rains have slowed them down."

I was glad Marc had made it across the border safely, courtesy of another fae favor—one who could league leap short distances. He'd been sent to try to drum up support from the south. The chessboard was set, the pieces in place. It was time to play.

For a moment, I wished Pedr was with us. He was always so much better at chess than me.

My eyes returned to the map, tracing the lines and markers. "I can try to stop the navy, with Destrian's help," I said, focusing on the immediate threats. "Fin, keep an eye on the battle and watch for any new threats. I'd be surprised if Elgar is the only sorcerer accompanying Sam."

Mellan was nodding. "The commander is used to using sorcerers in battle. I wouldn't doubt that there is a blaster or two on one or more of those ships."

"The outfittings are different from anything I've seen," Fin agreed. "I heard the name Del when I was spying too. I think she is the one who made the war machines."

I sighed. "Then we should be ready for anything." I

looked up at Luc. "Keep the men's morale high. An entire battle can hinge on hope.

"Work with Duke Kendrew and our new reinforcements to bolster the city's defenses," I added, locking eyes with the duke. "There's no telling when the Ayastaren force will decide to move, but we must be ready for anything."

As others filed out of the room to begin preparations for the looming battle, I felt a quiet sense of gratitude for the capable hands back in Helena. Sir Bernard was directing the others, with the help of Lady Vianne, Urdua, and Lady Maureen. Everyone had their role to play, and I trusted them to keep things in order. My eyes met Destrian's, and I thought about how much I owed him for helping me build such a strong support system early on.

I took his hand. The familiar squeeze reminded me I wasn't alone. His eyes flicked to Iranoct, the sword he'd crafted for me, now a permanent fixture on my waist.

"I don't want you to have to use that, Rowyn. Stay back and use your magic."

"We'll see," I replied noncommittedly.

"I'll be at your side, Rowyn, fear not," Mellan said, puffing out his chest.

Destrian shot him a glare, but Mellan just shrugged. "I know I'm responsible for all three of you now, but Rowyn will always be my favorite. After all, I've seen her breasts."

"If you stick around long enough, you'll get to see Fin's too," I retorted.

Luc shot me a venomous glare, even as Fin burst out laughing. Mellan's eyes twinkled suggestively.

When we arrived at the room the monarchs would share, Fin casually stripped off her dress and tossed her belt of knives onto a table before approaching the window. With fluid grace, she transformed into Arden and took to the skies, her feathers catching the last of the daylight as she vanished from sight.

Destrian began laying out weapons, rations, and a myriad of other essentials for the forthcoming battle. I followed suit, unburdening my own pack.

The room was silent for a moment before Destrian broke it. "About marriage," he started cautiously, looking me in the eyes. "Things are different now. Do you want to reconsider?"

I shrugged. I'd wondered about it during the time we were preparing to leave Helena, but every time it crossed my mind, I'd begin to talk myself out of it. What would it mean for Fin's part of the triarchy? Our work together felt more equal because we were not married. "Who says we need a formal wedding to be together or to have a family, should we choose to? We're the monarchs now. We can make the rules."

"As long as you know that I love you," Destrian said,

his eyes locking onto mine with an intensity that made me pause.

I smiled, a warm feeling spreading through me. "I love you too."

His expression turned serious, almost grave. "I know you're worried about the baron and Agramon."

He paused for a moment, as if weighing his next words carefully. "Fin and I have already talked about it. If they manage to take you, we will come after you."

"As long as you make sure that the kingdom won't crumble. That it will live on, even without me."

"I promise," Destrian said firmly, crossing his arms. "Morgania will always be the priority."

In a world that was crashing down around us, in a time when everything was uncertain, it was a pledge that steadied me, even if just a little.

"I should give our thanks to Onora," I said, breaking the silence. But when I turned to leave, Destrian pulled me back.

"Rowyn, wait."

His hands cupped my face, thumbs lightly brushing my cheeks. Then, his lips met mine.

"Morgania won't fall," he whispered against my lips. "The gods are in our favor."

"I don't care about the gods," I murmured back. "I care about you, Fin, and everyone else who's fighting for this dream we're building."

Chapter 28

IT TOOK TWO DAYS for the Grysian Navy to reach Eslin. Two days of tense preparation and hasty plans. Finally, we stood on the highest tower of Eslin, staring out at the sea that stretched to the East. The breeze played with my hair and filled the air with the salty scent of the ocean. For a moment, I was reminded of Solridge, of simpler times, and a pang of nostalgia hit me.

But the moment was short-lived. On the horizon, dark shapes materialized, a fleet of ships closing the distance, carrying with them the impending storm of battle. We stood dressed for war in each of our own ways. I wore a light-purple tunic with black breeches, my weapons carefully strapped to various parts of my body. The crown Destrian had made for me was braided into my hair so the added gems could boost my powers. Destrian, Mellan, and Luc had donned armor, and Fin a robe. Graywind was sitting patiently beside Luc, watching us all shift nervously as we waited for the Grysian ships to crawl closer.

I locked eyes with Fin. "Are you ready?"

She nodded. "As ready as I'll ever be."

"If anything happens, if you find yourself in trouble, you get behind Destrian's ward. He's set it up to protect this part of the tower. And watch for lightning."

Fin nodded again, then took a deep breath. She sprinted toward the edge of the tower. Her robe slipped off her shoulders and fluttered to the ground behind her. She leaped, naked, over the railing, vanishing from sight for a split second before reappearing as the shadow falcon. Her wings unfolded gracefully, and she soared high, carried by the wind.

Luc pulled down his visor, then gripped Destrian's and Mellan's hands. Without another word, he marched toward the stairs to join the army on the beaches below, Graywind at his heels.

Returning my gaze to the approaching fleet, I felt a growing sense of urgency. "Echo, are you ready?" I whispered, almost to myself.

"*Yes*," came her soft reply.

Closing my eyes, I tuned in to Echo's senses, suddenly feeling the rush of air. We'd found that when I wore my crown, the added gems allowed her to move farther from me. My heart raced as she glided effortlessly over the castle and across the water, closing the distance between us and the enemy's fleet.

Finally, she found it—the ship where Sam stood, peering through a spyglass aimed directly at the towers of Eslin. My heart sank a little as I, through Echo, floated in front of him.

"She's there," Sam said gruffly to someone beside him. Echo veered to the side, trying to identify to whom Sam was speaking. That's when Pythia Golden-Eyes stepped into view, her burning gaze locked onto the spot where Echo floated.

A sudden, searing pain coursed through my senses, as if a hot iron was thrust into my mind. I gasped, stumbling back.

"Echo?" I asked, my eyes flying open. I looked around myself, then closed my eyes again, trying to find her mind. "Echo!" I screamed.

She was gone—extinguished like a candle in a gale.

Tears spilled from my eyes. Destrian was quick to grasp my arm, steadying me, while Mellan handed me a goblet of water.

"Pythia is there," I managed to say through trembling in my voice. Echo had always been afraid of her. At the capital, I never had visions of Pythia and Agramon, though I'd known her and Elgar to be close. As a necromancer, she had the ability to raise the dead and see their spirits. She must've also had the ability to send them to true death too.

Echo had been with me through everything in Somme. When I had no one else, I always had Echo. She'd witnessed every triumph. Mourned every mistake. She had been my family through it all.

And now she was gone.

Emotion choked me. I wiped my eyes, wondering why fate had been so kind to some and so cruel to others. Echo had wanted to die. She'd told me as much when I worried about Pythia before. She'd seen too much of life and lived too little of it. I supposed I would never know the reasons of the gods, but I hoped that she found peace with her husband and child, long dead centuries past.

"Elgar must've brought her," Destrian was saying, his voice lined with burgeoning dread.

Drawing myself up, I whispered a silent prayer to Imor, asking for Echo's soul to find peace among the stars. My aunt from ages past had been with me through so much; she deserved an eternity away from strife and pain.

But as my eyes returned to the direction of Sam's ship, an overwhelming swell of anger washed over me. There would be a reckoning.

The opal gems embedded in the back of my hands and forehead warmed. I'd stopped the rain over Ayastaren days before to save magic, and now it surged inside me like the restless sea.

Destrian was beside me, peering through a spyglass in the same manner as Sam. "One of the ships is warded," he said.

"Do you think it's Owain?"

"It's hard to be sure," Destrian replied, still studying the fleet through the spyglass. "I would think Agramon would want him at his side."

"He's got so many protections already though," I said, leaning onto the balustrade.

"That's true." Destrian set down the spyglass and stared out at the sea. As he did, a glint of sunlight caught my eye. The war machines on the ships had moved, and I felt a sudden wave of alarm.

"Get down!" Destrian shouted almost simultaneously. Mellan and I didn't hesitate and threw ourselves onto the stone floor of the tower.

With a resounding crack, the first missile hit, a fireball bursting into the sky. The ward Destrian had set up shimmered as it intercepted a blast that came too close. A wave of heat and light filled the air, and my ears rang with the aftershock.

"Del is on one of the ships," Destrian said.

A pang of misgiving shot through me, but I pushed it aside. I'd never particularly cared for Del, though I couldn't put a finger on why. There was nothing really wrong with the girl, but now was not the time for sentiments.

The sound of more missiles filled the air, cutting short any further reflections. The marble towers of Eslin shook as several hit, plumes of smoke rising into the sky. I felt the tremors beneath me.

"Rowyn!" Destrian shouted. "We need to take out those ships!"

I stood. The magic inside me roiled like a storm, waiting to be unleashed. I nodded to Destrian.

It was time.

The wind whipped wildly like a living thing. I remembered the Nightlands, the dragon I'd bested there, and the funnel of wind I'd conjured to do it. I brought that memory to the forefront of my mind, channeling it into the magic I was weaving. A smile touched my lips as I felt the winds shift, aligning with my will. Two funnels began to dance over the waters below us.

With a fixed glare, I directed the twin funnels across the choppy waves of the Ballerian Sea. Mellan cursed softly behind me and took a step back, but I hardly noticed. My focus was on the ships.

As if summoned by the wrath of the gods, bolts of lightning began to crash into the sea. With a flick of my wrist, I directed them toward the Grysian Navy, and each bolt found its mark with deadly accuracy. One of the ships took a direct hit and erupted in flames, the fire spreading quickly over its sails and deck.

A memory surfaced unbidden—watching a symphony at Agramon's court in Solin, the conductor weaving a tapestry of sound and emotion. Only now, I was the conductor, and my orchestra played a symphony of destruction.

Sam's ship was warded, immune to my magical assault. But oh, how I wished I could see his face in this moment, to see his reaction to the true scope of my abilities. I'd been holding back when I was in the capital, but no more. They were coming for everything I loved, and I'd be damned if I let them take it away from me.

The twin funnels of wind danced like vengeful spirits, tearing through ship after ship. A missile was loosed from a vessel, but the funnel swept it up and sent it crashing onto another. Bolts of lightning followed my every command, striking down more of the fleet. One by one, they started to sink, dragged into the depths of the Ballerian Sea. Rain fell lightly around us, but it did nothing to dampen the rage within.

All my ire was directed at the ship with the ward. I could feel it there, a wall against my power, but it was weakening, cracking under the pressure of my onslaught. With gritted teeth, I channeled more energy, more fury, more of everything I had into breaking that ward.

Then it happened—the ward buckled, shattering like glass under a hammer. The wind did the rest and ripped the ship to splinters and shreds. I let out a breath and felt my magic start to wane, like a flame flickering at the end of its wick.

And then, suddenly, Fin was at my side.

Fin's eyes were wide, her gaze frantic. "Pythia and Sam

weren't on that ship, Rowyn. We have a big problem on the beach. Pythia's raised the drowned sailors."

I nodded sharply. "Meet us there."

Turning to Destrian and Mellan, I clasped their hands. "Ready to fly?"

A powerful wind swept us off the tower toward the beach below. The sight that greeted us was chilling—undead sailors were marching out of the water, a grotesque parade of the damned. Some had mangled feet; others were wrapped in tendrils of seaweed, their eyes vacant and mouths agape.

Just as we touched down, Fin landed next to us, transforming back into her human form, her nudity momentarily ignored in the face of the crisis. She raised her hands, and her gem glowed a soft blue.

"What are you doing?" I asked, stumbling forward. Destrian grabbed my arm and held me back.

"Let her handle this," he said, nodding at Fin.

The sea began to froth. I unsheathed my sword, my instincts screaming at me to run at the dead men and take them down once and for all. My eyes locked on one undead soldier dragging his body through the water toward the shore. Suddenly, he went under the water, and though I waited for him to resurface, he did not. Then the man next to him flailed as he disappeared beneath the waves. Within seconds, the undead were being pulled back beneath the surf, the water boiling into a violent, bloody frenzy.

My eyes widened as the sea turned red with blood. "What . . ." I asked, then covered my mouth as it filled with bile at the sight of limbs bobbing in the water. Shark fins cut through the sea, yanking pieces off the men who still doggedly tried to break toward shore.

Destrian moved forward, his palm lighting up with the ember of a fireball. He launched it, and it exploded among the undead who'd cleared the beach.

Just then, Luc's army descended on the soldiers, their weapons flashing in the sunlight as they engaged the reanimated sailors, lopping off heads and arms as the undead fumbled to reach the Morganian cavalry.

I raised my sword, ready to join the fray, but Fin caught my arm. "Stay with me," she urged. "The battle is won; there's no need to put ourselves in harm's way."

I looked around and realized she was right. The sea was littered with the debris of shattered ships, and the sky echoed with the screams of dying men. We had decimated their fleet and shattered their ranks within minutes. I was breathing hard, my chest heaving with the intensity of it all.

"We need to kill Pythia," I said, locking eyes with Fin.

She grinned fiercely. "Oh, I wholeheartedly agree. I'll get on that."

"Wait—" But before I could finish, Arden took to the

skies.

I cursed under my breath and turned to Mellan. "You should've stopped her."

Mellan raised an eyebrow. "Fin is a queen, Rowyn. She can think for herself."

I sighed, realizing the truth in his words even as I worried about what lay ahead.

Destrian returned with horses, and we mounted quickly, then rode through the wreckage of the battle. The rain still dripped from the sky. My reserves of magic felt drained, leaving me more vulnerable than I would've liked.

Luc galloped toward us, the wear and tear of battle evident in his armor and the set of his jaw. "The Ayastaren Army launched a brief assault before retreating to their towers," he reported.

Destrian's eyes met mine, a silent thought passing between us.

"What now?" I asked.

Destrian hesitated, then squared his shoulders. "We march on Ayastaren. We end this once and for all."

I looked at Fin, and I knew we were in agreement. "We're with you," we said almost in unison.

Mellan grinned. "I can help with that."

After a grueling day of battle, soaked through and muddied from the beach, I found myself craving the simple comforts of a hot bath and dry clothes. The tide of war had started to turn, if only slightly, in our favor, but the nervous tension from earlier still hummed under my skin. We'd come through the first clash of swords relatively un-scathed—fewer casualties on our side than I'd dared to hope for—but the knot in my stomach refused to com-pletely untangle.

Fin had returned from her scouting mission with unset-tling but useful news. Pythia and Sam were alive and in Ayastaren. They'd managed to avoid my wind funnels and Fin's sharks. It was a relief to know where they were, but it also meant the threat wasn't gone; it had merely retreated to fight another day.

On a more hopeful note, most of the Gryse men who survived were conscripts. I wanted to believe they had no real loyalty to Sam and Pythia, and would rather not fight for a lost cause. For now, they remained in chains under Duke Kendrew's care.

Fin breezed into the room where Destrian and I were sprawled, exhausted, on a couch before the fire. Mellan had left to take a break after our baths, while Destrian, even with his depleted magic, had managed to conjure a simple ward for a sense of added security.

"I thought we did quite well today, for our first show-ing," Fin said, grabbing a roll from the plate on the table and plopping on a chair to warm herself by the fire. "Luc said it would be beneficial to have more support for the soldiers on the ground. The Ayastaren troops and merce-naries only fled when they saw Rowyn's magic. They won't be surprised by it next time."

"You're saying we should split up," I said, unwinding myself from Destrian's arms and sitting up.

Destrian glowered at Fin as he swung his feet over the side of the couch and punched a pillow into his side. "I don't like that idea at all."

Fin met my eyes before turning back to Destrian. "We will be stronger if we are apart. We need to take out the other sorcerers and won't be able to do that from the other side of the battlefield."

Destrian's glower deepened. "What are you suggest-ing?"

Fin used her tongue to clean her lips of frosting. "I think that once the Morganian Army is in place, Rowyn and I can use the cover of clouds and darkness to get to Ayastaren castle and take out as many key people as we can. Pythia, Elgar, and anyone else who has the potential to get in our way."

Destrian leaned onto his knees. "Absolutely not. You're practically delivering Rowyn to them if you do that."

"Well, I wouldn't do much good trying to take them out all by myself," Fin snapped. "We shouldn't be so foolhardy with the lives of those in our army. We have to take their sorcerers out to spare men. Why should they fight for us if we don't do our best to protect them?"

"Then I'll go with you," Destrian offered. "Rowyn's magic would be better served behind our lines anyway."

"You can't fly!" Fin scoffed. "And I can't get you over the lines. It has to be Rowyn and me."

Destrian shook his head. "No, there has to be another way."

"You don't get final say," Fin said, taking another bite as her eyes shot to me. "What do you think, Rowyn?"

I was glad I was no longer in Destrian's arms with the way smoke began rising from his hair. "Fin's right. If we go at night, chances are they won't be able to see us. I can hide on the roof while Fin locates targets for me to take out. At the very least, I could disable any war machines they have."

"Could you at least take Mellan with you?" Destrian asked, seeing his battle was lost. "I won't be able to ward you from so far."

I shook my head. "Mellan would be best guarding you and helping choose targets. It takes more magic than I want to use taking someone else with me when I fly. Fin will be enough. She's watched my back plenty before and done a wonderful job of it."

"This is the worst idea," Destrian groaned, rubbing his hands over his face.

I rubbed his back. "There are three of us. We have to

know when to embrace the times when our separation will give us more power. You and Luc can handle the soldiers while Fin and I take out their magic. We have to make sure Pythia can't turn the tides of battle."

"I know," Destrian admitted. "I know we have to do it; I just hate the possibility of something happening to you."

Fin rose, brushing crumbs from her robe. "I'm spending the night in Luc's room to work through some post-battle jitters. So unless there is something more we need to discuss before tomorrow, I will let you two enjoy your night."

I couldn't help but snort a laugh. "Go easy on him."

Destrian shook his head as Fin slipped out of the room.

"I know you're capable," Destrian murmured, looking wearily over to me. "I'm just afraid."

"We all are," I whispered back, my arms around his shoulders as I climbed into his lap. "But we cannot let it rule us."

Destrian gripped my waist and kissed me smartly on the lips. "I also have some post-battle jitters to work off," he said, his voice low and warm.

I laughed, grateful for the change of mood. "Well, I can think a few ways to unwind."

Chapter 29

I SAT ON THE banks of the river that served as a boundary between Eslin and Ayastaren. Across the water, the marble towers of Ayastaren Castle rose into the sky, touched by the last light of the setting sun.

I thought back to my first and only other visit. How Duke Roland Lyon had greeted me with false courtesies, his eyes calculating even as he offered wine and bread. All seven of the Lyon brothers had been alive then, and present at the table of their father, save Mellan the Hero. Though later I would be blamed for both the Lyons' deaths, I was only truly responsible for one of them. I held no regrets over slaying Teilo Lyon at the Battle of Espiria and took full credit of the kill. But Elias's death was his own fault.

No, I didn't see a future where I would live the rest of my life with Duke Roland as a neighbor. I just wished I hadn't made it quite so easy for my enemies to join each other in the vendetta of taking me down. But I'd proven, time and again, I could take a Lyon. The battle at Eslin had gone *so* well, and *so* smoothly, that I felt more than confident to take Ayastaren. I was going to conquer it and bring it in as part of Morgania, settling the border feud once and for all. Marc Trinidan could have the duchy for all I cared. If his father and Korballis joined Morgania's fold along with Ayastaren, then he could control the entire southern border of Morgania. The ideal job for Marc, who already agreed to serve as ambassador to the consulships and provinces of southern Adair and The Fens.

I hated to admit that Destrian was right, and Marc actually was intuitive about a great many things that I was not, which I found out on frequent occasions during council meetings. Though I wouldn't characterize our relationship as warm—it was tepid on the best of days—I did respect his knowledge, even if that understanding came from being pampered with endless wealth and knowledge at his fingertips in the type of comfort that the rank of nobility afforded him.

Needless to say, Marc was extremely pleased when I appointed Destrian as king alongside Fin and me, which was almost enough for me to rescind the offer altogether. The one good thing about it was that Destrian could meet with Marc on his own, leaving me to all other more preferable tasks.

I heard footsteps approach behind me and turned, finding Mellan Lyon, his eyes on the distant towers of his childhood home. His usually easygoing expression had hardened into a frown. I didn't have to be a mind reader to know what he was contemplating. Aureliana, the woman he loved.

At the capital Mellan and I had put on an act of being interested in each other, to keep up appearances. It had been easy enough to pull off, considering we were both from the West, and relatively young, good-looking, and of unequal social standing. We were a perfect excuse for gossip with the old romantics at court. Some swooned over the love story of handsome Mellan Lyon, the fool in love with the woman who killed his brothers and whom his father vowed to hate. How tragic!

Nothing, of course, compared to reality. Perhaps I might've felt something for Mellan if I saw any chance at all of my feelings being reciprocated, but from the very beginning, Mellan's heart had already been given to another, and there was nothing I nor his father could do about it. Aureliana held Mellan's affection from the very moment he'd first laid eyes on her at Solridge. Though he'd had casual dalliances at court, I counted myself lucky as his friend instead of someone who met him for a brief night of pleasure and forgetting.

"How does it feel to be home?" I ventured to ask, though I suspected I already knew the answer. It was no secret how Mellan felt about his family.

Mellan's grip tightened on his sword hilt; his knuckles were white. "Home," he scoffed softly. "More like a prison than a sanctuary."

"I haven't forgotten your wish. If I see your father, I will leave him to you." As much anger as I harbored for the Duke of Ayastaren, it didn't hold a candle to the fury felt by his son.

Mellan's eyes were a shade darker than I'd ever seen them. "I always knew it would come to this," he said, more to himself than to me. "Ashes and smoke, mud and dust."

AFTER DINNER, many of us huddled together, plotting over the favors from the fae we'd been accumulating. Fin had been keeping track of the offers using a magical parchment that she used to communicate with the gatekeepers.

"What did you tell them?" I asked, already guessing her answer.

"I told them no," she said, shaking her head. "Even if they could help us now, they'd be a problem later."

Destrian and I nodded in agreement. We didn't need a future filled with blood-sucking complications, which is what would happen if we let any vampiric fae through the border.

Afterward, Fin and I readied ourselves to go after the sorcerers, while Destrian, Mellan, and Luc prepared to take on Sam and the forces surrounding Ayastaren.

As the threat of dawn approached, Destrian's arms enveloped me in a surge of warmth around my body. "I worry I won't see you again," he murmured into my hair. "Your path is far more dangerous than my own when dawn breaks."

"Not if we don't take Pythia out," I replied, rubbing my face into his chest.

Destrian pulled back, his dark eyes searching mine. "Please promise me that you won't take any unnecessary risks behind the lines."

"I won't take any risks *I* deem unnecessary," I assured him. "But if there is something I can do to make the battle shorter, and secure us the winners, I will absolutely do it."

Destrian cupped my cheeks with his hands, stroking my skin with his fingers. "But if you see the Butcher or Elgar, I want you to run."

"If I feel I need to, then yes, I will," I promised.

Under the cover of darkness, Fin and I soared, our eyes peeled for the dark shapes of Ayastaren's castle towers peeking through the shroud of low clouds. The murky sky shielded our approach behind Ayastaren's lines of soldiers who had begun preparations to attack the lines of Morgania's soldiers just across the river.

Finally, we found a spot Mellan suggested and landed softly on the castle roof. "Stay here," Fin whispered. "I'll go find as many targets as I can." With a slight rustle of feathers, she disappeared into the shadows.

I moved further into the shadows, watching the sun break over the horizon, the sky burning a deep red, heralding a bloody day ahead.

The rumblings of battle preparations echoed below. I watched Sam's troops and their war machines stationed by the river. Men scurried around catapults and scorpions, unaware of the storm I was about to unleash.

Nothing was warded. Fin had figured the warder had been killed at Eslin, and the only sorcerers she'd seen on surveillance were Elgar, Pythia, and Del. I raised my arms, the air crackling with tension. I could feel my magic connecting with the swirling mass of clouds above me, each one a floating cauldron of potential energy. Then, I released it. Lightning spears rained down like vengeful gods, their white-hot arcs lancing through the dark morning, illuminating men and machines alike as they shattered wood and melted iron.

Panicked screams were cut off by the booming thunder that shook the castle walls. Men dove for cover, abandoning their posts. All I could do now was wait for Fin and hope she would find Pythia soon.

I focused, my eyes narrowing as I scanned the enemy lines for signs of magic at work. My gaze zeroed in on a familiar figure standing on one of the ramparts. It was Del, her curls whipping behind her. Spectacles hid her eyes, though her skin looked pale beneath her dark freckles. Her gem was aglow, clearly holding some sway over the war machines that Sam had brought from the East.

Once, Del had tried to befriend me. She was kind, in her way, and had never shown me any malice. But now, she was working on Agramon's side. There was no room for hesitation.

The largest catapult's barrel aimed toward the river, where our Morganian forces were stationed. My heart tightened; I couldn't let that missile fire.

Channeling the pent-up magic in me, I raised my hand, fingers splayed. A bolt of lightning surged forth, crackling through the air and hurtling toward Del. When it struck her, she looked up. Her gem shattered into fragments, and her body convulsed as the electricity coursed through her. She let out a choked scream that I felt more than heard, then she collapsed onto the deck, smoke rising from her charred form.

A sudden emptiness filled the air where her magic had been. The catapult she had been controlling wavered, its aim thrown off. I felt a sharp, short-lived pang of guilt. She was young, like me, and we might have been friends under different circumstances. But she had chosen her side, just as I had chosen mine. In war, sentiments like these were luxuries I couldn't afford.

I shrugged it off. It was one fewer sorcerer to deal with.

Horns sounded, and the clash of swords and shouts of men filled the air as the soldiers on the ground began their assault. A ball of fire soared through the air, taking out a line of cavalry. Another blasted two scorpions that had survived my attack.

I refocused on the battlefield from my vantage point atop the tower, looking for more enemy sorcerers to eliminate, other pieces to remove from this deadly chessboard.

Fin reappeared, her eyes alight with urgency. "Follow me," she whispered. "Pythia's down there, near the line."

I called a wind and took to the air, following Fin as she darted through the sky. Below, soldiers caught sight of us, but there was little I could do about that now. All that mattered was stopping Pythia from robbing the Lord of Death.

As Arden swooped low, her wings practically grazing the tops of soldiers' heads, Pythia looked up. Her eyes narrowed on me. I descended, pulling the electric charge from the air once more. I unleashed a bolt of lightning over Pythia's head. I felt her own ward waver, almost cracking under the pressure. She must've had some gem or other talisman keeping her safe. But I'd learned that if you applied enough magic, enough pressure, you could break anything.

Another bolt exploded above her as the living soldiers

around her ducked and ran. Luckily, Pythia held no sway over the living.

Fin landed gracefully, her talons morphing into claws. Her gray feathers shifted into sleek black fur. With a ferocious snarl, the shadow panther darted toward Pythia, scattering more soldiers who had been close to the sorceress.

Seizing the moment, I sent another bolt at Pythia. This time, her ward shattered. Pythia convulsed violently before she steadied herself.

"The seer was right about you," she rasped, her voice tinged with malice. "The god of evil crafted you to break the world."

A dead soldier careened toward me, his sword raised despite the ax buried in his shoulder. I unsheathed Iranoct and blocked the dead man's swing before beheading him. His body lay still at my feet as another took his place.

Fin lunged onto Pythia's back. Her shadowy jaws clamped down on the sorceress's neck, snapping it with a dreadful finality. The dead man in front of me fell, along with others who'd risen around us.

I allowed myself a brief moment of relief before taking to the air again, my sword in hand. Arrows flew in my direction, but a quick gust of wind sent them veering off course. I couldn't afford to let my guard down—not now, not when so much was still at stake.

Fin had returned to the sky when a ball of fire sang

through the air above us. I looked up, following its path as it careened toward the lines of barrels that had been set up behind the war machines, now rendered useless. Several of the barrels had spilled, revealing black powder.

"Fin!" I screamed, reaching toward her winged figure. The ball of fire landed, and a wave of heat washed over me. Explosions erupted across the base of the castle. The force of the blasts knocked me down into the chaos. I hit the ground in a roll, losing my grip on Iranoct.

My eyes darted up to the castle. Flames engulfed the tower, and the screams from people trapped inside pierced the smoky air. By all the gods, what had we done?

Before I could think further, my gaze locked onto Sam standing just before me. His eyes widened as they met mine, and he began to cut his way through the fray, heading straight for me. Panic surged through my veins. I stumbled back, trying to locate Iranoct. My movements were frenzied when I found the sword and swung it in wide arcs, trying to ward off anyone who came close. I felt trapped, my heart pounding, as I scrambled away from Sam.

Smoke choked the air, and the clamor of battle mixed with the haunting cries from the burning tower. Someone large fell beside me. I gasped, stumbling to the side as I looked up and realized that some people had jumped to escape the flames.

Yet, there was still a battle to be won on the ground. I

swung, slashed, and stabbed, my actions guided by desperation more than skill. Suddenly, Mellan appeared in front of me. I recognized the distinctive engraving on his armor and seized him, gripping the metal as if it were a lifeline.

"Where is Destrian?" I implored.

Mellan shook his head, his eyes not meeting mine but staring at the burning tower above us. "Aureliana."

Mellan had someone he needed to save, just like I had people I needed to protect. Reluctantly, I loosened my grip, nodding for him to go.

As Mellan disappeared into the tower, I felt a new wave of determination mixed with gnawing fear. I needed to get out of this mess, and fast.

I shoved my way through the tumult, scanning for any sign of Fin. My vision blurred at the edges, tears threatening to fall, but I fought them back—not now, not yet.

I gathered the wind, preparing to launch myself into the sky, when a strong hand clamped onto my leather armor and yanked me back. I was thrown to the ground, Iranoct skidding out of reach. Dazed, I looked up to find Sam's eyes ablaze with a tempest of unspoken fury, as if he could seize my very soul and drag it back to the capital, kicking and screaming, against its will.

Then, a rumble like the growl of some monstrous beast filled the air. Sam and I turned our heads in unison, our gazes drawn to the towers of Ayastaren Castle. They wavered for a moment as if undecided and then, with a roar that shook the very earth beneath us, they crumbled. Stone and flame cascaded downward, obliterating everything in their path as a great cloud of smoke stampeded away from the castle in rippling waves.

I screamed for Mellan, imagining him caught in that. I had hope that he might've escaped until another tower collapsed, sending a tidal wave of dust and smoke billowing outward, swallowing soldiers and civilians alike. It was as if the very soul of Ayastaren had been ripped out, leaving behind nothing but smoky ruin and the horrified screams of those who'd survived to witness it.

I gasped a sob, the fighting momentarily forgotten as I mourned my friend. Where was Fin? Where was Destrian?

A cold, unyielding grip tightened around my neck. My hand shot to my throat, and I felt the alien sensation of metal. I turned sharply. Sam's expression contorted in fury and triumph. He held my wrist in an iron grip, and in his other hand, he raised a simple gold coin.

The wrenching sensation in my gut told me that we were league leaping.

"No, Sam, *no*!" I screamed as the world around us twisted and shifted. The battlefield, the burning city—all of it vanished.

I clawed at Sam, my voice raw as I yelled, "Take me back! What have you done? Take me back!"

I reached for him, for the coin—anything to reverse what had happened. But instead of answers, he shoved a cloth against my face. A pungent smell filled my nostrils, and a heavy fog rolled into my mind. My knees buckled, my energy sapped in an instant, and as my vision blurred, I felt myself slump into his arms. The last thing I knew before darkness swallowed me whole was the chilling satisfaction in Sam's eyes.

Chapter 30

A GENTLE ROCKING sensation chilled my stomach, sending me back into the hold with Omri. I felt around me, trying to locate the boy, when my eyes opened blearily and I realized I wasn't in a dark hold, but a cabin room. My brain caught up, and the memories of battle came screaming back to me.

Mellan. The people of Ayastaren. Even if we won the battle, it had come at too heavy a cost.

My arm felt heavy, and the clink of chains dragged over it. I felt around my throat. There was a collar buckled around it. I recognized the feel of it from when I'd been kidnapped by Alf Amun-doon. I thought back to my rescue. After Sam had killed Alim, he'd divested me of the collar and took it and the key with him.

At the time, I'd wondered how much the trinket had cost. There were sorcerers who could block the use of magic. After enough study, sorcerers could transfer their power into objects in interesting ways. Del would do it all the time with her marvelous works of architecture. Marc had imbued the essence of his magic into Destrian's and my swords so that they would find each other in the Nightlands. I was guessing the coin Sam had raised on the battlefield was a token manipulated by Elgar the Swift. Even Destrian could do it to an extent, with his own sword, and he could ward a room.

The collar had to have been made by a sorcerer. Someone who could block magic. I looked around the ship's cell. The scent of sea brine wafted in from between the boards, and I sank down onto the pallet, trying to hold back a sob.

Unfortunately, the chains were tighter than I'd have liked. I could stand up and just make it to the bucket in the corner to relieve myself, otherwise I couldn't make it near the door.

They were taking me to Somme.

They were taking me back to Agramon.

I looked down. My clothes were different. Panic sent my heart racing. The dirt and blood from battle was also gone. Someone had undressed and bathed me before putting me in a green dress that I'd worn when I was in Agramon's care. I took a deep breath. I'd last worn it in Maryse, when Sam and my romance had begun to heat up. How could I have been so blind when it came to him? Now, the very idea of him revolted me.

I gritted my teeth, noticing a tray of food near the door. I crept toward it, my stomach twisting with hunger. The chains rose the farther I went until they grabbed my hands and refused to let me take another step. I balanced on one foot, trying to drag the plate toward me with my toe, but to no avail. They'd taken no care in ensuring I could actually eat the food.

I fought the tears threatening the corners of my eyes, but they fell anyway. What could I do now?

Some queen I turned out to be. No sooner had I gained my crown than I let myself be kidnapped and taken back to the empire that I'd fought to escape. I sorely wanted news. Had they captured Destrian? Fin? How many others were getting dragged back from Morgania to the capital?

What would Agramon do to me?

What would Sam do to me?

I crouched, feeling the sharp pangs of hunger deep in my gut. I sat that way for hours. I wished I knew where I was. The only light came from the ship's window, high up in the cell, with three iron bars over it. How would anybody find me if I didn't give off a magical signature?

Would Marc's tracking power work if I'd been taken by a league leaper? I doubted his powers would be much help. Everyone knew where I was going.

Worry gnawed at my insides, along with hunger. What had happened to the others?

A DAY PASSED. I ran my fingers over the wood within my

cell, thinking of all the people I'd left behind. I was a queen now. Even with the charge of treason against me, they wouldn't be able to hold me for long. Not without doing something with me. If Sam gave me to Agramon, I knew in my heart that he would make an example of me. He would have to be merciless, to instill fear in the other nobles and consulships around the empire who were waiting to see where the cards would fall. He would want to scare them into siding with him.

Agramon was all about image, and he would need to look like he was winning. My power wouldn't matter. In the end, it probably would make it worse. If he could take me down, the most powerful sorcerer in the entire empire, then others would think they didn't stand a chance. The empire would be his. The Sons of Sol would side with Agramon. Chassandre would finally be on his side. I wondered if that was his plan all along. Had he wanted the others to hate me?

But what if Agramon didn't have me yet? What if Sam was planning to take me back with him? I bit my lip, finding a little splinter on the floor beside me. I lifted it and scratched the wall.

Sam would have to return me to Agramon. Even if he'd wanted to steal away with me to Bruin instead, Elgar could stop him. Elgar was Agramon's man, not Sam's. It occurred to me that with Sam bringing me back to the East in Elgar's company, the army in Ayastaren was without its great leader. Would the army return as well? Would Destrian and the others be safe now?

Maybe it was just as well. Destrian and Fin would be good leaders. The empire was fighting a losing battle in Morgania, and Agramon would be able to read between the lines. He might let Morgania go to save face. He would still have the rest of the empire, including both shores, to rule over. What would he do next?

He'd mentioned once that I'd never asked him why he wanted to rule the empire. I wondered what he would do now that he had it at his fingertips. Would he be a good ruler? I doubted it. He was too bent on revenge. I wondered how long Maryse would last in Lyrica's hold. Or Ardent, or even Ember Innes. The island nation would not take kindly to its daughter being murdered. The treaty there would fall, and war would ensue, but Ember Innes, no matter how ruthless and strong, was still pea-sized compared to the gargantuan Lyrican Empire.

Just as I was contemplating the possible ramifications of my capture, I heard voices on the other side of the locked door. My ears perked up, straining and eager to hear any shred of information.

The lock clicked, and the door creaked open. Sam walked in and closed it carefully behind him. I rose to my feet, my eyes narrowed in a hard glare.

"What the gods do you think you're doing with me?" I demanded, standing straight as I could. "I demand you take me back to Morgania!"

"You know damned well that I'm not going to do that," Sam said simply. He leaned against the door, out of my reach, watching me intently.

I hid my clenched fists in the green skirt. "Who changed my clothes? Who touched me while I was unconscious?"

Sam's nostrils flared. "You think I'd let anyone else touch you?"

My glare intensified. "So it was you." I hated Sam. I hated Sam with every fiber of my being. I'd bet he enjoyed every minute of me all to himself. The thought of it almost made me retch right then and there.

Sam's expression twisted into something ugly, something irate. "You think this is easy for me? You betrayed me, Rowyn!"

"Betrayed you?" The chains rattled when I stepped closer to him, hindered but defiant. "You kidnapped me, Sam. You drugged me. You put me in this cell and took me away from my people. You are just as bad as Agramon. I must return to my home. I am their queen!"

"Was I ever anything more than a pawn in your game? All that time, and you never told me you were a Morganite princess. Were you just waiting to make a fool out of me? Was I just a stepping stone to the throne?" His voice trembled as he stared me down.

"Don't you dare turn this around on me," I hissed. "You're the one who decided to enact some twisted fairy tale revenge. You're the one who decided to reduce us to pawns and captors."

"What would you have had me do, Rowyn?" Sam asked, his voice deceptively calm. "What other option did you leave me?"

"You could have let me go," I gasped. "You could have wanted me to be happy."

For a moment, we simply stood there. We nursed our own blend of betrayal, bitterness, and broken trust. There was so much to say, but words, it seemed, would solve nothing. And as much as I hated to admit it, I was too overwhelmed to fully process the emotional wreckage strewn before us. All I knew was that I needed to escape, get back to my people, and fix what had been so disastrously broken.

His eyes locked onto mine, his voice seething with bitterness. "Must've been fun, playing queen with your young hero."

"Destrian is a good man," I retorted, unwilling to let him tarnish another person I cared for.

"A good man? Is that all?" Sam's eyes sharpened. "Maybe I should've slept with you first. Then you could've crowned me king."

I recoiled, feeling a sharp pain in my chest at his words. How had we gotten to this point where love—or what had once felt like love—could be weaponized like this?

"Sam . . ." I paused, struggling to keep my voice steady. "This was never about crowns or thrones. It was about trust, something you shattered the moment you threw the knife."

"You ran!" he thundered. "I would've given my life for you, and you ran from me as though I were the enemy! I always knew loving you would be a gamble."

I let Sam shout at me, shaking my head. "I'm glad to know all I was to you was a gamble," I said when he quieted.

He let out an exasperated sigh. "Was there nothing you felt of affection toward me? Was there no hope for us?"

He wanted reprieve, but reprieve was something I couldn't give. "You are the one who pushed me away. You never chose me first. You always chose your position above everything else. Even your own honor."

"And what of your honor, wife?" Sam asked, his brow crooked.

I shook my head. "You may take my body back to Somme, but my heart remains in Morgania with Destrian. You will never touch it again."

"You are a much better actress than I took you for," Sam snarled. "You certainly had me fooled. Really, I must applaud your efforts. To have maintained the act for so long. To keep me believing you actually may have cared."

I scoffed. My every sense was trained on Sam as he stepped toward me, his breathing soft, like the memories of so many nights lying beside him and being held in his arms.

"You invade my soul, until I can think of nothing but you, then you think you can just turn your back on me?" He seized my arm. "Was none of it real?"

He waited a moment, like he expected me to answer.

I didn't. I refused to even look at him. If he insisted on chaining me to get his answers, then he didn't deserve them to begin with.

"You listen to Agramon more than I give you credit for," he whispered. I glared at the wall. But Sam wouldn't be put off. "There was a moment . . . a moment when I thought you really cared for me. When I thought I saw the real you." I could tell he was preparing himself for the hurt, but he still wanted some hint it wasn't all a lie.

"I can't even stomach to know what I ever saw in you," I said, meeting his eye. "You are just like Agramon, taking what you want and bedamned how it affects the rest of us. I saw who you were in Morgania. The village? The knife? You've not a shred of loyalty in you, Sam. Not an ounce of mercy."

Pain seared his face before it grew stony. I couldn't

bring myself to give him any sense of hope though. I wasn't in the mood for it.

"You have committed treason. It is my duty to arrest you in the name of the crown."

"You would really choose him?" I asked. "You would choose Agramon over me. Why are you doing this for him?"

His jaw clenched, and for a moment, he looked like he was struggling to find words. "I did it because I had no choice. Because you left me no choice!"

His accusation stung more than I cared to admit. But I pushed the feeling away, focusing on the man in front of me. The man I once knew, now so different.

"I left Agramon and his schemes. I didn't leave because of you. *You* chose Agramon. You chose power."

For a moment, he was silent, his gaze flicking away from me. Then he gave a sharp nod, as if coming to a decision.

"Perhaps I did," he conceded, eyes locking onto mine. "But like you told me, Rowyn: I should follow my conscience."

And with that, he turned on his heel and left me alone with my chains.

Chapter 31

N O SOONER HAD the door shut behind Sam than a loud blast reverberated through the hull. I twisted around, craning my neck to see through the barred window. A plume of smoke billowed in the distance, mingling with the sea mist. My heart leaped. Was it—?

Then a gigantic tentacle, dark and slick, moved over the window, its suckers gripping the outer wall of the ship. My heart pounded in my chest with a mix of terror and exhilaration.

A kraken.

"I'm here! I'm here!" I screamed desperately, clinging to a shred of hope. It had to be Fin and Destrian. They had come to rescue me. They had to have.

Another blast, louder this time, shook the ship from stern to bow. I held my breath, awaiting the sweet sound of splintering wood, the rush of water that would signify my captors' defeat and my impending freedom.

The door burst open with a bang. Sam rushed in, his face flushed with anger and panic. Behind him was Elgar the Swift.

"Don't make me hurt you, Rowyn," Sam snapped,

ignoring my shouts that continued unabated.

"Fin! Destrian! I'm here!"

He quickly unlocked the chains around my wrists from the main line that bound me to the cell. I let him, because the last thing I wanted was to be chained to a sinking ship. I began fighting as his arm wrapped around me, holding me tight against his chest.

Elgar the Swift reached for us both and then, with a wrenching tug from deep within my gut, we were league leaping away from the ship, away from what I'd thought was my rescue.

Just like that, we were gone.

WHEN MY SENSES returned, the world around me had shifted once again. I was no longer on a ship or in some nondescript chamber. Instead, I found myself riding in a cart, its wooden planks rattling beneath me. My head throbbed; Sam must have knocked me out during our second leap. I raised myself, wincing at the stiffness in my body. I took in the cobblestone streets and timber-framed houses that surrounded me. Somme. They must have league leaped all the way to Somme just to cage me. My hope fell as the chances for rescue dwindled.

The crowd that lined the streets was unlike any I'd ever encountered. Faces twisted in loathing and scorn. Curses filled the air and more than one person actually spit in my direction. I struggled to my feet before standing tall, gripping the bars. I was Rowyn of Morgania. I was a queen, and I would not cower before these people.

Ahead of the cart, Sam rode on horseback. Though my eyes were drawn to him, I bit back any words that threatened to spill from my lips. They would fall on deaf ears; that much was clear. Sam glanced over his shoulder at me, his eyes shadowed with an emotion I couldn't—or perhaps wouldn't—read.

As the cart moved closer to the citadel, I noticed more and more of the Sons of Sol gathering in the streets. Their faces were twisted with hate and disdain, some even daring to hurl objects at me. Stones, rotten fruit—I forced myself to ignore them. Whatever awaited me in the palace would be worse than the scorn of a disillusioned populace.

When we reached the citadel, the cart came to an abrupt halt. Sam dismounted and made his way over, his boots echoing ominously on the cobblestones. He opened the cart and grasped the chain connected to my shackles, jerking me out with a scowl. I stumbled but regained my footing quickly. A ring of soldiers enclosed us as we were led into the palace, and my heart sank when we headed down several sets of stairs to a part of the castle I'd never seen before.

I knew about the cells, though, specifically designed to neutralize a sorcerer's magic. A futile spark of hope ignited within me. Maybe they'd remove this damned collar.

But when Sam led me into one such cell, he merely attached my chain to a wall hook, giving me just enough room to move around the cell but not enough to escape. Without another word, he turned on his heel and left, taking the soldiers with him and plunging the cell into near darkness.

There I was—captured, bound, magic-less. I looked around. There was a disgusting-looking pail in the corner, and the pallet was filled with mildewed straw. I sat anyway and took a deep breath of the stale air. With each passing moment, the likelihood of rescue seemed to dim, leaving me engulfed in an ever-growing darkness.

My stomach growled. Perhaps they would accidentally starve me to death. I would love to see the argument between Sam and Agramon then. I leaned against the damp wall, the green dress far too thin in the chill of the dungeon.

Soldiers' voices echoed through the hall before stopping outside of my cell door. They continued talking, seemingly guarding my cell.

"I will starve to death in here if I do not get food soon,"

I announced loudly.

The voices stopped, but there were no footsteps either. I huffed and rose from the disgusting mattress only to sink onto the floor, which seemed marginally cleaner. My back against the wall, I held my head in my hands, trying to come up with a plan.

I couldn't use my powers.

I couldn't fight.

The only thing left was to try to talk my way out of it. I needed to make a deal.

I heard more voices. Agramon's unmistakable tone resonated through the stone walls, laced with annoyance and anger. Sam's voice was there, too, equally tense. As they approached, their conversation became clearer.

"Why did you bring her back to Somme?" Agramon snapped. "Do you have any idea how many other concerns I have? Now I have a kidnapped queen in my capital!"

"Because she's valuable," Sam responded, the tension in his voice carrying through the walls. "Her capture weakens the Morganian alliance and sends a message to anyone thinking of betraying us."

The room fell quiet for a moment, so quiet that I could almost hear my own heartbeat pounding in my ears. Finally, Agramon spoke again.

"And did you intend for her to die, like Empress Lesedi?"

For a second, the walls of my cell seemed to close in. Agramon's words lingered in the air, filling my cell with an even deeper shade of despair.

"And look what you've done!" Agramon continued, not waiting for a response. "You got the Grysian Navy decimated. Admiral Abelard has taken control of the northern seas! Ayastaren is demolished, and now it's in the hands of the Trinidans!"

I couldn't suppress the smile that spread across my face. So Marc got what he wanted. Ayastaren was now a part of Morgania. For a moment, I mourned Mellan and the countless innocents who hadn't lived to see this new chapter. If only fate had been kinder to them.

The voices stopped right in front of my cell. I rose, steeling myself for the confrontation. Metal screeched as Agramon turned a wheel next to the cell door. My chains tightened, pulling my arms upward until it became a struggle to move. Then the door creaked open, and Agramon and Sam stepped inside my confined world.

Golden robes had replaced Agramon's white ones. His staff was held in his gloved hand. The rose-colored gem affixed to his brow glowed ominously.

"How are you today, Your Grace?" I asked, my tone dripping with honey. "Have you missed me?"

Agramon tilted his head to the side, his gaze narrowed. "I have to confess, I wasn't expecting you to take the young prince with you in your escape. I knew you would run, eventually, and that your marriage to your ill-fated suitor would precipitate those events, but I have to admit that you surprised me when you took the boy with you. I would say well done, but I'm sure it wasn't planned."

"It was not," I said, agreeing with him. "But I was happy to do the empress a favor."

"Yes, and how has that worked for you?" Agramon asked, looking around the cell. His nose wrinkled. "Quite different from your other prisons? I daresay you considered our rooms in the palace to be a jail. Tell me, my dear, how does it compare to this hole you've put yourself in?"

"Morgania will come for me," I replied, my voice low.

"I have a hard time believing that." Agramon studied me. "Your lord Destrian was quite happy to leave you to rot at the capital before. I'd imagine he'd do it again, especially if it got you out of the way for ruling Morgania."

I gritted my teeth. "You would begrudge us both a crown?"

Agramon scoffed, taking a step closer to me. "I hope you enjoyed your time on the throne, Rowyn. You won't be going back to it. And while your powers as a sorceress might have served you well in the West, let me assure you, in the East, I have sorcerers at my disposal. I can send them to protect Somme, to keep Destrian and your friend Fin from getting to you—or Morgania from ever getting you back."

I glared at Agramon. "I don't understand what your problem is. Why don't you use this as a chance to ally with Morgania against the Marendeslys? I have no loyalty to them anymore. You have enough on your plate with the rest of the empire. You could easily let Morgania go in order to gain an ally."

Sometimes fate played games with our lives. There I was, doing the one thing that Fin and Destrian had vowed never to do. I was ready to negotiate with Agramon.

Agramon lifted his brow and stepped closer. His fingers reached up to brush my cheek. "I offered to give you everything, do you remember? You wanted for nothing in my care. Yet, this is how you repay my generosity?"

"I'm offering to make you a deal," I said. "I'm offering to hear you out. What do you want?"

Agramon smiled. "Tell me where the boy is."

My jaw turned to stone. Agramon's fingers fell away and he stepped back. Sam was glowering at the both of us.

I straightened. "I will never give up his location. We can have a military alliance. I can send rain, whatever you want, but I won't tell you where the prince is."

Agramon turned his attention to Sam. "You should have killed her when you had the chance. Would have saved us all a lot of trouble."

I clenched my fists as my stomach growled loudly. "If

the plan was just to starve me to death then he's nearly succeeded."

Agramon's eyes shot daggers at Sam. "What is she talking about? Have you not fed her?"

Sam rolled his eyes. "I ordered the men to give her a tray."

"They set the tray too far away from my chains," I interjected, my voice laced with scorn. "I get to stare at food every day. A novel form of torture, I must say."

"For the love of Sol," Agramon spit out, glaring at Sam again.

There was a part of me that took grim satisfaction in the discomfort Sam felt, a tiny flicker of triumph. But it was a hollow victory. Whether or not they fed me, I was still a prisoner.

"I can't believe the two of you are running this empire," I grumbled.

"Don't start with me," Agramon sneered, his eyes locked onto mine. "It's extremely difficult to find reliable help these days. I actually missed you, you know. You could have been useful."

"What does that even mean?" I asked weakly.

Agramon shook his head dismissively, his eyes cutting to Sam once more. "You'll see," he muttered before turning back to me. "Gree will tend to you every morning and dress you."

I groaned inwardly. Gree was one of Agramon's most loyal attendants, someone who would report back every detail about my condition and actions. It was like replacing one jailer with another, but at least I wouldn't starve.

"You should be grateful," Agramon added, as if reading my thoughts.

Grateful? The word echoed mockingly in my mind. Every fiber of my being screamed in rebellion against the notion. But I kept my face impassive; Agramon had already shown me that he took great delight in any visible sign of my suffering. So I would give him none. Still, the foreboding in my heart grew. Agramon had plans for me, and whatever they were, they couldn't be good.

In my mind, it felt just like old times—except now, the chains were a lot more literal, a lot more cold. "I suppose thanks are in order."

Agramon shook his head, as if unable to fathom any form of gratitude from me. "I'll see you later." He turned on his heel and stepped through the door. Sam glanced over his shoulder at me as he followed.

As they walked down the hall, Agramon's voice rose. "Send her food immediately, Butcher, or I swear I'll have your head!"

It could be worse, I thought. Agramon always liked to keep his possessions in good condition, and it seemed I was no exception. That would work in favor of my comfort, if nothing else. I settled down as best as I could, my chains jingling softly, and waited.

It wasn't long before a servant entered my cell, bearing a basket laden with peaches and a clean mattress filled with goose feathers. I lay down, eating through the basket of peaches, and schemed.

Chapter 32

VOICES ECHOED OUTSIDE of my door. The chains clinked as I adjusted myself, my eyes opening groggily.

Sam strode in, shortly followed by Gree and a host of young serving boys who carried all manner of things.

Agramon's torture had begun.

Gree crossed her arms as she studied me, her face wrinkled in clear distaste.

I shot her a smirk.

"You've certainly made a great mess of things, haven't you?" she barked, her eyes sliding to Sam who glowered in the corner, clutching his sword hilt.

Two servant boys came in dragging a tub behind them. They left and came back with buckets that they slowly lowered into the tub and began pouring the water carefully in.

So, they would bathe me. That was good. I hadn't bathed properly in days, and I was starting to smell bad. Good thing Agramon abhorred bad smells.

Sam crossed his arms and leaned against the wall as though planning to stay awhile.

"What are you doing here?" I asked. He could give me some dignity, at the very least.

"We must unchain you in order for you to bathe. Someone has to be here to make sure you don't try to escape."

I gritted my teeth. "Let me guess, you insisted it be you?"

Sam's eyes hardened. "I'm the only one in the capital besides Gree who has seen you naked. I thought you would prefer it to the guards outside your cell."

I clenched my teeth. "You couldn't have sent a woman to do it? There's plenty of sorcerers who could easily guard me."

Sam didn't respond. He just approached, slowly, and began unlocking my chains. He glanced at the collar around my throat and I raised my brows.

"That isn't coming off," Sam said, brushing his fingertips along my skin before he inserted a key into the lock on my wrists.

I didn't know what to say to him, or what to do, so I did nothing. Just rubbed the raw skin on my wrist the moment my hand was free.

"Don't try anything stupid," he murmured, grabbing my chin and tilting my face up to his.

I bit back a retort and turned my back to him as Gree helped me out of the cursed green gown. When I was naked, I turned to climb into the tub, but Gree motioned to Sam. "His Grace requested that the chains be kept on her unless dressing."

Sam stepped toward me. Heat rushed to my cheeks. He met my eye and held it as he placed the chains back on my wrists. I glared at him, seething, despite the fact that he was trying to keep his eyes on mine. I'd never been so humiliated in my life. Whether it was Agramon's or Sam's doing I'd no idea. I just knew I wanted them all to burn. Every last one of them.

Sam helped shove the tub closer to where the chains attached to the wall, though I still had to keep my hands raised in the bath. Gree dumped water over my head and roughly scrubbed the soap into my hair and skin, not caring at all that she was surely taking off a layer of flesh with it. I'd not missed her at all in Morgania.

Not. One. Moment.

"Stand up," Gree snapped. I sighed and rose, the water dripping down my body as she began scrubbing soap over my chest and stomach. Suddenly, my heart fell deep into the pit of my stomach.

I'd always scrubbed myself around my waist and private areas when I'd been in Agramon's care with Gree. That was the only way I could keep the Girdle of Ephema hidden. She'd never put her hands on me, at least there. She'd never remarked on my preference. Now, her hands ran down the skin on my waist and I held my breath. For the love of the gods. I felt the moment her finger met with the enchanted girdle. She paused, another finger joining it, feeling along the outline of the jewelry. She met my eye.

"She's chained now. You don't have to stare at her," Gree snapped over my shoulder. I looked up. Sam was turning red. A muscle in his jaw flexed. He turned away, leaning against the door.

"Don't take it off," I whispered, filling my voice with every trace of hope. "Please."

"It's either I do it, or His Grace does it himself," Gree whispered, her voice hard. She lifted the girdle, and it magically appeared in her hands. She found the clasp easily, undid it, and slipped it into her pocket with Sam none the wiser. My breath quickened into a panic as she hurriedly finished bathing me, then waited patiently for Sam to unchain me again, then dressed me in a simple gown, before hurrying out of the room as Sam chained me back on the wall for good.

"Was it worth it?" Sam asked, turning the key in the lock as I distractedly looked over his shoulder after Gree. I wished she wouldn't leave me with him. By all the gods, what would Agramon do when he found out?

"You've thrown everything away, and for what? A throne long torn apart? A prison cell? The love of some boy you barely knew?"

I couldn't wrap my mind around what he was saying. I was so distracted with my eyes on the cell door, sure that Agramon was about to walk through at any moment. "I didn't know you very long, either," I said, though my tone was more weary than angry. "All is not yet lost."

"Do you think they are going to come for you?" Sam asked, his voice dropping. I backed further along the wall, trying to keep a healthy distance from him. "Somme is impenetrable. You are here to stay, Rowyn, whether you like it or not."

"So why are you here?" I sighed.

"You need to tell me where the boy is," Sam said, stepping forward.

I scooted as far as the chains would allow. "And give up the only information keeping me alive? I don't think so."

"We will find him eventually. Agramon is prepared to be lenient if you make this as quick and painless as possible."

"What does lenient mean? A quick death?"

Sam shook his head. "He will let you return to Bruin with me. You would be required to bring rain on a specific schedule, touring the land and such, and you would be under guard in Bruin by both my men and soldiers from Somme, but you would live."

I raised my brows. "That sounds like it would be your dream."

Sam's nostrils flared. "I would have to give up my position as general. This is not my *dream*, Rowyn."

"Why bother?" I asked, seething. "I've told you I don't want you. I love Destrian. I want to spend the rest of my life with him. How many times must I tell you this before it sinks in?"

"I could get you better quarters. Since we have the collar that negates your powers, we could move you into rooms in the palace even. Up higher, with a bigger window." Sam stroked my cheek. "I want to advocate for you, but I have to know you will not run. Honor our vows, and I will champion you."

I frowned. "Are you serious?"

"It's the only way forward for you now, Rowyn. Let me save you."

I tried to shove him away but was hampered by the chains. "You honestly think I would come back to you after this? After you sold me out to Agramon? We are done, Sam. I wish we'd never been."

Sam stepped closer, his voice barely above a whisper, his eyes hardened granite. "You would choose death over being with me? Are you sure?"

I could feel Sam's breath on my face. His fingers went around my throat, and he leaned in. "I told you this already. You *will* be mine. Not even the gods themselves will be able to keep you from me. No matter where you go. No matter how you try to conceal yourself from me, I will find you and drag you home with me, where you belong."

"I belong in Morgania, Sam. You know this," I murmured as he squeezed my throat a fraction, a clear threat.

"You are my wife, and I will not have you running off to be with your lover in Morgania, playing at being queen, and embarrassing me across the empire. Now you *will* agree with Agramon's terms, or I will agree for you and drag you to Bruin in chains if I have to, but you will go."

"What then?" I choked. Tears welled in my eyes as he squeezed tighter. "Will you take me by force?"

"You forget," Sam murmured in my ear. "I seem to remember our time in Bruin quite differently. Did you tell your young lord? How I had you moaning, screaming into the sheets of my bed well into the night?"

My skin prickled as his warm breath swept across my cheeks. "You don't fool me, Rowyn. I know you remember the time well. Your body responds even now. It remembers me, even if you refuse to." He reached to caress my cheek, and I turned my face away.

He recaptured my chin, forcing me to meet his gaze. His eyes were a dark and tumultuous storm, and I saw the hurt in them. My heart clenched, guilt twisting like a knife in my gut.

"Sam," I whispered, my voice trembling, but he didn't let me finish.

Leaning in, he tried to kiss me. I clenched my teeth and bit his lower lip. He yelped and pulled back, pressing a hand to his bleeding mouth.

The sharp sting of his hand resonated across my face as my cheek slammed into stone and I winced, feeling the bitter taste of blood in my mouth.

"Why do you make me be cruel to you?" he growled.

I glared at him, his face pale in the torchlight, blood trickling from his lip. "You're a monster." The chains had rubbed my wrists raw, yet I still pulled against them. I didn't want Sam coming closer. I wanted him as far away from me as he could go.

"I will change your mind," Sam whispered. "In Bruin, I will be able to change your mind. You'll have Nirah there. You'll be in the lands of your ancestors. You'll want for nothing."

"Agramon was right," I said, mostly to myself. "Marrying you would only ever have been exchanging one cage for another."

Sam's eyes narrowed. "You think so little of me, then. You think I'd keep you in a cage?"

"You've already shown you would," I said, my eyes stinging with unshed tears. "I'm in one right now, aren't I?"

His eyes met mine, and for a split second, I saw a glimmer of the man I once thought I liked. A flicker of regret, but it was quickly snuffed out.

"I'll send for the food," he said abruptly, turning and

walking out of the cell, locking the door behind him.

I sank against the cold stone wall, the weight of my chains reminding me of the life I'd left behind and the uncertainty that lay ahead.

My mind went back to my people in Morgania, to Echo and Mellan, Lord Alexander, the empress. My heart ached for them. I wept, not just for myself, but for all the innocents caught in the calamity that seemed to have no end. Why was it that I'd been deemed worthy enough to continue on.

At least it felt as though Morgania was in safe hands. And if something did happen to me, I took solace in the fact that Morgania would continue to be the sanctuary I had always envisioned it to be.

I was left with nothing to do except cry and wait for Agramon to realize that I would now be putty in his hands. He would know *everything*.

Chapter 33

A GRAMON'S FOOTSTEPS ECHOED on the stone floor as he moved toward my cell. I could tell it was him. The distinct, deliberate rhythm of his boots halted just outside my door, where he engaged in a muffled conversation with someone. Whoever it was, their footsteps retreated, accompanied by the clinking of plate metal armor. I realized Agramon had probably dismissed my guard.

I rose to my feet, my heart pounding in my chest. The hackles on the back of my neck stood up. Gree had dressed me in one of my simpler dresses, a leftover from my time in Solridge, making me feel oddly vulnerable.

The door creaked open and Agramon stepped inside. His gem blazed in its pinkish light, reflecting off the stone walls of my cell. Searing pain cobwebbed through my mind, and I clenched my fists to my head, holding back a scream. It felt as if he was creeping through my mind like a spider. I could sense him sifting through my memories, lingering on each one, analyzing and dissecting them. His eyes closed, as if savoring a delicacy, relishing every moment he extracted from the depths of my consciousness.

He leaned in, pressing his forehead against mine,

inhaling deeply as if my very scent was egging him on. My thoughts clouded over, muddled by his influence, and before I knew it, I was overwhelmed by an inexplicable urge.

I reached up to wrap my arms around his neck, pressing my lips against his, deepening the kiss in a way that felt as unnatural as it was involuntary.

I kissed him with a fervor I couldn't comprehend, our mouths melding as if guided by an invisible hand. Agramon gripped my waist, and he pulled me against him. My eyes flickered open for just a moment, and for that brief second, I saw, not Agramon, but Destrian. My heart stuttered.

It was all there—those intense dark eyes, the crown of red hair that I had come to adore, even the phantom sensation of his beard's texture against my skin. My emotions churned in a blend of elation and confusion. It was as if my subconscious was trying to tell me something, but my conscious mind was lagging behind, struggling to make sense of the clash between reality and desire.

Without really thinking, I wrapped a leg around his waist, trying to draw my arms around him to bring him closer still. The feeling was intense, like the pull of a magnet that I was powerless to resist. It was as if the universe itself had ordained this strange, fateful moment.

He pressed into me, his kiss lingering on my lips, over my cheeks, and disappearing as he brushed against the collar at my throat.

"We could've had so much fun," Agramon murmured in a caustic blend of allure and menace, his fingers crawling up my leg. "I could hear your fear the moment I stepped out of the stairwell. How I would've loved this."

Reality crashed back like a tidal wave. I gagged, my arms flailing as I tried to shove him away from me, revolted by what he'd made me do, by what he'd made me feel. The chains dug into my wrists, cutting deep.

Agramon leaned in close, his fingers digging into my shoulder with a painful intensity. "Now tell me, where is the little emperor?"

I drew upon every ounce of Vianne's teachings on mental barriers, trying to lock away the information he sought behind walls of willpower. My thoughts became a fortress, each rampart constructed from sheer defiance and loathing for this man.

His grip tightened, biting into my flesh. I gasped. Tears stung, every instinct screaming to protect myself from him.

He closed his eyes and rested his forehead against mine as if we were sharing some intimate moment. I trembled at his proximity, the air thick with his magic. My heart thudded in my chest, still racing from having kissed Agramon. The disgust spiraled, leaving a bitter taste in my mouth.

"It's admirable that you would share your power," Agramon continued, his tone dripping with false sincerity.

"Insisting on three crowns instead of one. Many wouldn't. But it doesn't matter. I will bring Morgania back into the fold, and all your little traitorous friends will die."

I felt like I was falling, and there was nothing to catch me.

Princess Willene appeared at the cell door, scanning the room until her eyes locked onto mine. The older sister of the emperor, who Agramon had killed, and, to my further revulsion, someone Agramon had been involved with during my time at the capital.

"Has the girl revealed where my nephew is hiding?" Willene asked, a cruel glint in her eyes.

My glare intensified. "Are you going to do the same thing to your little nephew that you did to your brother?" I couldn't keep the disdain from my voice.

Willene scoffed, looking down her nose at me. "My brother didn't understand what it means to rule. He thought being born a male Marendesly meant he deserved a crown."

Every word that escaped her lips increased the revulsion I felt, both for her and Agramon. They were peas in a poisonous pod, each reinforcing the other's worst qualities.

"The only way to get a crown," Willene continued, relishing each word as if she were delivering some grand truth, "is through building power."

And there it was: the philosophy that had led to so much suffering, her justification for all the atrocities she and Agramon had committed. Power. That single, intoxicating word that justified any act, for them, no matter how cruel or heartless. It explained everything and yet nothing, least of all how people could become so blinded by ambition that they'd betray even their own flesh and blood.

Willene stepped forward, her eyes blue chips of ice. I glared at her, my mind locking down, refusing to think of the prince. I wouldn't give them that—wouldn't think of the one thing they sought so desperately to know. Instead, I focused on how much I loathed her, how much I loathed them both.

"I always wished I could correct that smart mouth of yours," Willene said before her hand connected with one side of my face and then the other. My cheeks stung, the slaps echoing in my ears and resonating in the pit of my stomach. I thought of a hundred pleasurable ways I'd love to end her life and then my eyes met Agramon's.

His eyes sparkled with mirth. He relished the chaos he'd orchestrated. He came up behind Willene and whispered something in her ear. "I don't want my empress to exert herself. I'll finish up here shortly."

Willene curled her lip as she regarded me one last time. "Don't play with her too long. We need to discuss the attacks on the border of Yliria. It seems the desertmen are no longer honoring the treaty, now that the emperor who signed it is dead."

As Willene strode out of my cell, my mind filled with increasingly imaginative ways I'd enjoy seeing her end. It was a grotesque sort of comfort, but it was all I had in the moment. My attention snapped back to Agramon as he turned his eyes to me, his hand reaching up to stroke my cheek. My skin crawled under his touch, every fiber of my being screaming for escape.

"I do wish things had been different between us, Rowyn," he mused. "We would have made quite a pair."

"Princess Willene not to your liking?"

Agramon smiled, a predator reveling in the trap he'd set. "One must do what they must to rise. Willene has her uses. Namely, the friendship of the older court women who can influence their noble husbands. Votes for the throne don't earn themselves, after all."

My mind raced. Why would Willene turn so decisively against her own family? "Wouldn't Duke Eldred be disappointed in her? Going against her own blood?"

Agramon's eyes narrowed, but he said nothing. He seemed to linger, his eyes still prying into my mind as though he wanted to uncover every secret, every hidden crevice. He planted a disconcerting kiss on my cheek and murmured, "I'll be seeing you shortly."

As he left, I couldn't shake the chilling sensation that it

was only a matter of time before he found what he was truly looking for—the location of the young prince. We were on borrowed time, and I couldn't help but hope that either rescue or death would come sooner rather than later. The longer I was in his grip, the higher the risk that I'd involuntarily divulge the prince's whereabouts.

My thoughts briefly drifted to Destrian and Fin. What were they doing right now? Did they have any clue where I was? Was there any hope of rescue in this godsforsaken place?

Questions with no answers. And time was running out.

The Morganian Army was too far away to be of any help, especially since we lacked a navy. The Marendeslys with Admiral Abelard were potential allies, but alliances were tricky things, and we didn't have one in place yet.

So, who was left to come to my aid? Just Destrian and Fin? The thought was as comforting as it was horrifying. The idea of both monarchs coming after me, taking such an immense risk—it seemed foolish, in hindsight.

Feeling utterly dejected, I sat back in bed, thankful that the chains hadn't been tightened. I sighed, drawing my knees up to my chest.

And so I was left alone, chained in a dark cell, with only my thoughts for company. Thoughts that meandered through the choices and mistakes, the turns and twists of fate that had brought me to this point. And, invariably, to the things I would have done differently if given a second chance.

Chapter 34

DAYS DRAGGED ON like years in that dungeon. With a loose stone, I'd taken to scratching marks on the wall, each one representing another day in my little hole. Every line was a tally of my failures, of moments lost and opportunities squandered. No sign of Destrian or Fin or any hope of rescue.

And then one morning, I overheard the guards murmuring outside my cell. "He's pushing the trial to tomorrow. They think the attack will come soon," one of them said.

A trial? What mockery of justice would this be?

Before I had time to mull over it, the door screeched open and in came Gree, clicking her tongue disapprovingly as she always did.

"Gree, what's this trial?" I croaked as she helped me to stand in a bucket to wash up.

"That's for His Grace to tell you," she said curtly.

Gods, how I despised that woman. But my feelings for her were like a flickering candle compared to the bonfire of loathing I had for Agramon and Princess Willene.

When she left, I was overwhelmed with a mishmash of boredom, nervousness, and despair. There was so much work left undone in Morgania, so much I'd left behind. I allowed myself a flicker of hope, envisioning a day I might return to finish what I'd started. But I quickly snuffed it out. Sam would come for me—of that, I was certain.

Sam had been a frequent visitor during my imprisonment, standing against the far wall of my cell, eyes fixed on me as if peeling layers off my soul. Each time he told me all I had to do was agree to be his, and he would get me out of this nightmare.

"It's in the gods' hands now," I'd respond each time, refusing to give him the satisfaction of seeing me break. But with a trial looming, I wondered just how much more I could take.

The next morning, Gree bathed me with more care than usual. The dress she chose for me was different as well— finer, with elaborate stitching and an intricate design. I ran my fingers down the fabric. Was this how I would meet my fate? Cloaked in false opulence in a farce of a trial?

Before I could dwell on it further, the heavy, synchronized footsteps of a troop of guards echoed down the corridor. I stood up, my eyes hardening as they approached. The collar at my throat had long ago bruised my collarbone, but its discomfort was a minor inconvenience now.

Sam was waiting outside the cell. His arms were crossed, his eyes dark and unreadable. As the door swung open, one of the guards reached for the lead of my chains to detach it from the wall. Another reached to grab my arm, ostensibly to guide me out.

"Don't touch her," Sam barked, his voice tinged with a ferocity I hadn't expected. He took the chain from the guard, placing his hand on my lower back.

The sensation was intrusive and oddly gentle, but I couldn't afford to focus on that now. As we walked through the twisting corridors of the dungeon, my heart pounded with a mixed sense of dread and—dare I say it— relief. Finally, something was happening.

As we stepped out into the open, I squinted, allowing my eyes a moment to adjust to the sunlight. For the briefest moment, hope fluttered in my chest. Maybe I was leaving the dungeon forever.

It was a fool's hope.

We moved through the castle, winding our way through its labyrinthine halls. Onlookers filled the corridors, their eyes wide as they took in the spectacle of a chained queen being paraded before them. I kept my head high, my shoulders squared. If they thought they'd see me cowed or broken, they were sorely mistaken.

Each gaze that met mine, each whisper that rippled through the crowd, fueled a growing fire within me. I made a promise to myself as I walked: if my end was near, I wouldn't go quietly. I'd take as many of these traitors down with me as I could. My mind raced, circling back again and again to the collar that bound my magical abilities. I'd tried before to break its enchantment, but its binding seemed unbreakable.

We finally arrived at the great hall. The doors swung open, revealing a space so filled with people, it seemed almost to burst at its seams. My heart drummed in my chest as I took it all in.

As I was led into the hall, my eyes immediately caught Agramon and Princess Willene seated in the emperor's and empress's thrones at the far end of the room. But what really stole my breath was the figure seated beside them— a woman in a long, brown gown. A sleek, black braid fell to her waist. Her skin was darker, more Ylirian in tone. But her eyes—two sets of inky black irises in each—were what marked her.

A seer. Chassandre. My heart pounded as the import of her presence sank in.

Sam's hand on my back guided me forward until I stood before the grotesque audience for whatever mockery of justice awaited me. Unexpectedly, Sam took my hand and slipped a small piece of paper into my palm. He raised it, kissing my fingers in a gesture that would have seemed tender under any other circumstance. I frowned, my fingers subtly caressing the concealed paper as he finally released me and stepped back.

I looked back to the dais where Chassandre sat with

Agramon and Willene and noticed members of the Sons of Sol lined up behind the seer. Their faces were twisted in ugly snarls. Standing beside the seer was Seith Lyon, clothed in a golden robe. Of course, a Lyon would be present to oversee my so-called "judgment." The bards would love how poetic it was.

Chassandre began speaking in a voice clipped by her unique accent. "Rowyn of Espiria, you stand before this court, a court of both man and gods, to answer for your crimes: conspiring in the murder of the emperor and causing untold devastation to the empire."

As she laid out the charges in her otherworldly voice, I could hardly keep a straight face. I had worked with Miyu to sabotage negotiations with Lu Shen during preparations for the Rainbow Gala. I'd faked being struck by Lu Shen sorcerers just to cause diplomatic upheaval. And, as if that wasn't enough, I had orchestrated a bombing on my own wedding day to kill the emperor and then kidnapped the young prince. The allegations were so absurd, so far from the truth, that I almost laughed. Almost.

All the while, my eyes were locked on Agramon. My glare must have been as sharp as a dagger, for I hoped it would pierce right through him. How dare he? How dare he lay the groundwork for all this and then so conveniently place the blame squarely on my shoulders?

I could almost feel that cursed collar quivering, as if

sensing the storm brewing within me.

Chassandre continued with her farcical litany of so-called crimes. "Rowyn has committed treason against the empire. She has attempted to break Morgania away, declaring it her own territory and herself its sovereign queen. She has also incited others to follow her in this reckless, self-serving endeavor."

Boos and hisses erupted from the crowd, thick with hostility. Yet, I refused to avert my eyes from the evildoers before me. I would not give them the satisfaction.

"And now . . ." Chassandre sneered, looking at me as if I were something disgusting she'd stepped on. "What do you have to say for yourself? A usurper queen, raised from birth in treasonous ways, with not a shred of loyalty within her."

I was the disloyal one? The one who had been betrayed, kidnapped, and subjected to this mockery of justice? The gall of these people. But what disturbed me more was the kernel of truth in their lies—yes, I had sought to break Morgania away. Yet it was a freedom from this very corruption I was being falsely accused of. But would they listen? Did truth even matter?

Taking a deep breath, I stood as tall as my chains would allow. I looked past the throng, past the gilded surroundings. I focused solely on Chassandre. If the crowd was a churning storm of malice, she was its tempestuous eye.

"I have given my all for this empire," I began, my voice ringing clear and forceful through the hall. "I have wielded my powers responsibly, raised my voice for the cause of truth, and worked diligently toward a just society. Your accusations regarding the emperor are false, slander designed to mask the true face of treachery."

My eyes flicked to Agramon momentarily before returning to the seer. "I stand here accused of claiming Morgania, as if that were some heinous act. But I'm merely claiming my birthright as the last living descendant of the Morgan line."

My words set the crowd to murmuring. Even Chassandre seemed taken aback.

It was at that moment that Agramon stepped forward, and I noticed the rosy glow of his gem pulsing softly. I clenched my teeth. What was he planning?

My gaze returned to the seer. I had sown a seed of doubt, but the crowd's simmering anger seemed to deepen, as if guided by an invisible hand. My heart sank. Agramon was using his magic to turn the crowd against me with a flicker of his cursed gem.

How much had he been doing that, I wondered, my thoughts racing. When would he crown himself emperor? Would he dare to do it before extracting the whereabouts of the prince from me? Or, gods forbid, had he already scraped that secret from the depths of my mind?

If Agramon ascended to the throne, the empire was lost.

As my gaze lowered to the paper in my hand, I realized I had been clenching it so tightly that it was now almost torn to shreds. I carefully unfolded it, smoothing out the crinkles as best as I could. The words written on it were simple: *Demand a Trial by Combat.*

I took another breath, trying to steady my quaking nerves. If I went through with the trial as it was, there was no doubt that I'd be found guilty, especially with the Sons of Sol orchestrating things from their high perch. But a Trial by Combat? That was a gamble, a game of chance where the gods themselves would weigh in on my fate.

I locked eyes with Agramon, Willene, Chassandre, and each of the Sons of Sol. "I demand a Trial by Combat," I declared loudly, my voice reverberating through the hall. "Let the gods decide my fate."

As I spoke the words, I felt the ripple of surprise, then excitement spread throughout the room. For a moment, I felt a strange, almost reckless sense of freedom. The gods might be fickle, but at least they wouldn't be swayed by Agramon's magic.

Agramon stepped forward, a slight smirk on his lips, as if savoring his next words. "Very well," he announced. "The empire will name our greatest swordsman, Baron Samael of Bruin, as our champion."

I stopped breathing as I glanced back at Sam. His face had gone ghostly pale, and in that moment, I understood. He had planned to be my champion. That was his secret plot to save me, to get me out of this mess. But Agramon had effectively tied his hands by naming him as the empire's swordsman.

My head swung back to Agramon, who was smiling down at me, fully aware that he had just dismantled any hope Sam had for an easy way out. "In three days' time, you must name your own champion to defend your honor among the gods," he continued. "Choose wisely."

My eyes met his one final time before I turned away. "Choose wisely," he'd said. As if I had any real choices left.

The crowd's boos followed me, growing louder with each step I took. This time, Sam wasn't beside me, shielding me from their touch. I was alone, fully exposed to the seething hatred of the masses.

I glared at the hissing crowd as they led me back to the very place I had yearned to leave—the dungeon. It was the last place I wanted to go, but it seemed Agramon had seen to it that I'd have nowhere else.

Once back in the cell, they roughly chained me to that damp, wretched wall that had been my unwanted companion for far too long. The doors hadn't even locked before I began pushing my power against the cursed collar.

Chapter 35

I SAT IN MY CELL, counting the hours and waiting for Sam to appear and explain himself. But he never did. I waited for Agramon, for anyone. But nobody came—except for Gree. Hours later, she showed up to bathe me and bring food. This time, the food was a notch above the usual slop—some sort of spiced meat with bread and cheese. An apology from Agramon? Unlikely.

I devoured the food more out of boredom than hunger, then sat on the cold, unforgiving floor as I pondered who to choose as my champion. Time was running out, and I had to make a decision that could quite literally mean life or death.

Sam had confessed once, a little too casually, that Mellan could best him in a duel. My heart wept at the thought of Mellan—brave, foolish Mellan.

There was Luc. An excellent swordsman and a man who owed me for the hell he'd put me through by betraying me in the capital. Given the guards' idle talk, I couldn't be sure whether my friends would reach me in time, but they had to go with my choice right?

Destrian, of course, was the most obvious choice. The best swordsman I knew. The man who had always been at my side, fighting for me, with me. But the notion of him facing Sam shuttered my thinking. What if Sam won? I couldn't bear to lose Destrian; the very thought left an ache in my chest that was nearly unbearable.

For a moment, I entertained the idea of naming Lord Achille of Maryse as my champion, just to see the look on his face. He had been nothing short of abominable during my visit to Maryse, and the thought of throwing him into the chaos was delightfully vindictive. I found myself smiling at the idea, despite the gravity of my situation.

I knew I had to make a choice soon, but every path seemed to hold a terrible cost, one that I wasn't sure I was ready to pay. So there I sat, trapped in indecision, as I waited for anything else to happen.

IT WASN'T UNTIL the next day that I received my first visitor, and it was the last person I expected.

"They said I could come pray for her," a voice floated in from outside.

The metal lock clanged as the guard thrust the door open. I squinted, the Solston stepping into the shadows, and finally my eyes focused enough for me to know I should be wary. Startled, I stood, grabbing the chains as if they could save me from Seith Lyon.

"What do you want?" I asked, trying not to show my fear. It was probably too late.

Seith looked different than I remembered. The chubby face I'd known at Solridge had become sallow, his features sunken. He'd lost weight since I'd first met him in Ayastaren, though I wouldn't say religious extremism had been good to him. The youthful arrogance was gone, replaced by a hardness that seemed to age him prematurely. I saw the tattoo on his forehead, his own marking denoting that he was a follower of Chassandre and Sol's word. Naturally, one of the Lyons managed to join my most powerful enemy.

Seith sneered. "I'm going to enjoy watching you die, Rowyn. The Butcher of Bruin will make sure that whatever champion you choose will be sent to the dark gods and you with them. A fitting punishment for what you did to my family."

"Your family destroyed itself," I retorted bitterly. "Almost all of you were poisoned apples."

"And I am the last of them," Seith said, drawing himself up. "With the strength to outlast them all."

"So your father didn't make it out of Ayastaren?" I asked. I'd already heard from Agramon that Ayastaren had been taken. I hadn't heard much else though. "I'm sorry I missed it," I added, dripping with sincerity. He didn't like that.

"I will have your head, whore!" Seith strode forward and struck me on the cheek. I turned my head with the force of the blow and spit some blood out of my mouth. I was starting to get really tired of people hitting me while I was chained.

"It's up to the gods to decide," I said with a smile, sure that my teeth were bloody.

Seith raised his hand to strike again, but someone stepped from the shadows of the doorway.

"Don't," Sam said with a frown.

Seith turned, looking over his shoulder. "Remember, Baron, Sol will reward those who walk in the light." He looked back to me. "I look forward to the moment I can dip my fingers in your blood and taste vengeance for what you have done to us."

"I didn't do anything to your family except hold them accountable," I snapped, ignoring Sam who was sidling closer. "They merely got what the gods decided was coming to them. Did you ever think about that?"

Seith didn't respond. Instead he turned, his head held high as he left me to my presumed doom.

Sam stepped forward. His eyes were bright.

"Don't," I whispered. "Haven't we hurt each other enough?"

A muscle in Sam's cheek flexed, his eyes haunted. Sam looked terrible, like he hadn't slept in days. His eyes had dark circles under them, and his normally robust color had turned sallow. He quickly locked the door behind him.

"I have the key for your collar," he whispered urgently. "You need to come with me. Now."

I stared at him, a mix of feelings roiling within me. Anger, confusion, and a bitter kind of hope. "I'm staying for the trial," I finally said. I would rather my fate be placed in the gods' hands then Sam's any day.

Sam slammed his fist into the stone wall, filling the cell with the echoing thud of impact. "What is so wrong with me that you would choose death over escape?" he hissed, his face inches from mine.

His question had no simple answer. And yet, I felt a strange calm. My choice to stay, illogical as it might seem to him, had given me a small measure of control in a situation that seemed utterly hopeless. And control was something I needed, even if it was only over how I met my end.

He stepped closer, his eyes intense, fists still clenched. "Very well, call forth your king, your beloved champion, to defend you. I will cross swords with him, spill his blood upon the earth, and when he lies defeated, you will be left with no choice but to be mine."

THE TIME CRAWLED BY. For two days, I was left in that suffocating solitude. I picked at the loose threads on my gown, traced the cold chain that held me to the wall, and stared into the flickering darkness.

Finally, Agramon appeared in the doorway, an unexpected interruption in the endless cycle of waiting. As he stepped inside, his eyes met mine, and I saw something I hadn't expected: regret. It flickered there, momentarily unguarded, before vanishing behind his usual veneer of control. Was all of this as much out of his hands as it was out of mine?

Had he tried to save me? He'd all but said so himself. But with the presence of the seer, Chassandre, the scales had tipped. He was no longer the puppet master; he, too, was dangling on strings.

"Stand," he commanded softly, and I did, forced through the glow of his gem. Agramon reached and cupped my cheeks.

I wondered if Agramon had ever cared for me, then immediately quashed the thought. Agramon probably didn't have that capability within him. He was a creature of ambition and political maneuvering, not one of love or regret.

His hands dropped and he stepped back, the moment of almost-intimacy shattered. "I wish things had been different," Agramon admitted. Was it genuine sorrow or another layer of deceit?

I refused to cow before him. I met his eye. "What about the prince?" I needed to know if he had penetrated my defenses and discovered the child's location.

Agramon leaned close, his lips hovering near my ear. "I'll make sure it's not painful," he whispered.

His words dropped into me like stones in still water. I lowered my head.

"As for other matters," Agramon said, distancing himself from our closeness, "you should know, Lord Destrian is a better swordsman than the Butcher, and younger too."

I looked up, our eyes locking for a moment.

Without another word, he turned and left, the cell door swinging shut behind him.

I sat on my bed, waiting as the minutes ticked by. Just before dawn, as the first light began to seep into the sky, heralding the day of my trial, the cell door creaked open once more. Gree appeared, her arms full of bathing supplies and a dress folded neatly on top. I took one look at the dress and shook my head.

"Breeches and a tunic," I commanded.

Gree looked surprised but didn't argue. She returned shortly with the requested clothing. As she helped me bathe and dress, I could sense a sort of compliance in her actions, an unusual willingness to listen to my every wish. Maybe it was her way of offering some final human kindness, considering she likely believed I'd be dead by sundown.

"Will you braid my hair into a crown?" I asked as she began to comb through my wet locks.

"Of course," she said, deftly weaving the strands into an intricate design that sat atop my head like a halo.

She stepped back when she was done, her eyes meeting mine briefly in the mirror. I couldn't read her expression, but it didn't matter. Whether out of genuine compassion or some morbid fascination with my imminent fate, she had made me look the part of a queen, and I was grateful for that small dignity.

I couldn't help but think that her unusual willingness to accommodate me was likely due to the belief that these would be my final requests. But little did she know, I had no intention of letting this day be my last.

I actually enjoyed the walk through the palace, considering it had been a while since I'd been allowed to move freely. I followed the guards obediently as we wound past corridors and stairways I had once walked as the pet of a noble.

Finally, we reached the gaming yards just outside the palace walls. The morning sun was too bright, a stark contrast to the gloom I had gotten used to. I squinted, my eyes adjusting as I looked up to see the emperor's box. Chassandre occupied the central seat, a throne really, her aura of power unmistakable even from this distance. To her side sat Duke Agramon and Princess Willene, the former looking concerned, and the latter as though they'd already tasted victory.

I let my gaze drift downward, finding the Sons of Sol lined up before the box. This time they were armed, their swords and maces gleaming in the sunlight, as if they'd be the ones to execute divine punishment should the Trial by Combat go awry. Perhaps they were.

I gritted my teeth, my fists clenching involuntarily. If it was a spectacle they wanted, I'd give them one they'd never forget.

They led me down the line, the chains around my wrists and ankles rattling with each step. It was hard to maintain a sense of regality in such a state, but I did my best to keep my chin high. The emperor's box was nothing more than a glorified wooden stand shaded by an overhead covering.

My eyes caught movement above the box. Perched atop the covering was Arden. My breath caught in my throat. The presence of Fin ignited a flicker of hope which roared into a fire within moments. I had allies, watching and waiting for the right moment. My gaze lingered on Arden for a heartbeat longer before drifting back down to the assembly rising before me—Chassandre, Agramon, Willene, and the Sons of Sol, along with the crowd of people who, a year ago, had screamed my name to save them.

Agramon took a few steps forward, his eyes locked with mine. "You have been given three days, as decreed in the Rites Under the Sun. Who do you name as your champion to wield sword and shield in your stead, defending your honor in the eyes of the gods?"

The crowd held its collective breath. I felt my own heart pause in that moment. Then, inhaling deeply, I spoke, my voice reverberating over the hushed yard.

"I name no one but myself," I declared, each word enunciated with clarity. "For there exists no soul better suited to stand before the heavens, in an arena cast by divine judgment, to wield the blade of my honor. I, Rowyn, Queen of Morgania, am my own champion."

The crowd erupted into murmurs. I focused on Agramon, challenging him to accept or deny the proclamation I'd so boldly made. He tilted his head down, a flicker of a smile playing at his lips.

Then my eyes found Sam. A shadow darkened his face. I caught a fleeting glimpse of his internal struggle as he realized that he would have to cross blades with me and not the young man he'd been so bent on destroying. But almost as soon as it appeared, that shadow lifted. His jaw tightened, his mouth set in a grim line as his hand settled on the hilt of his sword.

A guard approached and handed me a sword. I wished I had Iranoct. I wondered, briefly, what happened to it.

Gripping the hilt of the sword, I took my place in the fighting ring.

Breathe. I needed to breathe.

Sam had always been better than me when it came to sword-fighting. He had far more techniqu, and was stronger. The only thing I had going for me was the possibility that he might not actually want to hurt me. I knew he was capable of it—he'd proven as much before—but I still held out hope that he didn't really wish to see my fall.

I swung the blade a few times, testing its heft and getting a feel for its edge. It cut through the air with a satisfying hiss. I leaned and stretched, trying to work out the days I'd spent cramped in the cells of Somme. At least they'd finally gotten around to feeding me.

Breathe.

I was ready, as ready as one could ever be for a moment like this.

The air was humid, its dampness clinging to my shirt as though it, too, held its breath in anticipation. I couldn't help but wonder if my unspent magic, a pool of untapped power strangled by my collar, was causing the clouds to gather above. Lyrica had been locked in a drought, and I felt the irony of the looming rain on this of all days.

Chassandre rose. "Let the gods decide," she intoned, her voice echoing in the sudden hush that enveloped the crowd. I wondered how hard it was to kill a seer.

Sam and I took our places in the ring's center. His sword was raised, poised for an attack that would likely be both calculated and savage.

As for me, the collar chafed my skin. They wouldn't remove it for the duel. As much as I loathed it, I knew it made sense; they wouldn't want me invoking my abilities to tip the scales or, more to the point, to destroy the crowd. I would've gleefully done both, if given the chance.

Just breathe.

We squared off, the tips of our blades nearly touching but not quite. The world seemed to shrink until it was just the two of us, our futures hinging on the speed of our blades. For a moment, neither of us moved. Our eyes locked, both of us searching for something—answers, forgiveness, an end to this twisted path fate had forced us on.

The tension finally shattered as Sam swung his sword at me. My blade came up just in time to parry, steel ringing through the air. We broke apart only to clash again in a series of thrusts, parries, and lunges that sent us circling the arena. We'd crossed swords several times, Sam showing me different moves, but never in earnest. Now, it seemed we resorted to our old routine for want of wanting to hurt each other.

I wasn't a fool though. The gods wouldn't allow us to waste too much time.

I was fast, my movements guided by years of training

and an instinct for survival. But Sam was undeniably strong, each of his blows landing with a force that reverberated up my arms. Despite my speed, the impact of his strikes began to wear on me. My arms ached, a dull burn settling into my muscles, and I stumbled.

Thunder rumbled in the heavens above, a deep, sonorous growl that seemed to echo the tension crackling between Sam and me. The audience shifted nervously, their gazes flicking from the darkening sky to me and then back again.

I caught a fleeting glimpse of Agramon stepping forward, his concerned eyes raised to the unsettled clouds. I quickly scanned the perch atop the emperor's box; Arden was gone. My eyes darted around the arena. Even though there was no sign of my allies, they were close. I felt it in my bones. But this was my battle, my moment to stand alone.

I pivoted back toward Sam. Drawing a deep breath that tasted of rain and earth, I raised my sword, its blade glinting with the refracted light of an overcast sky. My arms trembled, with a kind of electric anticipation.

I took in great gasps of breath. Thunder rolled again, a heralding drum. In a burst of frenetic energy, I lunged at Sam, my blade fast as I spun in movements I'd learned in Espiria. Thunder answered my calls as steel met ringing steel. Lightning darted across the distant sky, fracturing the heavens in a momentary blaze.

Distracted, Sam glanced upward. Seizing the moment, my blade sliced through the air, cutting a shallow line across his arm. He stumbled back, clutching the wounded limb, his eyes widening in surprise.

I couldn't let his shock pass. I continued my strikes, which he countered with a series of powerful blows that fell like hammer strikes. Rain began to pour, turning the ground beneath us into a mire of mud and splattered earth. Lightning cracked again, unnervingly close.

My focus wavered; I knew that wasn't my doing. In that split second of doubt, his blade found its mark, cutting into my leg. Pain flared up like wildfire, and I staggered, nearly losing my footing.

Sam stepped toward me, arm outstretched, as though he'd forgotten we were in the midst of a duel. His face drained of color. His grip on his sword slackened. Our eyes met—his filled with a complex mix of emotions I couldn't quite decipher. He seemed as confused by his action as I was, his hand hanging awkwardly between us.

Time seemed to slow, the raindrops suspended before me.

I lunged, driving my sword through his gut.

Sam's eyes widened. Disbelief shadowed his gaze as he looked down at the steel embedded in his abdomen.

Sam crumpled, his knees hitting the mud with a spatter.

The reality of what I'd done began to sink in when his hand gripped my tunic. I sank to my knees in the mud before him, tears mingling with the relentless rain that soaked us both.

Suddenly, the vulnerability on his face, the way his sad eyes looked upon mine, he was again the man I'd remembered at the capital. He was the man I'd almost grown to love.

Gently, as if he were something breakable, I cupped his face in my hands. His eyes, once filled with conflicting emotions, now looked at me with a clarity that broke my heart. "I'm sorry I couldn't be a better man for you," he rasped, his voice barely rising above the sound of the falling rain and screams from the mob.

Sobs racked my body, each one a raw, jagged edge tearing at me. "I'm sorry," was all I could manage, the words choked out between tears.

His body went slack, falling back onto the sodden earth. I cradled his head in my lap, my tears falling freely onto his face. "I loved you in the only way I knew how," he said, his voice tinged with a regret that was too late to amend.

Then his hand moved, shaky and slow, lifting something toward me. Through the blur of my tears, I saw it—the key. The key to the collar that had kept my magic bound, a constant pressure against my throat. My fingers closed around the cold metal.

428

Sam's eyes met mine one last time. And then, as the rain continued to fall, his eyes glazed over, his body going limp. He died there, in my arms, leaving me alone in the mud and the rain, holding a key that had come far too late to save us both.

Chapter 36

THE KEY TURNED smoothly in the lock, and as the collar fell away, it was like inhaling after being submerged for too long. My magic surged back, rushing through my veins. I stood. Rain cascaded over me, mingling with the blood and the mud, my eyes locking onto Chassandre and Agramon. There was no need for words; in the eyes of the gods, I had proven my innocence.

Just then, the air erupted with the screams of the crowd. A ball of fire arced through the sky, crashing into the stands, incinerating wood and flesh alike. I shielded my eyes from the blaze, my heart pounding relentlessly.

Fin landed beside me, her wings folding into her back as she transformed into a woman. "The Marendesly forces are attacking the city gates," she said urgently, her eyes aflame with intensity. "But Bald Walden is holding them off."

Before I could respond, my gaze shifted over her shoulder. Destrian leaped over the back of a burning stand. In his clenched fist, Phyranox was ablaze.

Torrents of rain intensified, and lightning descended from the heavens to lash at the capital. I was bursting with anger and heartbreak. The charade was over. It was time to end this.

With blade in hand, I set my sights on the emperor's box where Agramon presided. But first, I had to cut through the intervening ranks of the Sons of Sol, arrayed before me like a human barricade.

They advanced, swords raised, eyes narrowed. I met the first with a disdainful parry, the scrape of metal on metal ringing out. He was too slow, his thrusts too predictable. I dodged, and my blade found the gap in his armor, and he fell with a cry on his lips.

The second fared no better. He lunged but over-reached, his blade aimed for my head. A simple sidestep was his undoing. I spun and carved an arc in the air, severing his hand from his arm. He screamed, clutching the bleeding stump, and staggered back into the chaos.

A third came at me, sword swinging in a wide arc. I ducked beneath the blade. In one fluid movement, I pivoted on my heel and slashed upward. He barely had time to gasp before he joined his fallen comrades.

They were uncoordinated, their attacks lacking any semblance of real strategy or skill. It was clear they were novices in the art of war, unfamiliar with the weapons they foolishly brandished. I was no such amateur. My eyes never left Agramon, my ultimate aim. But first, his pawns had to fall.

I fought my way to the emperor's box, catching

glimpses of pandemonium erupting in the stands. The trial had devolved into sheer chaos. People pushed and shoved, their screams merging with the violent song of thunder and rainfall.

Fin, meanwhile, had barely dodged a blaster shot. She pivoted in midair, landing gracefully but with a look of pure vengeance. She charged toward the man who dared to aim at her, her expression promising a swift and painful retribution as she morphed into a shadow panther.

But then, another obstacle appeared before me—Seith Lyon. His eyes were almost glassy, his gaze crazed.

"Get the abomination!" he screamed, brandishing a sword. When he lunged, he aimed straight for my heart.

Just as Seith Lyon's blade was about to meet its mark, a fiery sword appeared through his middle. The man howled, a wretched sound that got lost in the clamor around us. Destrian pulled his sword free, and Seith Lyon crumpled to the ground, his eyes frozen with disbelief and pain.

Before I could process what had just happened, Destrian's arms were around me, pulling me into a fierce kiss. His hand gripped the back of my hair with urgency. He pulled away only slightly. His breath felt warm against my ear.

"Get Agramon," he whispered. "We've got your back."

Nodding, I turned my gaze toward the emperor's balcony. Agramon was there, fumbling his way toward what I presumed was an escape route. Another blast rocketed through the air, landing somewhere in the crowd with a resounding explosion. In the swirling chaos, I even thought I saw a fairy zigzagging above us while it shrieked what sounded like curses.

Amid the clang of steel and the cacophony of war cries, the fae entered the fray, adding a new layer of chaos over the already frenetic battlefield. I cast my eyes across the pandemonium, trying to make sense of it all.

Off to one side, a sorceress was being bombarded by an onslaught of food—rotten tomatoes, stale bread, you name it—hurled at her with gleeful precision by a group of cackling pixies. They seemed to be having the time of their lives, darting in and out of view as they pelted their target, who was clearly overwhelmed.

Then I spotted Elgar the Swift desperately trying to league leap, but a persistent goblin had latched onto him like a bloodhound. The goblin's sharp teeth were bared, and its eyes had locked onto Elgar as though he were the main course at a banquet. Elgar popped in and out of visibility, reappearing a few yards away each time, but the goblin remained attached. Finally, Elgar disappeared from view entirely, but whether he'd escaped or met a gruesome end, I couldn't say.

Everything had turned into a landscape of madness and fury, but my mission was clear. I had to get Agramon.

I climbed the steps of the emperor's balcony, my boots slipping slightly on the rain-soaked stone. Agramon stood there, surrounded by a small cadre of guards, his gem glowing like a malevolent star. The insidious light flickered, a weak command that tingled against my mind. I shrugged it off, feeling more alive than I ever had.

A smile tugged at my lips as I advanced. One guard, sword unsheathed, moved to intercept me. Our blades clashed. It took mere moments for my sword to find its mark, slicing through his defense and ending his life. He fell with a look of surprise. The rain washed the blood off my blade.

Just as I was about to take my final steps toward Agramon, an explosion roared behind me, a thunderous sound that shook the ground. I flinched but did not turn.

But when I looked up, my eyes widened. Someone was already there, standing before Agramon.

It was Lady Vianne. A dagger glinted in her hand, its blade trembling slightly as she held it out to him. Her gem glowed vividly, pulsing in time with some rhythm I couldn't hear. Agramon's eyes met hers, and for a second, I saw the emotions play out on his face—adoration laced with horror. Love laced with hate. Desire with revulsion.

As if against his will, he took the dagger from Lady Vianne with a shaky hand. For a moment, they were frozen in the midst of chaos. A bolt of lightning rented the sky, illuminating them in a ghostly light.

I looked over my shoulder to gauge how my allies were faring. A shadow panther was snarling over the body of Princess Willene while Destrian was locked in battle with a guard. Chassandre was nowhere to be seen, but Luc was there, his great sword swinging toward the Sons of Sol. I tried not to look too hard at what the fae were doing. They looked as though they were having the time of their lives.

With that fleeting glance, my attention snapped back to Lady Vianne and Agramon. Lady Vianne leaned in close, her eyes fixed on Agramon's as the tip of the dagger made contact with his chest. Her voice, when she spoke, was tense. "Drive it in, Your Grace," she whispered. She lightly stroked his cheek. Her tone and gesture were paradoxically both sweet and venomous.

Agramon's hand trembled, but the dagger started to pierce his flesh. Just then, Lady Vianne's gaze shifted to me.

"His Grace never had a gem to protect his own mind from control," she said, never taking her eyes off mine. "He'd always relied on superior power, not cunning or precaution. And now that he's spent, drained from exerting himself too lavishly, he's mine to command."

Agramon's arrogance and overuse of his abilities had left him vulnerable, even to someone ostensibly weaker. Lady Vianne's gem shone even brighter for a moment, as if affirming her triumph over him.

With a trembling hand and sweat beading on his fore-head, Agramon finally drove the dagger deep into his own chest. The blade slid through flesh and muscle until it met the resistance of bone. A choked gasp escaped his lips; his eyes sought Lady Vianne's. It was a pitiful look, a desperate and final plea for some form of absolution.

He reached toward her, his fingers quivering, as if a mere touch could undo the fatal moment. But Lady Vianne stepped back, her eyes cold. She wouldn't allow him the consolation of her touch, not in his dying moment. Agramon's outstretched hand met nothing but empty air, and with a look of despair that would haunt me for weeks after the battle, he crumpled to the ground, life fleeing from his eyes as his body went limp.

I felt a myriad of emotions rush through me—relief, guilt, and an odd, hollow kind of victory. I stepped toward her.

"I had plans for him." I stared down at his lifeless form.

Lady Vianne faced me, her own gem dimming as if sated. "He was never yours to kill," she said, her voice softer than I expected.

As her words sank in, I took stock of the chaos. A scene of untamed destruction and frenzied fighting filled my gaze, and for a moment, I was pulled away from the gravity of Agramon's death, back into the relentless tide of war.

The Marendeslys had breached the castle walls and were spilling into the capital, their numbers overwhelming what remained of the city's defenses. Swords clashed less frequently now; the cacophony of battle was giving way to the discordant symphony of retreat and flight. The fallen littered the war-torn ground, the air thick with the coppery scent of blood and the stinging smoke of black powder.

As I walked toward Destrian, my heart pounded with a newfound sense of freedom and hope. Fin caught up with us, her face flushed from exertion but her eyes twinkling with triumph.

"You won't believe what we had to do to get here," Fin began, launching into an elaborate tale. "I called in every favor I had with the fae. Brindlewings were excellent for reconnaissance, and don't even get me started on how useful the dustsprites were for obscuring vision . . ."

She rambled on, but I found myself drifting.

I let out a sigh of relief, for among the remnants of a shattered empire and the dying echoes of war, I allowed myself to believe that I was finally going home—for good.

Chapter 37

FTER THE TRIAL BY COMBAT, the Marendeslys assumed control over Somme with surprising efficiency. The city, so recently a stage for spectacles of power, was oddly quiet under their rule, as if holding its breath.

I studied Duke Eldred as he looked over Fin, Destrian, and me, disappointment plain on his face. Next to him stood General Ivar, his similarities to Fin making her parentage unmistakable.

"You've left quite a mess for me to clean up," Eldred remarked. He actually seemed *more* cordial to me, probably because neither Agramon nor Sam were standing beside me, as they'd been in Maryse.

"So I've heard," I replied, keeping my voice measured.

"A coven of vampires has taken residence near the harbor, if rumors are to be believed," he continued. "And pixies, of all creatures, have decided that the kitchens at the castle are their new playground. Do you have any idea how much sugar they've eaten?"

Fin chuckled and leaned forward. "Well, if you're interested in containing the fae who helped you overthrow Agramon, you might want to discuss terms with their king," she suggested.

General Ivar's eyes had been lingering on Fin as if seeing her for the first time. "I must say, I'm impressed with you," he said, finally. "Daughter. You fought well against the usurpers."

Fin's eyes narrowed, her jaw clenched. "To you, it's 'Your Majesty,'" she corrected, an icy edge to her words.

I wanted to grab her hand, but I resisted. Thankfully, Destrian shifted the conversation. "We'd like to see Chassandre the seer contained. She's proven to be a threat to Rowyn, as have the Sons of Sol."

Duke Eldred sighed. "We're doing what we can to root out the extremists, but Chassandre is . . . unpredictable. She answers to no one but herself. It's complicated."

The duke then shifted his gaze to me. "And what of the young prince? Where is he?"

I met his eyes squarely. "I will be leaving it to his guardian to disclose his whereabouts when they feel it is time. Our hope is that he'll come into his own without the toxicity of the capital. Until then, his safety and that of the princesses is my utmost concern."

Eldred searched my gaze, perhaps looking for a sign of weakness or indecision. He found none. "The princesses are still in Ardent," he explained. "The count and countess have completely taken over their care. Neither has any sorcery to speak of, so we thought it best that they grow up close to their aunt."

I nodded. That left only one last burning question. "Who killed Empress Lesedi?"

General Ivar's eyes met mine. "We've decided not to pursue Morgania." I figured he was now high commander of the Lyrican forces. The job he'd always envied of Sam. "We have enough work here rebuilding an empire that has seen too much strife." Diplomacy coated his words like armor, and I was left to ponder the question unanswered.

We concluded our dealings under the gilded ceilings of the capital, but as I walked away, I couldn't shake the feeling that the story was far from over. The Marendeslys might have gained control, but it was a tentative grasp, fingers curling around the reins of an empire that had bucked its previous riders.

As I exited the palace, I wondered what this new chapter held for Somme, Morgania, and me. And somewhere in those thoughts, the unanswered question about Lesedi lingered, a whisper that refused to be silenced.

We made our way to the ships that would ferry us back to the shores of Somme. Luc and an assortment of fae, who had rendered their services in return for sanctuary in Morgania, accompanied us. As we cast off, the robust ships slicing through the choppy waters, I stood at the stern, watching the coastline of Somme shrink and blur on the horizon.

My burdens of the East seemed to fall away, sinking beneath the surf of the Ballerian. The salty breeze carried away the weight of my recent trials, and I silently vowed never to set foot on that accursed soil again. My gaze moved from the fading shore to the open sea, and beyond it to the sky, tinged with the first hues of evening. There was an entire world out there, and it suddenly seemed full of endless possibilities and held no one else to chase me.

My hands found their way around Destrian's arm. He wasn't content with that. Instead, he pulled me into a tight hug, resting his chin on top of my head as his arms wound around me. He was probably smelling my hair again.

Suddenly, Arden dove into the sea and a dolphin emerged, leaping out of the water at the bow of the ship. I smiled as, together, we turned our eyes westward, toward home, toward our future. I thought of the rolling hills, the verdant forests, and the ancient stones of Morgania. I thought of the challenges that awaited us but also of the peace and happiness that seemed finally within reach.

As the ship sailed on, my grip tightened, and Destrian's arms squeezed me in return. In that moment, whatever lay ahead seemed manageable because I knew we'd face it side by side. And for the first time in what felt like an eternity, I allowed myself to truly hope.

Epilogue

THE AIR WAS THICK with the scent of incense as we sat down to negotiate with Alf Amun-doon, an Ylirian warlord whose influence stretched across the dunes like the shadows at sundown. Destrian, Fin, and I were discussing a possible alliance with Yliria, and he'd traveled a ways to see us.

Alf Amun-doon leaned forward and pushed a box across the table toward us. "I heard you might be in need of these," he said, his eyes twinkling.

I opened the box to find it filled with rubies. For a moment, I was stunned. Then I looked at Destrian and remembered the tourmaline gems that King Valon had given us—gems that were already being used to fashion a crown for Fin. Now it seemed we would have stones for Destrian's crown as well. Destrian tried to conceal his excitement, but I knew he was already envisioning it.

Before we got lost in visions of the future, I had to ask the man, "Why did you try to kidnap me during my tour of the empire?"

Alf Amun-doon's expression sobered. "I had heard that you were lifted from the West. Anyone who is an enemy of the empire is a potential ally for me. I intended to save you from the emperor in exchange for harboring your power."

For the love of the gods. Save me? It was a phrase I'd heard often. Agramon had said it. So had Sam, Destrian, and Gillius. Everyone seemed to want to save me, but in different ways, for different reasons, and with the hopes of different ends. Yet, as I sat there, I took a deep breath and realized that in the end, I'd had to save myself.

After our negotiations, I found myself standing on my balcony looking out over Helena, the capital that had stood the test of time and turmoil. The sprawling city was bathed in the soft golden light of the setting sun, its rooftops and towers glowing like amber. The scent of morwood pine filled the air, rich and grounding. It was a fragrance tied to so many memories, to so many years of my life. Clouds hung low over the mountains, nearly shielding them from sight. The shroud had been our protector for generations. It was a part of us, just as we were a part of this land.

In that moment, everything felt possible. I breathed in deeply, letting the smell of pine and damp earth fill my lungs. I felt immense gratitude for the journey that had led me to this moment—where anything I wanted for my life seemed within my grasp.

Fin swept into my room dressed in one of her royal gowns, the fabric shimmering around her form like liquid gold, a simple sash holding the dress together. She moved gracefully, settling on the plush couch with a regal air.

"I'm going to visit Thorn Beyond-the-Border," she announced, her voice laced with anticipation. "We've got some fae business to hash out."

I raised my brows. "Is Luc all right with this?"

"He has to be all right," Fin said, studying her nails, "because I am a queen. And as a queen, I get to decide how to give my love. They can either take it or leave it, but they don't get to tell me how to do it."

In that moment, I couldn't have been prouder to call her my friend.

The door creaked open, and Destrian walked in looking disheveled from his review of the new army recruits. "Will I see you at dinner later?"

"No, actually," I replied, letting my gaze drift back to Fin momentarily before focusing on Destrian again. "I'm planning to challenge Pedr to a game of chess, if I can pry him away from Simon for an hour or two."

Destrian chucked me under the chin. "Good luck with that."

I smiled at the thought, then remembered something that had been on my mind. "What's the decision about the vampires? Are we offering them refuge in Morgania? I thought we'd reconsidered."

Destrian moved to the chair where he'd left his coat the night before. Shrugging it on, he smoothed the borders down with care. "So, you changed your mind about the vampires?" He locked eyes with me through the mirror.

"Yes, I thought you had to," I said with a twinge of annoyance.

Destrian shook his head. "I have not, my love, and neither has Fin."

I glared at him. "If you claim to love me, then you should always take my side."

From the couch, Fin snorted, trying to disguise her laughter as a cough. "That's one way to govern."

"No," Destrian finally said, his reflection betraying a hint of a smirk. "Fin got to me first and presented a very convincing argument. So, I'm against allowing the vampires refuge, and that's final."

Fin grinned so wide that her eyes nearly closed; she was clearly pleased with herself. I could only sulk, crossing my arms over my chest in mock indignation.

"I'm ready." Destrian turned from the mirror to face me. He sauntered over and found the curve of my waist. Leaning in, he kissed my cheek softly. "Don't overdo it today," he murmured, a note of real concern in his voice.

As the door closed behind him, Fin's playful smile faded to a frown. She looked at me, her eyes searching. "What was that all about?"

Avoiding her gaze, I felt my cheeks flush a shade pinker.

"Are you?" Fin's mouth crooked into a half smile, her

eyes sparkling with mischief.

My blush deepened. "Yes."

Her mouth opened wide in a grin, all pretense of regality vanishing. "How did this happen?"

I laughed. "Well, Destrian and I worked off too many post-battle jitters, and there wasn't enough lady's tea to go around on the battlefield."

Fin smiled warmly, her eyes softening. "And how do you feel about it?"

For a moment, I hesitated, collecting my thoughts. Then the words came easily, as if they'd been waiting for just this moment to be spoken. "Excited," I confessed. "I'm happy that, finally, there's something in my life that I know can't be taken away from me. And besides, the child could be one of our heirs . . . Who knows?"

My heart sank as the weight of the promise I'd made to the fae king flooded back into my memory. My daughter would belong to the fae world, a price my ancestors forced us to pay.

I looked up at Fin. It was as if she knew, without needing to be told, the bittersweet mixture of happiness and dread within my thoughts.

"I'll bring you back some fae treats from Horan," she promised.

I forced a smile. "I like that plan."

Fin kissed my cheek, her lips cool against my skin. With

one last radiant smile tossed over her shoulder, she left the room.

Alone again, I stared out of the window, lost in thought. We would need to tell others about the baby. Aunt Maureen would be excited. She was still helping man the castle, and she and Pria actually got along quite well. I'd wanted to tell Fin first, especially since she was leaving soon. Now that she knew, we could spread the word a bit more.

It was funny. The moment we set foot on Morganian soil, a sense of rootedness filled me as if the very land recognized one of its own returning for good. My first task, however, was not one of reunions or celebrations. I'd sent Fin directly to Lady Noemi with specific instructions: she was to take full charge of all matters concerning Omri, and I absolved myself of any future decisions related to him. However, I advised caution in announcing his existence; the Lyrican public was still recovering from the political upheavals, and I had no wish to further engage with the Marendeslys on the matter.

Lady Vianne chose to take refuge in Morgania. An initial sanctuary had been offered in Maryse, but the burgeoning animosity against mind readers—thanks to Agramon's treacherous manipulations—made it unwise for her to stay there. Lady Vianne's expertise was not wasted; she quickly engaged with Urdua, both working tirelessly to draft more equitable laws and to expand educational opportunities within Morgania.

Gillius and Master Haris settled in Eslin. The two of them were like peas in a pod, scholars at heart, and Haris was particularly elated with the griffins that chose Eslin's shores for their summer roosting.

In the midst of rebuilding Ayastaren, Marc went to Caldeaon to smooth things over with the Byrnes. He came back with Ingrid as his bride, and she became the Duchess of Ayastaren, much to her great pleasure. Marc continued to travel, ensuring that trade and ideas passed freely between Morgania and the lands of Adair and The Fens.

It was easy to sink into a comfortable routine, surrounded by those who I loved and respected. Morgania, the land of my ancestors, was now a haven for all.

The reflection in the glass caught my eye. Behind me stood the specter of a woman watching me. At first, I thought it could be Echo. But no. She had finally gone to live among the stars, just as she'd wanted.

The woman stepped forward and I looked over my shoulder, already knowing that I would see nothing. Turning back to the window, I noticed she'd come right up to my shoulder. Every time I'd seen her before, she'd seemed restless, agitated, as though tethered to this world by some unfulfilled purpose. But now, she looked serene, as if some burden had been lifted from her ghostly shoulders.

The rich colors of the setting sun cast a warm glow over the rooftops, and my eyes followed the glow as it reached to touch the farthest edges of Helena. I laid my hand on my stomach, where new life stirred, and a different sort of glow filled me.

In the end, that's what it was all about, wasn't it? Giving those you love—and even those you may never know—a place they could always call home. A place where they felt safe, cherished, and most importantly, free.

As the last rays of the sun dipped beneath the horizon, I took one final, sweeping gaze at the land that had given me so much and to which I owed everything. Morgania, with all its flaws and beauty, was a part of me, as I was a part of it. I had finally made it home.

The End

Acknowledgments

Phew, the end of a series! There are so many people to thank for their assistance throughout this writing adventure, all of whom were integral to my success. I absolutely could not have done this alone.

I am deeply grateful to my husband and children for their patience as I sought a balance between work and family, and for giving me the time to explore and work on my craft. I will always be infinitely grateful for your support and love you dearly.

I would like to thank my father, mother, sister Olivia, and mother-in-law Debbie for stepping in and helping out when I needed time to work. I am fortunate to have such an incredible support system.

To my beta readers, Galen, Patrick, Aureece, Patricia, and the dozens more who came and went over the years: I am immensely grateful for all your feedback. It was incredibly kind of you to take the time to review my work.

For her unending patience and incredible skills, I extend my thanks to Cayce at Kingsman Editing Services. Working with her has always been amazing, and she took the time to ensure my published piece was something I could be proud of.

Finally, to my readers – my mother, Rachel, sister Hannah, Shanna, Dani, Anne, Sophie, and everyone else who gave me a chance to tell you a story: Thank you so much for reading this series and seeing it through to the end. Your support has meant the world to me. And now, onto the next adventure!